The television crew that had flown down from New York to cover Katherine Leslie's trial frantically dollied their mini-cams around to capture the frenzy of the crowd. The roiling mass of Jamaicans, the clouds of tear gas, flashing red lights and screaming police sirens.

Her attorney, Tyler Grayson, attempted to usher Katherine inside the courthouse, fending off the reporters who screamed questions. Suddenly, Kate twisted sharply about in the engulfing crush. Lifting her manacled hands with a single sweeping motion, she whipped off the dark glasses. Her lovely porcelain features had been battered. Although both her eyes had been badly blackened, they sparkled with green fire.

Angrily, defiantly, Kate cried out, "I killed Andreas Jaccard because he was an exquisite monster. He deserved to die. And I was the only one who could stop him!"

The Paramour Woman

Charles Rigdon

A Warner Communications Company

WARNER BOOKS EDITION

Cover photo by Anthony Loew

Warner Books, Inc.,
666 Fifth Avenue,
New York, N.Y. 10103

 A Warner Communications Company

Printed in the United States of America

First Printing: January, 1983

10 9 8 7 6 5 4 3 2 1

For Baba
and my good friend Jerry Dixon,
for whom this novel
was written

SHE is like a ring of lightning, folds of flaming fire, or a bar of pure gold.

When *SHE* breaks her bonds, she is like a star shooting through space, like the sun falling from its place in the sky, or a point of light bursting forth like a sprouting seed.

Kundalini the Mother Goddess
Janeshwar Maharaj

Contents

Prologue		15
PART ONE	*Spring Lightning*	21
PART TWO	*Summer Solstice*	147
PART THREE	*Autumn Interlude*	271
PART FOUR	*Winter Solstice—A Dark Star Rising*	315
PART FIVE	*A Point of Light—And Beyond*	395
Epilogue		445

The Caramour Woman

Prologue

Montego Bay was wilting in the fierce white Caribbean sunlight. It was sweltering; the thermometer had registered 98 degrees at high noon, and threatened to climb even higher as the day wore on.

The mood of the crowd gathered in front of the Montego Bay courthouse was angry and bristling. The faces were mostly black, and a mood of sullen hostility prevailed, as oppressive as the heat itself.

Then an aging Cadillac limousine swung around the corner on to Britannia Street and pulled up to the curb, accompanied by a squad of motorcycle escorts with screaming sirens. The crowd surged forward, spilling across the police barriers to surround the car, with jeering, hostile faces pressing up against the windows.

They received little more than a glimpse of the woman seated in the rear of the Cadillac. There was a desperate set to her features, while her eyes were masked by huge wrap-around dark glasses.

In the next moment the limo was rocked crazily back and forth. Overripe mangos splattered against the windshield, and rudely lettered placards began to wave wildly in the torpid tropic air. Then the riot police waded in to break up the crowd with swinging truncheons and exploding tear gas cannisters.

It was over as quickly as it had begun. But reports of the Montego Bay courthouse riot would appear via satellite on the major American news networks that same evening. The television crew that had flown down from New York to cover the Jaccard murder trial frantically dollied their minicams around to capture the frenzied rout—the roiling mass of Jamaicans, surging this way and that amid searing clouds of tear gas, flashing red lights, and screaming police sirens.

After slowly panning the scene for maximum dramatic effect, the camera swung about and zeroed in on the shapely figure of Katherine Leslie emerging from the Caddy's rear door. She was simply dressed in a tightly belted trench coat with a silk scarf tied about her hair. A gloved hand pressed against her face staving off the acrid fumes that still hung like a pall over the courthouse steps. Her lawyers quickly shouldered forward to surround her as flashbulbs exploded on every side.

Kate's eyes glowed with guarded intensity behind her huge amber-tinted sunglasses as she anxiously searched the surrounding crowd for a face. Where was Paul? Why wasn't he there when she needed him so desperately? Surely he must have seen the headlines flashed around the world: CARAMOUR WOMAN INDICTED IN MURDER OF NOBEL SCIENTIST.

"Don't you worry about a thing, Miss Leslie, I'll have you out on bail as soon as I find out who I have to bribe on this shit heap of an island." It was Tyler Grayson who spoke, leaning intimately close while mopping his florid, perspiring face with a silk handkerchief.

He was without question the most famous criminal lawyer in the country, an obese, flamboyantly attired figure noted for his dramatic courtroom theatrics, enormous legal fees, and seemingly uncanny ability to keep famous names and faces out of prison.

"May the record show that my client has appeared voluntarily to place herself in the court's charge," Grayson drawled to the Jamaican High Court Marshal, who stood waiting to take Kate into custody.

The eyes raking over her were pitiless, and the man's gleaming black face seemed as tightly closed as a clenched fist. He was clearly relishing his role, and played it with a flourish.

"Are you Miss Katherine Leslie?" he demanded in thick East Indian accents.

Kate nodded. "I am." The words scarcely left her lips.

The man reached out, and, before she fully realized what was taking place, had snapped a pair of handcuffs onto her slender wrists. "As High Court Marshal it is my duty to place you under arrest for the murder of Doctor Andreas Jaccard."

The crowd surged forward like an amorphous mass, threatening to engulf and destroy. It was a terrible, soul-searing moment for Kate. She could scarcely believe it was actually happening—the surrounding sea of hostile dark faces, the angry, jeering voices, and the throng of reporters pressing in upon her as she and her entourage began moving up the courthouse steps.

"Is it true that at least three prominent society women are dead as a result of receiving cell-rejuvenation therapy at Doctor Jaccard's Coral Key Spa?"

Kate remained tight lipped and unsmiling as a bouquet of

microphones were thrust rudely in her face by the clutch of reporters dogging her footsteps.

"My client is not at liberty to address herself to that question." Tyler Grayson hastily intervened.

"What about allegations made by the Manhattan District Attorney that saleswomen employed by Miss Leslie at Caramour Cosmetics were pressured into exchanging sexual favors in order to meet sales quotas?"

"During her tenure as president of Caramour, I can state unequivocally that my client was completely unaware that any such practices existed. Nor is she prepared to make any statement in response to either the SEC or FDA investigations of Caramour that are currently pending in the United States. Now please clear the way for the lady, gentlemen. We have an appointment with the Chief Magistrate."

Planting himself directly in their path, one persistent reporter refused intimidation from the blustering two-hundred-and-fifty-pound lawyer in his voluminous white suit and courtly Van Dyke.

"Perhaps Miss Leslie can confirm the rumor that she was Doctor Jaccard's mistress," the reporter pursued.

Just then two smartly uniformed Jamaican militiamen thrust forward to grab the man and drag him out of the way. The courthouse doors yawned open before her. But even as Tyler Grayson attempted to usher her inside, Kate twisted sharply about in the engulfing crush. With a single sweeping motion, Kate lifted her manacled hands and whipped off the dark glasses obscuring her features as a gasp went up from the crowd.

Part One

Spring Lightning

Chapter One

It had been the rarest of days; a lovely languid displacement of Caribbean warmth and luminosity driven prematurely north by Hurricane Carmen, swirling up out of the Grand Bahama Deeps. It was the kind of day that can only happen to New York City, late in the month of May.

It was a day full of sunlight and pretty girls in spring dresses. A soft breeze blew sweetly through barrows of fresh-cut flowers being sold on street corners. Somewhere in the burgeoning green fastness of Central Park, a Jamaican steel ban was playing, while the sky stretched over the spectacular Manhattan cityscape like an infinite cerulean dome.

It was a day of signs and portents. Ever since arising at six that morning, to throw her windows wide and start her Yoga breathing exercises, Kate had felt herself strongly beneath the spell of déjà vu. Almost, she thought, as if she were being propelled by an unknown destiny toward some intersecting point in time. It was a provocative idea, especially in light of the fact that she was one day short of her fortieth birthday.

Friday was always a very busy day, and by the time Kate left her office and caught a cab uptown to her apartment overlooking the East River, it was already seven-thirty in the evening. She was exhausted, and the wondrous sense of expectation with which she had greeted the new day had been swallowed up by meetings and responsibilities, the decisions and details that went to make up another Friday in her life.

The telephone was ringing as she entered the apartment, and by some extraordinary intuition she knew that it was Paul.

When he asked whether or not she was free to drop by his Olympic Towers duplex that evening, she lied, as she had done so often in the past. "Of course. I'd be delighted," Kate responded.

For the past eighteen years, Kate Leslie had always made herself available to Paul Osborn, no matter how inconvenient or last minute the summons might be.

The truth was that she had been planning to drive out to her country place in Amagansett. But, if you worked for Caramour Cosmetics, your time—all of it—belonged exclusively to the president and chairman of the board. Paul Osborn was known for riding roughshod over the lives of his executive staff. But for Kate there was a far more selfish reason involved.

She had been in love with Paul for as long as she could remember. It had probably happened the first day she walked into his office eighteen years before, she realized, sliding into the dimly luxurious interior of the chauffeured Rolls he had sent to pick her up. And the opportunity to spend a few hours with him, for any reason whatsoever, was far more compelling than anything else she might have had planned.

In spite of her own hectic and demanding schedule as vice

president in charge of advertising and promotion, scarcely a week passed in which Kate did not juggle her own affairs in order to meet Paul for lunch, dinner, or a hurried limousine conference on the way to the airport. Whenever and wherever Paul might choose to see her, Kate always made herself entirely available.

For whatever else he might or might not be—brilliant, insensitive, ruthless, charismatic, and hopelessly complicated—Kate was totally dedicated to serving Paul's needs. She accommodated his egocentric personality in myriad ways, and theirs had been a richly symbiotic relationship from the very beginning. Paul was totally, unreservedly, and pathologically devoted to the success of Caramour Cosmetics, and Kate was devoted to Paul.

Of course he was the often infuriating tyrant that everyone accused him of being, but she was used to that. Genius did, after all, have its prerogatives. And the fact that Paul, the Perfectionist, never seemed to be satisfied with anything, nor seldom expressed the slightest appreciation for a job well done, only enhanced his magnetism.

He always expected the very best and insisted upon total dedication. Nothing was ever going to be enough for Mr. Paul Osborn, Kate had long since realized. The sharp edge of tyranny honing his personality succeeded eminently in keeping all those who served vying like gladiators in a highly competitive corporate arena.

"Good evening, Miss Leslie," the doorman said as Kate slid from the sleek white Rolls with a flash of long, shapely legs. "Mr. Osborn's manservant rang down to say that you were expected. You're to go right up."

Heads turned as Kate made her way to the elevators through the opulently appointed lobby. Paul was definitely a man who appreciated attractive women, and it had always flattered Kate enormously to be considered his corporate mistress. The continual buzz and whisper of gossip about the nature of their relationship had only served to enhance her own aura of power, as well as insure against frontal attacks by the more aggressive denizens of the corporate shark tank. Over the years, it had in fact proven to be a major factor that had allowed Kate to become the creative Cassandra in residence; the high priestess behind Caramour's most successful cosmetic promotions, who always seemed to sense a trend in the making.

Even so, it was often necessary to prop up her own feminine ego by reminding herself that Paul was deliberately avoiding the obvious temptation of taking her to bed. Kate was only too well aware that he often conducted one-night stands with a variety of beautiful young women—expensive call girls, models, or just about anything female and gorgeous that happened to catch his roving eye.

But in that regard, Kate had become rather sanguine. The other women in Paul Osborn's life had never really been a threat. She was secure in the knowledge that none of them could really compete with what she so willingly provided. Even when Paul announced his intention of marrying the glacially poised and socially prominent Cristina Dayne, Kate had understood. Trading up from Flatbush to a Park Avenue pedigree had all been part of the game. Paul married Cristina in order to upgrade his own image in the cosmetic marketplace. And in the process, a platinum gloss of social câchét had rubbed off on the company he had founded and nurtured to such phenomenal success.

Reflected in the smoky, mirrored walls of the elevator carrying her soundlessly upward, Kate appeared to be several years older than her thirty-nine years. Her chestnut hair drawn back smoothly from her face, her clothes expensively tailored and unobtrusive in color, she had the look of a woman committed to a serious career; sleek, sophisticated, and ready to tackle the job at hand.

Kate had always thought her eyes to be her very best feature, along with good bone structure and the flawless complexion with which she had always been blessed. They were the color of autumn wood smoke beneath naturally arched brows. The large tortoise-rimmed glasses she wore were only a partial necessity, due to being slightly nearsighted. More importantly, they provided the requisite distance she needed, allowing her to retain certain options with her colleagues that would have otherwise been denied her.

Her voice had a distinctively low and smoky quality that men found highly intriguing. Women for the most part were envious and wary of her at first meeting; and where their husbands were concerned, Kate always made it a habit to wear her success as lightly as possible, striving always to strike a balance between her own femininity and the fact that she was first and foremost a highly dedicated corporate executive. Envy, she supposed, was only to be expected. Still, she always went out of her way to avoid the petty vindictiveness and overemotional behavior of which so many women in positions of authority were often accused.

Being a ball-breaker was simply not her style, and she tried always to accept her setbacks as calmly as she accepted her victories. At least that was the image of cool, can-do competence she had always succeeded in projecting.

Kate was admitted to Paul's palatial duplex by Miguel, his beaming Filipino houseman. "Mr. Osborn will be joining you shortly, Miss Leslie. May I prepare you something to drink?"

"No thank you, Miguel. I can manage." Kate's footsteps rang against the marble floor as she crossed the foyer to the library. She was in fact as familiar with Paul's lavish surroundings as she was with her own eight and one-half rooms overlooking the East River. Upon Cristina's death some eight months before, it had seemed perfectly natural for her to step in to fill the void, and she had slipped easily into the role of Paul's official hostess.

Kate had never really been sure what Paul had felt about his wife's passing; Cristina's death had been so totally unexpected. Ultimately it was Kate who handled all the funeral arrangements and the disposal of her personal effects, while the bereaved husband simply went on with business as usual.

But then Paul had never been one to display his emotions; and Kate for her part seldom missed any opportunity to make herself indispensable.

The library was warmly inviting with its crackling log fire and subdued lighting. It was a spacious, purely masculine statement in contemporary decor, with a grand sense of scale. There were shelves of fine books, rare oriental carpets, and over two million dollars' worth of contemporary art splashed dramatically across the eggshell-white walls.

Crossing to the oak-panelled bar, Kate splashed a heavy crystal tumbler with Stolichnaya vodka. She added crushed ice, then crossed the room to stand thoughtfully before the floor-to-ceiling windows. The view was spectacular at any time of the day, but Kate never ceased to marvel at the glittering panorama of Manhattan by night. Now, standing there staring out, she felt the awesome power of its enchantment.

Ostensibly Paul had asked her over that evening in order to discuss Caramour's new Hypo-Allergenic line. It was already many months behind schedule in going into production, and the problems of how to promote it had begun to seem overwhelming.

Still, when Paul had called her earlier that evening, there had been something in his voice. A quality of strangeness that alerted Kate to the fact that something else was very much on his mind.

Then she remembered having awakened that morning with an overwhelming sense that something important was imminent. The realization struck her as if she had been slapped. Of course. Tonight Paul was going to ask her to become his wife. Kate wasn't exactly sure just how she knew. Rather it was something she felt on a deep, almost subliminal level.

Marriage was of course a natural enough extension of their long relationship. The prospect of becoming Mrs. Paul Osborn was not only an eminently satisfying thought, but entirely suitable as well. There had, in fact, always been a sense of ultimate inevitability about her and Paul. They balanced one another perfectly. He depended upon Kate totally, and, as far as she herself was concerned, there had simply never been anyone else.

Kate's hand trembled slightly as she hurriedly crossed the room to retrieve her purse from the bar. Removing a platinum compact, she quickly applied fresh lipstick. Then, pulling the pins from her hair, she arranged it with a few deft brush strokes to curl softly about her face, endowing her features with a different look altogether; an illusive aura that was softer, more fragile, and totally feminine.

Kate had never been possessed of classic beauty, but it was fully within her powers to create whatever image she chose. Her face was an arresting configuration of unusual features: the nose a bit too strong, the smooth clear brow with its definite widow's peak a shade too high, and the mouth rather too generous, at least by Kate's own estimation.

There was a soft clicking sound as she snapped her compact closed. Then Kate splashed some more vodka into her glass, and composed her features into a smoothly stylized mask. It was a look that would betray nothing of her true feelings. At least not until the right and perfect moment.

Kate was smiling softly to herself, however, as she turned down the lights, and curled up on the low velvet couch before the fire. At last her time had come, she realized. Why else would Tiffany's have made a decidedly mysterious delivery to Paul's office that day, with two armoured guards in attendance?

About twenty minutes later, Kate failed to hear when Paul entered the library and soundlessly drew the double doors closed behind him. She still sat curled upon the couch, staring into the fire, completely absorbed in her own thoughts.

Then without warning Paul's hands were resting upon her shoulders, and he bent to kiss the top of her head very lightly. At first Kate started at his touch, then sank back to clasp his hand with her fingers as she smiled up at him. "You startled me," she said. "I didn't hear you come in."

"Come on, Katie, admit it. Your mind was back at the office working on the new campaign, wasn't it?" He laughed lightly. "I know all about those twelve- and fourteen-hour days you've been putting in lately. You're working much too hard, too many long hours."

He squeezed her hand. "Frankly, Katie, I don't know what I'd ever have done without you, over the years. We turned out to be one hell of a team, you and I. And we took Caramour right to the top."

Kate searched his face as they lingered there before the fire, noting the signs of stress and tension that had become increasingly apparent during the past months. Still, at fifty-six years of age, there was something compellingly masculine about Paul Osborn, with his handsome square-cut features, the commanding jawline, and the chin intersected by a resolute cleft.

Paul carried himself like a man half his age, and yet on that particular evening there seemed to be a sense of hesitancy in his movements, along with a certain brooding resignation and something measured and distant in his voice.

In the soft lamplight Kate saw that his sideburns were

almost completely white now while his wavy dark hair was thickly threaded with gray.

"How was your trip to Tokyo?" she asked, trying to break through the distance that seemed to linger between them. "Three weeks is the longest you've ever been away. I was beginning to think that you'd been kidnapped by a hoard of sex-crazed geishas."

Kate was trying for lightness, but Paul only scowled. Taking the empty glass from her hand, he crossed to the bar, where he poured them each a drink with thoughtful deliberation.

"I wasn't in Tokyo for business or for fun, Katie. You see, I had a slight heart attack while I was in Hong Kong. I've been recovering at a private hospital near Tokyo, and undergoing a series of tests."

Kate lurched forward on the couch. "Paul . . ." she gasped. "I had no idea . . . why didn't you call me . . . let me know. Of course I'd have been there within twenty-four hours. From the daily Telex reports, everyone here thought you were working on the Japanese cosmetic franchise deal."

"Which is exactly what I wanted you all to think," Paul informed her. Slowly he recrossed the room, and when he handed Kate her drink their fingers briefly touched. Paul's slate-gray eyes were commanding. "The truth is, Katie . . . I seem to find myself with a bum ticker, and a one-way ticket to nowhere."

"I don't understand," Kate voiced, her eyes pleading.

Turning away from her, Paul took a long Monte Cristo thin from the leather humidor on the coffee table and lit the end with a heavy crystal lighter. Then, nursing his double Scotch, he began to pace the rug before the fire.

"I'm under doctor's orders to get totally out of the cosmetic business, Kate. There's even a pretty good chance that I'll need to have a pacemaker implanted, if I suffer any more of these attacks."

Paul stopped pacing and sat down beside her on the couch, taking both her hands in his and gripping them tightly. "I'll be leaving for the French Riviera in two weeks," he announced. "The *Caramour II* is being refitted for an around-the-world cruise, at Cannes. I'll be away for at least a year, maybe even longer. The doctors haven't really given me any choice in the matter."

Kate's thoughts were whirling, and she felt the bright, hot burn of tears as they brimmed and spilled.

"You're going away," she murmured. The words were like sharp talons of pain, sinking deep. "Look at me," Paul commanded. When she did, his clear gray eyes were very serious and direct. "Believe me, Katie, I need you now more than ever. You see, I'm throwing the ball to you."

"To me?" Kate repeated, taking the white handkerchief he held out to her and quickly dabbing at her eyes. "I don't understand."

Paul sat back to draw on his cigar. "At next week's board of directors meeting, I have every intention of appointing you president of Caramour, as well as acting chairman of the board."

Kate was utterly stunned at the news. She tried to speak, but no words came as her fingers knotted and twisted the linen handkerchief.

"It's true," Paul confirmed. "You're the only one I can trust."

They were interrupted at this point by the sound of the doors opening behind them.

"I do hope I'm not interrupting anything personal?"

The voice was a syrupy, southern confection that Kate immediately recognized. She shot Paul a sharp, questioning look, and then turned abruptly to find Allison Jeffries standing in the doorway.

Allison was wearing a filmy flesh-colored peignoir, and the

shock of discovering her there in Paul's library on a Friday evening caused all the color to drain from Kate's face. Then Allison was gliding across the room toward them, and cold, sick comprehension turned inside her like a knife.

Staring as if mesmerized, Kate watched Allison's lush, tawny body moving in shadowy profile beneath the gauzy sheerness of her gown. She was naked underneath.

"I told you to go to bed," Paul said sharply. "You knew that I didn't want to be disturbed for any reason whatsoever."

"I simply couldn't resist coming down to give Kate the good news." Allison smiled. She had joined them by now, trailing the aura of her sexuality like an exotic scent. "After all, Paul, darling. We do have Kate to thank for bringing us together in the first place."

As Kate struggled desperately to recover her composure, Allison settled herself on the arm of the couch. She draped one hand languidly about Paul's shoulder in order to better display the huge square-cut diamond glittering on her finger.

"Well, what do you think, Katie? Paul's finally going to make an honest woman of me," Allison announced with brightly malicious intent. "Of course he's tried to keep the whole thing very hush-hush, but I wanted you to be the very first to know.

"Just imagine," she sighed, "yours truly is going to become Mrs. Paul Osborn, and you are going to become president of Caramour Cosmetics. Isn't it utterly fabulous, Kate? Just like in the movies. Both of us got exactly what we wanted most."

Chapter Two

Kate fled Manhattan in a desperate race to outrun the panic that was fast overtaking her. After leaving The Olympic Towers, she returned to her own apartment only long enough to hastily pack a bag and leave a note for Maria-Luz, the Cuban woman who came three days a week to clean, shop, do laundry, and generally maintain order in Kate's domestic affairs.

It had been a night of endings. The fact that Paul had ultimately taken her totally for granted while spurning and humiliating her in the bargain, only convinced Kate that there had to be something terribly wrong with herself. Loyal, intelligent, attractive, and superbly efficient, she was all of these—yet Paul had cast her aside for a shallow, superficial little nothing like Allison Jeffries.

By the time that Kate gunned her Bentley out of the basement garage with a burning screech of tires, the inevitable realization had begun to sink in.

For the past eighteen years she had been living in a comfortably restricted emotional vacuum. She had simply refused to see what everyone else recognized. From the very beginning she had consistently refused to view Paul Osborn as the man he really was.

Now quite suddenly she had been awakened to the truth, not really because she wanted to know and acknowledge it, but because she had been given no choice in the matter.

She had preferred to live with a myth. To idealize the perfect phantom lover. Never to reveal herself openly to the charismatic and dynamic man who, she instinctively realized, was ultimately inaccessible.

Perhaps, Kate thought as she sped through the Midtown Tunnel en route to her country place in Amagansett, it was the fact that in over eighteen years together Paul had never taken her to bed that had always held her own sexual insecurity at bay.

The storm front that had been pushing up out of the Carribbean throughout the day finally broke with torrential force and vehemence when Kate was halfway out to Montauk Point. With the rain slashing and streaking against the windows, Kate kept her foot pressed relentlessly to the accelerator, sending the beige and cream Bentley rocketing ahead into the rain-wet night.

Glancing down at the softly illuminated speedometer, she realized that she was driving a great deal faster than was her habit, and taking risks upon the slippery highway she never would have considered under ordinary circumstances.

The circumstances, however, were anything but ordinary, and caution was cast to the winds. Kate strained to see through the downpour. She refused to slacken speed or give way, while weaving steadily back and forth through twisting lanes of slowly moving Friday evening traffic.

By now her emotional state was a turbulent maelstrom of

doubt and uncertainty, as the seemingly endless stream of headlights fell steadily away in the rearview mirror. Visibility had been sorely reduced, and as lightning streaked the inky, inchoate blackness, Kate became possessed by the feeling that nature itself had become an untamable entity, raging and swirling about her. The rain was sluicing across the highway in blinding sheets, as it was driven against the car by gale-force winds. The weekend lay ahead of her, empty and bleak.

Then suddenly the figure of a woman materialized ahead in the road in the glare of the Bentley's powerful headlights. A ghostly, stark, and immobile figure, the woman was standing naked in the middle of the highway, with her wet hair streaming about an utterly blank and empty face.

Instinctively Kate's hands gripped the wheel as the road suddenly narrowed into two lanes. In a desperate and perilous gamble, she swerved the heavy car directly into the path of an onrushing truck in order to avoid the waiting, willing victim, who had appeared so ominously. So suddenly. . . and out of nowhere.

There was a wailing blare of the diesel's airhorns. The glare of powerful headlamps shone directly into her eyes. Adrenalin raced and pulsed through her veins. Then, almost miraculously, the diesel hurtled past along the highway, and the ghostly, spectral figure was swallowed up by the dark, the night, and the storm.

Kate was so thoroughly shaken by the incident that when several miles farther on she spotted a garishly illuminated roadhouse with shiny silver siding, she pulled off the road and swung into the parking lot.

The windows facing the highway were steamy with moisture, yet warmly inviting. With the hood of her mink coat drawn up over her head, Kate paused for a moment in the doorway as a wash of laughter, hearty male voices, and blaring Country-Western music spilled out into the night.

Immediately Kate felt herself to be the focus of all attention. The tables were crowded with truckers, and as she stepped inside and closed the door behind her, she could sense the sexual tension in the atmosphere.

It was nearly midnight. The tension was like an electromagnetic force field, and the smell of fried eggs scorching on the griddle was enough to make Kate's stomach turn over inside her. She hadn't had anything to eat since lunch. Feeling suddenly nauseous, she hurried through the tables and made her way to the ladies' restroom at the end of a narrow, dimly lit corridor.

The room was windowless, small, and claustrophobic, with walls painted a sickly institutional green. The air was close and reeked of strong urine. Kate barely had time to latch the door behind her before retching miserably into the filthy toilet bowl.

Never in her life had she felt more miserable, lonely, and depressed.

Finally, after the nausea had passed, she splashed cold water on her face, and, swallowing two valiums, lifted her eyes to confront her own image in the cracked and yellowed mirror.

For a moment Kate felt as if she were viewing the strained and ashen visage of a total stranger. She hadn't been sleeping well of late, and without makeup her ghostly pallor only served to accentuate the bruised shadows beneath her eyes. She looked haggard, drawn, and desperate.

Kate stood there clutching the basin for support as her own mirrored image continued to shatter and re-form into the ravaged, empty countenance of the woman on the highway whose sudden appearance that evening had slashed Kate's confidence like a razor.

Like a malign shadow, it was herself she had seen out there

in the storm and the dark. The face behind the perfect mask that she had always worn.

The fear had always been there, running chill and deep just beneath the smoothly ordered surface of her day-to-day life.

Kate stepped back outside, to be engulfed by strident laughter, blaring music from the jukebox, and a confusion of booming male voices. Stopping at a roadside diner had definitely been a mistake, and she couldn't wait to get outside into the fresh, cool air.

The two valiums had begun to work immediately on her empty stomach, and Kate was in such a dazed and shaky state that she nearly collided with a shadowy hulking figure lounging at the end of the long, dimly lit hall.

He seemed to loom there against the light. A tall and powerfully built black man, with massive shoulders, narrow waist, and powerful arms that suddenly reached out to pull her hard against him. "Ain't you kind of off your beat, pretty lady? You got those boys pretty well stirred up. You know the animals get kind of restless, about this time of night."

The black's voice was a deep, slangy baritone. Liquor flamed on his breath, and the raw sexuality of his hard, muscular body pressing along the length of her stirred something deep inside her.

"What do you say, pretty lady? How about you an' me gettin' real friendly over at the motel next door?" His eyes were smouldering and volcanic. Kate felt his sex stiffening against her, and shivered as his big spatulate hands moved up beneath her coat and over her body with easy familiarity.

"Please . . ." she gasped in a hushed, slightly breathless voice. "I have to get out of here."

"I'm willing to pay," he said. "So what's your problem?"

Kate was too stunned to reply.

"You heard what the lady said, my friend. So just take your paws off her, and move on out of the way, all right?

You've made a mistake, and I definitely think an apology is in order.''

The deeply resonant male voice belonged to a young man standing at the end of the bar. He was darkly blond and athletically built, with attractive regular features, a luxuriant growth of beard, and the clearest, bluest eyes that Kate had ever seen.

It was a face to which Kate was instinctively drawn, and she experienced a wave of grateful relief as he stepped forward to intervene.

Everything after that happened with startling speed. Suddenly Kate felt herself being thrust aside as the black swung around to land a brutal powerhouse right squarely in the young man's gut.

It was a solid, damaging blow, and Kate looked on in horror as he doubled over with a groan. Once again the black hurtled forward with a deadly left hook. This time, however, he was taken completely unaware. His blunt, brutal features expressed startled surprise as he was deftly drawn in close, flipped over the young man's shoulder with a judo roll, and cold-cocked senseless with a powerful karate chop.

But by then Kate was already in full panicky flight, with a riot of angry voices, flying fists, and crashing tables exploding in her wake.

Chapter Three

Kate's country place at Amagansett had always been her refuge from Manhattan's brutally competitive marketplace. She loved the verdant Montauk Peninsula jutting out into the pounding waters of the Atlantic, with its thousands of woodland acres, starkly magnificent cliffs, high dunes, and endless miles of wide, white sandy beaches.

It was a naturalist's paradise, and during the spring and summer months Kate loved to sketch among the dunes, grow fresh vegetables in her garden, and cook marvelous gourmet dinners, which she usually ended up eating quite alone.

In lieu of the career as an artist she had always dreamed of having, photography had become her passion. She regularly indulged herself on weekends by taking hundreds of photographs of animals and birds; of the sea and the sky and the dunes. Stieglitz had always been her idol, and Kate sought to emulate his photographic artistry in every way she could.

The house at the end of Hushabye Lane was an old shingled-sided carriage house that had been converted into a large, high-ceilinged studio, with a wide expanse of skylight windows overlooking the beach. There was a huge fieldstone fireplace, antique early-American furnishings, brightly hand-woven rag-rugs, chintz-covered sofas, and over all an airy sense of light and space.

The cottage, as Kate called it, was secluded on three acres of beachfront property with lots of trees, a wildwood walk, and a spacious redwood sundeck that commanded a lovely view of the dunes and the sea shining beyond.

It was almost one in the morning by the time Kate reached Amagansett. The rain had stopped, and the confused and frightening emotions triggered by Paul's betrayal had begun to focus on the person of Allison Jeffries. Allison, the Caramour Platinum Girl, whose face smiled mockingly down at Kate from the numerous photographic enlargements and advertising layouts covering the knotty-pine walls.

Before Kate launched Allison Jeffries as the fabulous face that sold fifty million dollars' worth of Caramour cosmetics, she had been just another pretty profile making the rounds of the modeling agencies. A plastic bundle of teased hair, long legs, and stiletto heels, whose guileless smile could stop traffic at fifty yards.

Never mind that Allison had done a six-month stint at the Nirvana Massage Parlor on West Forty-sixth upon first arriving in New York City. Ultimately Kate had transformed her into the Caramour Platinum Girl, a captivating vision of blonde, blue-eyed loveliness and physical well-being that managed to suggest the healthy uncomplicated sexuality of the girl next door, while exuding the most outrageously inviting possibilities.

Allison had been Kate's most successful creation, and within a matter of months after her face and figure hit the billboards and T.V. screens across America, the wholesome look was most definitely in. While all those gaunt and ghastly beautiful survivors of some private Dachau were suddenly out of work, and out of style. Consigned forever to the trash heap of fashion out of fashion. The feminine ideal whose time had not only passed into infinity, but unceremoniously expired without so much as a death rattle.

For the past three years the public couldn't seem to get enough of Allison Jeffries, and, as things had turned out, it appeared that neither could Paul Osborn. He had fallen in love with a beautiful illusion, Kate realized. And she herself had been the enchantress who had taught Allison how to move, to smile and to beguile, while making maximum use of her lush proportions and candid, youthful allure.

For the next twenty minutes Kate slashed, ripped, and tore hundreds of Allison's photographs into shreds, before feeding them into the roaring blaze she had started in the fireplace. Then she poured herself a stiff double shot, and collapsed sobbing on the couch to watch a million-dollar advertising campaign go up in smoke.

Thinking of the past was so much more appealing than contemplating the uncertainties of the future and the bleak emptiness of the present moment. Nursing a bottle of vodka and chain-smoking Pall Malls, Kate allowed the memories to surface and float across her mind like drifting clouds reflected on the surface of a still pond.

Going to work for Paul Osborn because she had fallen in love with him had proven to be the very worst of reasons. Paul was looking for a business arrangement, and Kate had exactly suited his requirements. He was obsessed with his dream of building Caramour Cosmetics in his own image, and there was no room in his life for complications. First and foremost, Paul was always the total pragmatist.

Kate laughed a little, cried a lot, and managed to get very

drunk in the process as she remembered those early years together. She recalled her own plain Jane appearance, ill-concealed insecurity, and determination to prove herself equal to Paul's highest expectations, regardless of Spartan working conditions, low pay, and long hours.

Yet, in spite of everything, Paul Osborn had always been able to inspire her belief. It was Paul who had been the first to encourage Kate to believe in herself and in her own creative abilities. He always had an aura about him that promised wonderful things were going to happen.

He also knew a great deal about the female psyche. He knew about women and their dreams. It was under his exacting tutelage that Kate had begun to bloom into a sophisticated career-oriented woman, actively and importantly involved in building Caramour, Inc., into one of the great success stories of the beauty industry.

Paul had always been a driven man. With little formal education, he had been forced to make it strictly on daring, guts, hard work, and determination. He had always been someone with the ability to make things happen. But his style of doing business was so abrasive, his personality so egocentric, and his success so stunning that he was one of the most disliked men in the industry. Fast, aggressive, and more often than not lethal in a confrontation.

Yet perhaps more than anyone else, Paul Osborn had been responsible for building the beauty business into a five-billion-dollar-a-year bonanza. In so doing he changed the appearance of women throughout the world. He completely transformed them, both in how they looked to others and how they saw and felt about themselves.

The bitter irony of it all, Kate realized, was that for all his intuitive brilliance, Paul was a man who held women in virtual contempt.

At some point as the years, the hope, the pain, the regret,

and the sorrow washed over her in waves, Kate realized that her fortieth birthday was upon her. Almost two-thirds of her life had slipped away, and what the hell did she have to show for it, besides an impressive block of Caramour stock, more money than she could comfortably spend, a position of importance, and a certain amount of power within the company.

Her life gave every appearance of being enormously successful. Yet now, sitting alone before the fire in a room with the door locked behind her, she could feel no personal center of gravity or sense of self.

After finishing off the bottle of vodka, taking a long, hot bath, and drugging her senses into submission with two Seconal, Kate finally slipped off into troubled sleep.

It seemed that almost immediately she was dreaming. Running down an endless corridor, with doors opening off on either side. Strange, high-pitched voices kept crying out warnings of loss and despair. Yet no matter how frantically she pounded and pleaded at each of the locked doors, the voices consistently refused to allow her entry, until she finally found herself at the corridor's end.

A powerful wind was now howling and wailing about her, but somehow Kate managed to hold on with clawing fingers and clutching hands. For what seemed an eternity she clung there on the edge of the void with gale-force winds shrieking about her, threatening to carry her over the precipice and into the whirling black vortex of howling nothingness.

Then it was morning. Brilliant sunlight poured in through the wide expanse of windows to illuminate Kate's own familiar surroundings. On every side were her most familiar and cherished possessions, all those things from which at any other time she would have been able to draw some measure of reassurance.

On that particular morning, however, the easel standing before the windows, her paints and drawing things, all the expensive photographic equipment only served to confirm the death of her own most creative aspirations in service to Paul Osborn and Caramour Cosmetics.

The awareness that she had passed into the fourth decade of her life was like a suffocating weight pressing down upon her. She was forty years old. There was no steady man in her life and few real friends. Her career and a certain amount of status were all she had to show for it.

Kate had never had either the interest or the time to pursue more than a modest social life. Her career had always been too demanding and she herself too much of a perfectionist to give less than her total effort, which meant she usually ended up doing everyone else's job as well as her own.

Kate took a sip of scalding hot coffee and lit her first cigarette of the morning. Work had of course always been her crutch. When she was totally involved in her work, nothing else seemed to matter. Not her own emotionally sterile existence, nor her own doubts about the course, content, and ultimate disposition of her life.

Ambition had never really had much to do with it. Kate had been brought up to pursue a career, and that was precisely what she had done. In a way, it was rather like being an actress—playing a role for so long that finally she had turned into the character portrayed.

Now the full, stunning realization that she was going to be appointed president of Caramour at Monday's board of directors meeting engendered a sudden wrenching sense of desperation. A terrible feeling of bleakness pressed down upon her like a heavy physical weight.

The coffee cup slipped from her fingers and crashed to the tiles, but Kate just sat there staring down at it. She found herself utterly unable or unwilling to summon up the energy to move, and conscience-stricken that she cared so little.

Never in her life had Kate experienced such a wrenching

emptiness. A dreadful sense of despair seemed to be spreading through her veins like ice water, numbing the remotest extremities of her body.

As the fear began to grow, Kate held on to the edge of the breakfast bar, trying to connect with some kind of reality. She bit her lip hard in order to feel something, anything.

But there was only the cold visceral terror that seemed suddenly to inhabit her mind and body like an alien presence.

It was as if she had been walking a high wire that had been suddenly and inexplicably loosened by some malign, unseen hand.

She would have gone with the man at the truck stop the night before, Kate realized. She would have done anything to have kept from being alone.

Kate jumped as the phone shrilled at her elbow. But when she lifted the receiver to hear Celia Randolph's distinctively Bostonian accents her sense of relief was palpable. Celia was singing "Happy Birthday." Never in her life had Kate been happier to hear another human voice.

For whatever reasons—tuning, instinct, or habit—Kate had never gone out of her way to make women friends. For the most part she found her own sex devious and self-centered. Celia Randolph, however, was different. That difference went far beyond the expensive designer wardrobe, her fabulous collection of jewelry and even her unshakable and optimistic self-confidence.

First and foremost, Celia Randolph was a star, transcending all lesser luminaries. She was the charismatic *grande dame* of American interior design, whose enormous vitality, unequaled social clout, and hardheaded business sense had propelled her over the years into the ultrararified climes of what passed for the very best society in Manhattan, Palm Beach, and the Hamptons.

Although she had been born to the purple of an old Boston Brahmin family who had made millions in railroads at the turn of the century, Celia Randolph was most definitely among the working rich.

As a designer, Celia's forte was the ability to bestow the Right Look on anyone rich enough to afford the perfect stage setting for their lives; a look that proclaimed social câchét peer-group status, and a glowing well-tended appearance, due primarily to Celia's penchant for softly diffused lighting.

Celia Randolph was invited everywhere, and everywhere she went she invariably imparted a certain unmistakable sense of exquisitely casual elegance, as original and unique as her unequaled taste in clothes, labels, and decor.

Celia was a trend setter who passionately abhorred anything déclassé and was justly proud of her ability to command vast sums of money simply by telling people how to live their lives, decorate their homes, and spend their wealth to stylish effect. She was always first off the mark with anything new, and was famous for giving the most fabulous parties imaginable.

Celia Randolph was many things to many people, but to Kate she was the only close woman friend she had in the world.

Oakmore Manor, Celia's Southhampton country home, crested a high bluff above Georgica Pond. A two-story Palladian mansion surrounded by perfectly barbered lawns, it was flanked by tennis courts, the sea, and a kidney-shaped swimming pool of clearest aquamarine blue, with an artificial waterfall cascading into the deep end.

At the far end of the rose garden stood the century-old windmill that Celia had only recently converted into her own private gymnasium. Keeping herself physically fit had always been Celia's favorite fix along with organic health foods and the liberal sprinkling of conversational banalities that she invariably tossed off in cryptic French.

"Katie, *ma cher*!" Celia cried as Kate was shown inside. The exterior of the historic old mill had been perfectly restored with exactly the right shade of weathered shingle siding, while the interior was strictly neo-Romanesque with a soupçon of Jack LaLanne Baroque. There was indirect lighting, deep pile carpeting, mirrored walls, and environmental music piped in to soothe even the most frazzled nerves. Various pieces of shiny chrome exercise equipment gleamed like surrealistic sculpture in the early afternoon light streaming in through high stained-glass dormer windows. The inimitable Celia Randolph reposed languidly in a steaming redwood hot tub with the water swirling around her from a Jaccuzzi whirlpool bath.

"You're just in time to join me in a little preluncheon libation." Celia gestured toward a magnum of Möêt Chandon cooling in a silver urn. "I had my butler bring some excellent champagne up from the wine cellar, since a celebration is most definitely in order."

Celia's body rippled like pale marble beneath the foamy surface of the surging whirlpool bath. Her platinum hair was drawn up turban-style beneath a white towel, and her face was faintly beaded with moisture. She wore diamonds in her ears, although her really important jewelry was kept safely tucked away in a midtown Manhattan bank vault within easy access to her townhouse on Sutton Place.

"If you're referring to my untimely arrival at middle age, I'd just as soon forget this one," Kate advised her tartly. "From now on, I'm only keeping track of which decade I'm living in."

Celia's laughter was a sparkling crescendo of musical notes. "Wouldn't we all simply love to stop counting, *mon ange*. But time waits for no woman, or man either, so we might as well live it up. You know what they say about me. I'd turn up to celebrate the opening of an envelope."

The honors were done with oriental grace by Celia's Japanese masseuse, who was currently all the rage. Her flat, featureless face wore a look of beatific serenity. Kate had always thought of her as the "madonna of martial arts" in her white gym instructor's uniform. Yukiko was reputed to possess a black belt in karate as well as formidable, if not mythic, skills in the arts of shiatzu, zone therapy, and tai chi.

After popping the champagne cork with a flick of her thumb, Yukiko presented each of them with a glass of champagne as though presiding at a ritual Japanese tea ceremony.

"Here's to the new president of Caramour," Celia announced, lifting her glass in toast.

"How did you hear?"

"My dear, you should know by now that I make it my business to know absolutely everything," Celia responded with one of her glorious cornflower-blue-eyed smiles. "After all, Katherine, I am one of the company's major stockholders."

Kate realized that her hand was trembling slightly as she lifted the glass to her lips. "Did you also know that Paul was having an affair with Allison Jeffries?"

Celia did a quick double take. "Well." She shrugged. "I won't say that I haven't heard some pretty spicy rumors to that effect. But of course I just assumed that Allison was merely a passing fancy, rather like hula hoops and pet rocks. I mean after all, darling, even the prettiest face in the world has to say something eventually. Little miss round-heels isn't exactly the intellect of the decade, now is she?"

"She must have been doing something right," Kate responded in a brittle, biting tone. Then, with an edge of desperation honing and sharpening her voice, she announced, "Paul's decided to marry her, Celia. In two weeks they're flying off to the French Riviera to be joined in blissful matrimony aboard the *Caramour II*."

Celia's blue eyes widened in disbelief. "I think my hearing must be going. For one instant moment, I thought I heard you say that Paul was going to marry Allison."

"You heard correctly."

"But you've simply got to be kidding!" Celia exclaimed. "*Quel horreur,* Paul...marrying Allison...with a heart condition, yet?"

Kate nodded bleakly. "It's true. He asked me over to Olympic Towers last night, and Allison was there. As you might imagine, she simply couldn't wait to let me in on the happy secret."

Keeping her voice as cooly unemotional as possible, Kate proceeded to fill Celia in on all that had taken place at Olympic Towers the night before. When she was through, Celia finished off her champagne in a single gulp, then tossed her glass over her head, where it smashed against a chrome Exer-cycle.

"Well, *c'est la vie,*" she sighed. "Although I must admit I suspected all along that something like this might happen eventually, Katie. While you've never actually come out and admitted your feelings for Paul, one didn't have to have X-Ray vision in order to see that you were in love with the bastard."

Celia shook her head, sending her diamond pendant earrings dancing. "Trust me, Kate. I know it's difficult to accept, but you're well enough out of it where Mr. Paul Osborn is concerned. As you know, Cristina and I were the very best of friends. Take it from me. That marriage was no bed of roses, no matter what the press clippings said. The poor woman literally went to her grave trying to live up to the role of being the glamorous, charming, and *oh so very social* Mrs. Paul Osborn. In the end—when Cristina was drinking heavily and of no more use to him—Paul treated her like a piece of junk mail. Paul isn't really capable of love, Kate.

Only lust. If you ask me, I think he's finally gotten exactly what he deserves."

"I just don't know how I could have believed that Paul really cared for me," Kate offered. "How could I have been such a fool . . . for so long."

Celia signaled the hovering masseuse for another glass of champagne, and then stepped from the tub, to be enfolded in an oversize towel. "Now I don't want you to get upset about what I'm going to say," Celia lectured with mock severity. "Because I fully intend to say it anyway. Paul may not have been in love with you *comme ça* . . . but you certainly have his fullest respect, or he wouldn't have made you president of Caramour. The truth of the matter is, he's offered you the moon. Why, any career woman worth her salt would consider the presidency of Caramour Cosmetics the chance of a lifetime."

"I can't go in there on Monday and accept the presidency," Kate confessed, twisting the stem of her champagne glass. "I never wanted that kind of responsibility. You know as well as I do that as soon as Paul leaves, the boardroom at Caramour is going to look like feeding time in the shark tank."

"Then don't go in on Monday," Celia advised. She climbed up on a padded massage table and stretched out lengthwise. "Lord knows you deserve some time off, with the kind of hours you put in on the job. Come with me to Coral Key. Tomorrow morning I'm flying down to Jamaica for a two-week stay at the most incredible beauty spa imaginable. It's an absolute miracle factory, run by a very sexy doctor by the name of Andreas Jaccard. I can call down there right now, and make you a reservation. You'd wait years on your own.

"It's lovely of you to ask," Kate responded. "But I just wouldn't know what to do with myself in a place like that. Besides, I've got so much work piled up on my desk I simply have to go in. I have no choice."

Celia's laughter rippled softly as Yukiko set to work massaging a thin coat of fragrant golden oil into her skin. "I can see I'm going to have to resort to desperate measures." Celia made a soft clucking sound, as if regretful of Kate's inability to immediately defer to her superior judgment.

"Just how old do you think I am?" she questioned blandly.

Kate pondered momentarily, but there was no easy answer. "I suppose you have to be somewhere in the neighborhood of fifty years old, although you certainly don't look it for a minute."

It was true. Celia at whatever age was an amazingly lovely and vital woman, with a flawless alabaster complexion and eyes that were full of blue sky. She simply brimmed with cheerful well-being, while fairly exuding a healthy vitality.

Celia laughed. Her voice rippled, and then fell into a husky, intimate purr. "Now I wouldn't want this to get around," she said, arching one finely penciled brow. "But seeing how you are now entering the rarefied realms of older womanhood, I'm going to let you in on a fabulous secret."

"And that is . . . ?" Kate questioned.

"That you don't really have to grow old, gracefully or otherwise," Celia announced.

She reached one hand around to pat her firmly contoured buttocks. "I'm sixty-five years old, and I owe everything to a man by the name of Doctor Andreas Jaccard and the process of cellular rejuvenation."

"Didn't this Jaccard once win a Nobel Prize for some kind of scientific breakthrough some years back?" Kate asked.

Celia nodded, and her smile was incandescent. "Jaccard's a medical genius," she confirmed, "who just happens to be as handsome as any movie star and simply oozing sex appeal. Come with me to Coral Key Spa, Katherine. You have absolutely everything to gain and nothing to lose."

Chapter Four

Kate's Air Jamaica flight dropped down out of the final wisps of cloud vapor, circling well out over the sea. Then the plane came sweeping in for a landing over ripening fields of sugar cane flashing quicksilver in the bright afternoon sunlight.

Below, the airport buildings were sagging beneath the weight of neglect. The corrugated tin roofs had long since rusted, paint was flaking, and the signs had letters missing.

The feeder flight from Montego Bay finally touched down upon the blistering macadam airstrip. Overgrown with tufts of withered grass, it was cratered and pitted with potholes.

It looked to Kate like some poor, hot, tropical backwater, and she immediately lamented her decision to come. But then where else could she have possibly run to? Kate wondered. There was no place. No one else, besides Celia.

* * *

On the previous Sunday Celia had left as scheduled for Coral Key without her. Yet when it came right down to returning to Manhattan, to Paul, the board of directors, and her own heady ascent to the company presidency, Kate had decided that her only choice was to take a three-week leave of absence. There was just no way in the world she could have faced all that in her present frame of mind.

The first few days had passed in planting a sea of yellow daisies in the garden behind the cottage. After that Kate gathered, stewed, and canned wild berry preserves. Then she set to work on the rag rug she'd been braiding for the past decade. She also spent an inordinate amount of time walking alone along the beach and sketching among the dunes.

It seemed, however, that nothing held her interest for very long, or invested her with any real sense of fulfillment or real pleasure of accomplishment. Worst of all, Kate lived in fear that it would happen again, that terrifying discontinuity of self that had struck like an inner earthquake on the morning of her fortieth birthday.

By midweek even the simplest tasks, like painting her nails or ordering groceries from the market by phone, had to be approached as if she were walking an aerialist's high wire. She was smoking two packs of cigarettes a day, drinking far too many martinis, and taking a rainbow-hued variety of pills that left her tense, moody, and deeply depressed.

But it wasn't until Thursday evening that something happened that left Kate stunned, uncomprehending, and wondering if she were beginning to lose her mind. It was on the following morning, during the long, dark hour before dawn, that she finally decided to join Celia on Coral Key.

Celia had been right all along. What could she possibly have to lose?

* * *

The transition from the cool, dimly illuminated interior of the plane to the humid, sun-blasted world outside came as something of a shock. Kate emerged from the cabin, nodding her thanks to the Jamaican flight crew. Then she started down the steep metal steps, where she was suddenly swept by a sickening sense of vertigo.

For several queasy moments everything seemed to spin crazily, moving in and out of focus, blurring even the familiar figure hurrying toward her across the buckling tarmac as Kate clutched the railing for support.

"Katherine, darling, *c'est fantastique* to have you here at last." Celia's presence was immediately reassuring, and it brought Kate back from the edge. "Quite frankly," Celia was saying with a look of very critical appraisal, "I've never seen a more likely candidate for cell rejuvenation. You look like you've been shell shocked. Now let's hurry along. I've got the most wonderful surprise waiting."

Kate scarcely had time to catch her breath before Celia had whisked her off through the open-shed terminal building, which displayed little more than a ticket counter, baggage claim, and fly-blown newsstand offering a variety of out-of-date magazines.

Outside, in front of the terminal, Kate found herself being propelled through the wilting heat to a dusty old La Salle sedan with the words *Coral Key Spa* painted across the door. A handsome young West Indian was lounging against the front fender, apparently in anticipation of their arrival. Kate simply assumed that he was to be their driver. At least until Celia skipped on ahead to slip both arms about the young man's waist, while pressing her silk-haltered breast against his well-muscled arm.

"This is my surprise," Celia announced gaily. "Katherine Leslie, I want you to meet Benny Valdez—the new man in my life."

Benny Valdez had the widest, whitest smile Kate had ever seen in a black face. His features were pure natal African, with broadly structured nose, full lips, and widely spaced brown eyes. But from that point onward he was strictly the Scarsdale Town and Country Club, with his faultless good manners, tennis whites, Adidas keds, and dark blue La Coste shirt.

Benny was over six feet tall, broad shouldered, narrow waisted, and beautifully muscled beneath his gleaming mahogany colored skin. At least that was the color that Celia insisted he was, after Benny had sprinted off to retrieve Kate's luggage.

"Benny used to be the tennis pro at Round Hill," Celia gushed as the two of them climbed into the rear of the vintage La Salle. "Of course, Andreas spotted his potential immediately. He hired him on the spot, to be athletic director at Coral Key. Oh Kate," she sighed, melting back against the seat, "don't you simply love those perfectly sculpted negroid features, and that darling accent with just the slightest soupçon of British Regency?"

"He seems like a very nice young man," Kate said, choosing her words with care. She was still in shock. "But honestly, Celia, aren't you getting rather carried away? This just doesn't seem like you."

"Isn't it madness?" Celia giggled as Benny returned and began strapping Kate's luggage to the top of the car. "But then what's the point of looking absolutely gorgeous if you're not going to get laid?" Celia nodded toward the window where Benny's tight white tennis shorts were straining against his dark skin.

"He's hung like a water buffalo," Celia whispered. Her features were radiant, and her eyes sparkled. "Oh Katie, I never dreamed it could really be like this. Can you imagine? A tough old bird like me falling head over heels in love with an ethnic Adonis. I must be totally out of my mind, and I'm loving every illicit minute of it."

Kate's sense of unreality deepened considerably during the drive into Porto Cristo from the airport. The island of Coral Key lay several miles off the northwestern coast of Jamaica, and could only be reached by boat.

As they sped along the narrow winding road beside the sea with Benny Valdez behind the wheel, Kate was absolutely amazed at Celia's dramatic transformation in less than a week. There was something laid back, languid, and luscious about her.

Fashionably bronzed and casually braceleted with jangling gold slave bangles halfway up her arms, Celia looked fantastic. Her platinum blonde hair was bound up native-style in a bright scarf. She appeared to have been poured into the tight white slacks worn along with a flowered silk halter, from which her buoyant breasts kept threatening to spill at the slightest provocation.

For all her exuberant spirits concerning Benny Valdez, there had not been a word spoken about Winstin Thornton. As Celia's perennial escort, Winstin was a southern gentleman with a faultless pedigree, neatly graying hair, and a middle-aged paunch. Celia often joked that he was "little more than a limp handful."

No one was ever quite sure of exactly what it was he did, besides dabble occasionally in the stock market. Mostly he was "eminently presentable."

Headwaiters always remembered his name, and he could be depended upon to show up appropriately dressed when black tie was required. Since he was functionally impotent and held his liquor tolerably well, Winstin had never been known to create problems.

It had always been obvious to Kate that Winstin was

slavishly devoted to Celia. And up until the unexpected appearance of Benny Valdez upon the scene, she had assumed, along with just about everybody else, that their ultimate union was all but inevitable. Now it appeared that all bets were off.

Kate had to admit that the ride in from the airport was spectacular, with ever more magnificent vistas of azure sea and verdant green mountains. There was a wild, untamed beauty to the unfolding panorama of craggy mountain peaks surfacing through tropical rain forests of exotic fern trees, palm, breadfruit, and tamarind.

Everywhere she looked there was natural beauty and vivid color. Yellow shower trees lined the road, and crimson poinsettia and splashes of pink and orange bougainvillea covered the ancient stone walls of dilapidated plantation houses.

But if there was an awesome beauty to the matchless island setting, there was also an underlying sense of malignant poverty. Tin-roofed shacks clustered together with pigs rooting in their muddy yards. As they sped past in a swirl of dust, ragged black children ran out of hovels to stare after them with wide and wondering eyes.

Porto Cristo, Kate rightly assumed, was not one of those rich white resorts with which the western coast of Jamaica seemed to abound. Neither did it take her long to discover why Celia laughingly referred to Benny as her "private kamikaze pilot." After twenty-five recklessly endangered minutes on the road, the old La Salle finally skidded into the narrow, twisting streets of Porto Cristo, scattering chickens, dogs, and ragged urchins before the blaring horns. The town was graced with a gemlike setting at the foot of verdant green hills surrounding a beautiful crescent bay. Yet Kate felt a vaguely disturbing sense of threat; of being too white in a black land. It seemed to hang suspended on the torpid, stifling air. She saw it flicker briefly in the surly looks cast by a cluster of arrogant young blacks lounging in front of the local rum shop.

Hot Caribbean sunlight poured over the ramshackle collection of polygot architecture with its rusting corrugated-tin roofs, grilled balconies, and deeply shaded verandas.

According to Benny, most of the local inhabitants slept through the hottest part of the day. The dusty central square was nearly empty as they pulled up in front of the old Saint George Hotel in the heat-drugged stillness of afternoon. Then Benny drove off to gas up the launch and transfer Kate's luggage for the boat ride out to Coral Key.

As far as rich white Americans were concerned, the racial situation in Jamaica was like a powder keg. During the past winter, the New York papers had been full of so many horror stories that tourists were routinely advised to remain inside their hotels after dark and travel only in groups when visiting the island's outlying towns and villages. Always there was the threat of violent and bloody ambush by militant young blacks, who had been known to tear pendant earrings from delicately pierced ears, and slice off fingers in order to steal diamond rings.

The tiled patio of the Saint George Hotel overlooked the harbor of Porto Cristo and was considerably cooler than the streets. Kate and Celia sat beneath century-old mahogany trees and sipped double banana daiquiries served up by a smiling white-coated waiter whose features appeared to have been carved from polished ebony.

The service was genial and faultless, while the hotel itself was like something out of an Evelyn Waugh novel. Inside the dimly cool dining room ceiling fans revolved slowly, gently wafting the coiled strips of flypaper. Small tables, neatly covered with red and white checkered oilcloth, faced the old mahogany bar, where a handful of white planters clustered together drinking tall pink gins and smoking long evil-smelling cheroots.

"Chin chin," Celia pronounced, hoisting her daiquiri and touching it to Kate's own frosted glass. "You might as well enjoy it, love, because it's the last booze you're going to see for the next two weeks. No liquor, cigarettes, or drugs of any kind are allowed while undergoing therapy."

Kate looked doubtful. "I'm not really convinced about taking the injections. I know enough about immunology to know that having unspecified animal tissue injected into the human system is a pretty risky business, at best."

Celia leaned back in her fan-back wicker chair and spread her arms expansively. "What you see before you is living proof that you aren't going to die from gas-gangrene, or shrivel up like the curse of the mummy's tomb. This is my fifth visit to Coral Key, and you yourself thought I was at least fifteen years younger than I am. Yours truly has every intention of living to be at least a hundred, and making a gorgeous corpse in the bargain."

"I'd be willing to settle for a lot less than that," Kate said dourly. "Just exactly what are these injections supposed to do?"

"Cell therapy is based on the premise that the death of the body's cells is what causes the ill effects of aging, not to mention most all of our basic health problems. Getting injected with the live cells of disease-free animals stimulates your own natural cell growth, and brings about the rejuvenation of tissue-specific organs. For instance, it's the first time Andreas has given me a series of injections that come directly from the ovaries of pregnant sheep."

"Proving what exactly?" Kate questioned, with one eyebrow arching up.

"Let the record speak for itself." Celia laughed. "It's

given me the sexual libido of a teenage girl. To be perfectly candid Katie, I now consider a day without sex to be a day of my life entirely wasted. It's incredible that I've spent all these years building a place for myself in society, when all I ever really needed was a lover like Benny Valdez and a good, strong dose of sheep ovaries."

Kate was feeling exceedingly uncomfortable with the subject of Celia's sexual emancipation at age sixty-five. Somehow there was something vaguely indecent about the whole subject. "Tell me about this Doctor Jaccard," Kate suggested, in hopes of changing the subject before Celia went on to tell her far more than she really wanted to know.

"Well, darling, Andreas is a rare phenomenon. He's been known to simply paralyze members of the opposite sex with just one look from those big brown eyes of his. He also happens to be a brilliant scientist, a Nobel Laureate, and an absolutely gorgeous hunk of man. He's always reminded me of Omar Sharif, only taller and much better looking."

"Is he European?" Kate questioned. "The name sounds French."

Celia signaled the hovering waiter for two more banana daiquiries. "Andreas is a little bit of everything. He was born in the Dominican Republic of an hispanic father and a French-Creole mother. Andreas' parents died while he was still quite young in some kind of epidemic. After that he was raised here in Jamaica, and got his higher education at the finest medical schools in France.

"He won the Nobel while still in his early thirties, after he had transferred his laboratory experiments to the Meyerhof Clinic in Switzerland. For many years Andreas was considered to be the heir apparent. He even married Meyerhof's daughter, but eventually they had some kind of falling out. Most likely one of those silly scientific disputes. You know what two huge competing male egos can be like . . . especially since Jaccard won the Nobel. I'm told that Meyerhof never really forgave him for that."

"Is he married?" Kate questioned.

Celia nodded. "To an absolute bitch. Madame Jaccard came to Jamaica originally as private nurse to an elderly planter living on Coral Key. He left her everything when he died, and then she met Andreas. They married and he moved his research here to the island. I suppose that Ingrid must have gotten some money as well, because Jaccard consistently refuses to accept more than a very select handful of patients a year."

"Where did you first hear about him?"

"Through Christina, Paul's wife. She used to go to the Meyerhof Clinic for rejuvenation therapy at least once a year."

Kate's smile was tinged with irony.

"I hate sounding cynical," she said. "But one does have to admit that Cristina made a beautiful and quite youthful-looking corpse."

Kate breathed in the clean salt-sea air and experienced a sudden surge of expectation. Celia had been right. She had needed desperately to get away from New York, and the prospect of two restful and relaxing weeks on a small isolated tropical island seemed like the perfect retreat. And a rather strategic one as well, considering the circumstances.

Seated in the back of the launch while Celia kept Benny company up front, Kate trained her 16mm movie camera on the lush and tantalizing vision emerging from the sea. As they drew closer, Coral Key began to take on the appearance of a tropical Eden, basking beneath a blue and cloudless sky.

The island was formed in the shape of a three-quarter moon, with a crystal-clear lagoon and sugar-white beaches lined with graceful palms. The incredible lush greenness of the low-lying landscape served as a backdrop for a magnificent white yacht riding serenely at anchor about a half mile offshore.

According to Celia, it had been originally built in the 1920s for King Farouk of Egypt. The *Sultana* had been the largest sailing yacht in the world. A virtual floating palace, it was now the private property of a woman by the name of Fiona Van Zandt, who many still considered to be the richest woman on earth.

The stories about Fiona Van Zandt were legion. Following her total withdrawal from international society some five years before, she had been variously labeled a prisoner of drugs in her secluded Moroccan villa, a woman permanently disfigured by a quack plastic surgeon, and an insatiable slave of sex, attended by a veritable regiment of dusky North African lovers.

Fiona Van Zandt had always caused a stir in the press, as the madcap daughter of Virginia tobacco magnate James B. Van Zandt. She had been married six times, and most of her husbands had possessed titles of varying degrees of authenticity. The first had been a groom who shared Fiona's lifelong love of horses. The last had been a Bedouin sheik who shared her white marble palace in the Casbah at Tangier and her passion for ancient Sanskrit poetry.

In between there had been an English duke, an Austrian count, an exiled Russian prince, and the undisputed king of the silver screen. Yet neither marriage, motherhood, titles, nor a yearly tax-free income of nearly twenty-five million dollars had brought Fiona Van Zandt happiness.

As a woman possessed by an unquenchable thirst for love, Fiona had always managed to capture the imagination of large numbers of people through her romantic exploits. Yet less than six months earlier Kate had seen a photo of her being carried from a private plane at Orly Airport, en route to a Paris hospital where she was to undergo emergency surgery for cancer. Now, as Kate turned her camera upon Fiona's magnificent white yacht, she recalled that photograph.

It showed a pathetic wraith of a woman with pain-haunted eyes, a private fortune estimated to be over seven hundred millions, and almost no chance of survival.

The launch throttled down as it entered the lagoon and glided easily alongside the long wooden jetty extending out into the water. Benny jumped ashore to secure the boat, while Kate continued to pan the shoreline through her view-finder until the figure of a woman came sharply into focus.

She was striding purposefully across the beach toward the pier beneath a gaily flowered parasol held aloft by one of the most stunningly beautiful young mulatto women that Kate had ever seen.

The girl was somewhere in her late teens, exceedingly tall and graceful, with skin the color of old ivory. She had the delicate features of an African water bird, and her long, silky black hair was parted precisely in the middle, as if recently preened.

She carried herself with the lofty dignity of an African queen, and something in her manner managed to convey a subtle but unmistakable contempt for the white-clad figure marching briskly down the pier beneath the flowered parasol.

"Don't look now," Celia whispered, as Benny handed Kate out of the launch. "But you're about to be accosted, and I might as well give you fair warning that Madame Jaccard can be entirely lethal when properly aroused. She watches Andreas like a hawk."

Kate disliked Ingrid Jaccard from the moment she set eyes on her. Madame carried herself more like a man than a woman, and her gaze was as direct as a laser beam.

Ingrid thrust her hand forward as Celia made the introduction, but her handshake was brief and rudely perfunctory. "You're quite fortunate that Mrs. Van Zandt prefers the privacy of her yacht, *Miss* Leslie. Otherwise there would not have been space available for you."

"I'm very pleased that you were willing to take me on such short notice," Kate responded, forcing a smile. "The island looks beautiful. I'm sure that I'm going to thoroughly enjoy my stay."

Ingrid's expression remained unchanged, while her voice was brusque and commanding with its heavy Germanic accents. "I might as well warn you," *Madame* pronounced, "this is not some glamorous vacation spa. We are very disciplined here. My husband's program requires a great deal of dedication to self-improvement. We take only a limited number of patients each year, and they are fully expected to participate with both discipline and self-effort. The rules must be followed absolutely. There will be no smoking, drinking alcohol, or drugs of any kind used on Coral Key. Everyone is treated exactly the same on this island, and we are not impressed by either celebrity or position." Kate shot Celia a veiled look while Benny removed her bags from the launch.

Ingrid Jaccard was an unusual-looking woman. Her complexion was very pale. No cosmetics were needed to enhance the snapping black Tartar eyes that endowed her features with an almost Asian cast. Her face was more Slavic, an arresting study in planes and hollows with widely prominent cheekbones and a thin, tightly drawn mouth. Her lustrous straight dark hair was worn high on her head in a coronet of braids, while beneath the starched white nurse's uniform she wore a black high-necked leotard that completely enshrouded her sturdy frame.

"I quite understand the need to observe rules and discipline,'' Kate said as agreeably as possible. ''Now if you don't mind, I'm very tired from the trip. I'd appreciate being shown to my quarters.''

Ingrid nodded shortly, pursed her lips, and turned her disapproving gaze upon Benny. ''I've put Miss Leslie in the Yellow Cottage,'' she instructed. Then with an air of dismissal, ''If Mrs. Randolph is no longer in need of your services this afternoon, I want you to take the bags, then report to the Great House. I have work for you there.''

Madame Jaccard turned abruptly once again to Kate, and nodded toward the statuesque young mulatto woman who stood so silently attentive in the bright, hot Caribbean sunlight. ''Solange will take care of any personal needs you might have while you're here. She's functionally deaf and dumb, but don't let that fool you. She doesn't miss anything.''

The girl's huge dark eyes had remained lowered throughout. But now, as if obeying some psychic impulse, she looked up, and something flickered in the liquid brown depths of her gaze. What it was she saw reflected there Kate was not exactly sure.

Perhaps intuitively she understood that she herself appeared to supply at least a possible solution to some unknown equation, that something unspoken had passed between them.

The Yellow Cottage, with its peaked roof, wide-screened veranda, and creaking, polished mahogany floors, reminded Kate of an old Key West conch house. The interior smelled faintly of insecticide. There were two day beds made up like couches, and the walls were framed with faded watercolors of local scenes. There were virtually no amenities beyond those necessary to basic comfort.

From what she had seen thus far, Coral Key did not appear to be the sort of beauty spa Kate would have expected Celia

Randolph to frequent. Everything in fact appeared a bit ramshackle and threadbare.

Privacy was obviously considered to be of the utmost importance, however, and each of the cottages surrounding an overgrown, grassy quadrangle was secluded by hedges of flowering hibiscus, while the surrounding gardens were a veritable jungle of tropical ferns, trees, vines, and flowers.

By the time Kate had finished unpacking, she was completely exhausted, and collapsed on one of the beds.

She lay there in the dimness, allowing her thoughts to simply drift away, lulled by the distant wash and whisper of the sea. She had traveled three thousand miles that day in order to escape the numbing emptiness, but only the geography had changed.

Kate felt herself to be suspended in space and time. She was filled with a sense of having trespassed onto strange and entirely new emotional geography. All of her perceptions seemed dazed and distracted, as if she were standing outside herself. Like a dual image standing in judgment of her every act, her every thought.

She was appalled at having allowed herself to simply fall into bed with a virtual stranger the night before. It was that perhaps more than anything else that had driven her to Coral Key, to Celia, and to Doctor Andreas Jaccard.

She had been desperately in need of masculine reassurance. And Brian Brophy had appeared at just the right moment to move her into the very center of her own desire, her own desperate need to make contact.

After returning from doing some shopping late on Friday afternoon, Kate had noticed a green van with a metal surf rack on top standing empty at the end of Hushabye Lane. It had been parked there for the past several days, and she assumed that it belonged to the lone wind-surfer determindedly braving the waves that came roiling in out of the Atlantic, thundering into the shallows along her private stretch of beach.

It was in the late spring that the sea came into its wild season along the southeastern shore of Long Island. The temperature could drop twenty degrees in a matter of hours, while the sky changed swiftly from the purest cerulean blue to monochromatic gray pierced by shafts of light. Kate had never seen anyone surf that particular stretch of water before. There were always dangerous riptides, and the waves came rushing into shore at a precipitous sixty-degree angle to hurl their seething mass upon the dunes.

It was five in the afternoon when the door chimes sounded. Kate had just fixed her first shaker of martinis of the evening, and put her favorite jazz-guitar record of Gabor Szabo on the stereo.

"Yes, what is it?" she questioned, after opening the front door barely a crack and securing the chain lock.

Her unexpected caller was wearing faded jeans, sandals, and a dark blue sweatshirt that hugged his muscular torso like the pelt of a healthy young animal. His face was deeply tanned and warmly smiling, with light, clear-water blue eyes and straight white teeth.

He looked to be somewhere in his middle twenties, and Kate realized that he also appeared to be vaguely familiar.

"Remember me?" he questioned in a pleasantly deep baritone.

It took only a moment for Kate to collect her thoughts. Then abruptly she did indeed remember the brawny, shaggy-haired young man with the golden beard and friendly manner. "Why yes, of course I remember you. You were the one who came to my rescue last Friday night at the diner on Sunrise Highway."

Kate quickly unlatched the door and swung it wide. "I'm very grateful for what you did Mr. . . ?"

"Brian Brophy is the name, but my friends call me Skip." He nodded back over his shoulder. "I'm afraid my van is stalled out in front. Would it be allright if I used your phone to call the service station up on the highway?"

Kate poured herself a martini while Brian Brophy made his call. Then she stood staring out through the darkening windows as he explained to someone about the van. The dunes were deserted, strewn with driftwood and streamers of seaweed washed up by the outgoing tide.

She shivered slightly, drawing the heavy cardigan sweater closer about her. Listening to the distant thunder of the surf, gently underlain with the whisper of the golden-bearded sea grass rippling across the dunes, Kate contemplated the long, empty evening stretching ahead of her. The lonely dinner. The drinking . . . the pills . . . the hours passing like mourners in a funeral procession.

For the first time in her life, Kate felt absolutely no interest in all the various projects that had always kept her so fully occupied.

Kate turned as Brian Brophy replaced the receiver, and suddenly she was very much aware of her own careless appearance. She wore no makeup, and her hair was tied negligently back from her face with a ribbon and needed washing.

"I'm afraid they won't be able to send anyone down," he informed her. "So I guess I'll just hitchhike back to my boat at Montauk Harbor, and come back for the van tomorrow. That is, if you wouldn't mind my leaving the van overnight?"

Kate made a distracted motion with one hand. "Look . . . Mr. Brophy. You were awfully decent about the other night. I was rather at loose ends, I'm afraid. Really, I don't know what I would have done if you hadn't stepped in."

Brian Brophy's smile was entirely reassuring. "Nothing to it. I just did what seemed best, and nobody really got hurt. Just a few skinned knuckles, that's all. I'm not all that great with my fists, but I do happen to hold a brown belt in karate."

His easy warmth and openness served to melt the awkwardness Kate felt. "Well, to tell you the truth, I was just about to fix myself some dinner. I'd like very much to have your company, and afterwards I can drive you wherever you like. Please do stay . . . won't you?" There was a plea in her voice.

Kate opened her eyes and lay there in the dimness listening to the feral pulse of the tropic dusk. There had been something incredible about the evening they had spent together. Something completely out of step with her previously very disciplined and tightly controlled existence.

Yet somehow making love to Brian Brophy had seemed a natural response, something right and unavoidable. There had been no need to make a decision, just the overwhelming desire to touch and to be touched. To feel his strong hands caressing her, and his lips on hers. Brian's touch had been gentle but sure. His gaze was open, loving, and benign; without judgment of any kind.

It had been so long that Kate needed desperately to feel what it was like to be a woman, if in fact she had ever really known. It was Brian Brophy who had given her back that part of herself. Yet confronted with all that had passed between them when she awoke the following morning, Kate was only too aware of all that was hollow, lost, and fearful within.

Ultimately she had fled New York for Coral Key because everything seemed to be sliding away from her. There just didn't seem to be anything left to hang on to.

Kate no longer knew who she was, where she was going, or how she was going to get there.

Chapter Five

Kate walked slowly along the gravel path that led to the beach. The morning was clear and sunny, and yet she felt as if she were submerged beneath the green, leafy canopy overhead. The air was pleasantly warm and lightly scented with jasmine, and brightly plumaged birds flitted in and out of the thick tropical vegetation.

Kate's breakfast tray had been served that morning by the same statuesque mulatto who had accompanied Madame Jaccard to the dock the previous afternoon. In spite of her affliction, the girl was clearly intelligent and more than eager to please.

She spoke with her eyes and her hands, and the name Solange suited her exactly.

But it wasn't until after Kate had finished eating and Solange had departed with her breakfast tray that she realized who the young deaf-mute girl really was.

It had happened the day before, when she and Celia were walking along the wharf in Porto Cristo after leaving the St. George Hotel. They had been approached by a ragged old man playing a hand-carved wooden flute.

He was drunk and disreputable, with a face as grizzled and seamed as old saddle leather. One eye was milky and moon-struck, and he wore a single golden earring in one ear, with a bright red bandanna tied about his head. Kate was particularly taken by his hands, for the fingers moving so lightly and gracefully over the wood flute were as dark and gnarled as old roots.

The music he played had a lovely haunting quality to it, with the notes trilling off into the heat haze of afternoon. There was an equally disreputable-looking monkey perched upon the old man's shoulder. When the ancient mariner doffed his battered straw hat and bowed low in their path, the monkey leaped to the ground and cartwheeled nimbly about them in a circle. His acrobatics were perfectly orchestrated to the wailing notes of the old man's flute as he upped the tempo to a sprightly sea chantey.

"Have you got a piece of silver for old Captain Blue?" he whined with a boozy toothless cackle. "Ya know it's God's own commandment to feed the poor." He fixed Celia with his single good eye. "An' from the look of those diamonds, you can well afford a few yankee dollars."

"Don't give the old reprobate a cent," Celia pronounced. "Andreas told me about this old fraud. He's the local crack-pot, and we've all been warned to stay completely away from him."

The old man's wizened features sobered abruptly, and he jerked the length of rope to return the monkey to his shoulder. "Aye, and I'm not surprised that Jaccard told you to stay away from old Captain Blue, Missus. But did he also tell you that he kidnapped my only daughter, and that he keeps her prisoner out there on that island of his?"

"If that were true," Celia informed him archly, "the police would have done something about it long ago. I know for a fact that you have been forbidden to molest your daughter in any way."

"Jaccard pays off the local police to look the other way," the old man said angrily. "But that doesn't mean the good doctor doesn't bleed red blood like any other man."

His words and the implied threat had stayed with Kate. But now as she emerged into the blinding white sunlight reflecting off the white sand beach, she deliberately put the disturbing encounter from her mind. She shaded her eyes against the glare, and stood for several moments scanning the beach.

It was empty except for the figure of a woman reclining against a wicker back rest about halfway down to the water's edge. Her brief two-piece bikini was bright orange and contrasted sharply with the fairness of her skin and the cloud of flaming red hair that cascaded to her shoulders. She was slim, small breasted, wore huge sunglasses, and was leisurely smoking a forbidden cigarette.

The sand was hot against Kate's bare feet as she hurried across the beach. "Hi there," she said. "My name is Kate Leslie. Would you happen to have a cigarette you could spare? I'm about to have a nicotine fit."

Raising herself on one elbow, the woman in the orange bikini removed her dark glasses and smiled, squinting up at Kate against the sunlight. It was a warm, engaging smile, and Kate felt drawn to her immediately. "I already know who you are," she said in a softly cultivated voice. "Celia Randolph told me all about you in the sauna yesterday, before she went to pick you up at the airport."

Kate spread her beach towel, removed the pink terrycloth robe provided by the spa, and sank down to accept a cigarette, from the pack of Virginia Slims the young woman extended. "You look incredibly familiar," Kate ventured. "But it's hard to believe that you could actually be Adrianna del Bario, the ballerina."

"I'm afraid I have to plead guilty as charged," the woman said, proferring a small platinum lighter. "And speaking of guilty, you do realize, I presume, that we are both currently in default of Madame Jaccard's antismoking ban. Ingrid's utterly paranoid on the subject. If she weren't even more paranoid about avoiding the sun's ultraviolet rays, she'd be out here checking up on us at this very moment."

They laughed easily together in the simmering hush of morning. Then Kate drew on her cigarette and exhaled with a sigh of purest satisfaction. "It's heaven," she breathed. "If I'd known that this island was both dry as a bone and completely nicotine free, I'd have stocked up on vodka and cigarettes at the duty-free shop in Montego Bay. I finished off my last pack of cigarettes last night and have been undergoing withdrawal symptoms ever since."

In spite of Adrianna del Bario's pleasant smile and gracious manner, her features seemed shadowed by a look of somber introspection, as if only moments before her mind had been a thousand miles away, and it was something of an effort to bring herself back to the present moment.

"So what do you think of our tight little island so far?" Adrianna questioned, as if feeling the need to bridge the silence that had fallen between them.

"I suppose I'm rather nervous about this whole cell injection thing," Kate replied candidly. "It never occurred to me that I'd ever become one of those women desperately in search of some fountain of eternal youth. Maybe I'm just getting cold feet."

"It's called the Dorian Gray syndrome," Adrianna informed her. "We all go through it in the beginning. But don't worry, it'll pass."

"Frankly I wasn't relieved in the slightest by Celia's solemn assurance that Doctor Jaccard's Rejuvenal-12 injections made a group of experimental dwarfs grow four inches." Kate kept her voice deliberately light and bantering.

"Well then, maybe it'll help if I tell you about how the Pope, Mao Tse Tung, and Pablo Picasso all got jacked up with youth drugs. In fact, since I've been on this island I've heard that Rejuvenal-12 can cure everything from dowager's hump to the heartbreak of psoriasis."

"Maybe it's just that I've always had a fear of injections of any kind," Kate mused. "I just don't like getting stuck with needles."

"Well, from the look of things, it doesn't seem to have done our friend Celia any harm," Adrianna observed a bit ruefully. "From what I've seen I'd say that all her vital organs seem to be chugging right along."

They laughed together like old and familiar friends. Then Kate said, "Celia and Benny do seem to be quite a hot item around here. By the way, do you happen to know where she is? I stopped by her cottage on the way down to the beach, but she wasn't there."

"Celia and Benny go off every morning to collect sea turtle eggs from a little island called Gull Cay. Doctor Jaccard puts the eggs under stress and makes us gulp them down twice a day." Adrianna made a wry face. "I know it sounds disgusting. But according to Andreas, it's disgustingly healthy. Something about bio-stimulins being produced that revive your body's own ability to restore itself. He says the process was developed after World War II, as an aid to bringing Nazi concentration camp victims back to life."

Kate lay back and closed her eyes, feeling the hot burn of

the sun against her flesh. This was what she really needed, she realized. To simply allow her emotions to shift into neutral, and her body to absorb the natural elements: the sun, the sea, and the incredibly pure ocean air.

It was like a benediction, melting the cold inner core of fear that had begun to harden inside her like a jagged shard of glacial ice.

There had been something extremely reassuring about her encounter with Adrianna del Bario. Although for a woman who had been ranked as one of the greatest ballerinas in the world, she seemed to be surprisingly shy and retiring. Her skin was very fair and lightly freckled, and without benefit of stage makeup Adrianna's features appeared rather pretty, but in no way remarkable.

With her long, angular arms and legs, Adrianna even seemed a bit awkward. But having seen her dance, Kate knew that when she stepped upon a stage, something magical took place. It was there, underneath the bright lights, that Adrianna del Bario became an ethereal presence. Not really a flesh and blood woman at all, but rather some rare fantasy creature, inhabiting another realm entirely.

For over five years Adrianna had been absent from the American ballet stage. While during that period she had appeared as a guest performer with some of the major ballet companies in Europe, *La Suprema's* star was no longer in the ascendant.

Adrianna had begun life as Peggy McPherson. Orphaned at birth, she had been raised by the Sisters of Charity in a St. Louis convent until the age of sixteen.

Gawky, painfully introverted, and often hopelessly naive, little Peggy McPherson had grown up to become the ravishing Adrianna, Prima Ballerina of the American National Ballet, a virtual goddess of the dance, and the exclusive personal property of one José del Bario, the most charismatic, daring, and original ballet director in America.

Del Bario was over thirty years older when they first met. But he immediately spotted Peggy McPherson's star potential during a ballet recital at the St. Louis Conservatory of Music. She was just seventeen.

By the time she was twenty-three, Adrianna had become the youngest prima ballerina of any major company in the world. She was the glittering jewel in the crown of the American National Ballet, over which José del Bario exercised benign but absolutely autocratic rule.

Not even his critics could deny that del Bario had a superb eye for talent, and Adrianna was everything he had ever dreamed of in a ballerina. Tall, long limbed, and capable of the most marvelous extensions, Adrianna exhibited a sinuous grace and ease of execution that invariably held her audience spellbound throughout each performance.

According to one adoring New York critic, "Adrianna del Bario is a superb technician, equipped with total muscular memory and an awesome amount of talent."

Her mentor was well into his fifties when they finally married. A flamboyant and highly creative man, he considered it his *droit de seigneur* to exercise complete sexual dominion over all members of his ballet company, whether male or female did not seem to play a decisive role in his choice of conquests. It was the dancer in each of them he wished to seduce, and all the rest was merely dross.

Working under del Bario's exacting direction, Adrianna soared from one heady triumph to another during their years together.

Then a Russian dancer named Sacha Dimitri defected suddenly from the Kirov Ballet Company during a presidential command performance in Washington D.C. After that, nothing was ever the same.

Eventually it was revealed that José del Bario had personally engineered Dimitri's dramatic "dash to freedom." Three months later Adrianna made the announcement that she was leaving both del Bario and the American National Ballet.

The need for "creative freedom" was the reason she gave the press for her defection. There was no divorce and no scandal; Adrianna simply went into voluntary exile. Almost overnight Sacha Dimitri became the star attraction on the international ballet scene.

It was his name that now seemed to be on everyone's lips. The critics raved that he was more daring and virile than Nureyev and more magically accomplished than Barishnikov.

Dimitri was enormously gifted and as handsome as a young god. He was fêted and lionized wherever he appeared in performance. Yet always there was the shadow of José del Bario hovering in the background like an unerring Svengali. There were the whispers, the bitterness and resentment of all those who had thrilled to the sight of Adrianna whirling across a stage, a diaphanous, shifting, moving field of energy and effortless grace.

At first, after leaving New York, she did perform occasionally with other major companies. But without del Bario's genius, imagination, and the sumptuous choreography that had always displayed Adrianna's talents to such perfection, something of the magic was gone. Her star still shone, but not nearly so brightly as before.

Adrianna took several short, hard puffs on her cigarette, then buried it quickly in the sand like something distasteful. Then she crumpled the empty pack and buried it as well.

After a long interval of silence, Kate asked the question that had been uppermost in her mind ever since their unexpected meeting. "I hope you'll forgive me for asking . . . but, of all people, why are *you* here? Somehow it just doesn't figure."

Adrianna picked up a handful of sand and allowed it to spill slowly through her fingers. Then she began to speak, but her voice was different now. The words strung together in short, tautly connected sentences, as if to stop or pause for even an instant might shatter her control.

"I'm an artist," she said. "But being a dancer isn't like being a writer, or an actress or a painter, someone whose career can span an entire lifetime. In ballet you're always working at your peak. The ease, harmony, and control come only after years of grinding hard work and personal sacrifice. Then, just when your dancing begins to fully mature, your muscles begin to knot and stiffen, and your bones turn brittle.

"A woman's prime as a ballerina," she continued, "is somewhere in her midthirties. Ironic, isn't it? I'm thirty-seven years old, and already my body has begun to fail me. I suppose that's why I came to Coral Key. You see, my husband has written a new ballet especially for me. I'm going to be dancing opposite Sacha Dimitri for the first time. It's called *Les Emerauds de la Reine*, and I have only four weeks of rehearsals before opening night at Lincoln Center."

Adrianna's laughter was as brittle as breaking glass. "I suppose the real reason that I'm here is because the comeback I so desperately wanted has come too late."

She removed her dark glasses and slowly rose to her full height. Her gaze was level and very direct. "The truth is, Kate, I'd give ten years of my life to be able to dance as I used to dance for just one more season. Perhaps . . . even for just one more performance."

When the sun became too hot to remain on the beach any longer, they decided to go swimming.

Kate was charmed by the underwater scenery on view through her snorkeling face mask. There were browsing parrot fish, gently waving sea ferns, schools of brilliant neons jetting off through pastel gardens of staghorn, brainhead, and delicately branched blue sponge coral. In places the coral arched up to form baroque pillars with towering castle keeps and cathedrallike vaults swarming with brightly colored reef fish.

For the first time since her arrival, Kate began to feel glad that she had come. Adrianna swam on ahead, her scissoring white legs paddling off into the hazy underwater greenness where the water began to deepen into submarine canyons inked a teary indigo blue.

Below on the sand a stingray the size of a manhole cover took hasty flight. Kate's shadow passed over a sunken wreck, whose skeletal remains were inhabited by several large groupers and a school of brightly patterned angel fish. Drawing in a deep breath, Kate paddled lazily down to skim along the sandy bottom through undulating gardens of delicately trailing sea fern.

Then, just as her air supply was beginning to dwindle, a shadowy figure emerged from beneath an overhanging shelf of brainhead coral. At first Kate thought that it was a large fish of some sort, until she recognized a face mask, flippers, and spear gun aimed directly at one of the large groupers swimming languidly just off to her left.

In the next instant the silver shaft was streaking through the water to impale the big fish. It was then, as the grouper writhed and twisted in widening clouds of blood, that panic struck. Suddenly Kate's heart was pounding erratically as she thrust herself upward toward the light.

By the time she reached the surface Kate's face mask had filled with warm, salty sea water, and she was coughing and gasping for breath. Kate began splashing frantically, arms and legs wildly out of control. The shore suddenly looked far away, and there was no sign of Adrianna.

Kate tried to cry out, but her nose and throat were filled with water. Her heart was thundering, pounding against her ribs by now, while her mind had become filled with blank, white terror.

Then she was sinking beneath the surface, plummeting downward into the depths with bursting lungs and cramping muscles. Overhead the sunlit surface glimmered and flashed quicksilver as the sea tilted crazily upward.

Kate felt herself falling away into fathomless black infinity.

Chapter Six

It had happened twice now—the sudden galloping heartbeat, the terrible sense of being unable to get her breath, the suffocation, the nausea and weakness invading her limbs. Perhaps worst of all was the total helplessness, the inability to affect her own fate.

Celia's telephone call had pulled her out of it the first time in Amagansett, and this time Andreas Jaccard had quite literally saved her life.

In spite of the unique circumstance surrounding their first meeting, Kate found Andreas Jaccard to be a compelling personality, whose deep French-accented voice and penetrating brown eyes had an almost mesmerizing quality.

Now, curled in a wicker chaise on the veranda of her cottage, Kate looked out across that incredibly blue expanse of water and found it difficult to believe how close she had come to drowning that morning.

"Now let's see . . ." Celia voiced. "If I subtract a prune whip from column B at forty calories, I can add a cranberry julienne from column A at twenty-six calories, and still have two slices of rye crisp left over."

Celia sprawled languidly on a gently swaying hammock, poring over her dietetic menu like a cost accountant poring over a complex set of profit and loss ledgers.

"How are you going to make up for those two banana daiquiries you had at the St. George?" Kate questioned.

Celia looked up sharply from her menu to fix her with an imperious look. "Katherine, darling. As you know I can be an extremely disciplined woman about eighty-five percent of the time. The other fifteen percent I am utterly wanton and completely without shame." She shrugged. "I mean, what's the good in having rules if you don't break them from time to time? *N'est-ce pas, ma petite?"*

"Ingrid says that unless you follow the dietary program to the letter, the benefits of the cellular injections might be lessened," Kate informed her with mock German-accented severity.

"Ingrid Jaccard is a tedious woman." Celia rolled her eyes heavenward and nibbled hungrily on one pink-enameled fingernail. "One of those dreadful Teutonic types, who seldom really understand anything at all about true hedonism. And speaking of that, I wonder where Benny has gotten to? Why I almost had a coronary when we arrived back from Gull Cay to find that you'd almost managed to drown yourself. *Quel horreur!"* she exclaimed. "I would never have forgiven myself for inviting you down here."

"That wasn't the way it was at all," Kate responded. "I already told you. I had just eaten breakfast and got a cramp. That's all there was to it. Now stop brooding over me like a mother hen. I'm feeling just fine," she lied. "Honestly."

"Well," Celia said, only slightly mollified, "all I can say is, thank God that Andreas was there in the crunch."

It was true, Kate realized. She would have drowned if Andreas hadn't been skindiving nearby and intervened to save her. Kate had in fact spent the remainder of the morning undergoing a full physical. Jaccard seemed to sense both Kate's precarious mental state and her reluctance to alert Celia to the fact that she was fast approaching emotional Armageddon.

Kate was extremely grateful that, after carrying her unconscious from the water, Jaccard had spared her needless embarrassment by ascribing her near drowning to a disabling muscle cramp. The innocent lie had formed an immediate bond of complicity between them.

Throughout the examination, which included an electrocardiogram analysis of blood and urine samples as well as a battery of other tests, Madame Jaccard had remained in sharp-eyed attendance. Her presence, however, had only succeeded in making Kate all the more aware of Doctor Andreas Jaccard as a man.

It was immediately clear that he possessed a powerful male ego that displayed itself in numerous ways. But he was also charming, subtle, humorous, and highly sensitive to the female psyche.

While Kate had been far too upset to remember much of what had actually passed between them during the examination, Andreas had reassured her greatly. He had also managed to convince her to begin cell injection therapy the following day.

In appearance Jaccard had measured up to Celia's rave advance review, and then some. Tall, broad shouldered, and well muscled, with piercing dark eyes and wavy black hair, he projected an erotic Latin sexuality that took itself entirely for granted. He exuded dominance like a musk, and considering all that had transpired, Kate was rather surprised to find she was not in the least immune.

Celia popped the cork on the bottle of Tattinger '58 she had smuggled onto the island in her luggage. "I was going to save this for a very special occasion," she announced as she filled Kate's glass to the brim. "But let's just live for today. *Ça va bien?*"

Celia lifted her glass in toast. "Here's to eliminating every last ounce of bulging adipose tissue, and draining all those poisonous toxins out of your metabolic pool. Chin Chin, *ma cherie*. Glad to have you aboard. Simply put all your trust in Doctor Jaccard, and by the time you get back to New York you're going to feel absolutely indestructible."

Kate sipped thoughtfully, and then looked deliberately away. "I've decided to resign the presidency," she said. "I'm just not equipped to handle that kind of pressure, Celia. With Paul gone . . . well, I feel as if the bottom had dropped out of my life. I just can't seem to pull myself together."

Celia stretched out one hand to examine the huge emerald ring she wore with a look of casual unconcern. "Look, Katie. I'm gonna give it to you straight from the shoulder. Like it or not, you've finally joined the world's largest sisterhood. You're not the only woman who ever gave her all to an absolute bastard. The truth is that you never really wanted Paul Osborn for the man he was. Only for the man you thought he was, the perfect phantom lover. If you'd stop wallowing in self-pity, my dear girl, you'd see that what Paul actually did was pay you the highest possible compliment. I mean he wouldn't have made you president of Caramour, Inc., unless he was pretty damn sure that you could carry it off."

In spite of the tough talk, Celia's smile was generous and encouraging. "You know yourself," she went on, "that most women in business who are able to achieve a certain level of success are seldom able to carry it farther. Sad to say, we broads are generally self-limiting by habit. It takes a very rare bird indeed to make it all the way to the top. It takes someone who's willing to say 'I'm going to totally re-create myself. I'm going to broaden my vision, assert my ambition, and think differently about everything from this moment onward.' "

"The price is higher than I'm willing to pay," Kate said.

"If you mean that you're going to have to take off the velvet gloves, and stop worrying so much about offending all those delicate male libidos, you're absolutely right. I happen to believe that you can do the job, Kate. But you're going to have to change your way of operating. You are going to have to get your act together, and walk into the Caramour executive suite as if you had balls of steel.

"Otherwise," she warned, "your erstwhile colleagues are going to come after you like hungry pirañás."

Celia was right, Kate realized. Paul had always been her rock, her shield against the voracious denizens of the corporate shark tank—the ubiquitous old boy network where systematic deception, treachery, and flesh peddling were the accepted coin of the realm. She had never even begun to involve herself in the highly competitive and sometimes deadly labyrinths of power, plunder, and acquisition, pretending instead that they simply didn't exist.

"I guess I just haven't got any real instinct for the jugular," Kate said. She rose abruptly and restlessly prowled the length of the veranda, finally coming to a halt at the far end with her hands resting lightly on the railing.

Kate stood staring off across the garden toward the Blue Cottage. The shutters were always closed, and the cottage itself was secreted in a dense growth of bougainvillea and towering bright red hibiscus.

"I wonder what the Duchess thinks about, shut up like

that all the time,'' Kate finally ventured. ''It's hard to imagine that she was once one of the most famous, and surely the most envied woman in the world.''

''I haven't so much as laid eyes on the old dragon since I set foot on the island,'' Celia chimed in. ''Can you imagine that kind of rudeness? To completely ignore me as if I didn't even exist? As if I hadn't decorated her home in Montego Bay and sat across from her at a hundred boring dinner parties! Believe me, I've tried, but I haven't been able to pry a word out of Andreas about her. And of course pumping Ingrid for gossip is like trying to squeeze blood from a stone. Nobody's dropping a stitch, and I'm just drooling to know what's going on over there.''

''I feel that she's watching us,'' Kate said softly. ''Just sitting there behind her shutters, and watching our every move. I've felt it ever since I arrived.''

The Duchess of Sutherland was almost ninety years old now, and largely forgotten by the world. But there had been a time when European royalty had been rocked to its already shaky foundations by a self-styled actress named Brenda Louise Scanlon from Titusville, Nebraska.

Thin as a snake, aggressively shrill in her nasal Midwestern accents, unforgivably American and hopelessly divorced, Brenda would have appeared to have had little enough to recommend the attentions of a royal prince of the blood, the heir to the British throne.

According to the gossip of the time, Brenda Scanlon was said to have found her way into Prince William's affections by employing a rather dominant form of sexual arousal. But there were others who insisted that Bonnie Prince Willy had long since become bored with being the most eligible royal bachelor in the world, and didn't really want to be king anyway. He was by then well into middle age, with a serious drinking problem, next to no ambition, and perhaps the only waxed mustache extant in the western world.

Following a constitutional crisis that very nearly succeeded in bringing down the royal family, Brenda and Willy were finally married in exile, after which they drifted easily and swiftly into the idle social pursuits of the international rich. To no one's surprise, Lady Brenda soon emerged as a ruthless, overbearing snob of the first water who was clearly intent upon squeezing every last diamond, emerald, ruby, and sapphire out of her position as the scandalous American actress-divorcée who almost became queen of England.

During the Second World War, the Duke's outspoken appreciation of Fascist dictators earned him an appointment by the English Crown to the largely titular position of Royal Governor of Jamaica. From that point on, Lady Brenda put their gilded social life on a strictly cash and carry basis.

Armies marched across Europe, dynasties fell, and new empires were born. The years passed. The Duke continued to drink and sometimes drifted off for days into a nonstop alcoholic stupor. He was an invariably polite though rather vague gentleman who smiled on cue, bowed politely over ladies hands, and sometimes nodded off over his brandy at dinner parties.

For eight months of the year the Duke and Duchess worked Palm Beach, the Hamptons, Acapulco, and Monte Carlo. It was the worst-kept secret around that they could be had for a price. Brenda and Willy were available for charity balls, society galas, and even funerals with a sliding escalator clause that rose by leaps and bounds. Brenda saw that contracts were duly signed and travel expenses reimbursed to the last penny-farthing. Everywhere they went they made the headlines.

Then, packing up their sixty-eight pieces of Vuitton luggage, eight servants, and six Schnauzers, the Duke and Duchess would eventually fly off to the Jamaican estate at Montego Bay, where they were the closest thing there was to real royalty.

Yet by the time of the Duke's death some five years before, the Duke and Duchess of Sutherland had become a steadily less marketable commodity. Youth, megabucks, and panache were what counted now. Among the international glitterati, royal titles had begun to lose much of their former luster.

"Brenda's old and ill and totally isolated now," Celia commented, as she poured herself another generous libation of champagne. "I've even heard tell that right up until the death of the Duke, she still held out the hope of someday being queen of England."

"What was she *really* like?" Kate softly questioned.

Celia swirled the champagne in her glass and stared off toward the shuttered Blue Cottage. "Brenda was always the queen of the ball-breakers," she pronounced. "But utterly fascinating."

Chapter Seven

The administration building crested the highest point on the island. It was surrounded by century-old trees and a profusion of overgrown tropical ferns, vines, and flowering bushes. The Great House, as it was called, had been built originally in the 1880s, with coral-block foundations, deeply shaded verandas, wrought-iron grillwork brought from Spain, and high vaulted ceilings with heavy mahogany beams.

Seated in a high-backed wicker queen's chair on the south veranda, Kate looked up from the myriad forms she had been requested to fill out and sighed deeply. The gardener was clipping hedges near the house, and from the tennis courts, hidden behind a screen of brightly hued hibiscus, Kate could hear the steady *plunk* of a tennis ball being batted leisurely back and forth.

It was ten in the morning. Kate heard Benny's voice call out something from the courts, then Celia's response and her almost girlish laughter. In that moment Kate envied her friend for a variety of reasons. Life seemed easier for Celia, and somehow luckier.

How peaceful and idyllic everything looked, Kate thought. Sunlight seemed to pour from the sky, while beyond the stately procession of royal palms encircling the lawn she could see the waters of the lagoon receding outward in ever widening bands that deepened and darkened to indigo blue.

The jagged subterranean patterns of the coral reef where she and Adrianna had gone swimming the previous morning were clearly visible. But Kate did not want to think about her narrow escape from death. Instead she stared out over the incredibly blue expanse of water toward the verdant green mountains of Jamaica with their serried ridges running east to west.

Porto Cristo was clearly visible from that vantage point, and seemed to climb the gently sloping hillsides surrounding the lovely crescent bay in a haphazard, ramshackle fashion. At the harbor entrance stood the old Spanish fort, with its ancient, impotent bronze cannon and crumbling stone walls standing sentinel beside the sea.

How far away it all seemed from the world she had left behind, Kate thought. From her life in Manhattan with its skyrocketing prices, uncollected garbage, terrible transportation, and rotten weather. Kate fully realized that in spite of Celia's pep talk the previous afternoon, she had no choice but to resign the presidency of Caramour. There was simply no other way out, considering her present state of mind. She also knew that she was still very much in love with Paul Osborn, even though she had come to hate him as well.

There were moments when she felt such a sense of futile rage that Kate was left trembling and shaken. Yet there were other moments when she was so overwhelmed by longing for Paul and their shared past that she could see no point in even trying to go on alone.

It took a deliberate act of will for Kate to bring herself back to the task at hand. For several minutes she tried to occupy her mind with the medical questionnaire Ingrid had given her, but the printed pages kept blurring before her eyes, and she found it almost impossible to concentrate.

Yes, she had measles as a child. Her height was *five foot seven inches* and she maintained her weight steadily at a slim *116 pounds* through relentless attention to diet. *Yes,* she did indeed have *trouble sleeping,* was *anxious much of the time* and had experienced an *irregular menstrual cycle* for the past several years.

Do you think you look your age? the questionnaire queried. *Do you look younger or older?*

The answer to that was only too evident, Kate realized, as once again the pen fell still in her hand. She did indeed look older than her years, and feared the cycle of deterioration was fast accelerating. There was a slight sag to her breasts now; a thickening of the thighs and the faintest hint of crêpiness to the skin of her throat. Nor did sleep, when it came, seem to ease the dark circles, the faint puffiness around the eyes.

What had happened to the sleekly coiffed and superbly confident woman she had been for so many years? Kate wondered. Had anyone really existed beneath the smoothly lacquered façade? Had there really been any purpose to her life at all, beyond her career and the blighted hope of someday becoming Paul's wife? Where had she lost sight of who she really was, and where she wanted to go?

From earliest childhood Kate had entertained one real ambition in life. That was to sail to Europe and study painting. But being an only child and the tragic death of her mother when Kate was thirteen had predicated a very different future.

She never remembered being young; only striving to become as close as possible to perfect. Kate had always been a master of organization, and around that lonely talent she organized her day-to-day life. Invariably her checkbook balanced. She was neat in her dress, tidy in her living habits, and considerate of others to a fault.

During the years following her mother's death, Kate became indispensable to the father she adored. Colin Leslie was a quiet and distantly preoccupied man, who had married late in life. He was a brilliant chemist and the sole proprietor of a small but prosperous chemical company, which supplied a variety of beauty products to some of the most prestigious cosmetic firms in the Northeast.

Bright, talented, and totally dedicated, Kate breezed through a series of exclusive Catholic girls' schools until finally graduating from Bennington with the very highest academic and artistic honors. But by then her dream of attending L' Academie des Beaux Arts in Paris had died stillborn.

Deferring to her father's wishes, Kate had finally ended up doing two years of graduate courses in business administration at the University of Pennsylvania, while living at home and working part time for the Leslie Chemical Company.

Her intellect had always proven a barrier with people her own age. Even during her college years Kate had few close friends, seldom dated, and generally found the young men of her acquaintance callow and without interest. Instead she devoted herself totally to Colin Leslie—a tall, spare, white-haired man who wore round rimless glasses and always retained traces of his native Wales in both manner and voice.

They were close, but never intimately so. While her father had always inspired Kate's deepest respect, he was a largely impenetrable man who remained locked behind a steely reserve.

Everything was changed, however, when Colin Leslie was discovered to have a rare form of cancer called aplastic anemia. In dying, as with everything else in his life, her father had acted with reason, forethought, and cold practicality.

After prior consultation with Kate, Leslie entered into negotiation with a man by the name of Paul Osborn, who had long expressed interest in purchasing Leslie Chemical Products. Caramour had of course been little more than a marginal operation in those days. Osborn's primary desire for acquisition lay mostly in the fact that Colin Leslie held the patent on a revolutionary new nail enamel.

Eventually Paul was to elaborately package the nail enamel with a matching lipstick. Upon that single innovation a cosmetics empire was born, and the course of Kate's own life had been irrevocably set.

"Good morning, Miss Leslie. I trust you slept well."

Kate's thoughts were abruptly interrupted by the sudden appearance of Ingrid Jaccard. She was standing there regarding Kate coolly from beneath heavy, straight dark brows. Ingrid stood severely erect in her starched white nurse's uniform and black leotard, and Kate was reminded of a judge about to pronounce a guilty verdict.

Seating herself on a chair across the table from Kate, Ingrid went on to say, "I understand that you are in the cosmetics business, Miss Leslie. It is *Miss,* isn't it? I believe Mrs. Randolph told me that you had never married because of your career."

It was more of an accusation than a question. "No . . . I've never married, and I'm an executive of the Caramour Cosmetic Company."

"As you can see, I myself use no artifice of any kind," Ingrid related rather archly. "As far as I'm concerned, next to exposing one's complexion to direct sunlight, the effects of cigarette smoking, and a generally unhealthy diet, cosmetics are the most damaging thing you can do to your skin."

"That's not necessarily true," Kate countered. "In fact, many reliable studies have shown that cosmetics can give a definite lift to a woman's ego. Everyone, after all, wants to look her best."

"I suppose that depends on just what kind of an impression a woman wants to create." Ingrid sniffed.

Kate was in no mood to argue, and decided to change the subject. "Here are the forms you asked me to fill out last night at dinner. I'm afraid I'm still pretty sketchy, though, on just what is involved in cellular therapy."

"My husband's primary concern as a scientific researcher is in finding a medical solution to counteract the disastrous pressures and erosions of contemporary life. For the past ten years he has been developing a cellular rejuvenation serum to combat such symptoms as chronic fatigue, loss of sexual vigor, impotence in men, frigidity in women, anxiety and premature aging due to stress. It's called Rejuvenal-12.

"Following extensive testing," Ingrid went on in her clipped Germanic accents, "each patient's individual needs are determined, and a systematic therapeutic program is worked out."

"How long does it take before you can actually see signs of improvement?" Kate questioned rather anxiously.

"Certain symptoms are alleviated almost immediately. But the long-term benefits generally are achieved within three to four months."

"And the injections themselves . . ."

"The Rejuvenal-12 injections are given over a two- to-three-week-period under closely monitored circumstances. Primarily live cells from disease-resistant laboratory animals are used. But my husband has also devised a method for rehydrating literally hundreds of different cell types. The process is very similar to the long-term cryogenic freezing system used in sperm banks."

Ingrid turned slightly in her chair, and Kate followed her gaze to find the figure of Solange standing in the doorway.

Then she was moving toward them, carrying a small tray with a white styrofoam cup.

Once again Kate was impressed by the girl's natural elegance of movement. It was almost impossible to believe that the old man she had encountered on the wharf in Porto Cristo could actually have fathered such an elegantly exquisite creature.

"Here's Solange now, with your placental cocktail," Ingrid announced, rising to her feet.

Taking the cup Solange presented to her, Kate made a wry face. "It looks pretty disgusting," she said. "What on earth is it good for?"

"The bio-stimulins produced in turtle eggs, put under gravity stress for extended periods of time, act as a generalized stimulant to the ovaries, hypothalamus, and pituitary glands. There have even been cases of sterile women becoming fertile again."

"I'm not in the least surprised." God knows Celia was a testament to something near miraculous, Kate thought as she hurriedly gulped down the disgusting concoction. Only that morning over breakfast Celia had announced that she was experiencing The curse for the first time in over fifteen years.

Solange disappeared into the cool dim interior of the old house like a shadow melting into water. "She's a stunning young woman," Kate observed. "I'm curious about her racial background."

Ingrid regarded her for a long moment before answering. "Jamaica is the melting pot of the Caribbean. Everybody's come through here over the centuries, and the blood is a blend of African, Arab, Irish, Scottish, Chinese, Spanish, French, and English. Solange could be anything . . . or everything. There's no telling with a girl like that."

Ingrid's tone was condescending, but Kate decided to blunder on.

"Something odd happened on the day I arrived." Kate leaned slightly forward and dropped her voice. "Celia and I were on the wharf in Porto Cristo, when we were approached by an old man who called himself Captain Blue. He said something about his daughter being held on this island against her will. I can only assume that he was talking about Solange."

Ingrid's broadly structured face remained totally without expression, but her voice rose sharply, defensively. Her eyes narrowed until they were like chips of anthracite coal. "That old degenerate was selling the girl to sailors in the streets of Montego Bay when she was barely thirteen years old. My husband brought her here two years ago in order to protect the poor unfortunate. Certainly not to imprison or restrict her in any way."

Ingrid glanced pointedly down at her watch. "Now if you have no further questions, Miss Leslie, I'll show you to my husband's study. I must be getting on with my work, and he should be through soon in his laboratory. He's been working all morning preparing your injections."

The stark reality of her words sent a shiver of apprehension down Kate's spine like a chill. It must be the idea of all those damned needles, she reassured herself.

The doors of Jaccard's study slid closed behind her, and Kate turned to slowly survey the room. It was an old-fashioned library, with dark mahogany paneling, lofty bookcases, worn oriental carpeting, and tall French windows shuttered against the bright Caribbean sunlight.

Everything seemed to be submerged beneath a dimly brooding stillness, while sun motes drifted lazily through vagrant shafts of light sifting in through the tall louvered shutters.

Kate stood listening intently. From the dining salon farther down the hall came the sound of classical music, spooling out in scratchy rounds from a vintage record player. It was "Claire de Lune."

Adrianna was practicing for her comeback before the *barre* that Andreas had installed for her at the far end of the dining salon. This room was no longer used; and since there were never more than half a dozen patients in residence at any given time, meals were delivered to the cottages by Solange or one of the Haitians who worked for Andreas on the island.

The Haitians appeared an oddly primitive lot to Kate, but there was no question about their unswerving and complete dedication to Jaccard. Taller, darker, and more strongly built than the general run of the Jamaican population, they kept strictly to themselves, had blunt, almost brutal negroid features, and seemed always to be lurking silently somewhere in the background.

There were about half a dozen of them living and working on the island, and they did almost everything—assisting Jaccard in his laboratory, preparing meals, working on the grounds, and running errands to Porto Cristo in the power launch. All of them looked and dressed nearly alike, and from the time of her arrival Kate had been unable to tell one from another. If they had individual names, she had never heard them, and everyone just called them the Haitians.

Still listening to the haunting strains of the distant music, Kate moved across the highly polished parquet flooring to browse along the bookshelves. She wished she felt more confident about having the injections. It was risky, she knew, to have any kind of animal tissue injected into the human body, and you didn't have to be a crack immunologist to know that. Yet if Jaccard's Rejuvenal-12 injections even partially measured up to Celia's extraordinary claims, the risk might well be worth taking.

Or at least that was what Kate tried to tell herself, as she continued to browse through Jaccard's bookshelves.

She noted immediately that his taste in reading material ranged widely, from Proust in the original French edition to the very latest scientific journals, with every sort of subject matter represented in between, including an entire section given over to the study of psychiatry, with all of its major theorists represented.

Standing slightly on tiptoes, Kate reached up to pull out a copy of a book written by Jaccard himself. It was called *Psychosynthesis in Women,* and subtitled *Curing Emotional Disorders Through Live-Cell Therapy.*

Idly Kate began thumbing through the pages, until her eye fell upon a sentence that seemed suddenly to leap right off the printed page, totally galvanizing her interest.

Standing there in that silent room, she began reading with rapt attention.

> . . . Many women fear success and competition, but of course they desire it as well. In a recent study it was discovered that a significant number of intelligent, capable, and highly self-sufficient female executives of major corporations began to develop a variety of phobias and other problems relating to their own sense of helplessness.
>
> Sometimes it happens suddenly and for no apparent reason. But more often the various phobias are triggered by a critical emotional upset such as the loss of a loved one. However the various phobic conditions make their appearance, their solution is never simple and invariably masks something on a far deeper level of the subconscious, which invariably dates back to unresolved childhood conflicts.
>
> In the study of over one thousand executive women, it immediately became apparent that *control* was the magic word. Every woman wants to be in charge of her actions

and emotions, her body, career goals, and even her dreams.

Each woman in her own way must come to terms with the struggle to gain control of her life. Yet it can never be completely won as long as deeply rooted childhood traumas remain unresolved. Inevitably, the loss of a parent at certain critical periods in sexual maturation has long and far-reaching effects that tend to replicate dominant behavior patterns.

"Suicide . . ." Kate's lips barely moved as she spoke the word. Had she ever really come to terms with her own mother's suicide? Kate wondered. She'd been only thirteen at the time, and communicating with her mother had always been like trying to talk to someone through gauze. Then suddenly she was dead.

Standing there among the drifting dust motes and pencil-slender beams of light, Kate remembered the blood on the white bathroom tiles. At first she hadn't recognized the body floating there just beneath the surface of the oddly russet-tinted bathwater. Her father's straight razor had fallen to the porcelain tiles from pale, lifeless fingers. Then quite suddenly she knew that it was her mother, and that she had deliberately taken her own life.

There was the sound of a door opening behind her, and as she turned Kate caught a glimpse of herself in a tall gilt rococo mirror and was startled by what she saw. Her features looked strained and ghostly, as if some inner storm had dislocated all the original elements, leaving only a sort of wreckage.

"Good morning, Miss Leslie. I trust you slept well."

Jaccard smiled easily, displaying strong white teeth. Then, after closing the door opening into the lab, he crossed to his desk and seated himself behind it. He motioned for Kate to take the chair drawn up close by. "You appear at least somewhat recovered from your mishap yesterday morning. How are you feeling?"

"I'm feeling rather better," she lied, replacing the book on the shelf and then moving slowly to take the chair Jaccard indicated beside the massive walnut desk. Kate was very much aware of her close proximity to Jaccard. Near enough to smell the strong, dark tobacco smell, underlain with the merest trace of an expensive French cologne.

She pulled the robe closer about her, and leaned back. "I am of course extremely grateful to you, Doctor Jaccard."

Jaccard leaned back in his chair, reaching to stroke his heavy dark mustache. It was the way a healthy animal would have preened its fur. "I am a trained observer of both the human psyche and the human body, Miss Leslie. Perhaps I can be of help. But only if you are willing to tell me what really happened out there in the water yesterday. According to your friend Mrs. Randolph, you're a strong, accomplished swimmer. We both know that you didn't almost drown because you suddenly got muscle cramps."

Kate shook her head slightly as if to clear it. "I guess that's really the problem. I'm not sure exactly what happened. One minute I was fine, and the next I panicked. If you hadn't been skindiving nearby . . . well, I rather doubt that I'd be sitting here right now."

Jaccard tapped his fingertips lightly together. "Fear lurks deep in each of us, Miss Leslie. It's always there, like a clear, cold pool somewhere in the catacombs of the subconscious. At times of intense stress, reflections of that fear rise up to overwhelm all the mental and emotional barriers we have built like dikes in order to contain it. The heart pounds, the body perspires, the lungs refuse to draw breath, and something close to a lethal shot of adrenalin races throughout the bloodstream."

Jaccard shrugged as if to soften the picture he had so vividly portrayed. "It's at least partially an atavistic response. Something left over from the days when our ancestors crept out of their caves after the last ice age, to discover a violent and hostile universe seemingly intent upon their destruction. Then again, it can be something natural to the human aging process, the first warning signals of incipient menopause."

"Menopause," Kate repeated. "But I'm only forty years old."

Andreas leaned forward, adjusted his stethoscope, and then pressed the cold metalic diaphragm against her breast just inside the robe. His hands looked very strong. They were heavily veined, his fingers long and articulate.

He spoke in his deep, slightly accented voice. "To a large degree, Miss Leslie, the onset of menopause has everything to do with what kind of sex life a woman has."

Kate sat very still in the pink terrycloth robe provided by the management, inscribed with the words *Coral Key Spa*. "Perhaps I can be more specific," he said. "It's no mystery that a woman who feels sexually insecure and increasingly unfulfilled is far more likely to experience the type of phobic symptoms that you've described to me."

Kate didn't know why he made her feel the way she did. Perhaps she wouldn't have been so terribly aware of his almost scalding sexuality if her own emotional state had not been so vulnerable and chaotic. Yet it was actually a relief to be able to focus her thoughts on someone other than herself, at least for awhile.

Kate felt strongly drawn to Jaccard. She was terribly aware of the rapid beating of her heart and the faint flush of perspiration moistening her body beneath the terrycloth robe.

There was something elegantly feline about the way Jaccard leaned back and extracted a pack of Gauloise Bleu from the pocket of his white nylon physician's smock. Andreas was powerfully built through the shoulders, and the thick cloud of curly black hair matting his chest showed through the thin material. It reminded Kate of the healthy pelt of some sleek, dark, male animal.

"No doubt you are already aware that cigarettes, alcohol, and perscription drugs are off limits while you're undergoing therapy. But the condemned are entitled to have a last smoke, if you like."

Kate reached gratefully for a cigarette, then bent her head to accept a light from the slim gold Dupont lighter he proferred. "Thanks, I needed that. Your wife had me convinced that smoking was strictly *verboten.*"

Jaccard's laugh was low and full of sensual indulgence. "I'm afraid Ingrid is a purist. She's totally addicted to rules and procedures. A facet of her personality that, I must admit, has been extremely helpful in my research. By the way, how old do you think she is?"

Kate exhaled the aromatic blue smoke through her nostrils. The tension had eased, and she felt surer now of being completely straightforward with him. "My best guess would be that she's somewhere in her mid forties."

"Ingrid is in her late fifties," Jaccard informed her. "She's been receiving cell injections for over a decade."

"I have to be perfectly honest, Doctor Jaccard. I still have some strong reservations about having the injections."

He nodded, and then began speaking softly in a deeply resonant and reassuring voice. Jaccard spoke with a definite accent, although its source was never clearly defined. "You came to this island," he informed her, "because you are a frustrated, harried, insecure, and increasingly less productive woman."

Jaccard was staring directly into her eyes as he spoke, and his gaze was riveting, entirely compelling. "You came here because you are desperately in need of help. In simplest terms, what I can offer you through cellular therapy is a scientifically proven and clinically safe method of rejuvenating your entire cellular structure, of changing both your mental and emotional outlook on life."

Jaccard waved his cigarette like a conjuring rod. "To be entirely candid, Miss Leslie, you are courting both a physical and emotional breakdown, with a few phobias thrown in for good measure."

"You mean this feeling of fear, of losing control of my life, is an actual phobia?"

"According to psychoanalytic theory, we fear that which we most desire. And that desire almost always has highly sexual connotations. There are, for instance, a good many doctors, analysts and psychiatrists, who believe that a woman who is terrified of snakes is really fearful of sex. Actually, she may unconsciously desire to be raped, even while living the most chaste and virtuous kind of life. A fear of crowds is often related to the fear of sexual intimacy, of closeness. While the fear of open spaces is usually related to the complete abandonment of all control. To just letting go, and acting out one's most primary sexual fantasies."

Once again Jaccard leaned forward. He tamped out his half-smoked cigarette in an ashtray, and then reached to take Kate's left hand in both his own. "You are a desperate woman, Miss Leslie, and what I am offering you is the chance to live fully for perhaps the first time in your life. By starting cellular therapy now, you have a good chance of forestalling menopause, and requiring future injections at far less frequent intervals."

Kate nodded. "All right, Doctor. I'll rely entirely on whatever you suggest."

"Good," Jaccard pronounced. Then he pulled forward a folder containing her medical records and opened it up. "Based on the battery of tests I have already given you, I suggest that we start out with a maximum of four different kinds of cells: conjunctive tissue to keep your skin elastic; placental cells for a generalized stimulation of the cerebral centers; and hypothalamus cells to stimulate the glands and ovaries."

Jaccard reached into the pocket of his white smock and produced a small plastic phial of yellow capsules, which he placed in her hand. "Now I want you to go back to your cottage and take two of these pills. Afterward go straight to bed, because they are going to make you very groggy. What I'm going to do is to keep you heavily sedated for the next several days. It's a sort of sleep cure. During that time you will receive intravenous feedings every four hours, and cellular injections every twelve hours, until we've completed the first series."

Jaccard glanced down at his watch. "Now, do you have any further questions?"

"What are the chances of a serious, or even fatal reaction to Rejuvenal-12? I've heard of people getting gas-gangrene from cellular injections."

Jaccard shrugged with typically Gallic nonchalance. "You will no doubt have a reaction rather like a twenty-four-hour flu virus. There will be some topical swelling, perhaps fever, nausea, and maybe even hallucinations—a sort of generalized sense of disorientation. But that only lasts for the first twenty-four hours. In answer to your question, your chances of having a fatal rejection syndrome are about the same as being hit by lightning."

Jaccard's smile was like a beneficence. "Just let go, relax, and leave everything to me, Miss Leslie. Within a matter of days, you're going to feel as if you had been *reborn*."

Chapter Eight

Kate blinked her eyes, trying to focus in the dimness. The only light came through the open bathroom door, illuminating the shadowy figure of a man moving slowly toward the bed where she lay.

The man's sex hung obscenely tumescent from a bristling thicket of curling black hair, while with one huge dark hand he was slowly stroking himself into erection. Kate felt frozen within that timeless moment, without speech or breath or even heartbeat. She was simply there—a waiting victim.

The man moved toward her with the easy feline grace of a stalking panther, and with a single violent motion tore away the sheet she held clutched against her nakedness. Then the weight of him was upon her, and he was sundering her with his sex, as if it were a weapon of destruction.

Kate was startled awake by the touch of a cool, reassuring hand upon her brow. She heard a strong, familiar voice commanding her to return from the void where breakers of luminous gray light crashed like waves upon some deserted shore.

It had only been a dream. Blinking against the light through eyelids scarcely open, Kate looked up into the face of Andreas Jaccard. His features were blurred and insubstantial, swimming in and out of vision as she tried to focus. Some essential reality had been shattered, and she wasn't even sure she wanted to piece it back together again.

All she seemed to remember were the needles, the intravenous feedings, and muffled voices speaking somewhere in the room beyond her vision. It seemed as if she had been sleeping for days. She felt ill and feverish. Her head throbbed and a shuddery chill passed through her limbs, as bits and pieces of the nightmare from which she had just awakened continued to dart and flash through her sleep-drugged consciousness.

"Please . . . some water," Kate whispered. Her throat was parched. As Jaccard poured her a glass from a silver carafe on the bedside table, Kate tried to lift her head from the pillows, but fell back with a soft gasp.

"It's all right," Andreas assured her. He held the glass to Kate's lips as she drank thirstily. "Everything is going to be just fine. You're coming along very well indeed."

"How long . . . have I . . . have I been out?" she managed.

"About thirty-six hours so far!" Jaccard opened his bag and took out a hypodermic needle sealed in a paper wrapping. He tore it off, removed a small phial from his black medical bag, and then began filling the hypodermic syringe as Kate looked on in a daze. She seemed scarcely able to keep her eyes open.

Jaccard's voice was soft, deep, and entirely compelling. Like a metronome. "I want you to go back to sleep remembering that the basis of all healing is belief. We create illness, age, and disharmony by harboring doubt and negativity. By storing away all our guilts and repressing our truest emotions."

Jaccard lifted the hypodermic and held it poised against the light as a single crystalline drop ran down the shining steel shaft. Kate turned her face away into the pillow as the needle pierced the vein.

After rubbing her inner arm with a piece of alcohol-soaked cotton, Jaccard folded her hands upon the sheet and moved away from the bed. Kate heard the sound of the door opening and a brief hushed murmur of conversation with someone else in the room. But immediately thereafter, everything began to grow dim once again.

She actually felt very little beyond the languid heaviness that seemed to be overtaking her limbs. The hazy dullness that began to steep her mind in forgetfulness.

Yes, that was it exactly, Kate realized. All she had to do was relax and let go; to allow Andreas to make all the decisions for her. Kate didn't want to think about Paul or Caramour or nearly drowning. It was so peaceful to just remain like a blank slate upon which nothing had yet been written. To become the child she had never been; to shed all the excess emotional baggage she was so very tired of bearing.

A creeping numbness seemed to be moving stealthily through her body, and there was a soft roaring in her ears like surf breaking on some pure and natal shore. Kate began to experience a lovely, languid, peaceful sensation.

Perhaps this is what death is really like, she thought. Perhaps it was just letting go and floating away like a feather cast to the winds.

Chapter Nine

Kate embraced the religion of physical rejuvenation as if she had undergone a powerful spiritual conversion, and the change was apparent to everyone by the beginning of her second week on Coral Key.

There were of course a variety of factors involved, besides the first round of RJ-12 injections she had thus far received. Normally the shots were given on the second, fourth, eighth, and twelfth days of a two-week stay, although Celia, Adrianna, and Kate had been convinced by Jaccard to prolong their treatment for an additional week of therapy.

Considering the surprisingly immediate results, Kate could not have been more willing to comply, and the daily, almost hourly rituals involved with her body and health had quickly begun to absorb her completely. All of a sudden the obsessive-compulsive qualities she had exercised all her life began to work for her. The stern self-discipline, the willingness to struggle toward achievement on a day-to-day basis, and the determination to strive relentlessly toward a projected ideal.

She and Adrianna began each day with an early morning swim, in order to avoid the sun's most powerful burning rays. Then, following breakfast, there was a brisk jog along the beach.

After running for over an hour, Kate felt absolutely terrific. Her body felt supple and strong. Each day she and Adrianna kept increasing their distance, until finally they were able to encircle the entire circumference of the island by running along the hard, wet sand at the water's edge.

Following that, there was an hour of calisthenics orchestrated beneath the energetic guidance of Benny Valdez. In spite of certain reservations regarding his relationship with Celia, Kate found Benny to be a disarmingly candid and altogether charming young man, brimming over with good-natured affability.

By lunchtime Kate was always ravenous, and promptly thereafter came her favorite part of the schedule. There were therapeutic warm springs on the island, and directly after lunch Kate stepped into an oversized hot tub filled with warm, bouyant, softly circulating water. Vapors of health-giving aromatic oils and herbs filled the room with a bewitching fragrance. Settling back, Kate closed her eyes, emptied her mind, and began to practice yogic deep-breathing techniques.

For an hour it seemed as if her entire being was absorbed in a gently flowing mist while various nozzles provided a soothing underwater massage from head to foot. It was in fact exactly the kind of relaxation she needed in order to prepare herself for what came next. For each afternoon the highly therapeutic and relaxing aqua therapy was followed by a grueling deep massage beneath the strong, capable hands of Madame Jaccard.

From her very first day on the island, Kate had harbored

the suspicion that Ingrid had it in for her. That suspicion seemed to be borne out every afternoon as she pounded, kneaded, and twisted every muscle, sinew, and limb into pliant submissiveness.

Resolute and unsmiling, Ingrid seemed to revel in working out what she dourly referred to as "all those poisonous toxins," she insisted were harbored within "all those billions of alcohol- and nicotine-saturated cells."

As the days began to fall away beneath a beneficent Caribbean sun, it became increasingly more apparent to Kate that some fundamental change was in process.

She had never looked or felt better in her life. Her complexion had taken on a more youthful, radiant glow, and the carefully formulated diet had begun to add additional pounds in all the right places.

Yet the most profound difference was her own awareness of herself, the objectivity with which she was able to look back over her life with a clear and unobstructed view. There were so many things she now saw in a totally different perspective.

Ever since childhood, Kate had readily believed that no woman, no matter how clever and determined, could really make it on her own. Throughout her developmental years, she had defined herself totally in terms of the father she adored. She never had time to be young; to grow, to dream, and to ripen.

Then, upon the death of Colin Leslie when she was in her early twenties, Kate had transferred all of her hopes and ambitions to the paternalistic figure of Paul Osborn, a man to whom she had never really been more than a superbly functioning corporate asset. At the very center of his being, Paul's essential self was a frozen waste. He had always taken her completely for granted.

Yet Kate could now see that their relationship had also served to insulate her against looking too closely at her own ambitions. As long as she had kept working hard enough, there was never really any time for personal introspection. Never before had Kate stopped to think about the meaning of her life. Her aspirations had always been measured by external goals.

It was not her career to which she had been devoted, but to work for its own sake. Just the way other people became addicted to liquor, sex, or drugs.

Now all that had changed. The anxiety, depression, and pervading sense of inner emptiness that had beset her upon arriving on Coral Key seemed to be part of another world. Kate felt extremely grateful to Andreas Jaccard, and there was no question of having to sustain his powerful male ego at her own expense. Andreas was far too secure within himself for that.

It had been such a long time since Kate had felt like a woman, with any man. In her career, where she had done little else but deal with men daily, she had learned to ignore the fact that she was a woman, in hopes of making the men surrounding her forget about it too. But Andreas, with his blatant virility and dramatic good looks, was unlike any other man she had ever met.

Just sitting talking to him endowed their almost daily meetings with an aura of shared intimacy. Kate was extremely grateful for his innate understanding. She was also increasingly aware of the compelling physical attraction that Andreas held for her. But Andreas was married, and to Kate that still meant something.

During her stay on the island, Kate's friendship with Adrianna del Bario had deepened. During the late afternoons she would join her in the dining salon of the Great House to practice stretching and limbering exercises while Adrianna prepared for her comeback at Lincoln Center.

The dining salon, with its polished parquet flooring and

crystal chandeliers swathed in ghostly dust covers, was empty of furnishings. Late afternoon sunlight flooded in through banks of French windows. There was often a cooling breeze billowing the yellowed lace curtains, so they cast fluttering shadows upon the faded gold damask walls.

For Kate, to watch Adrianna dance was to experience a sense of timeless, exquisite truth. She never ceased to marvel at the ease, harmony, and control with which Adrianna invested each soaring jump, floating *arpeggio,* and exquisite *pirouette en point;* the dazzling turns in midair and heart-stopping off-center balances.

With her long limbs, fine head, and elongated neck, Adrianna expressed a gift for dramatizing whatever kind of music came spooling out of the vintage record player, with its collection of old classical records. Her dancing was a lovely, seamless flow. Yet there were moments when Kate had the eerie feeling that Adrianna seemed to be whirling on the very edge of some awesome abyss.

More than anything, Kate wanted her comeback performance to be an enormous success. No one, she believed, could have possibly deserved it more.

Celia spent most of her spare time happily preoccupied with Benny Valdez. But each evening just before sunset they all gathered on her veranda to drink prairie oyster cocktails and engage in the most outrageous gossip sessions imaginable.

After a long and arduous day, it was a pleasant respite to watch the glorious Caribbean sunset from the breezy veranda of Celia's Hot-Pink Cottage. There were cooing zenaida doves nesting in the eves, and grackles strutting on the lawn. Lavender clouds reared up in the west to march across the sky at sunset, and then, abruptly, the sun dipped into the sea like a flaming shard of molten metal.

Gossip was the coin of the realm on Coral Key, and Celia took delight in regaling them with the all too vivid details of her various sexual couplings with Benny, "the brown bomber." As for Ingrid Jaccard, it was always open season where she was concerned, and the speculation was endless regarding the Duchess of Sutherland, who still remained secluded in the Blue Cottage.

Kate had seen her only once, walking on the outer beach at dusk. Lady Brenda was gowned in deepest mourning, and in spite of Celia's contention that she was nearly senile and virtually bedridden, the Duchess still managed to carry herself with an imperious hauteur. Beneath her dark mourning veil fluttering in the wind, her features had remained shadowed and distant. Absolutely nothing about her gave anything away.

Fiona Van Zandt was another popular topic of speculation. Often, just before retiring for the evening around ten o'clock, Kate would take a walk along the beach. Invariably she would pause and look out toward the sleek white yacht with its towering masts.

Riding at anchor, the *Sultana* always looked so white and ghostly in the moonlight while the lights of Porto Cristo flickered fitfully along the farther shore.

Kate couldn't help but wonder about the woman dying on board.

Fiona Van Zandt had been blessed with a name akin to Croesus. Her birth had been heralded in the *New York Times* along with headlines proclaiming the financial crash of 1929.

Ever since, the tabloids had serialized her life like a long-running soap opera. The bitter parental custody battle. Her million-dollar début, and her ultimate ascension to Superheiress at twenty-one years of age.

Celia insisted that Fiona had always been far prettier in person than in her thousands of newspaper and magazine photographs.

Fiona had always looked breakable. There had been the

spindly child with the eerily adult face. The vulnerable teenager with too knowing eyes. During her marriages to six world-famous lovers she had appeared frequently within the pages of *Vogue* and *Paris-Match*. Then finally, signaling her withdrawal from society, she had been photographed as the veiled bride in a Moslem wedding ceremony when she had ultimately married a minor Moroccan princeling.

"Of course Andreas is in the business of producing miracles," Celia pronounced. "But I doubt that even he can make the dead walk. Fiona may be the richest woman in the world, but even two billion bucks isn't going to buy immortality."

As the days passed, Kate felt increasingly drawn to the dying woman. Finally, and for no reason Kate could clearly justify, she sent Fiona a note at the end of her second week on the island, and received an answer the following day.

"I'll be expecting you at teatime tomorrow," Fiona had written in her spidery, faltering hand.

With Benny at the wheel, the launch shot away from the dock with a roar. Kate tied a scarf about her head as she looked off toward where the *Sultana* rode the gentle swell, halfway to the mainland. She was almost sorry now that she had agreed to come. It was too much like going back into a past that Kate believed had been long forgotten.

For twenty-four long months she had remained steadfastly at her father's side in the family summer home on Martha's Vineyard. They had both known from the beginning that there was not the slightest chance Colin Leslie would recover from the cancer slowly draining his life.

It left him a gaunt and pitiful specter. Yet never once in all those months had Kate betrayed the numbing awareness of his impending death.

Instead she had done everything possible to ease her father's passage from the world, just as she had dedicated herself to serving his comfort and convenience for as long as she could remember.

Toward the end, when the painkilling drugs would cause his mind to wander and his sight was nearly gone, Colin Leslie would sit for hours beside the window, staring blankly out over beaches swept clean by wind and surf. The house on Martha's Vineyard was an old two-story saltbox perched high above the dunes tufted with tall golden-bearded sea grass that rippled in the offshore wind.

"Where are all the seagulls?" he would complain. "I can't see them anymore."

Sitting on the arm of her father's chair, Kate would assure him. "It's only because of the heavy mists. I'm sure you'll be able to see them tomorrow."

It was the kind of lie that Kate had become used to telling. The kind one told to tired and querulous children when the time had come for sleep.

Then came the day when there was no more need for lies. The day when Kate stood on a windswept bluff high above the sea and scattered her father's ashes to the winds. The crushed fragments of bone efficiently incinerated into handfuls of delicate filigree.

A human life reduced to handfuls of exotic coral polyps that had been kilned into subtle pastel shades of rose, ocher, and pale mauve. Kate had been deeply moved by their almost unearthly beauty, and her pain was bittersweet.

Accompanied by a shrill, tuneless cry like that of the wheeling, circling gulls, she had cast her father's final remains upon the winds, believing that Colin Leslie's passage into the beyond would finally set her free.

But even that was not to be. Two weeks later, while on her way to catch a boat for Europe, Kate had stopped in to see Paul Osborn in New York City. It was a purely business matter. There had been the final papers to sign, transferring the ownership of Leslie Chemical Products to Caramour Cosmetics.

Their meeting that afternoon had changed everything. For as soon as she had laid eyes upon him, Kate had been instantly caught up by the excitement of Paul's restless, boundless energy. Just being in his presence held the promise of exciting things to come. Almost from the very first moment, Kate knew that if Paul asked her, she would stay.

Now, eighteen years later, she was on her way to see a woman dying from aplastic anemia, just like her father. It wasn't going to be easy, she knew.

Benny throttled the launch down as they swung abreast of the *Sultana*'s gangway, which had been lowered in preparation for her arrival.

Kate was handed aboard by the ship's first officer, who led her through the luxurious main salon and up a flight of stairs to the *Sultana*'s master suite.

Like King Farouk, the yacht's original owner, Fiona was an avid collector of Eastern art, and there were treasures beyond price wherever Kate looked. There were inlaid screens, rare jade figurines and a priceless collection of Tang bronzes excavated from a twelfth-century Chinese tomb.

Kate's heart was racing by the time the ornately carved double doors were thrown open by a turbaned steward, salaaming low before her. The setting was an Arabian Nights dream, with silken hangings, the most beautiful Bohkara carpets imaginable, and a great gilded swan bed resting upon a low dais.

The atmosphere was perfumed. But nothing could mask the sickly sweet, foetid smell of cancer. Kate recognized it immediately, and recoiled from the cloying forewarning of impending death that seemed to waft over her in sickening waves.

Fiona herself was propped up against a froth of satin

pillows on a chaise lounge. She wore a ruffled pink dressing gown, and, as Kate slowly crossed the spacious cabin with its silk-paneled walls and rose damask upholstery, Fiona appeared to be sleeping.

Her respiration, however, was so shallow and rasping that the tragically wasted form outlined beneath the satin comforter scarcely seemed to draw breath. There was a respirator standing against the far wall, and it told the tale with shocking clarity as nothing else could.

The best that Fiona could hope for now, Kate realized, was a sudden blood clot moving swiftly through her veins. Unfelt and merciful, the clot would instantly put an end to all her pain, and most likely Fiona would never even awaken.

Kate had often wished during that long, agonizing twenty-four months on Martha's Vineyard that her father would be blessed with such an ending. But there just wasn't meant to be any easy way out. Not for either of them.

Fiona started suddenly. Then she lifted her head to slowly scan the room. "Is someone there?" she questioned. "Is that you, Miss Leslie?"

She looked softer than Kate had expected, more fragile and surprisingly pretty. The cancer had by now eaten away her flesh, to endow her bone structure with a sculptural elegance. Her pale skin was drawn taut, while her lovely hazel eyes were almost childlike and strangely serene.

Still, it was the mask of fatal illness that she wore, and it was a moment before Kate could bring herself to speak. "Yes . . . I'm here, Miss Van Zandt. I'm sorry if I awakened you."

"Come over here . . . where I can see you. There . . . in the light from the window."

Fiona was smiling wanly in welcome. She motioned toward a nearby chair, and Kate quickly moved forward to take her place across a small tea table inlaid with a mosaic of semiprecious stones.

"I've just had the strangest dream," Fiona said in a softly distant voice. "It was the kind of dream that would make one of those Park Avenue psychoanalysts simply drool."

Fiona laughed lightly, amused. Kate could not help a fleeting wisp of a smile. It seemed as if they had known one another forever. Two old and intimate friends, picking up a conversation where they had left off only days, or perhaps hours before.

"I dreamed I was standing on the edge of the desert," Fiona related. "I could hear the wind blowing through the pink tamarisk blossoms that bloom near the oasis at this time of year. I've always been mad for horses you know, and there, standing on a rocky promontory beneath that dazzling North African sky, was a magnificent white Arabian stallion. He had a thick wavy mane and tail, with a jeweled Bedouin saddle and woven horsehair reins."

As Fiona continued to relate the details of her dream, Kate could not help but notice the decided weakness in the movement of her hands. Whatever strength she had left was gathered now in her lightly musical voice and the calm intensity of her gaze.

Fiona's eyes shimmered, smiling softly in poised recollection. Then she continued. "The Stallion tossed its mane, snorted in the air, and danced a few slow, curving steps as I ran to pick up the reins. Then, as soon as my hand touched the curling mane, we were galloping away into the Sahara... like the wind."

For a moment her voice faltered. "Galloping endlessly... across that vast blinding desert, shimmering in the sunlight. The white stallion was death you see, and he had come to take me away so swiftly and so joyously that I wasn't even afraid."

Fiona turned slightly, staring directly at Kate. "You see, Miss Leslie . . . I think it's so terribly important to die well. Don't you?"

Before either of them could say anything further, refreshments were served by a robed and veiled servant, whose dark eyes flashed with fierce and primitive vitality. Fiona handed Kate a cup of fragrant-smelling tea, and motioned toward the several porcelain dishes bearing a selection of candied fruits, glazed dates, and various sweetmeats.

"It's rather frugal desert fare." She smiled. "But I thought you might enjoy some respite from the menu on Coral Key." Then, as Kate lifted the scalding tea to her lips, Fiona suddenly stiffened, intermittently racked by faint, shuddering tremors that seemed to spark and dim her eyes.

"What is it?" Kate asked, moving swiftly to sit beside her on the edge of the chaise. "Is there something I can do?"

"It's nothing," Fiona whispered. She was taken by a fit of coughing, her frail shoulders heaving and shuddering as Kate poured a glass of water from a silver carafe and pressed it to her lips.

"Perhaps I should be going," Kate suggested, as Fiona sought to gain her breath. "I don't want to tire you."

Fiona managed a fleeting smile. "You needn't worry about that. Where I'm going there will be plenty of time to rest, and no doubt about it."

"Have you stopped believing in miracles?" Kate questioned.

"I suppose I did come to Coral Key looking for some kind of miracle," Fiona admitted without the slightest trace of self-pity. "But then why should I have expected Jaccard to succeed where the finest cancer specialists in Europe had failed? They say you go through several stages when you discover you're dying. First there's disbelief, then anger and fear followed by something very close to complete despair. I suppose I've reached the point they refer to as 'resignation.'

Whatever happens . . . happens. I've made my farewells, put my financial affairs in order, and there's really nothing left to do before I die. *Insallah* the Arabs say. Whatever is the will of God. Then so be it."

Fiona gestured toward a silver-framed photograph standing on a table beside the chaise amidst a cluttered variety of various medications. It showed a younger Fiona, dressed in the style of the fifties. Standing next to her, with his arm placed protectively around her waist, was a young boy whose smiling features bore a striking resemblance to her own. In the background were pastures, stables, and several magnificent show horses, grazing in a field of tall grass.

"My son always used to ask me why I kept running away from home," she said. "But I was never able to give him an answer."

"Were you . . . are you close?" Kate asked.

"I'm afraid I was never much of a mother," Fiona admitted. "During the years when he was growing up, I was very much involved in marrying titles and gadding about the world. He was raised by his father on a horse farm in Virginia, but I haven't seen or heard from him in years. I suppose that now . . . that's my only real regret."

"Have you tried making contact?" Kate asked, taking one of Fiona's hands in both her own. Her flesh was hot and dry to the touch, and the skin of her painfully thin wrist had been punctured repeatedly with intravenous needles.

Fiona looked away, staring off toward where the sunlight filtered in through the curtained ports to illuminate the spacious and luxurious suite. "It would be too selfish to ask him to forgive me just because I'm dying," she replied finally. "Anyway, he's off somewhere climbing mountains in the Himalayas. He doesn't need or want anything from me. But I'd like him to know that I've stopped running away. That I've been happy with Prince Nessim these past five years."

Kate squeezed her frail, waxen hand. There seemed to be no need for words or explanations. Neither of them seemed to find anything in the least strange about the sudden depth of their shared intimacy. It was clear that whatever relationship they were to enjoy would of necessity have to happen quickly.

Fiona's voice was tentative.

"There's something I've been wanting to ask you ever since Andreas told me who you were. I was watching through binoculars that first morning when you went swimming with the tall redheaded girl . . . the ballerina. The day you almost drowned."

Fiona's grip on Kate's hand tightened. "Forgive me for asking, but I have to know."

"Ask me anything," Kate said. "I feel as if we've always been friends." It was true. Kate felt as if a powerful bond had been forged between them, somewhere back in the mists of time.

"What did you feel in those final moments, when you were very close to death?" Fiona asked. Her eyes were huge, bright, and questioning. "What was it like?"

"I wanted, more than anything else, to live," Kate gently assured her. "Just like you, Fiona . . . I wanted a miracle."

Chapter Ten

Kate stood staring up at the smooth white sculpture framed between the shuttered windows in Andreas' study. Beyond question, Doctor Andreas Jaccard was possessed of a unique creative talent that went well beyond his acknowledged genius as a medical researcher.

While strangely surrealistic, Andreas' work showed extraordinary technical and expressive quality. Yet invariably, each of the plaster-of-Paris castings had a claustrophobic quality Kate found disturbing, as if the fragmentary figures were being suffocated in some timeless vacuum, compressed within their own dense confines, even as the outer forms were nakedly revealed in smooth, luminous white plaster. All of the sculptures she had seen on Coral Key varied greatly in exposition. But all of them had in common this same psychological density. Introverted, thoughtful, often rather melancholy. Both in creative expression and physical attitude.

Kate had begged off when Andreas asked her to pose. But both Celia and Adrianna had been persuaded to undergo the grueling five-hour casting session that left them as limp and submissively compliant as rag dolls.

According to Celia's report that day at sundown, Andreas had spent at least an hour just selecting the proper pose. Then he had set to work, gradually encasing her entire body in plaster-soaked bandages.

Perhaps, Kate mused, it was the act of being wrapped and sealed in warm, wet plaster and gauze bandages that endowed the subjects with such introspective attitudes. Or perhaps it was the sensual molding of the model's body by Jaccard's hands, as he smoothed and shaped the anatomy until it perfectly suited his artistic vision.

Celia claimed to have experienced multiple orgasms during the process, but Kate hadn't really taken her all that seriously. Celia, it seemed, did little else these days besides experience multiple orgasms, and Kate wasn't even sure there was such a thing.

But of all the life-sculptures she had seen on Coral Key, it was the head and torso hanging on Andreas' study wall between the windows that totally captured Kate's imagination with its powerful existential statement.

It was like a human soul captured for all eternity. A woman's beautiful, haunted features frozen forever on the verge of some secret agony, or perhaps an exquisite orgasm. It was virtually impossible to tell which.

Standing there in the dimness, Kate closed her eyes to envision Andreas' large, articulate hands; heavily veined and very strong. She wondered what it would have been like to feel those powerful hands moving slowly over her body to shape and smooth, searching out the secret fount of her sexuality that had remained so deeply submerged for so many years.

The truth was, Kate realized, that she hadn't dared pose for

Andreas Jaccard. Because ever since their initial meeting over two weeks before, dark and sensual currents had been stirring within her.

But it wasn't only his blatant virility that attracted her so strongly. Andreas Jaccard fascinated her on many levels.

His intellect was prismatic, like a shimmering crystal whose facets never quite caught the light in exactly the same way. He exuded a highly sensual, almost hypnotic attraction. But there was something brooding and dimly mysterious about him as well. Something that suggested another age entirely to Kate.

He reminded her of a figure from an El Greco painting. Brilliant, creative, and infinitely complex, Andreas was in fact the modern equivalent of the prototype Renaissance Man.

Kate was so deeply engrossed in her thoughts that she started slightly as the door opened, and Andreas entered the room. "I'm flattered that you find my work so absorbing." He smiled.

"I think you're a very talented man," Kate responded. "Quite obviously you could have had a career in art, had you so chosen."

Andreas' expression was relaxed and easy. He had obviously just come in from the tennis courts, and was casually attired in white shorts and pullover, with a towel slung carelessly over one shoulder. He appeared to be in excellent physical condition, and Kate often saw him jogging on the beach, snorkeling in the lagoon, or playing tennis doubles with Benny, Celia, and Ingrid in the late afternoon.

"Or maybe even a tennis pro," Jaccard suggested wryly. "I just beat the pants off Benny Valdez, who's considered to be about the best there is around here." Andreas had by now crossed the room to his desk, where he lit up a Gauloise Bleu. "But you were wondering about the sculpture, weren't you? I could see it on your face as I came in."

"Who was she?" Kate asked, turning back to the smooth white sculpture hanging between the shuttered windows.

"That was done of my first wife, Angelique," he informed her evenly. "She died in a boating accident over ten years ago. Angelique was the daughter of Doctor Anton Meyerhof, the so-called father of cell-rejuvenation therapy."

"She was very beautiful," Kate observed. "You must have been very much in love with her."

"The only thing I've ever really loved was my work," Jaccard responded. "To pretend otherwise would be dishonest. You see, Kate, what I'm trying to accomplish in my research is far too important to allow anything or anyone to interfere. I don't know if you're aware of it, but I was forced to share the Nobel Prize with two other researchers in DNA. Next time I have no intention of being cheated out of what is justly mine, and mine alone."

Something in Jaccard's tone of voice forbade any further questions, and the sudden awkward silence between them left her feeling a bit foolish and ever so slightly chastened. Clearly she had intruded.

"Now please come and sit down," he suggested, settling into the chair behind his desk. "I've gone over all the various tests from your physical examination yesterday, and I'm happy to report that you appear to have made remarkable progress."

Andreas occupied himself in making some notations in the light green manila folder before him on the desk with Kate's name inscribed upon the face. Then looking up, he smiled as Kate took her seat beside him. "At this point, I think we can safely assume that the results of your cell-injection therapy have been completely successful. You won't be needing any further injections for at least two years, at which time I think we'll add some pituitary cells to your total program."

Jaccard's words only served to confirm what Kate already knew, but there were still some troubling doubts. "What if I were to stop the injections altogether?'' she asked. ''Are there any side effects?''

Jaccard shook his head. ''None whatever. You'll just go back to aging right along with the rest of mankind. Now this is not to say that Rejuvenal-12 can entirely stop biological aging. Nothing can do that, except death. But cell-injection therapy can go a long way toward slowing the aging process down and forestalling serious organic deterioration.''

''I don't suppose I've ever really known why people do age,'' Kate suggested, ''or even why they die. Are we biologically programmed to self-destruct?''

Jaccard leaned back in his chair to regard her intently through the drifting blue smoke of his burning cigarette. ''There are a variety of theories,'' he said. ''But my research has been based upon the premise that the most significant cause of actual aging lies in the brain's inability to keep a balance within the body's endocrine system.

''What I'm referring to are the body's regulators, such as insulin, adrenalin, and thyroxine. We are actually genetically programmed for death. As we grow older, the cells begin to make mistakes when they divide. They are no longer able to make exact copies of themselves; and it is these mistakes that are finally expressed as loose skin, shuffling gait, hair loss, and failing memory—everything we normally associate with the process of human aging.

''Before reaching approximately twenty-five years of age,'' he went on, ''sensitive repair mechanisms in the body's cells automatically correct these mistakes. But once the repair mechanisms begin to break down, the mistakes begin to exceed the body's ability to restore itself. And this is what leads us to the final catastrophe, which we refer to as clinical death.

''Ultimately we are all in possession of what I call a death clock,'' Jaccard declared. ''Evolution demands a fail-safe killing mechanism for multicellular animals. What I mean to say is, that if the immune system doesn't put an end to us through its failure to respond to disease, or we don't succumb to some kind of critical accident, then the cross-linkage in the body's chemical structure will finally do the job. I suppose that from one point of view, death is nature's way of giving us an evolutioary advantage over unicelled species, since it permits greater variations in the gene pool and increases opportunities for adaptation and survival to a far greater degree."

"Fascinating," Kate said. "But from what you've been telling me, it seems almost to go against nature if a woman the age of Celia Randolph can become fertile at the point where most women are starting to collect Social Security."

Jaccard smiled, tapping the ash off his cigarette. "First of all," Andreas said, "it is necessary to understand that the human body is not a thing or substance, but rather a flexible, fluid, energy field that is constantly in the process of change, from the moment of conception until the instant of clinical death. The flesh is not a solid, dense mass of cellular tissue, but rather a continuous creation, depending on your physical, mental, and emotional state, as well as millions of variable factors in both your external and internal environment. It is never static, but rather in a perpetual state of flux of self-construction and self-destruction. We must destroy . . . in order to make new.

"Rejuvenal-12 cannot make you immortal. But my experiments have proven beyond any doubt that cells in the human body can divide up to fifty times. Yet in theory, at least, fifty cellular divisions would give us an expected life span of one hundred ten or one hundred twenty years. Even conservatively speaking, we should all have a life span of ninety-five to one hundred years, yet most people have only the barest hope of reaching age seventy-five."

Andreas leaned forward to tamp out his cigarette. Then his

dark brown gaze came up to regard her intently. His look was mesmerizing. "In simplest terms, Katherine, my experiments have broken through the aging barrier for all time. You, Celia, Adrianna . . . you've all become part of a new genetic equation, unhampered by biological preprogramming. For each one of you, the death clock has been slowed by at least a quarter-century. Twenty-five years . . . depending, of course, on your individual life styles, diet, stress, and general health maintenance."

Kate found herself hanging on every word, and edged forward in her chair. "It all sounds so miraculous. Yet I can't help feeling terribly sad for Fiona Van Zandt. If only Rejuvenal-12 could have saved her."

Jaccard's expression remained inscrutable. Rising from his desk, he removed some X-rays from a manila envelope. Then, switching on an X-ray light box directly facing them, he slipped several clinical negatives beneath the metal clips.

"All four of these X-rays," he indicated, with a sweep of his hand, "have been taken of Mrs. Van Zandt over the past eight weeks." He tapped the first with his index finger. "In this one you can clearly see the dark cloudy areas in the lungs that were the result of the cancer metastasizing. The X-ray was taken when Fiona first arrived on Coral Key. What you see are a pair of lungs that can scarcely support life.

"Now here in the second picture, taken two weeks later, after Miss Van Zandt's second series of Rejuvenal-12 injections, the results are largely the same. No better and no worse. But then," he said, "here in the third X-ray the dark cloudy areas appear to be somewhat reduced. Yet at this point it was still impossible to be biologically sure that there was any real change in the course of the disease."

Jaccard tapped the light box with the end of a pencil, and there was a keen note of pride in his voice. "This fourth X-ray was taken only yesterday. You can see for yourself that the trend of remission is clear, after Fiona had been treated for only eight weeks with RJ-12."

By this point Kate was on her feet and peering intently at the illuminated transparencies. It was true. She could clearly see that one large spot on Fiona's right lung had disappeared entirely, while the dark cloudy area on the left lung had been considerably reduced.

Kate turned abruptly to Jaccard, imploring him with her eyes. "Are you telling me that Fiona is going to live?" Kate demanded, scarcely daring to believe.

Jaccard shrugged. "I'm saying only that there has been a remission. It could last for months, years, or even for a lifetime. But it may also last no more than a matter of weeks. There's simply no reliable way of telling."

The sea was a shining thing. As midnight approached the sky became a shimmer of pale light with flotillas of cotton-candy clouds trailing across the face of the moon at full. The lights of Porto Cristo flickered fitfully along the distant shoreline while the yacht *Sultana* rode serenely at anchor with all her portholes alight. Music drifted out onto the balmy night air, and figures were illuminated beneath Chinese lanterns strung around the awning on the aft deck.

"Let's all drink to the sisterhood of the Newborns," Fiona toasted, hoisting her champagne glass aloft. "Have you ever seen such a glorious moonlit night, ladies? Isn't it simply fabulous to be alive on such a night?"

Kate lifted her glass and drank along with the rest of them. Then she rose quietly and crossed the deck to stand at the railing, looking out over the shimmering bottle-glass sea.

Kate, Celia, and Adrianna had been invited aboard by Fiona that evening for what she had termed 'A celebration of Life.' "

Since having been informed of the cancer's remission,

Fiona had undergone her own transformation. She still looked dangerously frail, terribly gaunt, and hollow eyed. But there was definitely a change in both her manner and appearance. She was wearing a filmy Moroccan caftan of the palest peacock blue, and her eye makeup had been dramatically accented with Egyptian kohl, while a bright slash of red lip rouge was almost startling against her powdered, chalky pallor.

Yet they were all in a buoyant and expectant mood. As if the sudden and miraculous nature of Fiona's recovery had given them all exactly the reinforcement they needed to confirm the validity of their own personal miracles. It was the eve of parting, and they had been drawn together aboard the *Sultana* to form a mutual support system. Indeed, each of them felt herself to have become part of an exclusive sisterhood.

Fiona had treated them to an elaborate Bedouin banquet that evening. In the sumptuous dining salon of the *Sultana* they had been served an elaborate twelve-course dinner by a retinue of exotically garbed servants. The entire crew was made up of dusky North Africans, and the dining stewards seemed to come and go like slippered shadows as the feast progressed from one course to the next.

They dined off Limoges china and drank the finest vintage wines from Baccarat crystal goblets. All of them felt the close congeniality of sisterhood that evening, and there was even entertainment provided by members of the yacht's crew: a juggler, a trio of lute players, and a troupe of Saharan acrobats tumbling across the priceless Persian carpets as flutes wailed, cymbals crashed, and dark Berber eyes flashed with primitive vitality.

Now, after sharing Turkish coffee beneath the striped awning on the yacht's fantail, Celia was the next to propose a toast. "Here's to ecstasy," she pronounced. "I never even dreamed what it was like before I came to Coral Key and ran into the Brown Bomber. Andreas may have made me far younger than my years, but it took a twenty-three-year-old West Indian tennis pro to make me feel desirable once again as a woman."

Sitting with her legs curled beneath her on a deeply cushioned lounge, Celia did indeed look fabulous for a woman sixty-five years old. She was fifteen pounds lighter, and appeared to have been sleekly poured into her white sharkskin slacks and halter by Halston. Her firm throat was benignly choked by a savage ivory and gold necklace from Elsa Peretti, and she was drenched in Joy perfume, at one hundred dollars an ounce.

Celia reached up to tuck an errant blonde curl beneath the silk scarf tied babushka-style about her head. "Go right ahead—smirk and snicker if you will," she challenged. "Taking a much younger lover can be a very uplifting experience, let me tell you. Believe me, ladies, it's a real turn-on to climb into bed with a taut, well-muscled young male body simply pulsating with sexual excitement. There's just nothing like it to get all those tired juices flowing."

"You're beginning to sound like something out of a trashy novel," Adrianna good-naturedly admonished. "I mean, if your definition of ecstasy means falling in *lust* with some callow youth, you can count me out when my turn comes around to get all jacked up on sheep ovaries."

Celia looked exasperated. "Wouldn't you like to hear bells?" Celia questioned. "Just for the record, how long has it been since any of you had a man in bed who performed at peak efficiency? That's what ecstasy's all about."

"My definition is very different from yours," Adrianna said. "I've only experienced true ecstasy a very few times. And it was always during those perfectly exquisite moments on stage, when everything magically seemed to work. Suddenly I found myself a part of some kind of flowing universal rhythm, existing solely within that moment."

Sprawled upon a large silken cushion, Adrianna made a distracted motion, drawing her long red hair back from her face with both hands. "For me the very essence of ecstasy is to realize that I have actually become the dance . . . and that anything I do is going to be absolutely perfect. It only happens rarely. But when it does, nothing else in the world really seems to matter. That kind of ecstasy, even for an instant, is worth all the work, pain, despair, and frustration. It's worth everything . . . anything. Whatever price you have to pay."

They fell silent as a turbaned steward appeared to refill their champagne glasses. Then, as he disappeared down the companionway, Fiona spoke in a softly hesitant voice. "I've spent millions trying to purchase ecstasy, in one way or another. But believe me, I had no idea what it really was until Doctor Jaccard showed me the X-rays proving the cancer was in remission. I've cabled Nessim and asked him to meet me in Miami in two weeks. We're going to have a second honeymoon in the Bahamas," she excitedly informed them. "Andreas says that I should be well enough to travel by then. Afterward we're sailing north and should arrive in the Hamptons by the Fourth of July. Just in time to kick off the Hampton season with a marvelous party aboard the *Sultana*. It's going to be just like old times."

Throughout the conversation, Kate had been standing at the polished teakwood railing, staring off across the water toward the dark, velvety outlines of Coral Key. She felt the feral pulse of the tropic night all around her, as compelling as the hypnotic beat of distant drums.

Kate felt as if something were drawing her out of herself, carrying her beyond the narrow boundaries that had circumscribed her life up until that time. Everything had changed, and her meeting with Andreas Jaccard that afternoon just before sunset had confirmed that the future was ripe with promise.

* * *

Andreas was standing on the beach in the late afternoon sunlight as Kate came down the gravel path leading through the palmetto thicket. With his hands resting lightly on his hips and a beach robe slung casually over one shoulder, he was standing near the water's edge, staring after the departing launch as it sped off across the bay toward Porto Cristo.

The physical attraction she had begun to feel toward him was suddenly compelling. Kate could not take her eyes off his powerful physique: the muscular shoulders and long, well-defined runner's legs; the slim waist, with dark hair curling upward from the tight black nylon brief to blanket his belly and chest, like the pelt of some opulent male animal.

"Sorry to be late," she said in a smoky, slightly breathless voice.

"No problem." Jaccard smiled. "I came down early to see Ingrid off in the launch." Then, rather pointedly, Andreas went on to add, "I sent her to Montego Bay to pick up some laboratory supplies that got tied up in Jamaican customs. Ingrid won't be back until tomorrow afternoon."

His declaration jolted Kate slightly, like downing a jigger of strong whisky on an empty stomach. This was not going at all the way she had planned it, Kate realized, shading her eyes to look after the diminishing launch. Across the bay the sound of distant church bells pealed out across the water with clear, ringing purity.

Finally, when she felt sure enough to speak, Kate said, "To tell you the truth, Andreas, I did think your suggestion that we meet here on the beach at sunset might turn out to be . . . well, to be rather awkward, as far as Ingrid is concerned. You have an extremely attentive wife, Doctor. And I suspect a very jealous one where other women are concerned."

Andreas nodded toward the departing launch. "As you can see, I've already taken care of that little matter." His smile was very white and completely engaging in his bronze-tanned face. "Now how about going for that swim I promised you? It is your last full day on the island, after all, and diving over the coral reef is never more beautiful than just before sunset."

Together they ran down the beach, with Kate breaking away to slice the water with a shallow dive. After surfacing, she swam swiftly to the end of the jetty, where Andreas stood poised, ready to dive. Playfully Kate extended one hand to seize his ankle, after which they both went under, only to come up splashing and laughing.

"I wonder what happened to the lady with all the phobias?" Andreas teased. He moved closer to grip Kate firmly by the waist as they floated buoyantly in the crystalline water just off the end of the jetty. "Seems to me that I had to practically save you from drowning not so very long ago."

"That was someone else." Kate laughed. "A rather neurotic lady to whom I bear only a slight resemblance."

With that, Kate pushed him lightly away and swam off in pursuit of a school of brightly hued parrot fish. Diving down beneath the surface to skim along the sandy bottom, she glided languidly past shadowy caverns housing swarms of small tropical neon fish, as colorful and brightly luminous as miniature rainbows.

Andreas was right behind her, following her kicking feet into the hazy green dimness. Then he was swimming abreast and pulling Kate close against his chest, drawing her down toward the bottom amid undulating gardens of delicately trailing sea fern.

Down and down they drifted, with their bodies clinging and moving in graceful unison. Andreas held her tightly in his strong arms, kissing her deeply as Kate's hair became a silky veil enveloping both their faces.

The spell lasted for no more than a matter of seconds. No longer than it took for their bodies to drift upward. To float lightheaded toward the sunlit surface, sharing the last of their life-giving oxygen.

Then Kate twisted suddenly, sharply away with a strangled gasp, and started off stroking toward the beach. She was shaking by the time she finally walked out of the water and made her way up the sand without daring to look back. Kate's sun-bronzed skin glistened with tiny droplets of water, her hair was streaming about her shoulders, and the two-piece swimsuit clung wetly to her hips and breasts.

By the time Andreas reached her side Kate had managed to regain much of her composure. "We can't allow anything like that to happen again," she informed him, even though her limbs still tingled from their brief but highly sensual encounter. "You do understand, don't you?"

Andreas had begun drying himself. "As you wish," he replied, and his voice put some distance between them. "I guess that next you're going to tell me that you're just not the kind of woman who sleeps around with other women's husbands."

"Why do I have to be the kind of woman who sleeps around at all?" she asked rather sharply.

Then, relenting slightly, Kate slipped her arm through his, as together they began walking along the beach. "I don't mind admitting that I find you an extremely attractive man," she said, choosing her words with care. "Of course I'm attracted to you, and it is true that you're a very much married man. I happen to believe that there is a great deal that we—that you and I, Andreas—can accomplish together. But we can only do that by staying out of bed."

"Is that what you wanted to talk to me about?" he questioned.

Kate nodded, her head bound up turban-style in a pink towel. "Yes, that's why I asked to speak with you privately. You see, Andreas, I want to propose something of a partnership. I believe very much in the work you have been doing, and there is no longer any question in my mind but that Rejuvenal-12 is something very close to miraculous in its effectiveness. If you'll let me, I want to make at least a small piece of that miracle a reality for millions of women, everywhere. I want you to allow Caramour Cosmetics to produce, promote, and merchandise RJ-12 in the topical form you've developed through your research."

Andreas drew slightly away and plunged his hands deep into the pockets of his robe. "As I have already told you, Katherine, I am currently in the process of negotiating a contractual arrangement with a highly prestigious Swiss pharmaceutical company who plan to put RJ-12 on the European market as a Youth Masque. In fact, I'm flying to Switzerland next week in order to close the deal."

By now they had reached the series of coral block steps and ramps that led up from the beach through the terraced gardens surrounding the administration building. The sweet scent of flowering mimosa hung heavily on the air, and the royal palms rustled softly overhead in response to the faintest breath of wind. Dusk was coming on fast.

"I'd like to say that our relationship to date has been an extremely open and honest one, Andreas. Please hear me out, because I'm going to put all my cards on the table. I want you to formulate an entire line of skin-care products for Caramour, using RJ-12 as a base. Without any question, you can be assured of a multimillion-dollar advertising campaign with all the power and prestige of a major cosmetic company. In simplest terms, Andreas, I want to make your dream a reality."

"You're really quite serious about this, aren't you, Katherine? But I think you can understand my hesitation. No more than three weeks ago you appeared to be convinced that you were in no way capable of fulfilling your responsibilities as president of Caramour Cosmetics. Has everything changed so very much?''

''More than I ever would have imagined possible,'' she admitted. ''I've come to understand so many things. It was my father who really put Paul Osborn in the beauty business, and I've dedicated most of my life to Caramour. Now for the first time I actually have the power to bring about change. To work in developing new products that offer more to a woman than just a pretty coverup.

''In just three short weeks,'' Kate continued, ''you have converted me into a believer. Cellular rejuvenation could very well turn out to be the skin-care breakthrough of the decade. The possibilities are endless, and I have the very strong feeling that I'm the right woman in the right place at exactly the right time. To tell you the honest truth, Andreas, I feel absolutely indestructible.''

They laughed softly together as they crossed the lawn, and Andreas took Kate's arm as they mounted the steps to the veranda of the Great House to enter Andreas' study through the open French doors.

Kate stood waiting just inside the threshold while Andreas disappeared into the dimness only to materialize seconds later as he bent to light a single green-shaded hurricane lamp that softly illuminated the room with a pale wash of light.

''How about a brandy?'' he said, producing a bottle from the bottom drawer of his desk, and pouring each of them a stiff shot as Kate nodded and moved slowly to stand beside him at the desk. It was a lovely balmy evening, and a light breeze wafted in from the veranda.

''Well, doctor . . .?'' Kate said as she accepted the heavy crystal tumbler from his hand. ''What's it to be? New York or Zurich?''

Andreas sipped his drink while regarding her intently beneath hooded brows. ''I might as well be completely honest with you, Katherine. Money is a matter of prime concern. As you have seen for yourself during the past three weeks, everything on this island is old and run down. My laboratory is totally out of date for the kind of experimentation I want to do, and Geiger Pharmaceuticals has guaranteed me one million dollars in royalties. They are also willing to advance me enough money to at least upgrade my present laboratory capability, if I promise to give them first look at any new discoveries.''

Andreas paused to light one of his strong dark French cigarettes. He inhaled deeply, and then released a drifting blue veil of aromatic smoke. His laugh was low, sensual, and slightly bemused. ''Your offer is of course intriguing,'' he observed. ''But to be perfectly candid, even if the money were comparable, the powerful opposition of the American medical establishment to all forms of cell-rejuvenation therapy makes any thought of promoting RJ-12 in the United States extremely problematic. It would of course be perfectly legal to market a topical form. But then one simply can't compare the prestige of a highly reputable Swiss pharmaceutical company with an American cosmetic house.''

''The timing is right, Andreas. I can sense it. Women in America are ready to accept new and revolutionary concepts about their looks and health. Progress can no longer be stifled by the AMA. I'm willing to risk everything because I believe in Rejuvenal-12. My career, my reputation, every cent I have in the world is tied up in Caramour Stock. But you've got to give me the chance to show what I can do.''

Andreas swirled the amber liquor in his glass. ''I'm not questioning your commitment, Katherine. But what about your board of directors, and Mr. Paul Osborn? What makes you so sure that they will share your enthusiasm?''

''Paul Osborn and the board of directors can be managed,'' she assured him.

Throughout their conversation, Kate had been able to forget her personal attraction to Jaccard by concentrating completely on the business at hand. But now as he poured himself another drink and settled, half-sitting, on the edge of the desk, she was once again only too aware of the erotic potency of his total self-assurance. The arrogant sexuality he exuded like a musk.

"You're extremely convincing," Andreas conceded. "But I feel it's only fair to warn you in advance—I have earned rather more than my share of enemies. I have always been considered an outsider to the medical and scientific worlds, and there are those who bitterly resent all that I have been able to accomplish. There is an unbelievable amount of professional jealousy in scientific circles, and there have been times when I've been accused of the most heinous things imaginable."

"That doesn't matter," Kate voiced. "I believe in you, Andreas, and in your work. Caramour is prepared to match the offer you've had from Geiger, and I can guarantee you whatever money you need to completely refurbish Coral Key and bring your laboratory facilities up to date with the very latest equipment."

Andreas' dark eyes widened slightly. "Under the circumstances, Katherine, that seems an exceedingly equitable offer. But as far as the lab goes, you have to realize that the kind of facility you describe would cost a couple of million dollars at least."

Kate finished off her drink and held her glass out for a refill. "I've been giving this a lot of thought," she said as he poured her another brandy. "And while I still have to go back to New York to do battle with my colleagues at Caramour, I have already whispered the right words into the ear of a very rich and very grateful woman. Fiona has promised to arrange for a ten-million-dollar grant to the Andreas Jaccard Foundation for Life Research."

Jaccard flashed his smile. "You amaze me, Katherine. But such a foundation does not even exist."

Kate paused for several beats in order to fully savor her moment of triumph. "Not yet it doesn't," she finally responded. "But it soon will, I'll see to that. All you have to do is to trust me, Andreas. I can handle the rest of it. You have my word on that."

Kate lifted her glass. "Well, what do you say, Doctor? Do we have a deal?"

Andreas smiled that easy, confident, devastating smile of his and lofted his drink with a courtly flourish to softly clink against her own. "Yes, my dear Katherine. We do indeed have a deal."

His voice was very low, and his face, in the dimness, drew very close to hers. Close enough, Kate recalled, to feel his breath upon her cheek as they toasted the future. Now leaning against the railing on the fantail of the *Sultana*, Kate sipped her champagne and stared out across the moonlit water, wondering what that future would hold for all of them. For Andreas and herself. For Adrianna, Fiona, and Celia. For the Duchess of Sutherland and for Solange Wilkerson.

That morning she had left a neatly penciled note on Kate's breakfast tray begging her help in finding employment in New York City. Had she been mistaken? Kate wondered. Or had there been a look of tearful desperation glazing the girl's hauntingly lovely features as she was bidding her goodbye.

"Katherine," Celia called out. "Why don't you come and join the rest of us? Don't think for a moment that you're going to avoid this show and tell session by throwing yourself overboard. The subject is ecstasy, and we're all anxiously awaiting your definition."

Looking tanned, fit, and radiantly self-contained, Kate slowly crossed the afterdeck, to sweep her fellow reborns with a searchlight smile. "Three weeks ago, I would have had to say that I must have been behind the door when God was going around handing out ecstasy. But now, my dears, I know exactly what it's all about."

There were sprinkles of tipsy laughter and a brief smattering of applause that caused Kate to lift her hands, signaling for a respectful hearing. "My definition of ecstasy is accomplishing something that has never been done before. To chart a new course in life, knowing that for once in your life, you aren't going to let anything or anyone stop you from succeeding."

Kate reached into the pocket of her crêpe lounging pajamas to remove a clear plastic container filled with a creamy pink substance. She held it up to the light. "All of you are aware of the miraculous benefits of Rejuvenal-12. But what you don't know—at least not yet—is that Andreas has developed a topical form of RJ-12 that both preserves and rejuvenates the skin against stress, pollution, and aging."

Poised with the willowy grace of a fine actress, Kate paused in her recitation and poured a small amount of the liquified pink emulsion into the palm of her hand. "I want you three to be the first to know," she announced, allowing each of them to sample the creamy texture with her fingertips. "This afternoon, I signed a multimillion-dollar agreement with Andreas to incorporate his RJ-12 formula into a complete new line of cosmetic skin-care products for Caramour."

Kate lifted her champagne glass and flashed them a radiant confident smile. "*Bottoms up* might be the most appropriate toast I could offer. But instead, let's drink to Doctor Andreas Jaccard, and to Rejuvenal—the wonder drug of the age."

Part Two

Summer Solstice

Chapter Eleven

No woman who fell in love with Paul Osborn was ever quite the same, Kate realized. Cristina Dayne had been no exception. The only difference was that she had had the misfortune to marry him.

Kate stood on the sidewalk in front of the Plaza Hotel, staring up at a glossy vitrine window fronting Central Park South. It displayed a woman's perfect cameo profile, viewed through the window of a chauffeured Rolls Royce.

For that whisper of elegance, the copy read, *it's Cristina perfume by Caramour Cosmetics.*

An entirely new image was where it had to start, Kate thought to herself. Cristina perfume had been Caramour's top-selling fragrance for the better part of a decade, but sales had begun to slip badly in the last fiscal year.

It had all begun back when Caramour was in the process of making the transition from a small wholesale distributor of low-cost cosmetic products to a far more prestigious operation geared to the fashion-conscious woman.

Paul had decided that it was necessary to upgrade his own rather rough and tumble image. After equipping himself with Saville Row suits, the right club memberships, and a Rolls Silver Cloud, he began looking around for a wife with the requisite social câchét and a large enough dowry to expand his business into more lucrative areas.

By marrying Cristina Dayne, he had achieved both goals in short order. Paul had always been like that. The complete pragmatist.

There had, however, been problems from the very beginning. At the time of their marriage, Cristina was already well past first bloom and without visible prospects. She was always slightly overweight, basically insecure, and not nearly rich or pretty enough to satisfy Paul's ambitions.

What she did have going for her was a certain media recognition factor in society, and a wealthy stockbroker father who was willing to invest heavily in his future son-in-law when Caramour went public with an initial stock offering.

Henri Wexford Dayne got twelve percent of the company stock and a seat on the board of directors, while Paul got the five million dollars he so desperately needed, and a wife who measured up only marginally to his expectations.

Paul needed not only a rich and socially prominent wife, but a beautiful one as well. He wasted no time in making arrangements with a world-famous plastic surgeon to completely transform the woman he had so precipitously wooed and wed.

In truth, the too wide mouth and large hazel eyes that eventually came to smile out from thousands of newspaper photographs were all that Cristina could legitimately call her own.

Her original nose job had been such a huge success after the implantation of additional cartilege that during the ensuing months Paul easily persuaded his new bride to have her eyelids lifted, her brows heightened, and finally her ears pinned back.

But that was only the beginning. The Svengali-Trilby relationship continued to blossom on through breast implants, surgical thigh-reduction, and various silicone injections.

Ultimately, the finely chiseled and highly aristocratic profile that eventually came to replace Cristina's previously plain physiognomy had been selected feature by feature by Paul from photographs of the world's most beautiful women. It was a spectacular feat of cosmetic wizardry that cost close to a quarter-million dollars, and somehow managed to endow Cristina's beautiful frozen countenance with a perpetually perplexed expression, as if she couldn't quite believe in the reality of the woman she saw reflected in her mirror.

Later, after she began drinking heavily and throwing ugly jealous tantrums in public, Kate had felt very sorry for Cristina Osborn. She was so desperately in love with Paul, and yet they shared little beyond the same roof, and that was only on rare occasions.

By the time of her death, Cristina had become a pathetic wreck of a woman, obsessed by the idea of recapturing her husband's attentions. It was then that she flew off to Geneva, Switzerland, and checked into the famous Meyerhof Clinic to begin cell-injection therapy. Six months later she was dead.

Kate deliberately put such thoughts from her mind as she purchased a bouquet of pastel-colored peonies in the Plaza florist shop. Then she hurried her steps toward the Caramour corporate offices at the corner of Fifth Avenue and Fifty-ninth.

It was ten o'clock in the morning on her first day back in New York, and Kate dashed across Fifth in order to catch a green light.

Directly in front of her the General Dynamics building rose

shimmering in the morning sunlight from a broad plaza of placid reflecting pools and splashing fountains—a towering monolith of concrete, marble, glass, and chromium steel that seemed to pierce the Manhattan skyline with an effortless upward thrust.

As she made her way across the plaza, Kate felt as if she were viewing everything with new eyes. It was great to be back in New York City, and it was great to be alive.

Kate whirled through the spinning glass doors, and walked briskly across the marble rotunda toward the double banks of high-floor elevators at the rear.

"Good morning, Miss Leslie." The smartly uniformed and exceedingly garrulous elevator starter addressed her. "You're looking terrific. It's good to have you back from vacation, and congratulations on the new job."

Kate rewarded him with a radiant smile. "Good morning, Max," she called, stepping inside the elevator and reaching out to press the softly glowing button inscribed, CARAMOUR COSMETICS—RECEPTION: PENTHOUSE FLOOR.

The doors closed silently, and then she was rising upward, filled with a sense of heady anticipation.

The moment of beginning was something that Kate had always relished. That first tentative step toward creating some tangible reality out of a basically simple idea. All the challenges and problems still lay ahead of her to be mastered, while each and every step of the way would become an affirmation of who she was, and what she was capable of accomplishing.

As the elevator carried her upward for eighty-seven floors in a soundless vacuum, Kate reviewed her plans for developing RJ-12 into a complete line of skin-care products. Her enthusiasm for the project was almost like a physical sensation, like the initial vibrations of sudden, intense sexual desire.

But first there were problems that would have to be solved if she was to have any hope of success. Kate had always made it a policy never to threaten the corporate ambitions of her fellow executives. Having been considered to be Paul Osborn's *de facto* mistress had always given her a certain untouchable status. Yet the truth was now inescapable—she was going to be fair game.

Paul never made any secret of living by the rule of the jungle, which, roughly translated, meant that whatever he wanted he took. Opposition existed solely to be overcome—not only through his skill at bargaining and manipulation, but, if all else failed to produce the desired results, through fraud, cunning, and even blackmail. Or at least so Kate suspected.

There had been much that Kate had chosen not to see. Instead of playing corporate politics, she had worked long and hard to live up to her position as vice president in charge of advertising and promotion. Paul's patronage would have counted for very little had she not been willing to exercise a certain calculated daring coupled with a studious attention to detail and a nimble creative intelligence.

Perhaps most of all, she had always possessed an almost uncanny sense of how women wanted to see themselves. Kate's judgments in business matters were essentially conservative. Yet she was willing to take enormous risks, once she had convinced herself of the unshakable rightness of her chosen course.

With Paul as The Man in the executive suite, no one had dared to cross her. But now that he was gone, there was not the slightest doubt in Kate's mind that there would be a) a lot of people celebrating his departure with plans for their own ascension to power, and b) a lot of old scores still to be settled. The battles of the boardroom may not have drawn much real blood, but the wounds had gone deep, and they still continued to fester.

Paul had always been the ruthless manipulator *par excellence*. Fear had been the dominant emotion by which he ruled, and even as his creatively adept protegée, Kate had not completely escaped the tautly strung web of corrosive stress.

It started right at the top, and worked its way down from the executive suite in swiftly escalating shock waves to the lowliest janitorial employee.

Throughout the long years of their relationship, Paul's ruthless and demanding temperament had taken a terrible toll of both her fingernails and her nerves. Now, however, all that was going to change. Kate was determined to remake Caramour Cosmetics in her own image. And she was going to do it relying solely on the values, talents, and ability to excell that had already carried her so far.

A soft chiming note brought Kate back to the moment. The elevator had come to a halt at the penthouse floor, and Kate mentally composed herself as the doors slid open upon the luxuriously appointed reception area of Caramour Cosmetics, Incorporated.

Rich, almost subliminal strains of Muzak played in the background like gently falling rain. Across the richly carpeted foyer a remarkably beautiful young woman sat behind an excellent copy of a Louis XIV desk. There was a vase of long-stemmed red roses at her elbow, and from overhead a venetian crystal chandelier cast a muted aura of opulence over the dusky-rose and ivory-gilt foyer.

The receptionist's name was Beverly Farrell, a slim, green-eyed blonde with flawless skin and amazing breasts, who was widely reputed to have been one of Paul Osborn's favorite playmates.

Oblivious to Kate's arrival, Beverly was gently blowing on her freshly lacquered nails, and reading a copy of *Variety*.

"Excuse me for bothering you, Miss Farrell. But is this what you're being paid to do?"

The girl's eyes came up to meet Kate's coolly appraising stare, and an expression of startled recognition registered upon her perfect features.

"I'm terribly sorry, Miss Leslie. I didn't know you were expected in this morning." She held up one freshly lacquered hand to display long, perfectly shaped nails. They were the same bright red shade as the roses in the crystal vase. "Mr. Osborn always insisted I be color coordinated."

"What exactly can you do besides polish your nails, Miss Farrell? Can you type or take dictation?"

The girl shrugged prettily. "That sort of thing has never been part of my job," she explained. "Paul—I mean Mr. Osborn—always told me I only had to be 'decorative.' You see, I'm really an actress, more or less between jobs."

"Then you may consider yourself to be more, rather than less, unemployed. I'll see that your final check is ready for you at five o'clock today," Kate said in a voice far sharper than she intended. "Your performance here has been something less than memorable."

Beverly Farrell went pale beneath her bright and glossy makeup. But by then Kate had already turned on her heel and marched off down the corridor toward the executive suite at the far end. "Good morning, Iris," Kate said as she stepped through the door emblazoned with the title of PRESIDENT.

"Why, Miss Leslie! My goodness! I didn't expect you until Wednesday at the earliest."

"Relax, Iris. It's just a trial run today. I decided to slip in unannounced to try and get a jump on the paperwork."

Iris Quaid, Paul's formidable and highly efficient executive secretary, sat behind her desk in the stylishly appointed outer office of the executive suite. The striking focal point was a grouping of magnificent greenhouse orchids artfully arranged on a series of illuminated glass shelves displaying the full range of Caramour beauty products.

A single waxen *Laelia purpurata* stood beside the lavender-tinted phone console, while laying open upon Iris' desk was the morning paper, bearing bold headline type that read COSMETICS TYCOON WEDS GOLDEN GIRL IN RIVIERA NUPTIALS.

"I suppose you've seen the papers," Iris said, rising to her feet. She was an imposing-looking woman, whose perfectly coiffed bone-white hair framed sternly uncompromising features. Iris invariably wore black with pearls, and her scare power was enormous.

"I've read the papers," Kate pronounced. "I suppose that today is what you might call the beginning of a new era at Caramour."

"Well, I'm delighted to welcome you back," Iris responded. "I know that Mr. Osborn had the greatest faith in your abilities. I'm sure that you're going to make a fine president, Miss Leslie. Feel perfectly free to call upon me in any way that I can be of help."

Kate was momentarily taken back. She had not been at all sure how Iris would react to her own ascension to power. "Why . . . thank you, Iris. I'm very glad you've chosen to stay on. After being with Mr. Osborn for as long as you have, I know you must realize that I'm going to need all the help I can get. As you no doubt heard, my previous secretary got married and moved to California."

Kate's voice was firm, clear, and somewhat more assured than she actually felt. The incident with Beverly Farrell had upset her far more than she liked to admit. Yet the unexpected warmth of Iris Quaid's support did much to buoy her lagging spirits. Kate considered it an auspicious omen.

"Now then," Kate went on, "there are several important matters on the immediate agenda. First of all, I want you to notify everyone concerned that the board meeting scheduled for this Friday has been canceled. Then call personnel and tell them to arrange a replacement for Miss Farrell by the end of the day. I just fired her for incompetence."

As Kate spoke, Iris was rapidly taking notes in a steno notebook. "Type up an executive order for my signature, cancelling further production of Cristina perfume, and arrange a meeting with Scotty McPherson to discuss some ideas I have for a fragrance replacement."

As she reached the door of her office, Kate paused and turned to stare hard at Iris Quaid, as if seeing her clearly for the first time.

"Yes, Miss Leslie?" Iris questioned. "Is there something else?"

"No, Iris, it's nothing. Just hold all my calls for the rest of the morning."

Once the double doors to Paul's old office had closed behind her, Kate leaned back against the panels and exhaled a deep breath. Of course. Why hadn't she ever seen it before? Both she and Iris Quaid had been in love with the same man. Now, with Paul's marriage, they were even dressed like a couple of sod widows, in basic black with pearls.

The first thing Kate did was pull back the spun-glass curtains drawn across the wide expanse of windows and allow the bright morning sunlight to splash inside. Paul's spacious penthouse aerie, high in the sky above Manhattan, was strictly modern in decor. The furnishings had been kept to a minimum, allowing the spacious wood-panelled suite to make its own statement.

There was a single large Mondrian painting behind Paul's desk, and Kate realized as she took off her coat that it had always appealed to her deepest sense of order and infallible eye for design. For starters it was something she could moor herself to.

A panelled door blending into the wall opened onto a

dressing room with cedar closets and fireproof file-safe secreted behind a solid mahogany wall. Just beyond, and through another door, was a tiled bathroom with shower and sauna.

All of Paul's personal effects had already been removed. But as Kate swung open the closet door in order to put away her coat, she was amazed to find a full-length Russian sable hanging in the midst of all that resin-scented vacancy. In the pocket was one of Paul's business cards inscribed with the message: "Sorry I missed your birthday. But maybe this will help, if it turns out to be a long, cold winter."

How very like him, Kate thought as she slipped into the coat and turned slowly before the full-length mirror. But why would a newly wedded man give an expensive sable to a business associate? Paul had always been generous with presents, but this was the kind of gift a man would give to his mistress.

Anyway, she thought, returning to the outer office with her hands gently stroking the full sleeves, Paul was probably right about the long, cold winter to come. However you sliced it, Mr. Paul Osborn was going to be a very hard act to follow.

There was in fact such a powerful sense of Paul's presence still pervading the executive suite that as Kate ran her fingertips across the gleaming surface of his desk she was suddenly filled with a sense of terrible loss.

Paul had always been so able; so brilliant, sure, and decisive. How could she—how could anyone—ever hope to take his place? Kate didn't really even know where to start.

Thus far, she had been on the job for less than an hour and all she had managed to accomplish was to exorcise an old grudge and order the name of Paul's first wife, Cristina, stricken from its association with Caramour Cosmetics.

There was a soft buzzing from the intercom, and even as

she reached to press the flashing red button, Kate knew that it was Paul. "Yes, Iris," she said.

"It's Mr. Osborn calling on a ship-to-shore radio hookup from Cannes, Miss Leslie. I was sure you'd want to take his call."

Very slowly Kate sat down in Paul's high-backed leather chair. Whatever confidence she had felt upon arriving at Caramour that morning seemed to abruptly bleed away. "Yes, of course, Iris. You may put Mr. Osborn through."

Slipping off a single pearl earring, Kate lifted the receiver only to be greeted by a burst of static, interspersed with a chorus of garbled voices fading on and off the line.

"Hello, Katie . . .?" It was Paul's voice, sounding both strange and intimately familiar.

"Yes, Paul, I'm here." Kate's voice was taut and slightly breathless. "Is everything all right . . . I mean, are you feeling . . . well?"

"Never felt better." His voice boomed back at her as if rebounding through an echo chamber. "How about you? How was your vacation with Celia in the Caribbean?"

"Simply marvelous. I'm feeling a lot more rested. Today's my first day back in the office."

Once again the connection was interrupted by a prolonged burst of static, and Paul finally had to raise his voice to be heard. "I guess you've read about the wedding. The European press has played it up pretty big. There's *paparazzi* swarming all over the *Caramour II*. I've just about decided to pack it in and sail for the Costa Smeralda to get away from all the ruckus."

"I saw the papers," Kate said. Then, steeling herself against giving away too much, she went on to add, "Paul . . . I want to wish you the very best. Truly I do. And I want to thank you for the coat. It was a lovely birthday present."

There was a long pause. It was so long, in fact, that Kate began to wonder whether or not the connection might have been broken. Then once again Paul was speaking, although now there was a different note in his voice. "Look, Katie," he was saying. "Everything happened pretty fast over there, toward the last. I didn't mean it to be that way. You've always been someone very special to me. I'm sure that you know that."

"Yes," she responded softly. "Yes, Paul. I know that."

"Now I know it isn't going to be easy taking up the reins on such short notice," he went on. "But I haven't tossed you into the lions' den without some pretty heavy artillery to back you up. If you should get into a really tight spot, just remember that Max Drexel knows how to muscle his way around. Use him. That's what he's there for."

Kate stiffened almost imperceptibly. "You know I've never liked or trusted Max Drexel. There's something about the man that makes me terribly uncomfortable."

Once again Paul's tone had changed, and now he was strictly business. "I'm not suggesting that you jump into bed with him, Katie. No one in their right mind would actually trust the slippery son of a bitch. But the simple fact is, he's the kind of guy to get things done . . . one way or another."

"I've never really understood very much about corporate politics," Kate said. "Honestly, Paul, I don't even know where to start, as far as that's concerned."

"That's the main reason I called," Paul responded. "Now listen good, because I'm gonna tell you where to start. I never mentioned this to you before, but for the past half-dozen years I've had a team of private investigators developing what you might call dossiers, full of corporate intelligence. It's the locked blue file in the closet where you found your coat. Don't hesitate to use the information in that file if you get in a tight spot and can't reach me. Of course I'll be checking in on a regular basis just to see how things are going and advise you on any tough decisions.''

Kate was shaken by his words, but before she could respond there was another prolonged burst of static. Then she was listening to Allison's voice purring over the wire. ''Isn't it fabulous, Katie? Paul's taking me around the world for our honeymoon. Of course we were devastated you weren't able to attend the wedding, but then Paul said you were having some kind of emotional problem.

''Hello . . . hello? Katie, darling, are you there?''

As Kate sat there stiffly holding the phone, something very close to hatred turned inside her like a knife. She could still hear Allison's voice repeating her name. Kate's hand was shaking as she slowly replaced the receiver.

By the time that Celia breezed in about forty-five minutes later, however, Kate was seated at her desk, totally immersed in trying to bring order out of chaos. There were piles of correspondence, innumerable memoranda, and stacks of statistical reports that showed the company to be very much in the red.

''I come bearing tidings of great joy,'' Celia announced with a dramatic flourish. Directly behind her Iris was dogging Celia's heels with a dour and disapproving look. ''I'm terribly sorry, Miss Leslie. I told Mrs. Randolph that you did not wish to be disturbed under any circumstances.''

''It's all right, Iris, Mrs. Randolph is like gravity. There's just no point in trying to restrain a natural phenomenon. Just try and hold the rest of the world at bay for a while longer.''

''I do hope that you're going to replace the Dragon Lady with something a bit more engaging,'' Celia said as soon as the door had closed behind Iris Quaid's departing back. ''That one reminds me of the grim reaper.''

Kate leaned back in her chair, smiling. "Iris is a wonder, and she stays. Now to what do I owe the honor of this unexpected visitation?"

"Well, darling, to tell you the truth, it occurred to me when I got up this morning that you might just be having an attack of opening performance jitters. Sooo . . . I threw myself together in a trice and dashed over here on my errand of mercy, only to find you slaving away in a new sable coat. And it's the first week of June, yet."

Celia circled the desk to run her brightly enameled fingertips over the fur. "Not bad by the way, and *trés cher.* I'd say at least fifty thousand at Ben Kahn, and that ain't exactly chopped liver."

"It's Paul's birthday present," Kate informed her. "His card suggested that there might be a very long and cold winter ahead."

One of Celia's finely penciled brows shot up quizzically. "How very touching of Paul, and rather practical as well. It certainly wouldn't do for you to catch your death of pneumonia. That might just interrupt the honeymoon."

"Don't be bitchy, Celia. I'm just not in the mood. I've tons of work to catch up on, and there are a thousand important decisions that have to be made before the next meeting of the board. As for Paul and Allison, it isn't going to be just the Mediterranean. They're sailing around the world... indefinitely."

Celia marched to the center of the room, where she did a full three-hundred-and-sixty-degree turn, her blue eyes darting, shifting, scanning, and appraising with a thoroughly professional air. "Screw them," she announced. "As my own personal contribution to your dynamic new image, I've decided to completely redecorate this office. I think you need to get rid of every last trace of The Louse."

It was a moment before Kate answered. "I don't really want to change anything right now, Celia. Things are going to be getting pretty tight around here expenditure-wise if I have anything to say about it. I just took a look at the company's latest profit and loss statement. It's all loss."

"I wouldn't charge a cent beyond the forty or fifty thousand it'll take to give this corporate mausoleum a good face-lifting. Honestly, Kate, you owe it to the company to project the proper image."

"For now I want everything left just the way it is," Kate said in a softly hesitant voice.

"You mean you want things to be just the way they were, isn't that it?" Celia challenged. "Before Allison barged onto the scene, and destroyed your safe little fantasy world."

"You could be right," Kate admitted. "But that's the way it is right now. I'll get my act together before too long. I have to, if I'm going to survive."

"In that regard," Celia advised, "the time has definitely come for you to donate that little black dress of yours to the Salvation Army. The proverbial office uniform is as out of date as high-button shoes. Whether you know it or not, you could easily be mistaken for the directress of a funeral home instead of the president of a major cosmetics company."

"I've never been particularly interested in clothes." Kate defended herself. "You know I like to keep things simple."

"You won't have to try very hard to convince me of that," Celia decreed in her most impressive, take-charge voice. "Now I want you to cancel anything you might have planned for the rest of the day, because *tout ensêmble,* we are going out shopping for a whole new you."

Chapter Twelve

Kate sat staring down at the leather-bound portfolio embossed in gold lettering. It was entitled CARAMOUR'S REJUVENAL—PROSPECTUS: *Estimated Financing, Organizational Requirements, and Fiscal Projections.*

There were no more than a half-dozen copies in existence, and Kate's staff in the promotion department had been working around the clock for over two weeks to put the project together within the time allotted.

Kate was now ready to make her first important move.

Ever since returning from the Caribbean, she had been closeted with her closest creative people, those staff veterans of past campaigns, who had been surreptitiously scavenging all the various bits and pieces of information necessary to complete the Rejuvenal prospectus.

Their task was made all the more difficult by Kate's insistence on complete secrecy, but she had not the slightest intention of betraying her game plan until all the pieces were in place and the stage had been properly set.

As Kate sat at her desk scanning the pages of the prospectus one last time, she experienced a deep sense of pride and satisfaction. She herself had orchestrated the entire project, written most of the copy, done the photographic layouts, and narrated the promotional film that was to accompany her presentation to the board.

But it was the final page that confirmed her belief and enthusiasm. It was a confidential report from the research and development laboratories in New Jersey, where extensive testing had been feverishly in progress for the past two weeks. She read again the crucial paragraphs of their report:

> Our research strongly indicates that RJ-12 is a successful application that accelerates the skin's own ability to restore itself naturally. In short, RJ-12 appears to slow down the aging process of the skin's epidermal layer through a process of cellular osmosis.
>
> According to our own testing and the research material provided to us by Doctor Jaccard, the breakthrough in skin care has been achieved by extracting embryonic live cells from the unborn living tissue of a disease-resistant strain of mutant guinea pigs. These cell extracts are then freeze dried and preserved until they are incorporated in various preparations of the selected active substances already described in Part 1 of the report. . . .
>
> RJ-12 is indeed a unique preparation infused with preserved cell extracts in the form of placental tissue, collagen and elastin; which are the fundamental building blocks of a healthy complexion.

At the bottom of the report, Scotty McPherson, a man for whom Kate had the greatest professional respect, had scrawled,

"It looks like you're really onto something very big. From what I've seen so far, I wouldn't be at all surprised if Rejuvenal-12 were to revolutionize the cosmetic skin-care industry."

It was high praise indeed, since McPherson was considered to be one of the finest chemists in the business. Scotty had also worked for her father at Leslie Chemical Products, and had always been like a second father to her.

Kate rose from her desk to make a slow and thoughtful circuit of the room, with its loosely arranged grouping of deep suede chairs flanking a large, circular glass and chrome conference table. From the very first day she had felt herself entirely at home in Paul's old office.

It was the intelligently ordered working space of a busy, competent executive. Very functional and eclectic. Rather more like a living room than a corporate president's office, with its comfortable modular furnishings and lots of greenery arching upward toward the recessed lighting panels. There was nothing anywhere to conjure images of waste or indolence.

Paul had been right about Max Drexel, Kate realized. Whatever her personal feelings might be, he was absolutely crucial to the success of her plans.

As National Sales Director, Max Drexel was out on the road most of the time. But when he did manage to show up at the company's corporate headquarters in Manhattan, the most noticeable aspect of his presence was noise—the frantic clatter of typewriters, the constant ringing of telephones, and the cacaphony of urgent voices pitching the company products.

No matter where he was, Drexel operated in an atmosphere of continual crisis, and he always had an angle going. In fact his success since coming to work for Paul Osborn at Caramour was largely the result of a highly mobilized sales force of five hundred Beauty Reps, most of whom had formerly been models, actresses, or airline stewardesses. All of them were uniformly statuesque, invariably attractive, and, according to some reports, multiorgasmic.

Women were Max Drexel's fix. Through the skillful use of behavioral psychology, intense group competition, and some shrewd observations regarding what women wanted most out of life. Max had put together a strikingly motivated sales force who were rewarded for their efforts with huge commissions, expensive jewelry, fur coats, and custom-built cadillacs.

Most of them were divorcées. All of them had gone through beauty and charm school at the company's expense. Upon reaching their first $25,000 sales plateau, they uniformly were treated to a twenty-six-week physical fitness course, stressing thigh-reduction, muscular control, and breast enhancement.

Once a year, the Caramour Beauty Reps were flown to New York from all over the country for a full week's briefing on the company's newest products. While in residence at the Hilton, they attended various sales seminars, were coiffed in the best salons, allowed to buy fabulous fashions at discount prices, and ultimately treated to every available luxury in order to assure them that they were, indeed, a very select breed of women.

Paul Osborn had always referred to them as The Caramour Pussy Brigade, and Kate had always wondered just how many of them he had slept with. Yet their consistently high sales figures were a testament to their undisputed powers of persuasion with cosmetic wholesalers and retailers in all parts of the country.

It was widely rumored that Drexel ran his dynamic female sales force the way a pimp ran a stable of high-priced whores. But Kate had never given much credence to that kind of loose talk.

If Rejuvenal was to succeed, she needed Drexel and his

Beauty Reps playing on her team. For the moment, at least, that was all that really mattered.

At three o'clock that afternoon she was to preside over the first board meeting of her presidency, and the necessity of establishing a totally new image had called for desperate measures. Kate realized now that she never would have been able to achieve just the right look without Celia's takeover, makeover blitz.

Kate's metamorphosis from wren to butterfly had not been entirely without pain and effort, however.

Celia was like a missionary, passionately committed to enhancing the lives of those less fortunate with that indefinable quality called style. She firmly believed she had been born with an absolute sense of chic, the way that certain musicians were born with perfect pitch.

As Celia saw it, it was no less than a sacred duty to tend the frowsy, the rumpled, and the indifferent, who, according to the Randolph holy writ, had to be reassembled at all costs.

On her first day back in Manhattan, Kate had spent seven hours being restyled, manicured, pedicured and depilitated. At Celia's insistence, she placed herself totally in the hands of a variety of beauty technicians, while she languished in three swivel chairs, lay on two massage tables, wore four different smocks, and undressed and dressed partially or completely five different times.

She had been pampered, soothed, conned, manipulated, and ultimately reassured that she was indeed a very attractive woman. In fact, for the first time in her life, Kate had discovered what it was that rich women did with their time and their money. It was quite a revelation.

The total renovation was like a cocoon woven about her with lots of crisp green bills of large denominations, requiring the talents and unique abilities of a host of professional beautymakers. Those beauty technicians who, like Kate herself, were in the business of shaping and molding the entire fabric of how women looked, how they felt about themselves, and how they were perceived by the world at large.

It was a real education for Kate, who had never before been willing to devote the time and money necessary. Extravagance had never been something Kate could manage without an overriding sense of guilt. Helena Rubenstein's on Fifth Avenue had always taken care of her most pressing needs during a one-hour visit every two weeks. Her clothes had been bought to last, always in the same traditional tailored styles and conservative shades that had acted as a sort of camouflage or protective coloration.

But now Celia had changed all that, and Kate had the feeling she would never be the same again. On the previous Saturday morning they had started out on a whirlwind shopping spree that carried them through a variety of expensive Fifth Avenue shops and boutiques, and left Kate dazed and slightly stunned by the sheer velocity of their progress. Celia had been like a general, barking out orders, while in their wake the stores through which they marched took on the look of battlefields that had been the scene of a recent skirmish. All was chaos, with stacks of open boxes, clouds of tissue paper littering the rugs, discarded clothing tossed at random, and the exhausted sales personnel in a state of total collapse as they figured up stunning commissions.

Never in her entire life had Kate spent so much money in a single day. In fact, while earning more than a hundred thousand dollars a year for over a decade, she had always lived simply in the same unpretentious Upper East Side apartment, consistently reinvesting every possible cent in Caramour stock. When she did make a purchase of any consequence, like the house in Amagansett or the Bentley, she bought with an eye to quality and durability.

A brisk knock on her office door brought Kate abruptly out of her reverie. "Hi gorgeous," Wes said, sticking his head through the partially open door. "Do I detect a pensive, preoccupied look on that lovely face? Tsk Tsk," he clucked. "Now we don't want to develop lots of ugly frown lines, do we?"

Wesley Travis had been Kate's second in command for over five years. The creative chemistry existing between them had been responsible for many of Caramour's most successful and imaginative promotional campaigns.

At forty-four years of age, Wes had about him a casually decadent aura of sophistication, and looked like an aging Tab Hunter. He was an evenly tanned six-foot-tall Texan, who was slim as a snake, with longish wheat-colored hair, roguish good looks, a luxuriant blond mustache, and the kind of body that came from working out at a gym five days a week.

While he could appear to be the very picture of sartorial elegance in a satin-lapeled tux with ruffled shirt front and diamond studs, in the office Wes dressed invariably in designer jeans, form-fitting T-shirts in a variety of pastel shades, and Frye cowboy boots at three hundred fifty dollars a pair.

Wesley's habitual expression was bemused, and in spite of his addiction to smoking marijuana and snorting one hundred dollars' worth of cocaine in an evening, he could be counted upon to act as Kate's escort whenever she was required to attend important industry functions.

Over the years both their personal and working relationship had evolved to a point of intimacy she shared with no other male of her acquaintance. When Kate was feeling down, no one could give her spirits a lift and make her laugh the way Wes could. When she had a problem, his agile creative intelligence was never bound by conventional thinking.

Wesley Travis was utterly loyal to Kate, as well as being

her prime source of corporate gossip, since he made it his business to know absolutely everything that was going on at Caramour.

Now, as Wes hovered expectantly in the doorway, Kate beckoned him inside with a wave of her hand. ''I just finished going over the Rejuvenal prospectus,'' she announced. ''It looks terrific.''

Kate glanced down at her watch, and found that she had only twenty minutes before the start of the board meeting at three o'clock. ''You and the staff have done a great job, Wes. Now all I have to do is to go into that meeting and sell the board on giving me five million dollars to put Rejuvenal into production.''

Wes closed the door behind him. Then, walking as if he were treading on eggshells, he approached her desk and placed a copy of *Cosmetology Today* directly in front of her. It was the beauty industry's foremost trade paper, which had been founded by a maverick journalist by the name of Garrett Forbes.

Now Wesley flapped his long arms like a vulture, and his features assumed a dour, avian expression. He let out a couple of harsh squawks, while fluttering around in a circle. ''You know how I detest being the harbinger of ill tidings,'' he pronounced. ''But it looks to me as if the inmates are out to try and peddle the asylum.''

He nodded toward the copy of *Cosmetology Today* lying before her on the desk. ''This won't be hitting the newsstands before the first of next week. But I was able to get an advance copy through the good offices of a certain Puerto Rican typesetter of my fond acquaintance. He says that this is only the first article of a series that Garrett Forbes is going to do on major companies in the industry.''

Slipping on her glasses, Kate began reading with avid interest.

An Era Passes at Caramour, Inc.

Paul Osborn, long a legendary figure who was very much a part of the cosmetics scene for over twenty-five years, once complained to this reporter that he had little hope of ever finding a successor to relieve him of the responsibilities and complexities of running a major cosmetics company. Osborn claimed at the time that he wanted nothing more than to retire as early as possible and sail off on his fabulous yacht, the *Caramour II,* while a fit successor arose to inherit the mantle of his personal power.

Anyone who ever knew Paul Osborn knew also that he was bluffing. No one ever enjoyed the rough and tumble game of mass merchandising the way he did, and there were few who could match him as a formidable and at times lethal competitor.

Up until the time of Osborn's unexpected abdication, there still appeared to be no obvious successor who could step in and replace him as the driving force behind one of our most innovative cosmetics companies. Osborn's retirement, following a series of heart attacks, marks the passage of another titan of American business. Caramour, Inc., was one of only a handful of companies such as Revlon, Helena Rubenstein, and Esteé Lauder that soared to prominence amid enormous financial profits largely through the ingenuity and vigor of a single person.

In spite of his unquestioned abilities, perhaps Osborn's major failing during the course of his impressive career was in not attracting other top executives to the company he founded. Now, with the transition a fâit accômplí, a lot of bond and money people are asking questions about a very dedicated woman by the name of Katherine Leslie, who previously filled the slot of advertising v.p. before becoming Osborn's handpicked successor.

She appears to be one of those people who just happened to be in the right place at the right time. And yet it is considered to be highly unlikely that Miss Leslie has either the experience or the ambition to counter what is fast shaping up as a major power struggle in the Caramour boardroom.

As of this writing, any further questions of who will emerge victorious may be purely academic. Sources close to where the action is informed me privately that highly secret negotiations have now been in progress for several weeks.

International Consortium Export, which owns everything from oil tankers to fast-food outlets, is said to covet Caramour the way a prospective suitor covets a rich, young, and beautiful widow.

As of this writing, only time will tell. But it might very well turn out to be I.C.E. who ultimately dictates who is to sit in the president's chair at Caramour, Inc. For now, it would seem that everything is up for grabs, including the top slot.

Chapter Thirteen

They were gathered in the Caramour boardroom, with its deep brown lacquered walls, pale beige carpeting, Chippendale mirrors, and long glass and chrome conference table. Henri Dayne, Vice President and Director of International Operations, Theodore Baxley, Vice President and Company Treasurer, and Max Drexel, Vice President of Merchandising and Director of Domestic Sales.

At precisely three P.M. Iris Quaid entered through the bronze solar-panelled doors to announce, ''Miss Leslie will be joining you shortly, gentlemen. She's tied up on an overseas call.''

The board members exchanged looks as Iris proceeded to circle the table, making sure that everything was in perfect order. Pens, notepads, a crystal ashtray, and chilled water carafe at each place. Then she was gone, leaving the members of the board to doodle on their pads, tug at their ties, and cast futile, exasperated glances at their watches.

Not a word was exchanged between them, although Max Drexel took the opportunity to light up one of the torpedo-shaped Havana cigars that had become his trademark, due at least in part to their highly offensive odor.

Drexel was glowering and perspiring, his considerable bulk only barely accommodated by the suede conference chair. He had just flown into New York that morning from Topeka, Kansas, after being on the road for almost a month attending various beautician conventions around the country.

Henri Dayne, who made his headquarters in London, had flown in the previous day on the Concorde. He looked pensive and preoccupied, while Theodore Baxley appeared tanned and fit after his recent return from a Palm Springs invitational golf tournament.

They didn't speak among themselves. They sat silently around the conference table, scribbling on their notepads and glancing repeatedly at their watches as the minutes slid slowly past.

Kate paced the executive suite, glancing nervously at the clock from time to time. Her expression was tautly drawn, and invariably her gaze kept returning to the large pastel Mondrian painting slashing and bisecting the panelled wall with powerful linear certainty. Somehow it always managed to reassure her in ways that were not easily discernible. Then finally she was interrupted by a soft, buzzing sound.

Lifting her eyes heavenward in prayerful response, Kate hurriedly crossed to her desk, swiftly stubbed out her cigarette, and stabbed at the glowing red button pulsing on the intercom. "Yes, Iris!" she said with an air of breathless expectancy. "Have you been able to reach him?"

"I was finally able to locate Mr. Osborn at Taormina,

Sicily,'' Iris' disembodied voice responded. "I have him for you now on the overseas line.''

Kate slowly sank into her desk chair and removed a single pearl earring before picking up the phone and holding it to her ear. "Hello, Paul,'' she voiced.

"This is quite a coincidence,'' Paul responded in a hearty, well-remembered voice. "I was just getting ready to put in a call to you in New York. I've had some ideas about how to promote the hypo-allergenic line. I was too close to it before, Katie. But now with some perspective I can see exactly how to handle the thing. Now first of all get hold of Scotty over in New Jersey and tell him I want—''

"Paul,'' Kate cut in abruptly, "I called to tell you that I've cancelled the entire hypo-allergenic project. It's dead. *Finis*. An idea so far past its prime that the only intelligent thing to do was to take our losses and bury it . . . for good.''

There was a moment of distilled silence that seemed to almost crackle across the long-distance wire. "Are you out of your mind!'' Paul's voice boomed back at her. "Jesus, Kate, I've already sunk millions . . . what the hell's going on back there?''

Kate took a deep breath, sat back in her desk chair, and crossed her legs with a whisper of silk "Paul, there's something I have to speak to you about that is extremely important to me. Does the name Doctor Andreas Jaccard mean anything to you?''

"Didn't he used to work with Meyerhof at his clinic in Switzerland? I think Cristina mentioned him to me. Something about his winning a Nobel Prize for some kind of experiment he did. Pretty important stuff as I recall. Something to do with that DNA business. I remember she wanted me to invest in a sanitarium this guy was going to open somewhere.''

"I recently underwent cell-rejuvenation therapy at Doctor

Jaccard's Coral Key Spa in the Caribbean,'' Kate informed him coolly. ''And I have become convinced that Andreas has developed something very close to a miracle youth drug through his latest research. Paul, I want to develop an entire line of skin-care products based on a cellular extract Jaccard's developed called Rejuvenal-12.''

A sudden jagged burst of static intersected their conversation at that point. Then Kate once again heard the same familiar con job, from four thousand miles away. ''Look, Katie . . .'' Paul's voice had dropped into a lower, more intimate pitch. ''I know you're under a lot of pressure over there, but I also know that you can handle it.

''You know how much I've always valued your judgment. But you're sitting in the hot seat now with a responsibility to the stockholders you just didn't have before. It's going to take some time before you get your sea legs on the job, and I've already come to realize that we've got to keep in much closer communication. Maybe I could even get the doctors to let me fly back there in three or four months so I can help you to get a bigger perspective. Now until then—''

''Paul,'' Kate interrupted, ''the last twelve months of your presidency at Caramour were *all* red ink. Of course you couldn't have known when you left how bad things truly were, because the figures simply weren't in yet. But now they are, and the situation is desperate. Desperate measures are definitely in order.''

Paul's voice broke in angrily. ''The market's just too goddamned shaky to even think about launching a tricky gamble like this. The board will never buy it in a million years, and you can take my word for that. This whole discussion is purely academic. If you walk in there with this mad scheme, those bastards are going to eat you alive. I'm giving you fair warning.''

When Kate finally responded, her voice was very even and

controlled. "For the past eighteen years I have never asked you for anything, Paul. My reasons for doing that are strictly my own affair, but the simple truth is that I never stopped giving and you never stopped taking.

"I never wanted or asked for this responsibility," Kate continued, "but you walked out without even bothering to consult me on how I felt, or what I really wanted to do with my life. And that, Paul, was because you never really cared about anyone but yourself."

The distance between them seemed to widen and deepen into a bottomless void. Then, from what seemed to be very far away, Paul began speaking once again in a flat, hard voice.

"I don't really understand why you insist on backing me into a corner like this, Katie. It's just not like you at all."

"I told you that this was important to me," she said, "but I guess you just weren't listening."

"Just what the hell is it you want from me?" Paul demanded in a short, savage thrust of words.

Her response was very simple and direct.

"I need your total and complete support, Paul. You always had mine, and I never let you down. I think it's only fair to tell you that this job doesn't own me anymore, Mr. Osborn. I'm willing to give it my best shot. But this time . . . I'm going all the way."

At precisely three twenty-three Kate made her entrance into the boardroom, accompanied by an electric current of expectation. Preceded by Iris Quaid, she made her way to the head of the conference table as the other board members swiveled sullenly around in their chairs, and rose grudgingly to greet her.

"Good afternoon, Katherine." Henri Dayne addressed her in that characteristically clipped Down-east voice of his. "I must say you're looking exceedingly well after your, shall we say, prolonged absence."

As usual, Ted Baxley quickly seconded the opinion. "Yes, indeed, Katherine. The Caribbean certainly appears to have done you a world of good. You're looking positively radiant."

Drexel, who knew only too well of her dislike, merely nodded. Kate could feel his slush-colored eyes licking over her as she took her place at the head of the table and motioned them all to be seated.

She had dressed carefully for the occasion in a bone-colored designer original that clung in all the right places, while somehow managing to be both very feminine and strictly business. "Thank you, gentlemen," Kate offered as she slipped on the large tortoise-rimmed glasses that instantly added a stylishly severe look to her appearance. "I must apologize for keeping you waiting. Mr. Osborn was calling from aboard the *Caramour II* to discuss a matter of the utmost importance."

Kate just tossed it out and let it hang there as Iris proceeded to read the minutes from the previous meeting.

On Kate's right Henri Dayne impatiently drummed his fingers on the table top throughout the recitation. Tall, white haired, and patrician of feature, Dayne was, as always, immaculately dressed. He wore a conservative double-breasted pinstripe, and his posture was erect and commanding.

The chair on the left had previously been Kate's own and was now vacant, but seated just beyond was Theodore Baxley—a thin, bespectacled man, whose tanned and genial features managed to convey at least a modicum of sympathetic awareness. In spite of his slavish loyalty to Henri Dayne, Kate had always found Ted Baxley to be a pleasantly innocuous sort.

Before joining Caramour a decade earlier at Henri Dayne's behest, Theodore Baxley had been a career diplomat serving in a series of undistinguished locations around the world. At some point, however, he had displayed the good sense to marry a slaughterhouse heiress by whom he fathered four decidedly unattractive daughters, each of whom had been endowed with a considerable block of Caramour stock, which was beyond question their most agreeable asset.

Seated directly across from Ted Baxley was Max Drexel. He was resplendent in an electric-green double-knit suit with a florid Countess Mara tie, and a reddish brown toupée was carefully sculpted to his bullet-shaped skull.

He had the mashed and battered face of an ex-pugilist. While both his personal history and family antecedents remained largely obscure, Drexel was clearly an American classic—a self-proclaimed cosmetic colossus of the sun-belt circuit, who had made and lost a fortune selling cheap cosmetic franchises throughout the South and Midwest.

Drexel was part carnival barker, flim-flam man, and snake oil salesman, imbued with all the raw sexual energy and highly aggressive charisma of a fundamentalist faith healer.

Kate had always thought of him as Paul's personal enforcer, a man full of dangerous paradoxes who simply oozed lethal enigmas. Max Drexel repelled her in ways she couldn't even fathom.

After Iris had finished reading the minutes of the last meeting, Kate decided it was time to take charge. "We're running late, and in order to save time, gentlemen, we will dispense with the usual formalities."

She turned to Henri Dayne. "Since Paul appointed you *acting president* during my absence, Henri, perhaps you'll bring us up to date."

Dayne responded with a courtly inclination of his leonine, white-maned head. "The most important matter requiring discussion is what I must term a crisis of confidence. Something has to be done immediately in order to inspire support from within the financial community. I don't mind telling you, Katherine, there's a great deal of speculation regarding your ability to perform effectively in a role requiring firm executive leadership.

"We are, of course, only too well aware of your outstanding contribution to Caramour's success. You've done an often brilliant and quite selfless job, no question about it. I know how dedicated you were to Paul . . . and to the company. But there's simply too much at stake for us to flounder under, shall we say, *inexpert* leadership?"

Henri spread his hands and smiled benignly. "I mean, how could you possibly hope to cope with the kind of problems that Caramour is currently faced with?"

As Dayne was speaking, Kate lifted her eyes to the Jonathan Cartwright portrait of Paul mounted at the far end of the conference room. It was the same portrait that had been used for a *Time* magazine cover several years previously. Kate had always felt that it captured perfectly Paul's dynamic magnetism and powerful personal appeal.

Now, however, Paul's likeness seemed to stare blankly back at her, as clinically depersonalized as a Dunn and Bradstreet rating. She was totally on her own, Kate realized.

Henri Dayne was obviously prepared to accept Kate's immediate resignation, and had even gone to the trouble of having such a document prepared. He became almost fatherly as he placed it before her, with assurances that they all realized she was willing to do "whatever was best for the company."

All the while Kate's features remained impassive, as she allowed him to make the pitch. Directly behind her, the wide expanse of floor-to-ceiling windows provided a magnificent panoramic view of Central Park and the midtown skyline. Thank God for Iris, Kate thought. At least she had some moral support.

Seated at a discreet distance from the conference table, the keys of her stenotype machine continued to clack softly away beneath Iris' practiced fingers. Just having her there gave Kate a certain sense of continuity she needed desperately at that particular moment.

When Henri Dayne finally finished speaking, Kate chose her words with care. "I assume, Henri, that you have some alternative suggestion, do you not?"

He was prepared to be magnanimous. "Now I wouldn't want you to take this matter personally, Katherine. But surely you realize that I have large family stock holdings to protect. I had no choice but to consider possible alternatives."

"Your concern appears to be largely selfish," Kate assured him smoothly. "What about all those thousands of smaller stockholders? Who's going to look after their interests?"

Dayne's look was one of mild exasperation, a wordless reprimand for putting him on the spot. "Of course we are all committed to serving the stockholders' interests, first and foremost. That should go without saying. And it is precisely for that reason that we have no choice but to consider alternate possibilities."

Kate removed her glasses to regard him squarely with a long, cool, appraising look. "From what I understand, Henri, you've been doing a good deal more than considering possibilities. According to an article that will be coming out in next week's *Cosmetology,* you and the boys at International Consortium Export have been thick as thieves of late. That, of course, is merely an expression, and is not to be taken personally."

Drexel gave a short bark of a laugh, while Dayne and Baxley exchanged startled glances.

"You have been away at a very critical time," Henri suggested finally. "And while I hate to bring this sort of thing up, Katherine, there was a good deal of talk about your having a complete nervous breakdown. Certainly I can't be faulted for trying to work out an arrangement equitable enough that Caramour simply couldn't afford to refuse.''

Indeed, there were few enough companies that had survived the invitation to merge with I.C.E. That vast superconglomerate, whose tentacles spread out in all directions around the globe, had all started with parking lots in New York City. But by now I.C.E.'s operations had expanded to include an oil refinery in Kuwait, a string of luxury hotels with casino gambling in the Bahamas, a fast-growing fast-food franchise, and a once prestigious publishing house that was currently making millions by churning out paperback best-sellers of the romantic hysterical genre.

In spite of its nonstop mania for acquisition and impressive financial holdings, there had always been whispers about I.C.E.

There were even those bold enough to suggest International Consortium was an extremely productive conduit for all that drug and prostitution money funneled into legitimate business by mafia overlords.

''Let's face the facts,'' Drexel growled, speaking for the first time. ''The way things stand now, we're up shit creek without a paddle. We're still at least a year away from production on the hypo-allergenic line, and everybody else has already come out with practically the same thing. Sales are way down, the market's soft, and we've already dropped into fourth place behind Revlon, Lauder, and Rubenstein. Something has to be done fast . . . the question is what?''

''Please . . . Katherine,'' Ted Baxley pleaded. ''We have to think of the good of the company. Surely you don't want to preside over a corporate disaster. We simply have no new products competing on the market this year, and the old ones are not even holding their own. I.C.E. is willing to offer us top dollar on Caramour stock. As I see it, we really have no choice but to accept their offer, before the roof caves in.''

"I assume that you gentlemen are aware that the most recent federally funded study of conglomerate takeovers in the cosmetic industry has proven them to be disastrous beyond any shadow of a doubt. They're simply looted of all assets and left to go into bankruptcy. Is that what you want?" she questioned sharply. "To just take the money and run, and the hell with everybody else?"

"You've obviously been listening to a lot of scare stories," Baxley informed her in a reasonable, almost plaintive voice. "Of course I.C.E. is very rich and powerful. But they are willing to take us on with very little change in the present management. If you like, you can even remain as acting president of the company while the day-to-day operations of Caramour will be carried out by a management committee, consisting of Henri and myself."

Kate knew he had made a serious mistake by the sudden glowering look on Drexel's features. Baxley's theoretical division of the corporate pie had quite obviously not included a big enough slice to accommodate his lusty appetites. Kate decided she would have to move quickly in order to divide and diffuse the forces so swiftly gathering against her.

"We have an empty seat on the board, gentlemen. Who do you think I.C.E. will put in to oversee laundering of the cash flow? I understand they're very big on clean money."

Henri Dayne leaned back in his chair to regard her with cold, impersonal consideration. "Come now, Katherine," he admonished. "Surely you don't believe all those tired old mafia money stories. I hope you're not all that naive?"

"Not nearly as naive as you might suppose, Henri. Just suspicious and extremely skeptical. I am also unequivocally against seeing this company swallowed up in some voracious conglomerate's profit and loss statement."

Kate could feel Dayne's anger and frustration bristling like barbed wire between them. She was obviously proving to be far more difficult than expected. Kate assumed he had been prepared to see her disintegrate quickly in the face of what they had all obviously seen as a simple matter of exercising the proper leverage.

Dayne's smile was forced and condescending, as if pondering the least disagreeable compromise he would have to make. "Perhaps," he began with more equanimity, "you'd be more kindly disposed toward the whole idea after meeting and talking with the top I.C.E. people. Let me set up something, so you can make yourself familiar with the larger perspective in this matter."

Kate responded sharply. "I can assure you that won't be necessary, Henri. You see, I already have the big picture, and I'm simply not buying. You may feel entirely free to convey that sentiment to your friends, the parking lot people. It's just no dice."

Dayne's piercing gray eyes had always been unsettling to Kate, and in that moment they appeared entirely capable of stripping away her poised façade if she let down her guard for even a moment. The look on Ted Baxley's face was one of startled surprise mixed with aggrievement. Without looking at Drexel directly, Kate could feel his gaze lashing over her, as if he were searching for some soft and vulnerable spot.

Yet in spite of Dayne's bullying manner, and the obvious signs that a cabal had been set against her, there could have been no one present at the meeting who was not by now aware that some definitive change had come over "good old dependable Katie." She had never been known for making waves, only suggestions that could be easily brushed aside.

There was clearly more to her transformation than the extremely flattering new hair style, or the expensive designer dress she wore as casually as something she'd picked off the rack. Rather it was something in the eyes, and in the way she carried herself. A certain directness. A sense of cool calculation.

Sitting in Osborn's chair, with the panoramic skyline forming a dramatic scrim behind her, Kate appeared to embody an almost serenely confident sense of herself. It was something that had not really been there before, at least not readily discernible behind the competent reserve, and the total dedication she had always previously displayed.

Folding his neatly manicured hands before him like a judge preparing to deliver a stiff sentence, Dayne carefully examined his clear-lacquered nails. Then he looked up abruptly, piercing her with a look as cold as glacial ice. "I had hoped you could be reasonable about this matter, Katherine. But since you choose to remain obtuse, I might as well inform you that you're holding a losing hand. I.C.E. wants Caramour badly enough to have already accumulated a considerable amount of corporate stock. You can delay the inevitable if you like. But it's really only a question of time."

Kate graced him with a frosty smile. "In that regard, Henri, it may be a question of a great deal of time. In case you aren't already aware, I control a voting stock majority that amounts to roughly sixty-three percent. The scheme you are proposing would require not only a clear majority of fifty-one percent, but a quorum vote by the board to bring the merger up before the next general stockholders' meeting. I may as well add that while Mr. Osborn is no longer head of the company, he still retains his seat on the board.

"I spoke with Paul just before coming to this meeting, and he has fully empowered me to use his vote as I see fit. I can assure you, gentlemen, that he is completely opposed to any kind of conglomerate takeover."

Kate folded her hands and poised them beneath her chin. "Unless I'm mistaken, that makes the vote two against two. I suggest we consult Mr. Drexel, since I suspect his opinion on the subject might come as something of a surprise."

Drexel gave her a look of surprise. Then he reached up to

deliberately remove the half-smoked stub of his cigar from between his teeth. His hand was huge, with corpulent fingers and a glittering diamond pinky ring.

"Well, Drexel," Dayne demanded. "What's she talking about? You gave me to believe that you were willing to go along with us on this thing."

". . . if certain conditions could be met," Drexel finished for him. "I'm afraid that we live in fast-changing times, gentlemen. It looks to me like the entire I.C.E. business needs a lot more looking into. For now, I propose we table the offer and take up more pressing matters. Like for instance what the goddamn hell am I supposed to be selling instead of perfume—cow piss?

"I guess the word must have gotten around to you guys by now that our classy new lady president has canceled production of Lady Cristina perfume."

Drexel's hard-eyed gaze was fixed intently upon her, but Kate knew he was only raising a smoke screen, stalling for time and leverage. He had always been in pay to the highest bidder, and that was precisely what Kate had been counting on.

Their eyes locked and dueled. Drexel was wondering what kind of stakes she was willing to play for, Kate realized. And the answer to that was something she didn't even know herself.

Drexel spread his hands upon the table with his sausagelike fingers splayed wide. "I've decided to go along with the status quo for now," he pronounced. "It's my opinion that our Miss Katherine the Great deserves at least the chance to show what she can do."

"You're both making a big mistake," Henri Dayne cut in. He leaned slightly forward to return the sheaf of papers to his attaché case. "Without any major new products scheduled to go on the market within the next six months, there's bound to be a multimillion-dollar loss in the fourth quarter. And for that, Katherine, you are going to have to take full responsibility.''

Kate's smile was guileless. ''I'd be glad to, Henri. You see, we are going to have a new product line on the market by Christmas. I think it's safe to predict that by the end of the fourth quarter, Caramour stock will have gone up by at least five points. I'm willing to stake my job on it.''

Dayne and Baxley exchanged incredulous looks, while even Drexel's eyes widened in disbelief. He sat there staring hard at her, while a cloud of cigar smoke surrounded his head like a malign nimbus. ''Do you have any idea what it is you're saying?'' Drexel demanded. ''Sales would have to be up at least twenty-five percent during Christmas for that to happen.''

''It would take a miracle to drive the stock up even two points,'' Dayne charged. ''Just what the hell are you talking about, Katherine?''

''I'm talking about a miracle called Rejuvenal-12,'' she responded, drawing the leather-bound prospectus from her slim Gucci portfolio. Kate nodded for Iris to distribute copies to the others present. Then she pressed a button to alert the control booth that she was ready to proceed.

Within a matter of seconds heavy draperies moved across the expanse of windows on electronically operated tracks, while at the far end of the room Paul Osborn's portrait slid soundlessly from view to display a movie screen. The illuminated wall sconces began to dim, and a small portal opened in the wall to expose the lens of a movie projector.

In cutting and splicing the hundreds of feet of film that Kate shot on her visit to Jamaica with slides, stills, and various documentary footage, Wes had proven himself to be a master cinematographer.

The film opened with the camera panning in on Kate seated at her desk in the executive suite. She rose as if to meet it, then slowly circled the desk holding up a glass test tube containing a crystalline-pink emulsion.

As they all sat watching in the dimness, Kate's voice began to spool out of the hidden quadrophonic speakers to narrate the film.

"Throughout history, man has sought to discover the secret of extending life through various potions, miracle cures, and occult spells. Medieval alchemists prescribed gold and mercury in hopes of turning mortals to immortals. But only within the present century has medical science finally discovered a safe and viable method of prolonging and enriching the span of human life."

Following a slow dissolve, they were treated to the ravishing technicolor spectacle of luminous snow-capped peaks bathed in transparent silver light. Glaciers loomed and vanished as the airborne camera zeroed in to reveal the magnificent snow cone of the Swiss Matterhorn glistening in the distance like the cathedral spire of a higher kingdom.

"Live cell therapy," the narration continued, "is the process of injecting various organic cells of disease-resistant animals into humans for the purpose of transmitting their health and rejuvenating properties to the corresponding organs of the human body."

By now the aerial camera had panned down through alpine meadows to focus on an old Chalet-type edifice surrounded by gardens, and a cluster of small cottages secluded by mountain fir trees.

"One of the foremost pioneers of this revolutionary therapy was Doctor Anton Meyerhof of the famous Meyerhof Rejuvenation Clinic near Geneva, Switzerland. For over three decades, many of the world's most powerful and prominent personages have traveled to the Meyerhof Clinic to undergo this remarkable process, which may ultimately prove to be the key to human health and longevity. Among them have been a pope and at least a half-dozen heads of state as well as a galaxy of movie stars and internationally known celebrities.''

The Meyerhof Clinic was set amidst a pastoral scene of woods and alpine meadows, with a flock of woolly black sheep grazing in the background. ''Doctor Meyerhof has been acclaimed throughout the world for his work in cell rejuvenation therapy,'' Kate's narration continued. ''But it remained for his brilliant young heir apparent, Doctor Andreas Jaccard, to develop this remarkable youth therapy even further, through his own extensive research.''

Suddenly the snowy mountain ramparts dissolved into the emergence of a lush green tropical island materializing from an azure sea. Kate had taken the filmed footage upon the day of her arrival on Coral Key. It looked for all the world like a tropical Eden, basking beneath a blue and cloudless sky.

''Doctor Jaccard is presently operating Coral Key Spa on a small island off the coast of Jamaica. And it is in this setting that the full benefits of his research have finally culminated in the development of Rejuvenal-12. The drug is given through a series of injections, along with a rigorous exercise regimen, special diet, and various other therapies. The entire procedure is costly, time consuming, and available at present to only a small handful of wealthy people with both the time and money to make the pilgrimage to Coral Key.''

The scene had by now switched to Doctor Jaccard at work in his laboratory. A tall, commanding figure who looked the very epitome of the brilliant researcher and charismatic guru of the international youth and beauty cult.

''Since the full benefits of live cell rejuvenation therapy can only be fully realized through injections of one hundred percent potent, living cells, the procedure has not yet been recognized by the American medical establishment. Consequently, Doctor Jaccard has gone ahead to make the medical research breakthrough that will disseminate the benefits of live cell therapy in a topical form that can be easily absorbed directly into the skin.

"Radiant good health at any age is of course based upon proper diet and exercise. Yet with continued usage, Rejuvenal-12 opens up exciting possibilities for preserving the skin against the ravages of pollution, stress, and the inexorable effects of the aging process itself.

"For the discerning woman of any age who demands the very latest and the very finest in total skin care, the answer is Caramour's new Rejuvenal product line."

The promo film ended with the camera panning in for a closeup of Solange Wilkerson—a hauntingly beautiful face out of black Africa, whose perfectly sculpted features had somehow miraculously impacted upon the Indo-Aryan bone structure of the Asiatic steppes.

Solange stood in statuesque profile against a glorious Caribbean sunset. She wore a flame-colored gown with a bright red hibiscus in her long, straight black hair. Simply and unequivocally she looked gorgeous, yet with a certain futuristic quality that held the eye visually enraptured, spell-bound with her tawny, golden beauty.

In that moment Kate realized that all of them sitting there in that room might very well be looking into the face of the future.

Chapter Fourteen

Scotty McPherson was waiting for Kate at a secluded banquette in the grill room of the Algonquin Hotel. They exchanged fond greetings. But as always, Scotty Mac, as Kate had always called him, was a bit gruff and slightly awkward when she kissed him on the cheek.

How very like her father he was, Kate thought to herself. And how very much older he looked than Kate remembered. It had been over a year, and the realization gave her a momentary twinge of guilt. Scotty's strong Anglo-Saxon features were craggier now, and his bushy hair and ginger mustache were both amply frosted with white. McPherson had always taken his role as Kate's godfather extremely seriously. Tall and spare, thin to the point of gauntness, Scotty had always seemed middleaged. But now, suddenly, the physical changes and obvious signs of aging came as a shock.

Like her father, Scotty had been born in Glasgow, where the two of them had been raised together. Both had studied at Edinburgh University and emigrated to the United States immediately following the Second World War.

"How have you been, Scotty?" Kate asked with genuine warmth and affection in her voice. "It's been a long time, much too long, as far as I'm concerned. I've missed you."

Scotty leaned back and took a long drink of his bourbon, regarding her carefully with that pale, penetrating gaze she knew so very well. "Aye, Katherine, my girl. And I don't mind tellin' you that some of the stories drifting across the river from the headquarters office to the New Jersey plant have kept me wondering. Someone, and I think it was Mr. Henri Dayne, was even trying to convince me that our new lady president had cracked up somewhere along the way."

Scotty winked broadly. "But you know me, Katherine. I don't believe half of what I see, and almost nothin' of what I hear. Anyway, this new job of yours appears to agree with you. You're lookin' very good, Katherine."

"Well . . ." Kate smiled. "At least part of that glow you see is because of your report on Rejuvenal-12. I have great hopes for this project, Scotty, and I think it's important to do it. For the first time women are being offered an alternative to expensive cosmetic surgery and quack rejuvenation techniques."

Scotty took another long drink of his bourbon, then removed his familiar briar pipe from the pocket of his coat and began methodically tamping the scorched bowl full of Wings pipe tobacco. "I must agree that I think you're on to something here, Katherine, but it's never easy to break new ground. It's going to take at least another couple of months to run through all the necessary testing procedures before we know anything like the whole story."

Kate waited until her vodka martini had been placed before

her and the hovering waiter had departed, after having been informed that they would order luncheon later.

"Scotty . . . Rejuvenal works. I myself am a walking testament to that. One of the reasons I asked you to meet with me today was to tell you that we don't *have* the four to six months you want to complete the tests. I know you've seen the latest profit and loss figures. Sales way down . . . costs skyrocketing . . . and an extremely soft market. Unless I can get RJ-12 on the market by Christmas," Kate warned, "Caramour, Inc., is going to be in very serious trouble."

"At this point," Scotty advised her, "we only have Jaccard's own scientific documentation to work with, while the long-term effects are completely unknown. Sure it's possible to cut some corners, but you know as well as I do that the FDA gets delerium tremens over anything remotely connected to the whole cellular extract business. It's total anathema to the AMA."

"The man is a nobel scientist," Kate patiently recited. "And I'm convinced that cell rejuvenation is the wave of the future. But you know Washington. Nothing is going to change until someone has the courage to educate the public by demonstrating that cell rejuvenation actually works."

Scotty raised one bushy brow to give her a long, coolly appraising look as he lit his pipe, then exhaled a cloud of aromatic blue smoke. "And just what does Paul Osborn think about all this?"

"Paul has agreed to give me carte blanche. And speaking of cutting corners, just how many do you think he cut when he was trying to get on the market with something new and totally innovative?"

"Well," Scotty observed with a shrug, "you may have gotten Paul to go along with this whole scheme. But I think that your father would have approached the matter with a great deal of caution. You know what a stickler he was for testing.''

Something came over Kate's face, a fleeting expression of pain. Her gaze, however, remained direct and unflinching. ''There's something I have to ask you, Scotty. Something that I guess I have always suspected, but just never wanted to know for sure.''

''The past is best left to itself,'' Scotty warned. ''The truth is not always an easy thing to live with.''

''Did my father deliberately set me up with Paul Osborn before he died?''

Before answering, Scotty puffed thoughtfully on his pipe. ''Your father always did have a lot of respect for Paul Osborn, Katherine. Paul had ambition and your dad liked that. He always knew that Paul was going to amount to something in this business.''

''That isn't what I asked you,'' Kate stubbornly insisted.

''I don't think there was ever any question but that Colin Leslie always kind of hoped that you and Paul would tie the knot, Katherine. You know, sort of keep the business in the family sort of thing. I guess he figured that nature would just take its course if you were working together.''

''Well he figured wrong,'' Kate announced bluntly. ''The truth is that Paul never even took me to bed, Scotty. In fact, he never even bothered to try. I was merely a corporate asset who got stuck holding the bag in the final analysis. I guess the time has come when I *have* to know the truth, all of it. Did my father sell out Leslie Chemical on the cheap because he had some kind of deal with Paul where I was concerned?''

Scotty shrugged and his weathered features colored slightly. ''I guess you might put it that way,'' he finally answered. ''I mean, there was never anything in writing between them. But Paul did agree to put you to work once your father passed away. You know how he was. Colin just wasn't the kind of man to go off and die, leaving a lot of loose ends behind him. He was a very methodical and practical man, as you well know.''

Kate blinked rapidly against the sudden, unexpected burn of tears, and quickly brushed at her eyelids with a lightly perfumed handkerchief.

''Sorry, Scotty. I didn't mean to put you in the hot seat. It was just something I had to know.''

''Your father only did what he thought was best for you, Katherine. You do know that, don't you?''

Kate reached out to clasp the big, rough, rawboned hand resting upon the white linen cloth, and squeezed it affectionately. ''Yes, of course I know that, Scotty Mac. It's all in the past anyway, no one's fault. But now it's my turn to make the decisions. And I desperately need you on my side, Scotty, if I'm to have any chance of succeeding.''

Scotty's craggy, saturnine features softened into a reassuring smile that seemed to melt the years between them in a single instant. ''You know I've always had a soft spot in this cast-iron heart of mine where you're concerned, Miss Katherine Leslie. And besides that, I think it's time for you to show what you can do. I think they ought to see exactly what it is you're made of . . . and where you came from.''

''I want all the essential testing completed within three weeks,'' Kate informed him anxiously. ''Can you make it by putting your best people on the project, right around the clock?''

Scotty nodded and finished his drink in a single short draught. Then he bent confidentially closer, leaning his elbows on the table and folding his arms like a judge. ''You know you better be right about this one, Katie my girl. Because if you're not, you're going to be taking a lot of people over the cliff with you.''

''I know what I'm doing,'' Kate assured him. ''And I also

realize that this isn't going to be easy. All I'm asking is the chance to prove that I am right about Rejuvenal-12."

It was six o'clock in the evening, and for a long time Kate had been standing in the rushing hot shower with the steam clouding up around her. Slowly and sensuously she had been running a big soapy sponge over her entire body, allowing the muscles to relax, and the day's tensions to evaporate beneath the tingling spray.

Her meeting that afternoon with Scotty McPherson had been extremely gratifying in terms of his promised support. Come to think of it, Kate realized, the intervening weeks since her return from Coral Key had turned out to be an increasingly heady experience in the exercise of power.

Following her bravura performance before the assembled members of the Caramour board of directors, and due largely to the stunning impact of Kate's promotional film, her colleagues had ultimately voted the largest budget in Caramour's history in order to bring the new RJ-12 skin-care line onto the market by Christmas.

Before the close of the meeting and quite deliberately while things were still going her way, Kate proposed that Celia Randolph be named to the Caramour board. Her name had been seconded by Max Drexel, and ultimately the motion was passed.

That was precisely why she needed Max, Kate realized. His support was essential if she were to restructure the company according to her own design. Kate had always felt that the cosmetic industry was essentially a woman's business, and was now determined to bring a cadre of competent executive women into all levels of the Caramour corporate structure.

With her large stock holdings and impressive connections, Celia would be sure to prove an important ally during the difficult months to come. Following the initial skirmish with Henri Dayne, Kate realized only too well that she was going to need all the fire power she could get if she were to emerge victorious from the eventual bloody battles of the boardroom.

Max Drexel had proven himself indispensable to her plans, even while she loathed the man. But Paul had always liked hustlers, and with his hand-tailored Hong Kong suits, Havana cigars, and bright yellow Cadillac pimpmobile, Drexel was the very epitome of the street-tough corporate muscleman on the make.

Paul had even gone so far as to set Drexel up with a special Caramour bank account that no company controller had ever been permitted to question, no matter how outrageously exorbitant his expense vouchers might be. Drexel got things done, and no one in the company was eager to know too much about how he did it.

For Max Drexel not only had a reputation as a notorious con man who very probably had underworld connections, he was also considered by many in the business to be a virtual pariah. When it came to eliminating the competition and enforcing sales quotas, Paul had always found Drexel to be a very handy man to have around.

He was, however, everything that Kate detested, physically repulsive, ill mannered, and blatantly ostentatious.

Even so, Max Drexel was a very valuable ally to have on her team. It was precisely the talents that he possessed in such large measure that had convinced Kate to make him her second in command on the RF-12 project. Far better that Drexel was working with her rather than against her. At least that way, she reasoned, he'd be easier to watch.

After drying herself vigorously all over, Kate moved into the adjacent dressing room and turned slowly before the full-length mirror. ''Simply amazing,'' she breathed.

It was truly remarkable. Before her visit to Coral Key all

the signs of aging and decay were there, even though most were so slight as to be scarcely noticeable. Now, however, her breasts were fuller and more buoyant, while the long, smooth line of the leg seemed to start at the hip and run all the way to the floor.

Kate was in an expansive and expectant mood. She had never looked or felt better, and her mind was filled with creative ideas, a luminous sweep of lucidity that imbued even the most mundane details with fortuitous signs and portents for the success of the new line.

Tying the sash of a silk dressing gown about her waist, she moved into her bedroom and seated herself at the alcove dressing table where she kept a complete selection of Caramour cosmetic products. Then she switched on the merciless studio lights encircling the magnified mirror and began to meticulously apply her makeup.

Kate felt renewed and revitalized. It was as if her entire past life had been peeled away like a layer of exhausted skin. Her face in reflection, even though highly magnified, looked smooth and lustrous, almost luminous. She felt highly charged, while her body and limbs seemed strong and supple as never before.

Kate's face had always been unusual. But now the wide mouth and large gray-violet eyes combined to dramatize her features in an entirely new way. For the first time in her life she both felt and looked glamorous.

With her makeup complete, Kate undid the towel wrapped turban-style about her hair and quickly brushed it into a stylishly loose frame feathered about her face and glinting with reddish golden highlights. Then she rose and went to the closet to pull out the Jon-Claude Fabiani original she had purchased especially for Adrianna's début at Lincoln Center.

It was a filmy blue chiffon with sheer billowing sleeves and handkerchief hem that seemed to drift and flow about her slender figure. It was youthful, very feminine, and extremely flattering, exactly the dress and the look to suit her mood.

Since the weather was exceptionally cool on that particular evening, a reunion of the Newborns was exactly the right occasion, Kate decided, to wear her new sable coat for the first time.

Celia had taken a box for the Celebrity Gala at Lincoln Center, and after her performance in the premiere showing of *Les Emerauds de la Reine,* Adrianna had promised to join them for dinner at Tavern on the Green.

Kate had spoken briefly with Adrianna only that afternoon, and she could tell by her voice that all systems were go for that evening's performance. "I've got someone I want you to meet." Adrianna sounded breathless, excited. "Oh Kate, I was going to wait until tonight after the performance to tell you, but I just can't keep it to myself any longer. I'm in love with Sacha Dimitri and he's in love with me. Tonight we dance together for the first time in public. I'm so terribly glad that you're going to be there. I've never been so nervous in my life."

The news had come like a lightning bolt out of the blue. Then, just as Kate was gathering her things and getting ready to leave the apartment, the pink Princess phone rang on the table beside the bed.

"Hello," Kate answered in her uniquely smoky and slightly husky voice. "Yes, operator. This is Miss Leslie. Yes, of course I'll accept the call. Please put him on."

"Hello, Andreas!" Kate exclaimed. "Yes . . . yes, I feel perfectly fabulous. I've never felt better, and I have wonderful news. The board has given me virtual carte blanche on Rejuvenal. I'll be sending our lawyers down to handle the legal part of it next week. Isn't it marvelous, Andreas? They've approved everything."

Kate stood listening to Andreas' deep familiar voice. He

sounded distant, so far away, and yet so vibrantly compelling that she could picture him perfectly. His eyes, his slow, ironic smile. His hands, so strong and creative and capable.

"I have something else to tell you that I know you're going to be pleased about," Kate announced. "It's Solange. Everyone's so thrilled about the photographs I took of her that we've decided to have her launch the new line. Solange is going to be the new Caramour Girl. She's absolutely perfect. I can't wait for you to give her the good news."

As the silence on the line lengthened, Kate began to think that perhaps the connection had been broken. Then Andreas began to speak, and her smile flickered and died like a candle going out. Kate twisted the phone cord with her brightly lacquered nails.

"Yes, Andreas. Of course . . . I understand. But it's just so difficult to believe. This would have been the chance of a lifetime for Solange. I'm just very disappointed."

Kate suddenly remembered the time. She glanced quickly at her watch, and realized she was going to be late. "Yes, yes, Andreas. Of course. I realize you're doing everything possible to find her. But please call me as soon as you hear anything. Solange Wilkerson simply cannot have vanished off the face of the earth without leaving a trace."

Winstin Thornton was restlessly pacing the corridor and chain-smoking cigarettes as Kate was shown to Celia's box at Lincoln Center. Even as they exchanged greetings, she knew what was coming.

In his well-cut formal attire, Winstin's blandly attractive features were deeply etched with concern. "I have to talk to you," he announced, taking Kate's arm and leading her off to one side of the corridor. It was almost empty, and the curtain was due to go up at any moment.

"There isn't much time," Kate insisted. "I don't want to miss the beginning of Adrianna's performance."

"Kate, please," he begged. "What the hell happened down there on Coral Key? Celia's been treating me like junk mail ever since she got back."

"Why nothing happened," Kate lied. "I don't really know what you're talking about."

Angrily Winstin stubbed out his cigarette in a sand-filled urn and beseeched her with his eyes. A balding, middle-aged man with a paunch and soft white hands. "It's Jaccard, isn't it? Celia's fallen in love with him."

"That's utterly absurd," Kate insisted. "You're imagining things, Winstin. Andreas Jaccard is very much married."

"Am I imagining things?" he demanded. "Can you really look me in the eye and swear that you believe nothing has changed between Celia and me?"

Kate was saved from she didn't know what kind of dreadful scene by a series of soft chiming notes followed by the lights dimming. She quite deliberately drew her arm from his grip. "We have to go inside now," she said. "Celia will be wondering what's become of both of us, and the performance is about to start."

Reluctantly he opened the door, and Kate quickly stepped into the darkened box directly above the stage. She was furious at Celia for having involved her. But she also felt sorry for poor pathetic Winstin.

No question about it, Kate thought. Benny Valdez was definitely a tough act to follow, in Celia's present state of mind.

Lincoln Center had been sold out for weeks, and the press had been labeling Adrianna's comeback as the society gala of the summer season. Kate couldn't remember just which charity it was supposed to benefit. As she took her seat next to Celia at the front of the box there was a flurry of introductions, the rustle of programs, and the excited undercurrent of whispers ebbing and flowing throughout the audience.

In spite of the dimness and the brevity of briefly whispered introductions, Kate quickly realized that Celia was traveling with a much faster crowd since her return from Coral Key. Her guests that evening were immediately recognizable.

A flurry of celebrated names and vaguely familiar faces that were constantly flitting in and out of the gossip columns: a notorious Principesa, the discarded wife of a Greek shipping magnate, a best-selling author who wrote the most outrageous things about his jet-set intimates, a fading Broadway star exhibiting her latest face lift, and an extremely handsome young man whom Kate immediately recognized, since she was wearing one of his creations. It was the former Morris Lipschitz from Mosholu Parkway in the Bronx, who had taken to calling himself Fabiani while creating his highly stylized masterpieces for some of the richest and most famous women in the world.

It was instantly apparent to Kate that Celia's new crowd were all members in good standing of New York's hedonistic glitterati, those shimmering night birds who discoed the early morning hours away at Regine's or Studio 54 and dined with privileged ease at Elaine's or Pearl's, or the Russian Tea Room.

For them it was always La Dolce Vita American-style, and the name of the game was reportedly the continual pursuit of instant gratification. There could never be a moment of dead air. No space in their lives that wasn't filled with bright, clever, amusing, and highly decorative people, all in frantic search of the ultimate extended high—the drugs, the booze, and the sex that made everything appear to be a lot more fun than it really was.

Everything else was forgotten, however, when the curtain

finally lifted to expose an enormous empty stage. The on-stage backdrop was composed of flowing diaphanous draperies that seemed to be gently wafting in the breeze somewhere between sea and sky.

From the orchestra pit, the string section was lightly fingering the delicately unobtrusive theme of *Les Emerauds de la Reine*. Next came the woodwind section, and finally the entire orchestra, building slowly toward the cymbal-crashing climax that brought Adrianna soaring onto the stage.

From that moment on, Kate sat totally entranced.

Adrianna del Bario looked exactly like the prima ballerina she was. Yet her impact went far beyond the presence and grace with which she invested the slightest movement. Adrianna possessed that indefinable quality called magic. Everyone in the audience was aware of it from the moment she first appeared on stage.

After making a dramatic entrance, she appeared to be alone in some surrealistic landscape. Hesitantly, at first, she sketched a few dance steps, and then allowed her supple, lithe body to drift easily into the music, as if she was being carried away by the wind rippling the hanging draperies.

Moments later, Adrianna was whirling and spinning upon the stage as the wind quickened. No longer was she simply a flesh and blood woman, but rather an ethereal, other-worldly creature, with flaming tresses, pale porcelain skin, and the look of a startled fawn upon her expressive features.

Her dancing was a lovely seamless flow, effortless and abandoned, at once impetuous and yet serene. She continued to hold the audience spellbound, with heart-stopping off-center balances and dizzying spins that managed to convey the impression that she was whirling on the edge of some sheer abyss.

The opening sequence of *Les Emerauds* was a perfect showcase for Adrianna's talents as a superb sculptural dancer, capable of combining a haunting romanticism with exquisite grace and perfect muscular memory. Then she was joined on stage by Sacha Dimitri, and Kate immediately became aware of the intense physical chemistry existing between them.

Dimitri was justly celebrated as one of the truly select male ballet stars in the world, who perfectly fit the mold of the traditional *danseur noble*. He was tall and handsome as a young god, with a mane of golden hair and magnificently proportioned body. Elegance and virility were his trademarks, combined with an amazing verve and stunning versatility that carried every movement to perfect effect.

Like the unerring master he was, José del Bario had created a work of undisputed genius in which to pair his two most highly acclaimed protegés. It was a brilliant and highly spirited match, with very little to distract in the way of a story line. The presentation was a free-form progression from simplicity to sumptuousness; from youth to maturity and from illusion to the purest fantasy.

The second act portrayed the evolution of a great, although ultimately tragic, love story. While the third act was so richly permeated with the dancers' romantic feelings for one another, that when Dimitri strung the magical emerald necklace around Adrianna's long white stalk of a neck, the act became the perfect poignant symbol of matchless lost love.

Les Emerauds ran unbroken for ninety minutes, and was one of the longest nonstory ballets ever produced. It was in essence a showcase, displaying the mastery and excellence of its two dancers. In one unforgettable visual impression after another Adrianna and Sacha presented patterns and movements that seemed never to have been danced before.

Ultimately it was a journey of the spirit that carried the audience along through an entire cycle of life and love.

Then, all too suddenly it seemed, the dancers were back once again on that enormous empty stage. Shadows upon the landscape. Ghostly lovers dancing in perfect physical and spiritual union, as if for them, at least, the world beyond the blinding bright incandescence of the footlights had ceased to exist.

The performance ended with a rousing standing ovation. There were cheers, bravos, thundering applause, and long-stemmed red roses raining down upon the stage. Hand in hand, the two dancers stepped forward to take their bows, and the applause ignited into one wildly frenzied ovation after another.

The curtain was rung down at least a dozen times, only to have the radiantly smiling lovers recalled again and again to the footlights. Kate's eyes were brimming with tears, and her hands had begun to smart from clapping as she stood pressed against the railing of Celia's grande tier box.

Swathed in red chiffon and spirals of matching ostrich feathers that accentuated the powdered whiteness of her skin, Adrianna was now alone upon the stage. Kate was seated close enough to be able to see the exhaustion etched beneath the heavily rouged stage makeup, and the slight trembling of the hands clutching two dozen long-stemmed red roses.

Then quite suddenly Adrianna's widely smiling countenance seemed to dissolve before her eyes into a tortured mask of pain. It was like watching a mirror shattering; like looking into the eyes of someone whose inner darkness had suddenly been pierced by the light of a thousand suns.

Chapter Fifteen

With her sable collar turned up against the early morning chill, and her hands plunged deep into her coat pockets, Kate moved like a somnambulist.

It was almost dawn, and she felt dazed, emotionally drained. How could it have happened, she wondered dully. Why did it have to happen?

Kate threw back her head as she restlessly prowled the long avenue of trees leading south from the Bethesda Fountain. The buildings surrounding the park were illuminated like firebirds against the paling dawn sky. They looked like towers of molten light.

The morning stillness was broken by a vagrant gust of wind. It passed like a sigh through the leafy green branches overhead and scattered leaves before her feet along the path. There was still fresh dew on the summer grass, and the reflecting pool, where children came to sail their boats on summer afternoons, shimmered smooth and unruffled through the trees. It was almost six A.M. and the sky above was streaked with clouds of bright salmon pink. Already Kate could sense the heartbeat of the city quickening just beyond the leafy perimeter that circumscribed the park. Somewhere in the distance she heard the wail of a police siren.

By the time that Kate reached the Zoo near the Sixty-Fourth Street entrance, the seals were still drowsing on a rock above the pool. She heard the mournful calling of the big cats, and her steps were drawn past the wrought-iron avaries filled with brightly plumed tropical birds to where a solitary leopard paced relentlessly back and forth in his cage.

For an instant the animal paused behind the bars that stood between them, and Kate felt herself being drawn into that mystical, golden gaze. She felt dazed and benumbed by grief, exhausted and scarcely able to stay on her feet.

A peacock screamed, welcoming the dawn, and once again the leopard resumed his endless, restless pacing. With a shuddery sigh, Kate sank down on a stone bench across the way, and, dropping her face into her hands, she silently wept. Allowing her tears and her grief to flow outward in hopes of exorcising the fractured images that continued to flash through her consciousness like an endlessly running slide projector.

Even the sounds were part of the stillness that pervaded the ninth floor of New York Hospital like a numbing chill; the soft whisper of rubber-soled shoes on the vinyl floor and the rustle of starched uniforms as nurses passed along the dimly lit corridor. From the duty station at the far end of the hall came the steam wheeze of a sterilizing machine. High on the wall just outside the Intensive Care Unit, the sweeping red hand of a large circular clock counted off the passing seconds in short, pulsing spasms. It reminded Kate of a heart reluctant to beat.

"I'm afraid I can't offer you much besides hope," the doctor informed José del Bario. "That embolism exploded in your wife's brain like a grenade going off. We have no possible way of knowing just how much damage it may have done before we were able to arrest the intracranial bleeding."

"How is she now?" del Bario asked in his softly accented voice. The doctor shook his head. "I'm sorry to have to report that Mrs. del Bario is still in deep coma. At this point we still can't predict when, or even *if,* she will ever recover consciousness."

Kate remained standing a short distance away as the two men continued speaking in hushed tones. She had already heard enough, and, turning slowly, she stared in through the thick glass wall of the Intensive Care Unit where Adrianna lay immobilized upon a white-sheeted bed.

Her face had a waxen pallor, with great bruised shadows beneath the eyes and a turban of coiled bandages completely swathing her head. Adrianna's wrists had been bound to the bed with strips of white sheeting. Vaguely Kate supposed it had been done in order to prevent the displacement of various tubes and needles monitoring her vital signs and supplying her body with a necessary life support system.

According to Doctor Charboneau, Adrianna's heart had stopped beating twice while she was undergoing emergency brain surgery, but miraculously they had been able to resuscitate her by employing massive electrocardial shocks.

"For the moment we have done everything we possibly can," Charboneau advised in a colorless voice heavily freighted with his own fatigue. "It could be days, weeks, or even months before your wife regains the use of her faculties."

"If in fact she ever does recover," del Bario intoned bleakly. "Isn't that what you're telling me, Doctor?"

Charboneau nodded, removing the scorched briar pipe from between his lips. "We have absolutely no way of knowing whether or not she would survive the removal of her life support system. But for the moment we're not taking any chances. Later perhaps. It's a decision you yourself are going to have to make."

José del Bario, the great ballet director, looked like a man condemned to live an endlessly recurring nightmare. He was still wearing the tuxedo in which he had appeared for the performance of *Les Emerauds* earlier that evening at Lincoln Center. He was a short, wiry, intense man with mournful dark eyes and blade-thin Andalusian features.

Throughout the long hours during which Adrianna was undergoing surgery, he had paced continually and chain-smoked.

Sacha Dimitri was there as well, although he had been heavily sedated, and now sat huddled in a corner with his shaggy blond head buried in his hands, and a trench coat thrown about his shoulders.

All was bedlam following Adrianna's collapse on stage. Kate had tried to reach her in the ensuing chaos, but all to no avail. It had all happened so fast. Yet no more than fifteen minutes after Adrianna had been stricken at Lincoln Center, Kate had arrived by cab at New York Hospital to find a clutch of reporters clustered outside the emergency entrance, with powerful television arc lights bathing the scene in their lurid glare.

Screaming with a banshee wail, the ambulance had arrived only a matter of seconds later. It stopped short, and then backed up to the heavy glass doors of the hospital's emergency entrance.

Kate pushed forward through the surging crush as the doors of the ambulance were swung open by white-coated interns. Then, as Adrianna was lifted out on a rolling stretcher, a sizzling, crackling streak of lightning tore open the summer sky, and the pushing, jostling throng of reporters was suddenly inundated by a torrential downpour.

Somehow Kate found herself clinging to Adrianna's motionless white-sheeted form as the gurney upon which she lay was wheeled through the glass doors of the hospital's emergency entrance and into a waiting elevator.

"There's absolutely nothing that any of you can do by waiting here any longer," Charboneau said. "The hospital will advise you immediately if there is any change in your wife's condition. But for now, I suggest that you all go home and try to get some rest."

Kate didn't want to cry. At least not there in that impersonal hospital corridor at four o'clock in the morning. She was simply too drained, stunned, and dazed with a terrible sense of loss.

For two hours Kate had walked the streets after leaving the hospital, and she had already seen the headlines in the morning papers as they hit the stands: BALLERINA IN COMA FOLLOWING TRIUMPHAL COMEBACK.

Taking a handkerchief from her purse, Kate dabbed at her eyes and realized that there was nothing to do but return to her apartment and get ready for work. She rose and started walking toward Fifth Avenue with José del Bario's final words echoing eerily in her mind.

They had walked out of the hospital together, and his eyes had been fixed and staring, looking straight ahead at nothing. "It's such a tragedy you know . . . they . . . Adrianna and Sacha were so very much in love. What a team they could have made. What a future they could have had performing together. Adrianna had only begun to dance. Now the world will never know how truly magnificent she could have been."

Chapter Sixteen

Kate arrived at the Four Seasons a full fifteen minutes early for her luncheon engagement with Shanga Duprez.

"I would like to meet with you in order to discuss a matter of vital interest to both Caramour Cosmetics and yourself. I can promise that you will not regret accepting my invitation."

The brief message was intriguingly enigmatic, and, while Kate didn't really know much about Shanga Duprez, she was aware that the name carried a certain cachet among more militant feminists. Shanga was also the president of her own advertising agency, which had been responsible for some very innovative campaigns during the past several years.

"I'm meeting Miss Duprez for lunch," Kate informed the maître d', who stood awaiting her when she reached the top of the deeply carpeted staircase.

"Miss Duprez has not yet arrived." He smiled. "She

called to say that she would be a few minutes late, and asked that you be shown to her regular table."

The table in question turned out to be located in prime space beside the reflecting pool. After Kate was comfortably seated, the maître d' wished her "bon appetit," and a waiter immediately appeared to take her order for a vodka martini.

Over the years, Kate had dined only rarely at the Four Seasons, and, as she sipped her drink and waited for Shanga, she watched the surrounding tables begin to fill up with the typical media-oriented luncheon crowd: advertising executives, publishing people, several columnists of note, and a sprinkling of familiar faces to whom Kate was unable to attach names.

Eminently recognizable at the luncheon gathering was the ruggedly handsome pro-football quarterback who was probably even more celebrated for doing a variety of the most outrageous television commercials. He was seated in a corner banquette with a pair of blonde and blue-eyed Barbie Doll look-alikes.

The football player was a macho Italian type, with dreamy, melting brown eyes, a bushy dark mustache, and a mane of curly black hair. For a moment their eyes met, and his gaze was both admiring and rather startling to Kate.

She had never thought of herself as the kind of woman about whom younger men entertained sexual thoughts, and when he winked, she looked quickly away.

Kate realized suddenly that she hadn't even thought of Paul during the past twenty-four hours. In fact, even to think of him now brought only a strange absence of feeling.

Somehow, during the past three weeks, Kate's own future independent of Paul Osborn had begun to crystallize about her determination to have a life and a career entirely on her own.

Unbidden, thoughts of Adrianna slid uneasily through Kate's mind as she sat listening to the soft murmur of voices and the clink of silver on fine china. The previous evening she had been allowed to visit her for the first time since the massive cerebral accident had so suddenly struck her down.

Adrianna had been transferred to a private room. It was painted a sunny yellow and looked out on tall trees. Kate wondered if she would ever be able to see them.

As Kate entered the room Adrianna's eyes were open, and she was moving her head slowly from side to side. "We have no way of being certain at this stage," Doctor Charboneau informed her. "But it is my professional opinion that Mrs. del Bario has suffered extensive damage to the left cerebral hemisphere. She might very well remain in coma for an indefinite period of time."

"And if she does come out of it?" Kate had asked.

"We'll just have to wait and see," Charboneau responded. He nodded toward the bank of electronic monitoring devices that were keeping constant track of brain activity and heartbeat, as well as assisting Adrianna's respiration. "At present, Mrs. del Bario is at least partially dependent on all that machinery."

Kate remained sitting next to Adrianna for over an hour, as she kept lazily moving her head from side to side. Her body was rigid and twisted, curled foetally in upon itself, while her eyes seemed to scan the room, glancing at objects and then moving on.

After a while Adrianna's head slowed its restless movement and her eyes, sunken within great bruised hollows, fluttered closed. Limp and silent, she drifted away once again to dream her distant dreams.

Kate had risen then and bent to kiss her cheek. "It's going to be all right," she whispered in a choked, scarcely audible voice. Then after squeezing one of her pale, chill hands, she turned away and hurried from the room.

Adrianna's tragic collapse at Lincoln Center had been an

emotionally wrenching experience for Kate. And she had managed to get through the week only by throwing herself totally into her work. It was through concentrated and sternly disciplined work habits that she kept her sadness and concern from overwhelming her completely. It just wouldn't do anyone any good, Kate realized.

Kate also remembered only too well the hopeless drift and depression she had experienced over Paul's desertion, and she had no intention of ever going through that again.

Suddenly Kate's attention was drawn by a stir at the entrance to the restaurant, and she turned in that direction to see a stunning black woman engaged in animated conversation with the maître d'. In her swirling cape and colorful culottes, she looked as if she had just stepped out of the pages of a glossy high-fashion magazine. But the unique *something* that seemed to draw all eyes lay more in the way she carried herself like a queen.

She was tall, honey-beige in color and very slim, with an electric smile and flashing white teeth. Her hair was cut short and worn close to her finely sculpted head in a medusalike cascade of golden ornaments that flashed and shimmered with every movement she made.

Fascinated, Kate watched as the statuesque black beauty made her way around the reflecting pool, nodding, smiling, and waving as she came. Everyone seemed to know who she was, and there were stops at important tables along the way, where she was warmly greeted by the restaurant's most celebrated clientele.

After being embraced by the super-macho football star, who whispered something in her ear that made her laugh in deep, rich, bell-like tones, the dusky Nefertiti began moving in Kate's direction, her wide, white smile shining like the beam of a searchlight. Only then did Kate realize who it was.

"I'm sorry to have kept you waiting," she said, swirling

her cape off her shoulders and sliding gracefully into the banquette. "My name is Shanga Duprez, and I can't tell you how much I've looked forward to meeting you again."

Kate was momentarily flustered. "You mean we've met before?" she asked.

"It was a long time ago," Shanga informed her. "Twelve years to be exact. I don't blame you in the least for not remembering. I was green as hell and just off the bus from Detroit when you interviewed me for a modeling job. I wasn't right for the commercial you were doing, but I've never forgotten how kind, thoughtful, and encouraging you were to a gawky green kid from the hinterlands, trying desperately to land her first job."

Suddenly it all clicked, and Kate remembered a very different girl beneath the glamorous high-fashion veneer. The time had been winter, and Kate had been interviewing an endless stream of models for a new lipstick commercial. It was late in the day, and she was drinking coffee steadily to stay awake, when the most extraordinary young woman walked into the room where the auditions were being held.

She was tall. My God, but she was tall. There was simply no way that anyone could have missed her. It had been snowing outside, and she had been wearing one of those voluminous sheepskin coats, with knee-high boots and tight-fitting ski pants. Her long black hair was tucked up beneath a wool knit ski cap, and when she took it off and shook her head, her hair tumbled down around her shoulders like a lion's dark mane.

Immediately Kate was jolted out of the casting doldrums where everyone begins to look alike, and names and faces become part of a hazy montage.

The tall black girl with the dazzling white smile was truly a knockout, possessed of that special kind of magic that totally captured the imagination.

"Yes, of course I remember you." Kate laughed. "How could I ever forget that entrance? You looked like you had just gotten off a dog sled from Nome, Alaska."

"It was more like a bus from Detroit," Shanga responded. "I was broke, with about five dollars in my pocket, and convinced that I was going to take the New York modeling world by storm."

Kate leaned forward on one hand, smiling. "I think the quality I immediately liked about you was that you were definitely for real." For a moment Kate looked pensive. "But your name wasn't Shanga Duprez in those days. It was Carla . . . Carla Green, if I remember correctly."

Shanga flashed that incandescent smile of hers. "Good lord, what a memory you've got. But what you seem to have completely forgotten is that you fixed me up with a place to stay, and arranged for a top photographer to do my portfolio at no charge. Afterwards, you managed to convince someone at Famous Faces Agency to take me on spec, and teach me all the tricks of the trade."

After ordering a white wine cassis from the hovering waiter who presented them with luncheon menus, Shanga proceeded to relate her story. "Several months after we first met, I ended up in Paris, where I worked for all the great designers. Somewhere along the way I changed my name to Shanga, since all things African were terribly *in*. Then I managed to get myself married to a slick French dude by the name of Baron Marcel Duprez. He was rich, titled, and gay as Chinese pajamas, but he had this thing about tall black models. After Marcel and I split up, I decided to come back to New York and open my own advertising agency with the money I got from a whopping divorce settlement. That was five years ago, and as they say, the rest is history. All in all I probably didn't do too badly for a gawky black kid from

Detroit who never got beyond the seventh grade, and whose mother took in laundry to support twelve kids.''

They laughed warmly and fondly together in recollection.

''You always did have colossal ambition,'' Kate mused. ''It doesn't surprise me in the least that you've done so well in the world.''

Shanga Duprez, Inc., was at that moment the hottest new ad agency in New York, while Shanga herself was primarily known for her highly successful campaigns promoting various women's products. It was she who had put the handsome football star seated across the way into panty hose and a fur coat for TV commercials. It was also Shanga who had presided over the introduction of beauty products for black women into the market and in so doing had been named Advertising Woman of the Year.

Kate was impressed once again by Shanga Duprez's strong sense of personal pride and total self-assurance. She was clearly a woman of great strength who could lay it all on the line if she believed in something. At close range, Shanga's features were strong and angular, handsome rather than beautiful. Yet she possessed that unique quality that far more truly beautiful women tried without success to emulate.

Shanga Duprez had the ability to make you believe that she was anything she chose to be and was able to project an image capable of capturing the imagination of large numbers of people. She was, in a word, fascinating.

Throughout the salad course, they laughed and talked together with the warm and easy intimacy of old friends. Then, as the dishes were being cleared away and the maître d' was pouring the dark red wine accompanying the steak tartare they had both ordered, Kate lifted her glass and proposed a toast. ''Here's to success. You've done marvelously well,

Shanga. You should feel very proud of all that you've been able to accomplish."

"Well, you haven't exactly been loafing on the job yourself," Shanga responded. "I mean, after all, you are the president of a major cosmetics company, you look simply fabulous, and you're just about to get an offer that's much too good to refuse."

"I must admit that your invitation to lunch was intriguing," Kate said. "Just what is this matter of vital importance you wanted to discuss?"

Shanga laughed a deep, rich, bubbling laugh, full of ready mirth and secret ironies. "Look, Kate, I'm going to lay it on you straight out. I get around a lot in this business, and I hear a lot of inside dope. Right about now, you and Caramour, Inc., are a very hot topic in the beauty industry."

"And just exactly what is it you've heard?" Kate questioned, tracing the rim of her drink with one clear-lacquered fingertip.

Shanga leaned close, and her voice fell into a lower register. "The word is out that you have come up with a dynamite beauty package called Rejuvenal that's going to take the cosmetics business by storm. Everybody's talking, and it's no big secret that I.C.E. has got big eyes."

"I'm already aware that there's a contract out on my job," Kate confirmed. "But so far I'm still holding my own, and even managing to win most of the major battles."

"I've been in business long enough to know that just holding your own isn't going to make it. You just aren't going to be able to survive indefinitely on your own, Kate. We women have to begin sticking together, instead of waiting around for things to happen. It's time for us to begin to establish alliances. You know yourself there are a very limited number of women with whom you can discuss the problems you encounter in your work, women with whom you can establish parallel arrangements to those the male team players use to keep us in a state of continual psychological isolation.''

Kate sipped her wine, thoughtfully twisting the stem of her glass between her fingers. ''I've never really considered myself as a participant in the women's movement,'' she confessed. ''I guess I always just went my own way, and fought my own battles as best I could.''

''That was O.K. when you were playing in the minor leagues,'' Shanga insisted. ''But things are different now, and I'll bet you've already begun to discover that it can get pretty slippery at the top of the heap. Believe me, Kate, to put Rejuvenal over and stay in control of the action, you're gonna need all the help you can get. You'll do yourself a big favor by getting rid of the idea that you have to prove something by making it strictly under your own power.

''What I'm proposing,'' Shanga went on, ''is that we join forces. I want to handle the Rejuvenal campaign. Quite frankly, I'm convinced that you're onto something sensational. The potential is enormous, but first you're going to have to overcome the clinical effect. The idea of rejuvenation itself is still a little scary to people.''

Kate nodded, knowing instinctively that Shanga was right. ''And just how would you go about accomplishing that?'' she asked.

''First of all we need a symbol to capture the imagination of women everywhere. Rejuvenal Skin-Care Products have to become associated in the public consciousness with glamor, excitement, and success. I believe that *you* are that symbol, Kate. And if you'll give me the chance, I intend to make your name and face instantly recognizable to women around the world.''

Chapter Seventeen

As the launch skimmed across Shinnecock Bay, Kate breathed in the pure salt-sea air and felt a surge of adrenalin coursing through her veins. In the distance, the *Sultana* rode at anchor, illuminated like a floating palace in the gathering dusk.

It was the Fourth of July, and the occasion was the first in a series of media-oriented social spectaculars guaranteed to endow the Rejuvenal promotion with a highly sophisticated public image. Fiona had arrived in the Hamptons only the week before aboard the *Sultana*. She was accompanied by her husband, Prince Nessim, and the presence of the exotic royal couple aboard their fabulous yacht had already sparked the summer social season into a blaze.

Youth and Beauty Forevermore by Caramour had already begun to take on the hallmarks of a sensational advertising campaign. Shanga was a master of marketing strategy, who had begun to plot a shrewd course from the very beginning. But it was Kate herself who epitomized the prototype Caramour Woman, a highly marketable symbol of the newly liberated feminine consciousness in action. She was in essence the woman who had already made it to the top, and the multimillion-dollar advertising campaign was specifically geared to the beauty-conscious career woman who felt she owed it to herself to remain as radiantly youthful and physically attractive as possible. The target market would be the competitive and highly capable female who still gloried in being a woman.

According to Shanga's candid appraisal, with her streamlined air of chic, expertise, and corporate savy, Kate had already succeeded in establishing herself within the beauty industry as a force to be reckoned with. Ever since undergoing cell-rejuvenation therapy on Coral Key, Kate felt herself to be a greatly changed woman—a newer, more dynamic version of herself, industrious, resourceful, and brimming with a totally new sense of inner self-confidence. Yet even so, she was not exactly looking forward to the evening ahead.

It was Kate's first visit to the Hamptons that summer, and as she and Wes stepped from the bobbing launch onto the gangplank of the *Sultana*, it was obvious that the Hampton social season was well under way.

The yacht was mobbed, and Shanga Duprez was waiting to greet them as they came aboard. "I want you to meet Wesley Travis, my terrific art director," Kate said. "You two are going to be working very closely together from now on, so you might as well get acquainted."

"I don't mind in the least," Shanga purred, while giving Wes her double-whammy onceover from head to foot, without missing anything in between.

Wesley Travis did indeed look debonairly handsome in his

navy blazer, white trousers, and dark blue linen shirt open at the chest. Nor had Shanga herself ever looked more provocative, Kate thought, with her silver lamé gown slit to the thigh, and her multibraided dark hair shimmering with silver ornaments.

It was true, Kate thought a bit wistfully. They did make a very attractive duo, and there was not much question about the sudden sexual attraction they seemed to feel for one another. The question was not whether they would manage to jump into bed together, but rather how soon.

By now Shanga had slipped her arm through Wes' and was lightly stroking his cheek with her long, tapering silver-taloned fingers. "I'm afraid you're going to have to excuse us for a few minutes of girltalk," Kate informed him. "Shanga and I are both running on a pretty fast track these days. We have to catch each other when we can."

Turning her attention to Shanga, she went on, "I talked to Andreas Jaccard by phone today from Jamaica, and he seems extremely enthusiastic about your idea of arranging a Manhattan gallery showing of his sculpture. I'm going to see if I can talk Celia Randolph into sponsoring the exhibit and going public about her cell rejuvenation. I mean, after all, the woman is a walking testament to the miraculous benefits of RJ-12. And she knows absolutely everyone."

"That sounds great," Shanga agreed. "And it should sync in nicely with Fiona's announcement that she's making Jaccard a ten-million-dollar grant from the Van Zandt Foundation. In fact, while your friend Jaccard is in town for the gallery showing, why don't I book him for some major magazine interviews and a round of TV talk shows? He sounds like a natural for the tube, so let's just go ahead and make the most of it."

Shanga deliberately fluttered her long false eyelashes and

dropped her voice into a sexy purr. "The good doctor sounds utterly dreamy on the phone," she declared. "May I ask what he's like in the flesh?"

"Not bad," Kate observed. "Just your run of the mill gorgeous hunk of man who also happens to be brilliant, charming . . ."

"And the recipient of a Nobel Prize," Shanga finished for her. "I mean what on earth could you want unless a girl just happened to have a dirty mind?"

"Would one of you ladies be good enough to point me toward the bar?" Wes complained. "Suddenly I'm feeling all kind of left out."

"It's that way," Shanga instructed, pointing amidships. "Just follow your ears, while I run along and try to corral the video crew to get some footage on Kate. Tonight is *the night,* after all, that we're launching the Rejuvenal campaign into earth orbit."

As far as the fabled summer Hamptons were concerned, the *Sultana* was definitely the place to be that evening, for all those fun-loving types who buzzed constantly from one discotheque to another, to charity balls, and on into the social columns.

Everyone was there. The rich, the celebrated, and the merely beautiful; all the high rollers who made a career out of being seen in the right places at the right time. Yet the gathering aboard Fiona's yacht that evening also reflected the disparate ingredients of a typical New York media bash, and Fiona herself was of course the star attraction.

Her sudden reappearance on the social scene after nearly a ten-years' absence and her miraculous recovery from terminal cancer had sparked a sensation. Everyone wanted to have a piece of the action, and for one evening, at least, what passed for Society with a capital *S* had bedded down with a gaggle of

P.R. flacks, some major Madison Avenue heavies, and a sprinkling of stage and movie people.

Kate's own appearance aboard the *Sultana* that evening had been carefully orchestrated and planned for maximum effect. She looked stunning in a scarlet lace cocktail dress the color of opium poppies, with a matching feather boa trailing from her bare shoulders. Kate's new shorter and more flattering hair style was just the right length and shape to accentuate her elegantly slender neck and angular bone structure, while playing up the widely spaced gray-violet eyes beneath a thick dark fringe of false lashes.

Strolling arm in arm, Kate and Wes allowed their initial momentum to carry them down the deck to where a sudden surge of bodies circulating amidships swept them inside the sumptuous main salon. Once there, they found themselves to be at the party's heart and center. Loud disco music blared out over high amp speakers, while a glittering array of celebrated names and faces mixed, mingled, and swilled Moet Chandon amid an impressive display of Fiona's priceless Eastern artworks.

Flotillas of low marble-topped tables surrounded the dance floor beneath a silk-tented ceiling. Attractive, well-dressed people were to be seen everywhere. Lithe and golden women with ageless bodies, streaked hair, and stylishly contoured breasts moved easily among the tables, out onto the dance floor, and into the arms of men with lean, well-proportioned bodies and perfect tennis tans.

No one seemed to mind the heat, the crush, or the high-decible noise level. The service bar was in full swing, while a boozy wash of laughter, voices, music, and a mix of expensive perfume created a heady and intoxicating brew.

Kate gave an involuntary shudder as she glimpsed Winstin Thornton slumped over his drink at the bar. He looked drunk.

But he also looked brooding, sullen, and very much alone.

"Can you see Celia anyplace?" she asked Wes as he deftly lifted two glasses of champagne from a passing tray.

"No, but I do see the cannibal king in drag, and she's coming our way," he said in an urgent aside. "Forgive my cowardice, but I think I feel a migraine coming on."

"Well if it isn't *the* Katherine Leslie."

Kate spun around to find herself cheek to jowl with Cassandra Presley, the rag and beauty trade gossip columnist. For a fleeting moment, Kate wished that she herself had been able to slip away into the converging currents of social intercourse sweeping, eddying, and jostling about them.

It was, Kate supposed, in order to offset her rather severe appearance that Cassie had taken to wearing flouncy little-girl dresses and hair bows. She was tall and thin, with sharp, inquisitive features framed by a carbon-tinted Sassoon cut at least a decade out of date.

Cassie the Crocodile they called her, and when she sunk her teeth into a skewered shrimp, Kate had a pretty good idea why. Her ravaged face was painted like a China doll's, and when she spoke, the cloying southern voice was as seductively parasitic as hanging Spanish moss in ancient oaks.

Cassandra wagged a brightly taloned finger and smiled that crocodile smile. "Since you haven't returned my calls, I was almost ready to believe all those stories about your nervous breakdown. I mean, what other possible reason could you have for avoiding me, since I can give you the kind of press you're so desperately in need of right now? You don't exactly have everyone on your side, you know. I'd even go so far as to say you've been making some very powerful enemies."

"I've been swamped with work," Kate heard herself saying. "Quite frankly, Cassie, I haven't been returning anyone's calls. Let me go on record as saying that I'm well, happy, and extremely busy getting the new line off the drawing boards."

"Of course darlin', you know that Cassie understands. But one does hear such ugly rumors, and I am, after all, in the business of keeping the public abreast of what's going on, don't you see? I mean it's no secret that you and Paul Osborn were extremely close for absolutely donkey's years, and Allison did make such a beautiful bride. I couldn't help but wonder how you took it, being so sudden and all. I mean it *was* so terribly *sudden*, wasn't it, Katherine? What with you and Paul always havin' been so close?"

Cassandra batted her double tier of theatrically false mink lashes and snatched a canapé from a passing steward's tray as Kate tried to manage her best imitation of a smile. "Paul and I had a working arrangement for many years . . . nothing more. To be perfectly truthful, Cassie, I couldn't be happier that he finally found the right girl. It was time for Paul to begin leading a different kind of life. I wish them both the very best."

Something went hard in Cassandra's snapping black eyes.

"Of course you really don't have very much choice in the matter, now do you, darlin'? I mean, you are winging it on your own now, aren't you? If I were you, I'd go out of my way to be nice to me, Katherine. Then I can afford to be nice to you."

At that moment Celia appeared on a rescue mission, and Kate looked on gratefully as she and Cassandra exchanged a flurry of whispery little noncontact kisses. "I'm going to have to drag you away from what I'm sure just had to be a fascinating exchange of confidences." Then turning to Cassandra, Celia dead-panned, "How perfectly marvelous to see you looking so spry and chipper, Cassie darling. Still scavenging around for all sorts of malicious gossip to titillate your readers' vulgar little minds?"

"I haven't even begun to dig where you're concerned, Celia dear. But there are some very juicy rumors making the rounds about you scooping up some bronze-skinned young god off a Caribbean beach. I'll get to them eventually. Ta Ta, Katherine. We must lunch soon. I want to know all about the new product line and that fascinating Doctor Jaccard I've been hearing so much about. Remember now, you promised me an exclusive."

As soon as Cassandra was out of earshot, Celia said, "It looked to me like old Cassie was moving in for the kill. Did she strike an artery?"

"Not really." Kate laughed. "Just a large vein. I'll survive. Cassandra couldn't wait to tell me what a beautiful bride Allison was. I could have thrown up."

Celia rolled her blue eyes heavenward. "Well, darling, the evening is still young, and I'm here to warn you there are still some surprises in store."

"For instance?" Kate questioned.

"Your friend Fiona, for instance. Or should I say Princess Shama Al Laban, which means something on the order of 'may you be blessed by the fruitful udders of the white she-goat.' Of course one does have to watch those direct translations from the original *Bedowee. N'est-ce pas, cherie?* You just can't afford to take them too literally."

With that, Celia took Kate firmly by the arm and led her through the crush to where a video camera had been set up on the dance floor. As they edged closer, the cameras zoomed in to capture the casually sartorial figure of Ron Snieder. The News Center Eight On the Spot Report was preparing to go on the air. The video-cam whirred, and a sudden wash of arc lights bathed the scene in a white-hot glare.

"This is News Center Eight bringing you a televised on-the-spot report about one of the fastest-breaking stories of the day. We're here tonight aboard one of the most famous yachts in the world, anchored in Southhampton Harbor. The two hundred-eighty-foot *Sultana* is the floating palace of American-dollar princess Fiona Van Zandt, a woman considered by many to be perhaps the richest woman in the world.

Beyond any question, Fiona Van Zandt has been one of the most glittering ornaments of our time," Snieder went on in his cloying, insinuating way. "And considering the extravagance of her existence, the conspicuous consumption for which she has become world famous, along with the wild marital escapades and her highly publicized penchant for living life to the very fullest, it's not too surprising to learn of her near spiritual conversion to the cause of cell-injection therapy, which she credits with having saved her life after being afflicted with terminal cancer."

The video coverage was being beamed throughout the northeastern United States, and Kate shuddered at the way the whole thing was being handled. Snieder's presentation had the effect of making Fiona appear as a grotesque joke, and she was absolutely furious at Shanga for having permitted such a thing to happen.

Just then there was a sudden clash of cymbals and a rising wave of steadily mounting applause from the assembled guests. Then as all eyes turned to stare, and the video-cam swung slowly around to pan the scene, Fiona and her prince made their appearance through a teakwood arch festooned with silken banners and flashing mosaic mirrorwork.

Celia had been right to warn her, Kate realized, for whatever she may have been expecting, it was not even remotely connected with the scene playing itself out beneath the glare of the television lights.

Fiona, in the role of Princess Shama Al Laban, was scarcely recognizable.

She was fashionably bronzed and gaudily bejeweled; painted, powdered, and costumed in a filmy harem outfit, with a jeweled halter that prominently displayed newly siliconed breasts. Her kohl-rimmed eyes were glittering and unfocused, while the crown of diamond and emerald leaves she wore on her head trembled and shimmered with every faltering step she took.

Fiona was leaning heavily on the arm of the prince, and she was clearly stewed to the gills.

Then she was standing before the whirring video-cam and Ron Snieder was thrusting a microphone in her face. "During recent weeks, the columns have been full of stories about your miraculous recovery from terminal cancer. Can you tell us in your own words to what you attribute your amazing deliverance?"

When she spoke, Fiona's words were slightly slurred, even though her smile was serenely incandescent. "I was as good as six feet under, when Doctor Andreas Jaccard began giving me injections of Rejuvenal-12 at Coral Key Spa in the Caribbean. The finest cancer specialists in Europe had already given me up for lost, when within just six short weeks Jaccard was able to restore me to health and happiness."

"Are you saying that this Doctor Jaccard has discovered a cure for cancer?" Snieder interjected.

"I'm saying that Doctor Andreas Jaccard saved my life with injections of Rejuvenal-12. He's a brilliant scientist," Fiona went on, "and I have given instructions to the Van Zandt Foundation, founded by my father, to make available a ten-million-dollar research grant in order to further Jaccard's work."

Snieder turned back to the camera. "Well, ladies and gentlemen, you heard it from the lips of the miracle lady herself. The legendary Fiona Van Zandt, who appears to have found happiness at last, with two billion dollars and her Arab prince.

"This is Ron Snieder aboard the fabulous yacht *Sultana* in Southhampton Harbor, switching you back to our Manhattan studio in the heart of the Big Apple."

As the bright, hot camera lights switched off, Fiona hurried forward to embrace Kate in an exotic cloud of perfume and a swirl of filmy veils. "Dearest Katherine, how simply marvelous to see you again. And here is the wonderful man I wanted so much for you to meet."

Prince Nessim was wearing an ill-fitting dark blue suit with a traditional Arabic *kefia* draped about his lightly bearded Byzantine face. He was a short, lean, and esthetic-looking man. Not at all the Porfirio Rubirosa type Kate had been expecting.

Prince Nessim's dark eyes flashed in greeting, and he salaamed stiffly as Fiona introduced them. "My wife has spoken of you often," he expressed in his softly hesitant English. "You are our most welcome guest."

He seemed like a pleasantly unobtrusive man, but Kate's smile felt stiff and false. "I've always wanted to visit Morocco," she said to fill the awkward gap. "I've heard it's a very beautiful country with an ancient culture."

For a moment Nessim's hooded dark eyes searched hers as if questioning something. "It is true that our culture is very old, and our Moslem customs little understood here in the West." He made a short gesture of dismissal with one slim dark hand. "You understand that all of this . . . is entirely new and quite strange to me. I am hopeful that within a few days the *Sultana* will be sailing for North Africa. The life we lead there is far simpler, and I think better suited to my beloved Shama Al Laban's fullest recovery."

Fiona's heavily made-up features turned petulant, and her

voice was sharply brittle. "Oh, Nessim, you're not going to start harping on all that again."

She turned to Kate, exasperated. "My husband, the Prince, doesn't seem to realize that I've been reprieved from the grave. Surely you understand, Katie. I've got a lot of living to catch up on, and I don't want to miss out on a minute of it. The Hampton Season has just begun, and already Nessim wants to get back to the desert."

Kate wanted to say something about her concern, the need for Fiona to rest and fully recover her health. But the words just didn't seem to come, and Fiona wasn't really listening anyway. Like most everyone else, her attention had been drawn to the center of the dance floor, where Celia had fallen into the arms of a sleekly handsome young man wearing a white dinner jacket with a red carnation in his lapel.

They seemed to be drawn to one another like orbiting moons. Celia appeared oblivious to everything but the pulsing rhythm of the pounding disco beat. Nor was she concerned by her partner's hands, playing down over her swinging hips, to caress her softly rounded buttocks.

Kate was shocked, but she was not surprised. Celia's behavior had been growing increasingly frivolous of late. Most nights of the week she was flying high on diet pills, liquor, and the obvious desire to escape the all too predictable boredom of her relationship with a man she found intellectually stuffy and sexually uninspiring.

A man who in the very next moment lurched drunkenly onto the dance floor and began making a fool of himself trying to cut in. Winstin Thornton had become a pathetic figure to Kate, and she turned her eyes away, only to receive her second high-voltage shock of the night.

Kate blinked hard, staring in disbelief at the shaggy-haired, blond-bearded young man, expensively turned out in a dark blue blazer, tailored gray slacks, and Gucci loafers. His amber-tinted lenses were smoked to conceal clearwater-blue eyes, but Kate knew immediately who it was.

Skip Brophy was dancing with the most beautiful girl at the party, and she was pressing intimately against him. She looked to Kate like one of those coolly confident debutante types so often featured in society columns. The perfect features, the fashionably lean body, and silky, flaxen hair that hung in shimmering waves about her evenly tanned shoulders.

"Don't Skipper and Amanda make a simply gorgeous couple?" Fiona chirped. "I can't tell you how happy it's made me to be reunited with my son after all these years. It was like a second miracle!" Fiona exclaimed. "He just appeared on Coral Key about a week after you and Celia left."

Kate kept her voice deliberately casual. "You mean that bearded young man dancing with the beautiful blonde girl is your son?"

"You wouldn't believe how he's changed," Fiona observed. "Skipper's been traveling around India with some kind of super-guru. I mean there are millions of Indians who actually consider this man to be a living saint," she prattled on. "Skip came to Jamaica looking for me because he heard I was dying. This guru of his . . . this Muktananda is here in America, up in the Catskills somewhere, and people attribute all kinds of miraculous happenings to just being in his presence. Skipper was convinced he could cure me."

Kate placed her hand on Fiona's arm. "I'm afraid you'll have to forgive me," she said, "but I'm going to have to go outside and get some air." At that instant Winstin Thornton staggered onto the dance floor, to splash his drink into Celia's partner's face.

Suddenly Kate felt as if the heat, the crush of people, and the loud, pounding beat of the music were closing in on her. The last thing in the world she wanted was to get involved in another ugly scene involving Celia and Winston. Besides that, she'd had nothing to eat since a light lunch off a tray in her office; and the three glasses of champagne were beginning to work on her head.

There were a scattering of couples strung along the teak railing, and the lights of Southhampton hung against the dark shoreline like a shimmering jeweled necklace. Breathing in deep draughts of fresh air, Kate walked slowly along the deck. It was cooler now, and the light offshore breeze felt good against her overheated flesh. It ruffled her hair and fluttered the scarlet feather boa she held clasped about her shoulders.

So this was the shimmery glitter world of the restless rich with golden tennis tans, Kate thought to herself. She was up to her false eyelashes in gaudy and conspicuous consumption, but it failed to have even the remotest appeal. Kate was only sorry now that she had allowed Fiona to become involved in the promotion. But then she had never been entirely sure who was using whom. Everybody seemed to be playing some sort of game, and nobody had bothered to tell her the rules.

Kate breathed a sigh of relief as she reached the familiar fantail deck with its striped overhead awning and comfortable lounge chairs. There was no one there, and the deck was strung with colored lights that bled down into the dark water lapping against the hull. Kate paused to lean against the railing, and the music sounded as if it came from very far away.

Then she heard footsteps behind her, and a familiar male voice questioned, "Mind if I join you?"

Kate turned, and her face was a pale oval beneath the softly colored light. "I should imagine, Mr. Brophy, that you can do anything you like aboard this yacht."

Kate took a cigarette from her purse and placed it to her lips with a reflex action. She had tried to stop smoking, but was now back up to a pack a day. She bent her head to accept a light and then said, "I saw you dancing inside. Amanda . . . is very beautiful."

Skip was leaning against the railing next to her and she could feel his eyes. "Why did you disappear after that night we met?" he asked.

Kate exhaled a cloud of softly billowing smoke through her nostrils. "I had to get away. There were a lot of things in my life that needed sorting out. That's where I met *your mother* . . . at Coral Key Spa. We became friends. She told me about having a son she hadn't seen in many years, but I had no idea . . ." Her voice fell away.

"Contrary to popular opinion," Skip observed, "being the son of a very rich woman isn't necessarily any picnic. I don't normally make a habit of advertising the fact. It's been a long time since I belonged to that world in there."

"What about Amanda? She quite obviously belongs, and one doesn't have to be in possession of psychic powers to see that she's very much in love with you."

"We were engaged once," Skip volunteered. "But that was quite a while back, before I went to India. I guess my mother must have invited her to the party tonight, hoping to rekindle something that's been dead for a long time now. In case you haven't noticed, my mother is a hopeless romantic. Love has always been the dominant theme in her life. Love pursued, love won, love rejected . . . love turning to ashes, and then rising up to beckon her yet again."

"Maybe she read Byron as a girl," Kate suggested, trying to keep it light. "Anyway, I liked Prince Nessim very much. He couldn't be like the others. It's easy to see that he cares for Fiona. After all, they've lived quite happily together in Morocco for almost five years, and Fiona told me herself that she was very much in love with him."

It was several long moments before Skip responded, and when he did there was an edge of residual bitterness in his voice. "My mother has been in love with many men. Six months after I was born she ran off with an English duke who ended up relieving her of five million dollars. That roughly figured out to one million for each month they lived together."

Kate turned to search his strong, square-cut features. Something in his voice, in his candor, moved her deeply. She understood that behind his words lay a much deeper truth that made her own disappointment in Fiona's behavior easier to bear. She felt drawn to him by the power of his quietly confident sexuality, by his honesty and openness.

Once again, Brian Skip Brophy had managed to stir something in her. A sensual awareness. Skip had removed his smoked-lensed glasses by now, and his eyes were penetrating, a clear, sharp blue.

"Come have dinner with me," he proposed. "It's been a long time, and I've thought about you a lot."

"You don't know anything about me," she said. "A lot has changed since the night we met."

He reached out to touch her cheek with his fingertips, and she felt the scalding heat of his sexuality. "Change is what life is all about," he smiled. "And besides, I happen to know you have a passion for soft-shelled crabs. There's this Italian seafood restaurant out in Montauk we can go to, and watch the Fourth of July fireworks on the pier at midnight. Soft-shell crabs are their specialty."

In that moment Kate realized that she was enjoying herself for the first time that evening. "Since you seem to be in the habit of reading my mind," she said, slipping her arm through his, "I'm going to accept your kind offer, Mr. Brophy. But what about Amanda?"

Skip bent to kiss her lightly on the cheek, and they started moving up the deck toward the gangway. "Amanda isn't a real person," he uttered. "Just like my mother, she lives in a fantasy world. It doesn't really exist."

Chapter Eighteen

They drove out to the Blue Whaler Inn at Montauk. The restaurant was small, intimate, and located directly across from the wharf where Skip docked his forty-eight-foot schooner, the *Westwind*. He was obviously a favored customer, and the owner led them to a table overlooking the harbor. There was candlelight, flowers on the tables, and a crowd of Hampton summer people celebrating the Fourth of July at the adjoining tables.

After the waiter had poured each of them a glass of flinty white Bordeaux, Kate fixed him with a bemused look. "And so Mr. Brophy, just what *was* it like being the son of the legendary Fiona Van Zandt?"

"Do you really want to know?," he questioned.

"About you? Yes, indeed, I would. I really don't know anything about you. In many ways, you're almost a total mystery to me."

Skip shrugged. "I never really saw much of my mother when I was a kid. She always seemed like pretty much of a kid herself, with a lot of expensive toys. Maybe I grew up thinking I had to prove something to the world, because at times . . . my mother seemed like a pathetic joke. A selfish, rich, and indulgent woman who bought husbands and titles the same way she bought jewels and houses and yachts and racehorses. Of course there were always the headlines and expensive presents arriving with predictable regularity on important occasions like birthdays and graduations. But for the most part, my mother was always a stranger."

At Kate's urging, Skip went on to tell her about his boyhood in Virginia and in a series of exclusive Swiss boarding schools. He had always exhibited the talents of a natural-born athlete, and by the age of sixteen was being touted as having Olympic potential in downhill ski racing.

Skip was attending Harvard Law School by the time he finally reached the Olympic trials. But during his first year in competition, he abruptly switched from downhill racing and slalom to ski jumping, because it was faster, riskier, and played much closer to the edge.

On his twentieth birthday he participated in the Olympic trials at Kitzbuel, Austria, and managed to break both legs coming off an icy and treacherous ski jump at eighty miles an hour.

During the long months of convalescence, Skip had been forced to give up any idea he may have had of Olympic stardom. He also gave up the idea of becoming a lawyer, and decided to take up sports car racing instead. On his twenty-first birthday, Fiona had given him a buttercup-yellow Maserati and a five-million-dollar trust fund.

After that, Skip related, it was sleek women, faster cars, and an increasing addiction to speed, whether in chemical form or on the track.

"I guess I was always a participant," Skip related. "I never wanted to read about what it was like driving fast cars, ski diving, or climbing the highest mountains in the world. I wanted to know what it was like for myself. Challenge has always exhilarated me. I've always felt a need to create risks for myself."

As Skip talked Kate realized that there had been a powerful kind of chemistry between them from the very beginning. His light eyes were guileless and penetrating, expressing sensitivity, consideration, and a certain affection. Enthusiasm seemed to emanate from him in waves of energy, suggesting that anything was possible to anyone venturesome enough to tempt the fates.

In that, Kate thought, he was very much like Fiona, who had always nurtured the same wanderlust and hunger to experience life in all its variety. Yet with his quiet confidence Skip was very much in contrast to the egocentric type of men Kate dealt with every day in business. He made her feel feminine, relaxed, and very secure.

Skip's career as a race car driver ended in a fiery six-car smashup at Le Mans, in which three other drivers died a terrible death. Skip was dragged from his wrecked Lamborghini and managed to walk away miraculously unscathed, even though he was never again quite the same person he had been before.

"I guess I felt guilty about being alive after that," he informed her. "But taking incredible risks didn't only mean danger and excitement to me, it meant pushing back whatever limitation I felt. After the tragedy at Le Mans, I went big game hunting in Africa with just a bow and arrow. My first kill was a black leopard and I had to carry it for miles over my shoulders with its blood soaking into my skin. Later I found out that it was an endangered species. There were only a handful of the animals left in the world, and I had killed one of them. After that I could never kill anything again."

"Fiona said that you seemed very different," Kate suggested. "She said you'd changed so much while you were in India that she scarcely recognized you when you showed up on Coral Key."

Skip poured them each another glass of wine. "Something did happen to change me, but I'm not really sure myself exactly what it was. All I know is that between one moment and the next my entire perception of both myself and the world around me changed irrevocably and forever."

"Fiona said that you were traveling around India with an Indian holy man. Some kind of spiritual master, to whom people attributed all kinds of miracles."

Skip nodded and gazed out over the harbor with a faraway look in his eyes, a look that spoke of sky and distance.

"I went to Nepal to climb Annapurna," Skipper continued, "but on the way I stopped at Benares during a religious festival called the *Kumbala*. It was there I met a man called Baba Muktananda, and it seemed as if my entire life had been carrying me toward that place at that particular hour on that particular day. From the very first moment, I knew that he accepted me exactly as I was, without any kind of judgment. All the great spiritual masters are like that. They can just look at you and know everything there is to know. I guess I had always been looking for some way to approach life so that everything didn't always end up turning to crap. By the time I met Baba, I was carrying around one hell of a lot of unnecessary baggage. He gave me back *myself*. It wasn't really a question of being transformed into something or someone else. It was more like becoming the person that I was always meant to be."

At that moment their waiter appeared bearing bowls of clam chowder, plates of crisply fried soft-shell crabs, and a platter of steaming bright red lobsters. Kate was suddenly famished and very glad that she had come.

"The food looks fabulous," she said after taking a sip of her wine. "But what happened to the fireworks on the wharf you promised me? It is midnight, you know."

Skip looked sheepish as he began heaping her plate with the bounty of the bay. "I guess I was even willing to lie in order to get you to have dinner with me," he admitted. "I just made that up about the fireworks."

"You're forgiven," she said. "But what I'd really like to know is how you found out I have a passion for soft-shelled crabs."

It was three A.M., and their bodies lay entwined upon the deck of the *Westwind* beneath an infinite blue dome shimmering with stars. A soft, cool breeze caressed Kate's face and bare breasts and shoulders as she lay listening to the soft lapping of the waves against the hull, and the creaking of the gaff-rigged halyards straining against the masts.

The *Westwind* rode the light swell at the end of the Montauk fishing pier with a gentle rocking motion. Skip had just completed a total renovation of the schooner, and the eggshell-white hull was reflected in the dark harbor water. The masts and deck had been newly varnished, and the brightly polished brass work gleamed against the running lights strung from the bow to the stern. He had done it all himself, and Kate was exceedingly appreciative of the results.

Skip and Kate were lying together inside a heavily quilted sleeping bag. "Are you asleep?" she questioned, rising up on one elbow and running her fingers through his shaggy blond hair. His bare chest rose and fell with deep, even respirations.

"Uh . . . uh," he muttered. "Just resting my eyes."

"I'd like to know about *him*," Kate said after a moment.

"About this Baba Muktananda. You said that something happened. That afterwards you saw the world in a completely different perspective."

Skip opened his eyes and his gaze was guileless and penetrating. "I'm not sure if I have the words to explain exactly what happened. It was so strange . . . unlike anything I ever experienced, or even imagined. When he touched me, I found myself wrapped in a flame-colored cloud. For an instant I thought of fire, an immense conflagration. But in the very next moment I knew that the fire was within myself.

"Afterwards, Baba stood smiling down into my eyes, and I experienced a sense of incredible exultation. Of immense joyousness accompanied by an intellectual illumination that's just impossible to describe. I no longer believed the universe to be composed of dead matter, Kate. It's living presence, and I was fully conscious of being in possession of eternal life. Not just the conviction that I would have eternal life, but the actual awareness that we are all *immortal*."

Chapter Nineteen

Kate slept late on Saturday morning, and awakened only when the sun had reached in through the studio windows to warmly touch her face.

She stretched languidly, allowing her eyes to drift slowly about the familiar room with its chintz curtains, Early American furniture, and colorful scattering of rag rugs. Everything seemed brightly cheerful, and Kate was in no hurry to begin the all too familiar rituals of her life—all that would have previously kept her fully occupied until time to return to work in the city, early on Monday morning.

She snuggled down beneath the big fluffy down comforter. It was enough just to lie there. Not have to be or to do anything, just allow her imagination to drift like a feather on the breeze. As lightly as the hundreds of golden Monarch butterflies she could see drifting fitfully beyond the windows.

Once a year, and always in July, the Monarchs migrated

south, and the grass, trees, and foliage surrounding the cottage were dotted with the flutter of black and golden wings.

Kate thought of Skip, and for an intense, longing moment she wished he were lying there beside her. But instead, she had driven back from Montauk at five in the morning.

It disturbed her that Brian Brophy was at least fifteen years younger than she, and Kate had no intention of advertising the fact that she was sleeping with a youthful lover. Gossip traveled with the speed of light in the summer Hamptons, and behaving like some desperate middle-aged woman on the make definitely came under the heading of very unattractive behavior. God knows, she didn't want to begin acting like Celia Randolph.

Even so, there could be no question about the powerful sensual currents running just beneath the surface of her coolly competent reserve. Kate closed her eyes and wondered at the heady sense of arousal that caused her entire body to tingle expectantly.

She stroked her bare breasts lightly and allowed scenes from the previous evening to float lazily across her mind like drifting summer clouds.

After finishing dinner, she and Skip had walked hand in hand down the wharf to where the *Westwind* was moored. Once inside the commodious teakwood cabin, the instant sexuality was like an explosion between them.

Both of them had known all evening what was going to happen, and as Skip reached out to pull her close against him, Kate melted into his arms and sought his lips.

In that moment, she felt that somehow they had always been destined to be lovers. Their differences in age and life style meant absolutely nothing. At least for the moment. After all, she had not the slightest intention of falling in love with him.

For a long while they lay on one of the bunks, holding one another closely, touching and exploring as their bodies moved together, kissing long and deeply, like lovers reunited after a long and painful parting.

In the dimness of the cabin Kate looked like a young girl, slim and delicate, with softly molded contours over which his hands moved as if her body contained some rare treasure. His fingers seemed to sear her flesh as one by one the garments fell away. All that was alien, all that separated the necessary closeness of his hard and muscular body, arching and pressing along the length of her.

No words were spoken and none were necessary. Ultimately all the barriers had fallen away, and their mouths ground hungrily together. An urgency took possession of them, running in the blood like fever, until they were hovering on the very brink of orgasm.

Now, lying there with the sun splashing in upon her through the skylight windows, Kate shivered slightly as she conjured up Skip Brophy's regular, unlined features, the deep-set blue eyes crinkling at the corners when he smiled.

She'd have to watch herself, Kate realized. Brian "Skipper" Brophy wouldn't be all that hard to fall in love with.

Filled with sensual intoxication, Kate allowed another face to float across the screen of her mind. It was the darkly sensual visage of Doctor Andreas Jaccard.

Kate shuddered from head to foot with a violent whiplash spasm that left her gasping for breath. Then abruptly the phone shrilled beside the couch, and she lurched upward, blinking against the bright sunlight flooding the room.

Finally, after allowing the phone to ring a full five times, Kate lifted the receiver to her ear. "Hello," she finally answered in a breathless voice.

"I'm sorry Kate . . . but I'm afraid I have some bad news for you."

It was Skipper's voice coming from the other end of the line, sounding hollow and uncanny. ''I just got a call from the Southhampton Medical Center,'' he informed her. ''My mother was brought in by ambulance this morning.

''She's dead, Kate.''

Chapter Twenty

Fiona's grave was marked by a surprisingly simple marble gravestone bearing the date of her birth and the month and year of her death. Sheik Nessim had insisted on honoring the woman he loved by having her Bedouin name carved in Arabic, a sentimental touch that Kate found entirely appropriate for the extraordinary occupant of the simple grave beneath the sheltering limbs of beach and laurel.

Considering the extravagance of her existence, the conspicuous consumption in which she reveled, and Fiona's passion for living life to the fullest, it was actually a wonder that she had managed to survive so long, Kate mused. For from the very first moment of their meeting, she had realized that Fiona had always been extremely breakable.

There were of course the scandals, the heartbreaks, and the wild marital escapades. Yet always, just beneath the gilded mask of sophistication, was a real person. A woman of genuine warmth, compassion, and generosity, who lived beneath the platinum façade.

From the shady hillside where Fiona had been laid to final rest there was a fine view of Shinnecock Harbor, with the ghostly white *Sultana* still riding at anchor. Kate blinked hard against the tears that welled and brimmed. It had been only a week since the gala Fourth of July party aboard the yacht, and yet the world had already begun to seem a very different place.

Nothing could have possibly prepared Kate for the double tragedies she had so recently endured. First there had been Adrianna's tragic collapse at Lincoln Center, and now—Fiona.

Her passing had made headlines around the world. According to the doctor who signed the death certificate, Fiona had succumbed to cardiopulmonary arrest.

The crack paramedic team who had been called to the *Sultana* at six o'clock in the morning had made a desperate effort to revive her. But Fiona was pronounced dead upon arrival at the Southhampton Medical Center.

After placing a bunch of violets at the head of the grave, Kate dabbed at her eyes with a crumpled handkerchief, slipped on a pair of dark glasses, and started walking back down the gravel path to where she had parked her car. It was Friday afternoon and she had left the office and driven out from New York City immediately following lunch.

It had been a blistering day, but here in the shade of the trees it was cool. Kate walked slowly past the ancient graves pressed and crowded in death. The mouldering wreathes and faded floral tributes. The badly sculpted angels and mournful virgins with upturned sightless eyes. Underlying everything was the damp, pungent earth smell that spoke of the past and of death.

Kate could not help but recall Andreas Jaccard's words that day in his study, looking at Fiona's X-rays.

"What we have, Miss Leslie . . . is a remission. It could last a month, a year, or even a lifetime. There's just no way of knowing how long Fiona will survive."

Barely six weeks later she was gone. The cancer had been waiting for her like a loaded gun in the hands of a hired assassin.

Kate found Skipper waiting for her in front of the old stone church with its ivy-covered walls and lovely stained-glass windows. He had mysteriously disappeared after alerting her to Fiona's death, and his absence was widely noted by the press.

"I've been worried about you," Kate said as she approached the stone bench upon which he was sitting. Skip was dressed in sandals, faded jeans, and t-shirt, shaggy haired, sunburned, and slightly gaunter than she remembered.

He appeared somber and saddened as she sat down beside him and took his large, tanned hand in both her own. "I took the *Westwind* out to sea for a few days. I guess I just wasn't willing to face the funeral and all the publicity. It would have served no purpose. My mother's gone now. The sideshow is over."

Kate was unable to hold his eyes, to see his pain. "I was with Fiona aboard the *Sultana* when she thought she was going to die. We talked about it and I want you to know that she was at peace with herself. Death didn't frighten her anymore. Her only wish was to be reunited with you before she passed on. She knew there was no way of telling how long the cancer would stay in remission."

Skip shook his head with a dogged, weary motion. "I guess that's what's really bothering me, Kate. I've got this funny feeling that my mother didn't really die from cancer. I think it was something else."

"Something else . . . ?" Kate echoed.

Once again he nodded, drawing his hair back from his face with one hand. ''I've just got this eerie feeling that it had something to do with those injections that Jaccard was giving her on Coral Key.''

Chapter Twenty-one

It was a glorious summer morning with a hot July sun burning down from a clear and cloudless sky. They had started out from Amagansett at nine A.M. in Kate's Bentley. It was Saturday, and while Skip had steadfastly refused to inform her of their ultimate destination, Kate guessed where he was taking her as soon as they drove across the George Washington Bridge and headed north along the Palisades Parkway.

The Hudson River shimmered off through the trees on their right, spangled and molten in the bright morning sunlight. Skip was deeply immersed in one of his quiet, contemplative moods, and they spoke little on the journey north, each of them lost in silent thoughts.

The idea of an Indian holy man holding forth from an old borscht belt hotel in the Jewish Alps struck Kate as more than slightly ludicrous. But there was a great deal more than that behind her reluctance to come face to face with Skipper's highly touted Indian guru.

Perhaps, Kate pondered, the difficulty lay in the fact that among the trendy pace-setters of the whirlwind seventies, the title of *guru* had gained wide acceptance as instant media hype.

Kate had never involved herself with the art of being faddishly *au courant,* and instinctively distrusted most everything she had read or heard about the so-called Higher Consciousness Movement—all that Buddhist chanting, Zen meditation, zone therapy, and Transactional Analysis that came bubbling along the chic-speak pipeline, promising to eliminate pain entirely, or at least to lower the decibel count to an acceptable level of healthy neurosis.

It was the kind of talk one invariably heard studding the boozy wash of conversation in all those *chi chi* Manhattan hangouts frequented by the city's creative elite. All those ambitious, upwardly mobile types committed to the frantic business of shaping and molding the taste, style, and thinking of an entire culture run amuck with its own creative exuberance.

Brian Brophy was anything but part of that world. Nor was he a glassy-eyed space cadet, intent upon escaping reality. According to him, Baba Muktananda was the guru with a difference.

He was, in fact, a *Sadguru,* a highly respected spiritual master who had only recently come to America. As the guardian of an ancient and very powerful spiritual lineage, Muktananda in many ways was a direct throwback to distant antiquity. Back to the time when Hindu ascetics wandered alone in the wilderness, seeking enlightenment through a life of dedicated austerity.

According to Skipper, Muktananda could take away people's addictions. Anything from alcoholism and drug addiction to compulsive fear of failure. He also claimed that Baba was more than anything else a mirror, endlessly reflecting the truth about yourself.

The Catskill Mountains were a place of sweet summers, lush woodlands, numerous clearwater lakes, and broad mountain meadows covered with wildflowers. But then to the Hindus, Kate recalled, mountains had always symbolized immortality, and the source of all spiritual life.

Finally, at the end of a long and winding country road, they arrived at the old De Ville Hotel, which has been converted into a temporary ashram by Muktananda's American followers. Yet it wasn't at all the kind of monastic atmosphere that Kate had been expecting to find.

Instead she found herself walking up the steps of a comfortably shabby white-shingled structure overlain with an exotic Eastern veneer. In the spacious lobby there were garlanded shrines, hanging plants, fresh-cut flowers, and bamboo cages full of chirping birds.

The reception area was filled with men and women who were mostly attired in colorful Indian dress. Then quite suddenly the guru was among them, moving swiftly down a flight of carpeted stairs and into the lobby, surrounded by a scurrying entourage.

Muktananda didn't look anything like Kate's own preconception of what a living saint should look like. In fact, the small brown man in the bright red socks, dark glasses, and orange knitted ski cap cut a decidedly outrageous figure.

Yet all around her people were bowing and smiling, as if they were in possession of some profound personal awareness.

It was true that everything about Muktananda was vivid, and that he appeared to effortlessly radiate some quality that demanded recognition. It was as if a great actor had suddenly appeared on stage, instantly drawing his audience to him with magnetic certainty.

Was that all he was, Kate wondered? Just a consummate showman in the land of the large green dollar bills?

Muktananda appeared to have read her thoughts and turned sharply, allowing his amber-golden eyes to flicker over her as he and his entourage swept past.

It all happened very fast. Not a single word had passed between them, yet Kate had the strongest sense of having made contact with some kind of extraordinary phenomenon.

The meditation hall where Muktananda sat every afternoon was a cavernous high-ceilinged room with veils of drifting incense softly wreathing the scene with mystical intonations.

The guru sat upon a raised turquoise divan at the head of the room. Several hundred people had already gathered for Muktananda's afternoon *Darshan*. There was the sweet, dark smell of incense, the buzz of crickets, the lazy chimera of summer heat, and a feeling of deeply intense absorption.

It was the traditional gathering of the faithful at the feet of the guru for chanting, meditation, and questions about the ultimate meaning, content, and nature of human existence.

Everyone was staring at Muktananda, who sat easily on his thronelike chair, leaning forward to greet people and laughing occasionally with a rich, deep musical laughter that shook his entire body. He was gowned in orange silk, and his skin was dark and velvety.

Kate took a place at the back of the room among the women, who were separated from the men by a wide plush-carpeted aisle. At that particular moment it was lined with the guru's devotées, carrying various offerings of fruit, flowers, and gifts to lay at his red-stockinged feet.

The subdued wail of an Indian sitar played in the background, and in spite of the large number of people present, there was a familiar, easy intimacy to the proceedings. What seemed to Kate like a sense of family, as the waiting devotées bowed reverently at the guru's feet and placed their offerings in a large wicker basket. Baba appeared to be enjoying himself enormously as he genially swatted each of them with an opulent wand of shimmering peacock feathers.

Muktananda was possessed of an almost grandfatherly affability, but Kate sensed a deep inner remoteness in him as well. He had an essential dignity that defied containment or easy familiarity, and there was something quite lordly and avian in his movements. In the way he would suddenly swivel his head around, it was not in the least difficult for Kate to imagine an elegantly crested peacock with its proud neck scarved in rich plumage.

His eyes seemed to seek her out. They were amber bright and sharply intent. Momentarily they would narrow and then widen abruptly, as if scanning the proceedings from some incredible avian height, or perhaps even some other dimension of reality.

A translator had risen, and the questions being addressed to the guru were exactly the sort of questions that made Kate extremely uncomfortable with the entire Higher Consciousness Movement. They dealt mostly with swimming blue lights, esoteric visions, and mystical revelations of one sort or another.

As far as Kate was concerned, they were the kind of questions she instinctively distrusted. Questions that had passed some point of no return, and no longer dealt with any kind of tangible reality. Nothing, in any case, that she could encompass in her own day-to-day frame of reference.

Then, intruding suddenly upon the peacefully euphoric scene, came a voice that was honed to a razor's edge with intense psychic pain.

It came from a spectrally thin, pale-as-ashes young woman who had dropped to her knees at the guru's feet. Appearing ravaged and unkempt, she began to speak in short, painful gasps that immediately brought Kate forward in her seat, straining to catch every word.

As she spoke, the woman's voice became increasingly fragmented and emotionally charged. Then finally she broke down altogether, and her whip-thin body shook with dry, rasping sobs as it trembled uncontrollably.

The woman sketched a desperate plea toward the figure of Muktananda, and he began speaking to calm her in gentle, reassuring tones. It was then, quite suddenly, that Kate realized she herself was trembling with intense feeling.

She too had experienced the nightmares of which the woman spoke, and she had often known the cold, visceral horror of falling endlessly through a dark and swirling void.

Like the woman with the ravaged face and terror-haunted eyes, she too had awakened crying out in the darkness because she existed so far from the light.

Chapter Twenty-two

There was a new vibrance and electricity in the air at Caramour, and Kate herself had never before experienced such a sustained rush of creative energy. Her days were long, demanding, and often brutal. Yet they were also stimulating in a way that reminded her of working alongside Paul Osborn during those early years of empire building.

Kate liked the feel of being able to make things happen, and as far as Dayne and Baxley were concerned the long weeks of summer were a period of grace. While Paul remained out of touch somewhere in the Mediterranean, Kate was definitely calling all the shots, with Henri effectively exiled to the company's Paris headquarters and Ted spending most of his time on the golf links of the Westchester Country Club.

Overall, Kate had the feeling that her life was changing at a rate that made her sometimes suspect that she had lodged in a dream.

The truth of the matter was that the beauty business was the ultimate purveyor of dreams. A kaleidoscopically changing industry that took fish scales, seaweed, ambergris, flower oils, sulfides, acids, and a variety of distinctly unglamorous ingredients, and whipped them together into endlessly varied combinations that sold ten billion dollars' worth of hopes and dreams each year.

Kate had realized from the very beginning that she would have to change the company's corporate image completely if she was to have any hope of success. Under Paul Osborn, Caramour had ground out products in huge quantities, taken long risks with trendy new lines and as often as not, wound up getting back truckloads of unsold merchandise from stores when sales slumped or interest in the new products failed to materialize.

"Cash and Carry Katie" was what they had begun calling her during her first thirty days as president. Even though she had always considered herself to be most at home in the creative department, Kate discovered she was very good at analyzing balance sheets, quarterly reports, and profit and loss statements. Then she would pick up the phone and make dozens of calls to the firm's suppliers, wholesalers, and even competitors, in order to find the answers to questions she found endlessly engrossing.

Right off the mark, Kate had begun to change the way things were done at Caramour by instituting an austerity budget along with tight inventory controls and detailed accounting procedures for all departments. She also issued an Executive Order requiring that "customers must pay their bills within sixty days of delivery," or be forced to put up substantial security bonds.

It had been long-term company policy to borrow heavily from banks in order to finance the variety of new products that were always in development. Kate was horrified to discover that each year Caramour was paying millions of dollars in interest on back notes, and called a halt to the practice immediately.

As the weeks passed, the new corporate image that began to emerge was slim, trim, and of necessity self-supporting. But it didn't stop there.

Traditionally, Caramour had glutted the market with cosmetics, toiletries, and fragrances in every possible price range and available in a variety of outlets, from the most exclusive department stores to national retail drug chains.

Kate's approach to running the company far more profitably was to limit production and increase creativity, while reserving all major decisions subject to her own *Imprimatur.*

By the first week in August, Caramour was in the business of designing a very few innovative new products, launched with packaging and advertising, geared to carefully targeted markets. Rejuvenal was to be the first of the new product lines to hit the market, and Kate fervently hoped that it would serve to establish Caramour with an entirely new and highly streamlined corporate persona.

Industrious, resourceful, and brimming with a totally new sense of self-confidence, Kate had quickly become a force to be reckoned with in the cosmetic industry. Her revolutionary concept of a total skin-care package that promised almost immediate and near miraculous results had sent competitors scrambling to develop something similar in their labs.

But that as Kate was well aware, would take between twelve and twenty-four months, which quite literally gave Caramour a powerful corner on the market she was in the process of creating.

The ultimate success of Rejuvenal depended largely on Kate's ability to have it available in a select number of prestigious outlets across the country by mid-November. Almost one-third of all sales were rung up between Thanksgiving and Christmas when men indulged the women in their lives, and women tended to indulge themselves.

The entire beauty industry, in fact, revolved around making women feel attractive, and the growing national preoccupation with youthful appearance and total physical fitness at any age.

Kate found that it was also necessary to take demographic and social changes into consideration. As birth rates continued to drop, and the postwar baby boom reached their thirties, the population was aging. But perhaps most importantly, just over half of all American women now had jobs, and it was the working women who had both the need and the cash to buy cosmetics and the more expensive skin-care products. They also used 39 percent more cosmetics than nonworking women and demanded that the various products they purchased could be applied quickly and easily, as part of a daily beauty regimen for the modern woman continually on the go.

Through the use of Jaccard's exclusive formulations, the Rejuvenal line had blossomed into five individual products. An Antiwrinkle crème to counter the first signs of aging and loss of skin elasticity. A Crème du Jour to aid in fighting the environmental ills that so commonly attacked the skin.

Le Crème du Soir was a powerfully formulated application that miraculously strengthened the tone of the skin, while almost erasing overlarge pores and crêpiness around the throat. Kate herself had worked to help formulate the Placental Masque, which invariably provided a dramatic lift for tired-looking complexions.

Finally there was La Beauté du Lait, which was designed to cleanse away every last trace of makeup, in order to leave the skin fresh and moist after each application.

Kate often experienced a heady sense of accomplishment at having been able to bring Andreas Jaccard's miraculous formulations onto the market. And she had very specific ideas about how she wanted to promote the entirely new product line.

Kate firmly believed that merchandising any original beauty concept required the ability to zero in on a specific target. From the very beginning, the RJ-12 promotion had been geared toward the image-conscious career woman who felt that she owed it to herself to remain as youthfully radiant and attractive as possible, for as long as possible.

By the end of August Kate had surrounded herself with a talented staff of women who in themselves appeared to fit perfectly that description. The managerial staff at Caramour was no longer dominated by men, but was in fact run far more competently by a corps of lady lawyers, fashionably dressed accountants, and an impressive cadre of pants-suited sales personnel who smoked Virginia Slims and treated jobbers and wholesalers to three-martini luncheons.

Kate made it a point to involve herself with every aspect of Rejuvenal, following each new product from the conceptual stage on through development, production, and ultimately packaging and marketing. There was simply not enough time to commission the various research projects over which she had labored so assiduously in the past. In order to save time wherever possible, and cut corners when practical, Kate had to rely largely on her own instincts.

She quickly became a walking market survey, and there was no detail too small to escape her attention. Trying to fit the new product line into the mental picture that women had of themselves in the late 1970s was an intriguing and sometimes risky and complicated process. One in which the packaging and advertising had to work together in order to present a unified appeal to the emotions, from which Caramour expected to reap enormous prestige and financial rewards.

A decade earlier it had been Kate's ability to project what made women feel good about themselves that had been largely responsible for the New Natural Look in cosmetics. Now she was equally convinced that the trend of women's liberation had begun to shift from feminist to feminine, to an underlying yearning in women for glamor and allure.

Bearing that in mind, Kate had ordered production of a new Caramour fragrance that was guaranteed to capture the same seductive mood. It was called L'Immortal, and was destined to become the romantic accent note for the entire Rejuvenal products line, which was slated to expand eventually into a variety of cosmetic applications.

Kate had come under the spell of the tropics during her visit to the Caribbean, and she was fortunately blessed with what the fragrance industry called a "nose."

She knew exactly what she wanted in a new scent, and worked with Caramour's top chemists for over a week, experimenting with various combinations. Kate insisted from the beginning that she didn't want anything too obvious, and the price had to be affordable for mass marketing.

First she experimented by mixing jasmine and tuberose with iris and patchouli, in order to establish a basically floral high note. Then, on a more subliminal level, she added ambergris, sandalwood, and ylang ylang blossoms to capture the subtle lower notes that turned out to be as compelling as a balmy tropic breeze.

Ultimately, L'Immortal was a thoroughly modern fragrance that was still mysterious, feminine, and entirely compelling. Whenever Kate herself wore it during the testing period, she was pleased to discover that it always gave her mood a decided lift.

A lift was often exactly what she needed to keep up the consistently frenzied pace of twelve- to fourteen-hour days in the corporate pressure cooker. For the time being at least, Kate had been able to keep Dayne, Baxley, and I.C.E. at bay, but she knew that it was only a question of time. The vultures were circling, waiting patiently for her to make some fatal error, so they could swoop in to greedily divide the spoils.

Whenever she felt harried, pressed for time, and beset by on-the-job tensions, Kate turned her thoughts toward Muktananda, closed her eyes, and slipped off into meditation for five or ten minutes. The fascination had been there from the very beginning, planted like an exotic seed. Often she recalled in detail her visit to the Catskills. In her mind's eye the shabby old De Ville hotel seemed to shimmer and vibrate in the sunlight beneath a sky of cloudless blue, shining and luminous against the lush green woodland backdrop.

By the beginning of August she began seeing Muktananda's pictures all over New York. They were on posters inscribed with the enigmatic message BE WITH BABA. He seemed to be watching her with those incredible hypnotic eyes from billboards, the plywood walls surrounding Manhattan construction sites, on the exit doors of a porno movie house on Forty-second Street, and finally from a lamppost directly in front of her Upper East Side apartment building.

Suddenly everybody seemed to be talking about "the living saint from India." In *Time* and *Newsweek* magazines, he was billed as the newest "Ultra-Chic Guru" among afficionados of the Eastern mystical scene, a fully realized spiritual master who did something that nobody else was doing, at least not in America in 1976.

Muktananda embodied the rare capacity to transmit his own conscious spiritual energy to others. He was said to be able to energize that place deep within each human being where they were inherently perfect.

The Hindus had been calling the process of spiritual awakening by the name of *Shaktipat* for several thousand years. Those who had received this transmission of spiritual power during the guru's whirlwind visit to America were quoted in various articles as having experienced "brilliant flashes of light, esoteric visions, ethereal music, sudden rushes of love,'' and, among some female devotées, ''instant orgasm.''

During Kate's own encounter with the guru there had been no mystical visions or delphic revelations. She was still convinced that falling under the spell of even such a highly charismatic guru as Muktananda was tantamount to admitting that you simply couldn't make it on your own.

Even so, he was often in her thoughts. For just an instant, with Muktananda's eyes upon her, she had turned within to become aware of a bright, luminous point of inner consciousness, radiating light, warmth, and knowledge. A fundamental part of her being that she had never even known was there.

The beach was deserted, empty, and strewn with driftwood and long trailing streamers of seaweed washed up by the outgoing tide. Kate estimated that she must have walked at least a mile up the beach toward Montauk Point that afternoon. She was breathing hard and felt the chill bite of the offshore wind and the cool dampness of the sand beneath her feet.

It was only two o'clock in the afternoon. But already the sun was diffused with a hazy corona and banks of low-lying cloud.

Kate drew Skipper's heavy cardigan sweater closer about her, and paused to listen to the thunder of the surf. It was a low, soft, booming sound, gently underlain by the whispering of the golden-bearded sea grass rippling across the dunes.

Kate shielded her eyes against the hazy glare to watch the massive green combers pile in one upon another from the sea without break or pause. A solitary gull came winging in over the dunes, crying out in a shrill, tuneless voice.

She felt chilled and tired after the long walk up the beach, and, climbing higher into the dunes, Kate sought the refuge of an ancient tree trunk that lay half-buried in the sand. It had been bleached and scoured by the sea until the surface was smooth and satiny. The upturned roots beseeched the lowering gray sky, like the limbs of spirits in torment. It reminded Kate of Andreas Jaccard's sculpture.

Sheltering against the stiff wind blowing in from the sea, Kate shook a cigarette from her pack and drew the smoke deep into her lungs. The nicotine tasted bitter and dark on her palate. Kate realized suddenly that she was now back to smoking at least two packs a day. Back to what she was smoking when a young man by the name of Brian Skip Brophy stepped so confidently into her life.

Basically they had both always been loners. Skip seemed to sense exactly what Kate needed in the way of psychic space, and he had never intruded upon the hectic and demanding business life that absorbed her completely throughout the week.

Often when she arrived in Amagansett on Friday evening, utterly exhausted from her crushing work schedule, Skip would be waiting for her with a jug of dago red, a warm embrace, and a macrobiotic diet dinner for two in the wok.

From the beginning their relationship had been imbued with a sense of comfortable domesticity. But aside from being friends, they were highly passionate lovers as well.

Skip made love to her with great gentleness, thoughtfully yet naturally, and with complete understanding. She loved his lean young body, and had begun to sense something deeper in his caring for her. It seemed to Kate to be a very fragile and tender feeling, and she was almost afraid that by acknowledging the intensity of her own response the feeling might evaporate like the morning mists of autumn.

It wasn't quite love, at least not yet, but it was something very close to it.

Brian Brophy was the kind of man whose quiet strength and reasoned response to life had gradually begun to give

Kate a sense of emotional security and balance she needed in order to be able to function at her peak of performance.

By the time that Friday evening came around each week she found she was able to put Caramour completely behind her. Kate actually caught herself humming as she packed her clothes for the weekend, always with Skipper in mind. Just the thought of two nights and two days together made her feel lightheaded with excitement.

She felt a shiver of desire run through her in anticipation of their lovemaking. Of the weekend to be shared with long moonlit walks along the beach and lazy stolen mornings in bed with Irish coffee. Skip always seemed to comprehend her mood, and never failed to respond as they sailed, swam, jogged, rode horseback, and made love.

But there were long, quiet, contemplative periods as well, as they each read before the fireplace, or just lay side by side on the white fur rug, listening to music on the stereo. Kate had told no one about her affair with Brian Brophy, and the beach house in Amagansett had become their own secret sanctuary. A lovers' lair, entirely private and completely apart from their separate weekday lives.

For the first time since leaving college, Kate began to experience a renewed interest in her painting. Often she sketched and painted while Skip was out wind-surfing on Saturday and Sunday afternoons, and an entirely new sense of perspective had begun to emerge; a newly inspired depth of fulfillment that expressed itself with thick, flowing colors and firm, sure strokes.

Her work that summer was soaring, supple, and often daring in execution. Gradually Kate began to realize that she seemed to have developed a spontaneous feeling for the very nature and substance of things, coupled with a sense of freedom and proportion that seldom erred as long as she trusted it fully.

But now Kate realized, tamping out her cigarette and burying it in the sand, the summer was drawing to a close. Misty dawns had become a part of the season, and there were daisies and goldenrods nodding gently in the meadows as a filmy gauze of whiteness came rolling in from the sea to settle over the dunes.

She could smell the crisp breath of autumn in the air, and wondered what the coming months would bring.

It was almost four o'clock by the time Kate got back to the cottage. After fixing herself a shaker of martinis and putting her favorite Peggy Lee album on the stereo, she moved to stand behind the Hasselblad camera mounted on a tripod before the skylight windows overlooking the beach.

It was an exquisite piece of photographic equipment, with a 250mm tele-tessar lens. Kate took a sip of her martini, lit a cigarette she set burning in a nearby ashtray, and then pressed her eye to the view finder.

Ka-chung . . . Ka-chung went the Hasselblad. Kate leaned into the camera, adjusting the lens in order to draw the solitary figure of the surfer into closer magnification. Outside the house the wind was by now blustery and chill, and Skip was wearing a black rubber wet suit as she captured him crouching and balancing on the face of a huge wave.

Ka-chung . . . Ka-chung. Kate slid her body around the tripod, peering through the telephoto lens as Skip sent the fragile sailcraft shooting into the rushing whitewater. It was a mythic contest, Kate thought. The challenge of man's pure and primitive will to prevail over the elements. *Ka-chung . . . Ka-chung*.

As Kate scanned the scene in closeup, the intimacy of the photographic process in which she had become so raptly engaged began to take on a compelling and sensual aspect. She admired Skipper's courage enormously as he skillfully manned the slim twelve-foot polyurethane board with its twelve-foot mast and over forty square feet of bright red white and blue sail.

The sea was running high with dangerous riptides and erratic waves that gathered far out and then came rushing shoreward to hurtle their seething mass upon the beach. There wasn't really enough light to get the kind of photographic clarity she wanted, since the sun had already begun its descent into the sea, draining the light from the day.

Ka-chung . . . Ka-chung. The camera was like a metronome. *Ka-chung . . . Ka-chung.* An insistent sensual force, demanding that she give herself fully.

It seemed to Kate that Skip handled the sleek and slender sailcraft as if it were a lovely and sensuous woman. A woman fully conscious of her own beauty and grace as she tacked and faltered, then surged suddenly ahead in response to the slightest movement, trailing a graceful plume of whitewater.

Ka-chung . . . Ka-chung. The sound broke against the silence. The record had ended by now, and there was only the crackling of the fire and the sound of the wind in the catalpa trees outside.

Kate had finished her shaker of martinis and her cigarette had burned to ashes. Suddenly she felt the hot, scalding burn of tears, and didn't really know why.

Standing before her, the camera was now silent, with all her passion, yearning, and hope for the future safely locked inside.

Part Three

Autumn Interlude

Chapter Twenty-three

During the first week in October Andreas Jaccard arrived in New York. Kate had not seen him for over five months and she was entirely unsure what her reaction would be to the man she had previously found so sexually compelling.

Any doubts she may have had immediately vanished, however, as Kate saw Andreas striding toward her across the arrivals' lounge at Kennedy Airport. It was almost a shock to see him again—the startling dark eyes, the handsome bronzed features, his tall, commanding presence, causing passersby to turn and stare after him.

Kate felt a knot in the pit of her stomach as they moved toward each other, smiling in greeting. She couldn't seem to think of anything but the gripping compulsion to be in bed with Andreas, having him make love to her. People were looking and Kate wondered a bit absurdly if they could sense her thoughts.

But now it was forty-eight hours later, and Kate's doubts had resurfaced to the point that she was jittery with aprehension about Andreas' gallery showing that evening.

She and Wes were being chauffeured to the Winthrope Gallery in midtown Manhattan. They were already over an hour late as the sleek white Rolls moved slowly through the early evening traffic along Fifth Avenue, and Kate began to wonder if events were not beginning to move rather too fast for her.

"Why do I distinctly get the impression that you've been avoiding our wonder doctor ever since he arrived? Your man Jaccard seems to be charming the pants off just about everybody, and you act as if he's got the plague. Or at the very least, a low-grade venereal infection."

"I don't think that's funny," Kate snapped. "And I haven't been avoiding Andreas. It's just that he has a great many things to accomplish in a very short period of time. His meetings with Drexel . . . with Shanga . . . and with the chemists over at the factory . . . talks with the production people. There just hasn't been a spare moment since I picked Andreas up at the airport. I'm sure he understands the situation, so I don't see why it should be bothering you."

Wes flicked a bit of lint from the sleeve of his immaculately tailored tuxedo. "Funny," he observed a bit ruefully, "but I got the impression that there was more to it than that. I guess it must sound pretty silly, but I sort of got the idea that something might have happened between the two of you down in Jamaica. You know what I mean. A beautiful tropical island—the sea, the sand, and the stars. Who could resist?"

"Absolutely nothing happened," Kate snapped. "Andreas and I are strictly business. He's a married man and as far as I'm concerned, that's all there is to it."

But was that all there was to it? Kate wondered as she turned away to stare out through the window toward the brightly lit shop windows on Fifth Avenue. As usual, Wes was right on target. It was true that something about Andreas Jaccard seemed to act upon her like a highly potent aphrodisiac. How much longer, Kate wondered, could she continue to resist?

In spite of the fall chill in the air, there was a waiting crowd of onlookers clustered in front of the gallery as the Rolls pulled up to the curb. A uniformed doorman hurried across the sidewalk to open the rear door. Kate stepped out flashing long, lovely legs as she was ushered past the jostling throng and through the double glass doors.

Wes was no more than a few steps behind her, and they had scarcely stepped inside when Dwight Winthrope himself came bustling across the wine-red carpeting. "My dear . . . dear Miss Leslie." He beamed, lifting her extended hand to his lips with an absurdly courtly gesture.

"I'm awfully sorry to be so late," Kate responded. "It was something quite unavoidable."

Winthrope brushed the apology aside with an airy wave. He presented a slender, willowy, and faultlessly tailored figure, with suspiciously golden hair and finely manicured hands. Quite obviously he had big eyes for Wes.

"Simply everyone has turned up for the showing," he pronounced. "And *your friend* Doctor Jaccard is divine."

Kate tried not to visibly wince. It was already clear that the entire evening was something that would simply have to be endured. She smiled stiffly.

"How about showing us around?" Wes asked. "I'm anxious to have a look at Jaccard's work, and I know that Miss Leslie is equally anxious to congratulate the sculptor."

Kate could have kicked him in the shins for that. But instead she kept on smiling throughout a flurry of introductions as they made their way through the glittering array of Social Register guests. The gallery extended up a broad flight of stairs to another floor, and on through several long and narrow *gallerias* to the sunken sculpture garden entirely enclosed by glass.

Ever since seven that evening limousines had been pulling up to the curb out in front to disgorge a stream of formally attired guests. The atmosphere was expensively expectant; perfumed and murmurous with excited whisperings.

Quite obviously the mood of the crowd was exceedingly upbeat, and Kate worked hard to keep her smile intact. From the crystal chandeliers hanging overhead the light seemed to melt and pour over the shimmering white sculptures.

By now Wes and Dwight Winthrope were several steps ahead, sharing a convivial joint. They were chatting easily together about the showing, and Kate took the opportunity to fall further behind, moving slowly from one sculpture to the next while sipping from a glass of champagne with a gloved hand.

She wore a floor-length black-jet sheath that fit her willowy body like a glove, and there was a black lace veil drawn tightly across her features beneath a velvet turbaned hat. Her eye shadow was smoky. Her lipstick was dark red tinged with midnight blue, and she trailed an aura of L'Immortal perfume. It was the new Caramour Nightime Look, which had been labeled "the Aura of an Exceptional Woman" by the advertising department.

Dwight Winthrope was clearly enthusiastic about the showing, and as the three of them browsed among the sculptures, people turned to stare, sleekly lacquered women and stylishly attired men who leaned together in whispered conversation. Kate could feel their eyes upon her, and realized suddenly that she had become something of a celebrity in her own right.

"One of the critics who was here earlier suggested that

Jaccard's work reminded him of discarded chrysalises,'' Winthrope volunteered.

It was a chilling observation, Kate thought, as she deliberately put some space between herself and the garrulous Winthrope. She needed space in which to view Andreas' work, and even Wes had been getting on her nerves all evening.

Yes, the sculptures did remind her of ''discarded chrysalises.'' But they also took on aspects of terror, hallucination, and nightmare. A miscellany of disembodied torsos; of severed heads and anonymous arms and legs, entwined in deathless sleep. Invariably, each of Andreas' individual sculptures appeared ominously silent and muffled in form.

Kate wished she didn't find them so disturbing, but beyond any question there was brilliance evident as well. The sculptures were sensual and stirring. Firm and full in execution, with a flowing sense of scale, of expression and movement. The smooth white plaster had been thickly or thinly molded over the model's anatomy, according to some exquisitely rare aesthetic response. Andreas had mastered the art of forcing the viewer to comprehend the very nature of the human experience in an instant. It was a subtle kind of force.

Abruptly Kate stopped, spilling some of her champagne in the process. *It was Adrianna.* A perfect reproduction of her lovely, enigmatic features, mounted on a broken marble pillaster. It looked to Kate like a death mask.

''I had almost given you up for dead.'' Kate almost jumped out of her skin as Celia's boozy, breezy voice assaulted her from behind.

''It looks as if you invited half of New York,'' Kate observed, trying desperately to recover herself.

Celia flashed her smile. ''I used to think of it as the better half until I found out just how boring they all are. But you did say you wanted this to be a strictly class affair, so I took the hint and left all my new flash trash pals dancing their little tootsies off over at Regine's."

Beautifully coiffed, elegantly gowned, and enveloped in a cloud of Shalimar perfume, Celia looked to be at least three sheets to the wind. "Oh by the way, Katie, did you come with Wes? I just saw him comparing coke spoons with that old queen Winthrope on the way to the men's lounge." She giggled and slipped her arm through Kate's. "What do you think they do in there anyway?"

"I couldn't care less," Kate responded shortly. "Wes has been acting bitchy as hell all night, and I couldn't be happier to be rid of him."

"Well now that I've got you all to myself, Katherine, I'm going to take you down to the sculpture garden and show you the pièce de résistance. The one that Andreas did of me while we were on Coral Key. I was so disappointed that you didn't get here in time to see me unveiled, so to speak. My dear, the crowd went simply wild over my body. You could have heard the clapping and whistling."

"That must have reminded you of your days as a Ziegfeld Follies girl," Kate observed rather tartly.

By now they had started down a spacious flight of stairs descending along a series of suspended catwalks into the glass-enclosed sculpture garden at the rear. "Sshhh," Celia cautioned. "I'm not quite ready to advertise the fact that I was hoofing it around Broadway in the heyday of Florenz Ziegfeld. Anyway, I only did it long enough to marry a millionaire, and I was practically a child bride."

Celia prattled on as Kate swept the two-story tinted-glass enclosure with a glance. She saw him immediately. Like a magnet, Andreas had drawn everyone to him, and was surrounded by an avid cluster of fawning courtiers.

My God, but he was devastatingly handsome in his black

tuxedo, Kate thought. Jaccard was smiling and chatting easily in that sophisticated milieu, as if he somehow held dominion over it. He seemed to convey a subtle but distinctly sexual domination. Kate felt that now familiar knot in the pit of her stomach. The sudden tremor that made her catch her breath at just the sight of him.

It was a most impressive setting, and she herself had placed him in it, Kate realized. All this was her doing. This was what power felt like.

"I suppose that you've heard by now that Fiona didn't leave poor Andreas a sou of that multimillion-dollar research grant. She must have died before she could fill out all the necessary forms. You know how life does seem to be getting terribly complicated, and who can keep up with all the paperwork."

Kate felt numbed by the revelation, but there was still more to come. "The papers said she died before changing her will. Everything went to her son. You know, Katie—the young handsome one. I think his name is Brian something or other."

"I wonder where that leaves Andreas?" Kate mused, anxious to change the subject as quickly as possible. "He's been spending a fortune on this renovation he's doing down there. Wes just informed me tonight that you were planning to fly down to Coral Key to work out the decor."

"I'm off at the end of next week, darling, and I can hardly wait. Can you imagine being able to charge two weeks with Benny Valdez off on my corporate expense account?"

"I thought you were seeing a lot of Jon-Claude Fabiani?"

Celia's laughter was like the ringing of tiny silver bells. "Oh, of course. Jon-Claude is a darling boy," Celia gushed. "But compared to Benny Valdez, there's just no contest. I mean, he is ever so slightly swishy, and not really all that frisky when I do manage to get him into bed." Once again her laughter was a sparkling crescendo of notes. But it struck

Kate as being slightly off-key. She was relieved to see Shanga moving forward to greet them as they reached the bottom of the stairs.

"Before you talk to Andreas, I just wanted to mention that he's given me the most fantastic idea," Shanga breathlessly announced. "Instead of holding the big Rejuvenal kickoff bash at Studio Fifty-four, why don't we rent a plane, fill it full of columnists and social celebs, and fly them down to Coral Key? It's a natural tie-in, and we can get a lot of mileage by turning it into a media event. You couldn't buy that kind of publicity at any price. The hundred thousand or so it would cost is still peanuts."

"What an utterly fabulous idea," Celia chimed in.

"Not tonight, Shanga," Kate said patiently. "I just don't feel up to talking business. Why don't you drop by my office for lunch on Monday? I've got a lot of things I have to go over with you about those video-taped segments you want to film in the boardroom. We'll thrash it out over diet salads, rye crisp, and a couple of double martinis."

Kate placed her hand on Shanga's arm. "And by the way. If you want Wes back, your best chance of finding him is to raid the men's john on the second floor. I think there's a snowstorm blowing up inside."

With that Kate turned and started making her way across the room to where Andreas stood watching her approach. Without a word, he bent to give her a light, affectionate kiss on each cheek. Anyone who saw it might have considered the greeting almost overly casual. But to Kate it was anything but that.

Andreas poured her a glass of wine and placed it in Kate's hand. It was perfectly chilled as she sipped, and the stem crystal glass was cool against her fingertips. Momentarily it gave Kate an object of concentration. A fixed point of reference with which to pull herself together, without ever appearing to miss a beat. At least, she hoped that was the impression she managed to convey.

"Why have you been avoiding me?" he asked.

Kate swirled the champagne in her glass. There was just no way to avoid the truth, and after a moment she looked up to meet his eyes. "I suppose I have been avoiding you, Andreas. It was because I was—"

"Afraid of what would happen between us," he finished for her.

Kate nodded. "You're a very attractive man, you know. Any woman would be tempted."

Jaccard's smile was slightly mocking. "But you, my dear Katherine, have never been the kind of woman to sleep with married men. Isn't that it?"

"Yes," Kate admitted. "I'm afraid that is it."

Andreas sighed deeply and shook his head. "You know, Kate, there are so very many things I like about you, and one of them is your blatant honesty. Of course I hear what you're saying. But I also know you realize that our making love is . . . let's just say, inevitable."

There was a slight widening of Kate's gray-violet eyes as she searched his handsome aquiline features. "How about my putting it to you this way," he suggested. "You're looking incredibly beautiful tonight, my lovely, naive Katherine. We're here together in New York. My wife is three thousand miles away, and I want very much to take you to bed."

Chapter Twenty-four

The Hotel Grande Victoria on Forty-sixth Street east of Broadway spoke of another era. Kate lay gazing up at the ceiling in a streetfront room on the sixth floor with wide and unblinking eyes. Slowly she allowed her gaze to move about the room, assembling details.

The rococo ceiling cornice, painted with flaking floral swag. The sweetly fading cherubs. Badly framed reprints were askew on the garishly papered walls, and flashing neon streamed in through the dingy lace curtains to trace eerie spider-web patterns across the worn carpeting.

The room was strewn with a scattering of feminine apparel. Limp nylons, sheer silken undergarments, a crumpled black-jet evening dress, and ankle-strap heels. A black chiffon scarf was thrown over the single burning lamp, and Kate's Russian sable was tossed carelessly across the back of an old Morris chair.

There was a sense of emptiness inside her as she lay there in that huge ugly bed with its scarred headboard, creaking springs, and starchy linen. Kate felt irrevocably compromised.

She hated that room, but she also thought it was probably just exactly what she deserved.

Andreas Jaccard slept beside her on the bed. Kate turned to stare at him in the dimness, listening to his deep, strong breathing. As his bare chest rose and fell, she could see the slight pulsing of his heartbeat.

Kate thought of a time bomb, ticking away in some silent anonymous room.

It had all begun so differently. Upon arriving at the hotel with Andreas, Kate had been giddy with all the wine she had drunk, and the awareness of what was about to transpire between them.

Even the dreary hotel room had been nothing more than an amusing stage setting. They had even laughed about it. Then Kate was sitting on the edge of the bed and Andreas was bending over her, touching her and kissing her neck, her shoulder and her bare breasts, as her gown fell away beneath his hands.

There was something in the way that Andreas touched her that made Kate's body feel like a highly tuned instrument that he manipulated with infinite expertise. Each gesture, every caress carried the message that she was beautiful and desirable to him.

Lying naked in his arms, Kate felt as if she were being swept away on a rising tide of sensation. Then quite abruptly something changed.

Almost as if he were another person entirely, Andreas grew ruthless and self-serving. He appeared to be exorcising his own personal sexual demons to the exclusion of all else. Kate could not help feeling that, ultimately, her seduction had been nothing more than just another sexual conquest.

She meant nothing to him. Any one of the whores working the street below would have done as well.

But most troubling had been that part of her own sexuality that had responded. That other part of her that Kate had not even known to exist. The mirror-image persona she had seen writhing and twisting beneath him. The voice, so like her own voice, moaning, pleading, and crying out.

It had been pure carnal lust. A raw, desperate kind of sexuality, totally without tenderness or restraint.

There was something quite volatile and perhaps even dangerous about Andreas, Kate realized. Something that both compelled and threatened her in ways she could not begin to comprehend.

Slipping silently from the bed, Kate lit one of Andreas' strong, dark-tasting cigarettes and began to prowl the room with a chenille spread wrapped about her shoulders. She stopped before the open window and drew back the curtains to look down on Forty-sixth Street with its shadowy cotillion of whores.

It had rained sometime after midnight and the pavements were wet and glistening with reflected light. Kate could hear the shrill peal of distant laughter. The sharp tattoo of stiletto heels against the wet sidewalk.

The ice maiden had melted, Kate mused, wondering what Paul would think if he knew.

Even so, Kate realized she was still the daughter of a morally righteous and sternly disciplined father. The very idea of sleeping with another woman's husband had never even been a credible alternative.

There was a slight rustling sound of bed linen from behind her. Kate turned from the window to find that Andreas had awakened. He was lying propped up against the pillows, staring across the room at her with the sheet drawn up around his waist. He patted the empty space beside him and motioned for her to return to the bed. As if it were an arena and she had no choice but to comply.

Slowly and reluctantly Kate moved across the room to sit carefully beside him on the edge of the bed. The cigarette was still burning between her fingers, and there was a half-empty bottle of Stolichnaya vodka on the bed table with two mismatched drinking glasses from the bathroom.

Andreas poured himself a drink, and Kate's stomach turned at the smell of the liquor. Her head was pounding with the dull throbbing of a full-blown migraine. In that moment she could not have felt sorrier that she had come there with him that evening.

He took the burning cigarette from Kate's fingers and dragged deeply.

"I suppose you must have heard about the research grant," he said. "Fiona didn't sign the papers. It leaves me in a rather inconvenient position."

Kate spoke softly, maintaining her composure by an act of will. "I'm sorry, Andreas. I know how much your research means to you. It must have been a terrible disappointment."

His laugh was harsh and grating. "It was rather more than just a disappointment. Ten million dollars might have enabled me to solve the riddle of human aging. As it is, I went ahead with a total renovation of Coral Key. I've put a million dollars alone into rebuilding and modernizing my lab facilities. For the past five months, I haven't even accepted any patients. You, Celia, Adrianna, Fiona, and the Duchess were the last."

"You know I'll do anything I can to help," Kate volunteered. "I have a great deal of belief in your work, Andreas . . . it's changed the course of my own life."

For a moment Andreas continued smoking quietly. Finally he said, "I'm very glad you feel that way, Katherine. Because when we get down to the bottom line, I have no choice but to ask you to bail me out."

Kate was stunned. "What do you mean, bail you out? I'm afraid I don't understand."

"Well, consider this little scenario. What if you were to pick up the *New York Times* and read CARAMOUR STOCK PLUMMETS AS YOUTH-DRUG DOCTOR FILES FOR BANKRUPTCY." Andreas shrugged. "Let's face it, Katherine. It's going to look extremely bad for the Rejuvenal promotion if Coral Key is sold at auction and I'm forced to peddle my services elsewhere. Possibly even to one of your competitors."

Kate could scarcely believe what she was hearing. Andreas certainly didn't appear to be drunk, even though there was a slightly glazed and mocking irony sparking his dark eyes. Her mind reeled with the implications of what he was suggesting.

"Just think about it for a minute," he said, still wearing that half-bemused smile. "Because unless you're willing to make me an offer I can afford to accept, Caramour could stand to lose millions. And you, my lovely Kate, could lose everything you've worked to achieve."

"I . . . I just don't know what to say, Andreas. Somehow I feel as if you're almost threatening me."

"I don't think you should look at it that way," he assured her coolly. "But it is entirely necessary that you understand the urgency of the problem in its truest dimensions. If anything, you should blame your friend Fiona. She was too busy partying out in the Hamptons to even take time to sign the research grant. According to my sources, it was sitting on her desk for over a week awaiting her signature. I'm also told that it was her son Brian who advised her against giving me the money."

Brian Brophy's name, injected so suddenly and almost too casually into the conversation, gave Kate another start. Did Andreas know anything about their relationship? she wondered.

"What exactly is it you want?" Kate questioned, in order to forestall any further discussion on the subject. Ten million dollars was one hell of a lot of money to have slip through your fingers because of a procedural lapse. Perhaps, Kate reasoned, Andreas had a right to be both angry and frustrated. Fiona had clearly left both of them out on a limb.

"What I'm offering you in return for saving our collective necks," Andreas went on in an entirely reasonable voice, "is *exclusivity*. For the sum of five million dollars, I'm willing to sign over fifty-one percent of Coral Key Spa to Caramour, Inc., and give you the right to produce and merchandise any new products developed through my laboratory research for a period of five years. I think that's about right, don't you? Surely I'm worth at least a million dollars a year to Caramour. On the basis of Rejuvenal alone, your corporate stock is up two points already, and every cosmetic company in New York is rushing to put out some kind of facsimile."

Kate turned away from him and tried to rise, but his grip closed around her wrist, forceably restraining her.

"You've got this all figured out, haven't you, Andreas?" Her voice was cold and put distance between them. But Kate didn't say what she really thought. That he had brought her there to that sleazy hotel deliberately in order to compromise her.

Andreas was regarding her shrewdly. "You don't seem to understand, Katherine. My situation is desperate. I have no choice but to resort to desperate measures."

Everything that happened after that happened very fast, with the actual events racing, colliding, and blurring together. There was a loud crash as a heavy-booted heel splintered the door inward, and two men burst into the room, exploding flashbulbs as they came. Shrieking and cursing like an avenging fury, Ingrid Jaccard was right behind them, and in her hand she held a gun.

Chapter Twenty-five

Irma Weintraub sighed and wriggled her fingers through Kate's hair, gently tickling the scalp. "Ya know, Miss Leslie, that Doctor Jaccard is a real dreamboat, if you want my opinion. I saw him on the TV. Anytime he wants to, he can park his shoes under my bed."

Kate reclined in a horizontal position while Irma tipped her head back into the sink and began lathering up her hair with a fragrant herbal shampoo. A hot, steaming towel covered most of Kate's face, and she made no attempt to respond. Instead, she willed her taut muscles to relax in the padded lounge chair, which was adjusted to a semireclining position.

Irma was, of course, a pain. There was no secret about that. But she was also the best in the business, and Shanga had insisted on having her do Kate's hair for the commercial. She was a slender, fiftyish, bleached blonde, with a girlish figure and sharply pretty features. She wore a bright pink dacron smock with the sleeves pushed up to the elbows to accommodate a variety of jangling gold bangles. Her fingernails were her greatest source of personal pride. They were painted a matching hot pink, and were at least an inch long—like talons.

As Irma prattled on, Kate languished in a state of almost unbearable apprehension. Within the past twenty-four hours she seemed to have entered a netherworld of violence and intrigue. A place where the sudden, the unexpected, and the totally unforeseen could loom grotesquely, overshadowing the commonplace events of daily life.

Ever since going to the Grande Victoria Hotel with Andreas the previous Friday night, Kate felt herself to be inhabiting a new and unfamiliar terrain of dangerously shifting sands.

Andreas was something other than the man she had believed him to be. Beneath the sophisticated veneer, the charm, geniality, and fine looks lay another man entirely. Before her very eyes Andreas had undergone a strange and violent metamorphosis. Now Kate found herself inextricably enmeshed in exactly the kind of nightmare she had always abhorred. A sleazy sexual liaison in a cheap hotel with a married man.

Kate had been physically attacked by Ingrid Jaccard and threatened with a gun. Ingrid had struck her several times before Andreas had intervened to beat his wife unconscious with a barrage of naked fists.

Even now, after spending the rest of the weekend shut up in her darkened apartment in a state of shock, Kate could still scarcely believe it had all happened. The detectives with their flashing cameras. The taut faces, thrashing limbs, and garbled, angry voices. A mirror shattered, furniture overturned, and all the while Kate could think of nothing beyond trying to cover her nakedness.

Never, if she lived to be a hundred, would she forget the look in Jaccard's eyes. The nearly inhuman brightness as he bodily dragged Ingrid away from her, and smashed her skull against the wall. Hitting at her again and again with his naked fists.

How far would Andreas have gone if she hadn't intervened? Kate wondered. His fingers were imbedded at Ingrid's throat, and she was making an awful choking sound by the time that Kate was finally able to separate the two.

Ever since it happened, the scene had remained imprinted upon Kate's consciousness. She turned her thoughts away to the proposition with which Andreas had confronted her before Ingrid and the two detectives had broken into their hotel room.

At first she had been stunned by Andreas' coldly calculated assumption that she had no choice but to bail him out of a tight spot. But now, upon reflection, she realized it was a blessing in disguise. The bottom line was that Andreas had presented her with an opportunity of incalculable promise.

It was by now clear that Rejuvenal had vast marketing potential. The RJ-12 skin-care product line was only the beginning. Kate was entirely convinced that Caramour was destined to expand into the rejuvenation spa business on an international scale.

The FDA still refused to permit testing of cellular rejuvenation therapy within the United States, which made Coral Key an immediate and most expedient answer to the question of where to begin.

Kate no longer had any romantic illusions about Andreas Jaccard. The night they spent together at the Hotel Grande Victoria had taken care of that. Jaccard was playing her for all she was worth. But two could play at that game.

Maybe Andreas was right, she pondered. Perhaps they

were both in far too deep even to think of turning back. It was too late for doubts. The only thing now was to win, whatever the cost.

Kate was abruptly transported back into the present as Irma shifted her chair into an upright position, then turned on a hand-held blow-dryer that began moving a rush of hot, dry air over Kate's entire scalp.

Kate removed the hot towel from her face and lifted her head slightly to confront her own pale reflection in the mirror.

Her features appeared strained and tight, the eyes violet shadowed from long sleepless nights and the relentless tensions under which Kate had been laboring.

"I'd sue the ass off that cab company if I were you, Miss Leslie." Irma's intrusive Bronx-baroque accents were almost comic relief, but Kate was in no mood to be amused.

"How about whiplash?" Irma queried thoughtfully. "Did you get checked out by a doctor after the accident?"

"No," Kate murmured. "I didn't really think it was necessary." She reached up to touch her bruised cheek with her fingertips. "The swelling has gone down a lot already."

Irma looked dubious, but before she could comment further Wesley Travis' familiar knock sounded at the door.

"That'll be all for today, Irma," Kate said. "I can comb myself out after Wes does my makeup. He's an absolute magician, and I don't think he's going to have any trouble making me presentable."

"And how's my beauty today?" Wes questioned as Irma gathered her things in preparation to depart. He stood back, scowling at her in the mirror. "Well, the damage isn't exactly irreparable, especially with the right kind of lighting. But I do seem to detect some ugly frown lines around that lovely mouth that are guaranteed to make you look like Grandma Moses on a black and white screen. Are you sure you want to go ahead and film the video segment today? You're the boss, you know. You could call the whole thing off until you're feeling up to it."

Kate took a deep breath and willed her taut facial muscles to relax.

Wes was right. Nothing showed up on camera worse than nervous tension. The dark circles and bruised discoloration could be hidden easily enough with makeup, but tension was the kiss of death before the camera's all-seeing eye.

"That's simply not the way I operate," Kate informed him tartly. "Shanga's already getting the crew together in the boardroom, and this afternoon I have the 'Women on the Move' interview for *Time* magazine. Let's just get on with it, okay?"

She settled back in the padded lounger once again as Wes wrapped a white linen towel about her head. "Well at least this may teach you to stay out of kamikaze taxis in midtown Manhattan. I mean let's face it, Kate, the company does provide you with a chauffeur-driven Rolls Royce and you might as well take advantage of it."

"Taking advantage has never been something I did very well," Kate said acidly. "It's very simple, Wes. I take taxis when I'm in a hurry to get where I'm going and don't want to be saddled with a chauffeur waiting around for me. Now will you please just get on with my makeup? I've got one hell of a rough day ahead of me, and you're not helping."

"Trust me," Wes said, placing two bright yellow capsules in Kate's hand and running her a glass of water. "Just gulp these right down and don't ask any questions. I can guarantee the results."

Reluctantly Kate did as he suggested, and then dropped her head back against the chair. She closed her eyes as Wes began smoothing on a specially prepared liquid base to erase the telltale bruise and even up the dark circles. Then, using a sable-tipped artists' paintbrush, he applied a glistening application of dark red lipbase, before going on to select from a wide array of creme blushes, powders, tints, and various eye liners.

In less than twenty minutes he had created a smoothly stylized cosmetic mask that succeeded in totally transforming Kate's features. It was far more of a madeup look than she was used to wearing during working hours, but the dark carmine lipstick, dusky-rose glossed high on each cheekbone, and smoky mauve eye shadow had to be strong enough to stand up under the hot bright television lights without washing out in the process.

Almost immediately Kate began to relax beneath Wes' practiced and reassuring hands. The perfumed atmosphere became dreamlike and filmy. Kate felt as if she were slowly dissolving in it; succumbing to a luxurious sense of peaceful relaxation, where it just wasn't necessary to think about the traumatic events of the past weekend.

Then there was another brief knock on the door and Shanga Duprez breezed into the room like a minor whirlwind. "Good morning, Katie darling. And hi there, tall, blond, and virile. I haven't seen you since breakfast this morning. What are your plans for dinner and the rest of your life, by the way?"

"Now look, you two." Kate interrupted Shanga's breathless appearance on the scene. "I don't care what you do on your own time, but I'm just not in any mood for this. Now please . . . just read me Cassandra's review of the gallery showing."

"Here it is, hot off the presses, and it's an absolute rave," Shanga declared. "Just feast your ears on this . . .

"On Friday evening the bevy of Beautiful People thronging the Winthrope Gallery were treated to cinéma vérité at its best. The production was sponsored by Caramour Cosmetics, directed by ex-cover-girl Shanga

Duprez, turned ad agency whiz, and hosted by Celia Randolph, society's own interior decorator extraordinaire.

"According to Katherine Leslie, the glamorous high-powered lady president of Caramour, the purpose of the evening was to introduce the sculpture of Doctor Andreas Jaccard to Manhattan's haute monde culture groupies. Jaccard, just in case you've been off hunting reindeer in Lapland or something, is the brilliant, handsome, and oh so charming Nobel Laureate who developed the fountain of youth beauty formula that Caramour is marketing under the trade name of Rejuvenal.

"Not the least of the evening's surprises was the unveiling of a nearly life-size nude statue, for which Celia Randolph posed during a visit to Jaccard's Coral Key Spa in the Caribbean. Clocking in somewhere between midlife crisis and Lost Horizons, Celia is definitely a walking advertisement for cellular rejuvenation. She admits to having been a patient of Doctor Jaccard's for at least a half-dozen years, and there are those who insist that she's pushing close to her seventh decade on earth.

"I don't know much about applied biology, but I do know for a fact that Celia has been kicking up her heels in all the very best places of late with a variety of attractive young men. Romance is definitely in the air, and if the nude statue Jaccard did of the blue-blooded former Ziegfeld Follies girl is any indication, I'm ready to sign up for a visit to Coral Key."

The floor-to-ceiling windows of the Caramour boardroom framed the magnificent panoramic view of midtown Manhattan, with Kate seated at the head of the long, gleaming conference table. She lifted her chin slightly, and her smile was coolly self-confident as she held the pose. The camera shutter clicked, and then clicked again.

"All right, that's a wrap on the still shots." Shanga's voice cut in. "We'll have a ten-minute break for the crew before we shoot the video segment."

Everyone began talking at once as they headed for the coffee urn. The elegantly appointed boardroom was wreathed with cigarette smoke, populated by a variety of technicians, and booby-trapped with long, snaking cables leading to an impressive battery of equipment. There was a video camera set up on tracks, and a dollying mini-cam for closeups and tight-angle shots.

Wes had been right about the mysterious yellow capsules, Kate realized as she sat calmly studying her lines for the taping. The atmosphere surrounding her was electric with tension, and yet Kate felt herself to be totally in control. Calm, cool, and very much collected.

"All right, everybody, let's keep down the noise and get some airconditioning going in here to clear the smoke." Once again Shanga turned to consult with the photographer with whom she had been going over the script for a five-minute video segment that was to be used in the Rejuvenal promotion.

"Now what I'm trying to capture," Shanga informed him, "is a certain aura of sophistication. It's a *power* look, but there is also an underlying sense of refined eroticism. The woman we see on camera knows her own self-worth. But she is also possessed of a high degree of personal integrity. Her basic message is, 'Take a look at me, girls. I did it . . . and so can you.'"

The photographer was peering closely at Kate through the lens of the videocam. He was young and attractive, and his jeans were stretched tightly across his muscular buttocks. His physique was lean, lanky, and very sexy, Kate found herself thinking. His name was Kelly something or other, and he was smiling at her in a way that Kate had begun to recognize of late.

Nor was Kate herself totally immune from the kind of attention she was getting from men. Competition in the male-dominated marketplace was like a highly potent aphrodisiac.

Kate had never thought of herself as being highly attractive, and yet soon her image would be gracing television commercials, billboards, and magazine advertisements all over the country. Yet she had a distinct advantage over those who had gone before her to become symbols of feminine beauty in their own time.

After almost twenty years in the business of image building, Kate knew how to project a particular mood or mental attitude. She also had an innate understanding of what the camera could and could not do, as well as an inborn awareness of how to project herself to best advantage.

It was something they called *presence* in modeling, and it was a rare enough quality, even among truly beautiful women. It was that special something that made the difference. *Something* in the eyes, and in the way she walked. It was the attention she now seemed to command whenever she entered a room.

"All right now, Katie," Shanga instructed. "We're ready to roll, and if you need to consult the cue cards, Wes will be turning them as you speak."

Kate winked at him as Wes hoisted the first cue card.

She was feeling highly charged and anxious to get on with the taping session and to get it out of the way as quickly as possible. Coping was turning out to be easier than she had thought.

"People!" Shanga called out. "Let's exercise a little discipline . . . and patience. Miss Leslie is a very busy woman, on a very tight schedule. We'd like to get this down with just as few takes as possible. Okay, everybody . . . quiet on the set. All right Kelly . . . roll the camera."

Wearing a black Chanel suit and high-necked silk blouse in bright coral, Kate turned slowly from the wide expanse of glass with the Manhattan cityscape rising beyond her like the towers and spires of some mythical kingdom. Removing her stylishly severe horn-rimmed glasses, she leaned slightly forward in her high-backed chair, and smiled directly into the camera.

"My name is Katherine Leslie," she announced. "I'm the president of Caramour Cosmetics Company, and I want to tell you about a miraculous new scientific discovery called Rejuvenal-12.

"Caramour's new Rejuvenal Skin-Care Line is something entirely unique in the way you cherish your own special brand of beauty. And yet it is not just a new system or regime. But rather a total beauty package developed by Doctor Andreas Jaccard, who has long been recognized as a foremost expert in the science of cellular rejuvenation.

"Rejuvenal is not a random collection of unrelated skin-care products that have little or no bearing on the way a woman really wants to look and to feel about herself. Rejuvenal is you. A carefully designed beauty regimen that really works.

"No matter what your age or life style, I am inviting you to share the complexion care secrets of rich, beautiful, and renowned women the world over.

"Remember. Being a beautiful woman is more a matter of intellect and self-appreciation than it is youth or just good basic bone structure. The truly self-assured woman of today is intelligent enough to seek out the very best advice, and then put it to good use.

"For youth and beauty forevermore . . . it's Rejuvenal by

Caramour Cosmetics. With Caramour . . . your face can become the face of the future."

It was all over in a single take, and as the bright hot lights were switched off, and the noise level rose, Kate looked across the boardroom to note a rather ominous unfamiliar face. He was a stockily built man with a florid countenance, untidy ginger-colored hair, and the slightly battered features of an Irish cop.

But it wasn't his looks or generally unkempt appearance that bothered her. Rather it was the intensely quiet air of coiled inner tension. The man was staring directly and pointedly at her, and his eyes were as pale, wintry, and predatory as the eyes of a hunting wolf.

Kate walked over to Shanga and drew her slightly aside. "Who is that man over there?" she asked. "The one fixing himself coffee at the electric urn."

Shanga did a slow reconnaissance of the room, and then rolled her eyes heavenward in prayerful response. "That, I'm afraid, is Garrett the Terrible. He's the turkey who runs *Cosmetology Today,* and wrote that poison pen piece on you right after Paul bowed out. I don't know why, but ever since then I've kind of had the feeling that he was out to fasten your scalp to his belt."

"All right, I'll handle it," Kate said. "You'd better run along and set up for the *Time* Magazine interview in my office. Order some lunch and I'll meet you there as soon as I can."

By now Garrett Forbes was moving toward her, and Kate stepped forward to greet him with her hand extended. "I've been told that you can be a very dangerous man to have as an enemy, Mr. Forbes. I'd prefer that we be friends."

For just a beat Forbes gazed, unsmiling, at Kate's outstretched palm before slipping his own hands into the pockets of his baggy tweed coat. "I don't plan to make any friends in my business," he grunted. "I think it makes it easier that way."

Kate dropped her hand to pick up her slim leather Gucci portfolio. "Just what is it you want, Mr. Forbes? I have a very busy day still ahead of me, and quite frankly I despise bad manners."

Forbes chose to ignore the comment and wasted no time in stating the reason for his unexpected visit. "I came here to ask you a question I know you aren't going to like," he informed her as he sloshed steaming black coffee around in his styrofoam cup. "Just how much do you really know about this Doctor Andreas Jaccard?"

Kate's features remained totally without expression. "I think that has been well documented already in Shanga's press release. I'll see that a copy is sent over to your office."

For the first time Garrett Forbes smiled, but Kate didn't like the result. It was a belligerent, wolfish smile, and it didn't reach his eyes. "You don't seem to understand, Miss Leslie. I already know all that crap about the brilliant young heir apparent to the highly respected Doctor Christian Meyerhof. But that just isn't good enough. Last week I read an interview in the *Frankfurter Zeitgeist* with Meyerhof, where he referred to Jaccard as a scientific *wunderkind* all right. But he also called him 'a man of badly flawed character,' who should never have been awarded the Nobel Prize."

"Bad press is not a crime, Mr. Forbes. It's merely an opinion, and could very possibly have been taken entirely out of context from what Doctor Meyerhof actually said. But even if what you report is true, it wouldn't be too difficult to assume that professional jealousy had something to do with it."

"You may have a point there," Forbes drawled. He extracted a pouch of Bull Durham tobacco from the pocket of his baggy sport coat. Then proceeded to roll himself a cigarette, strike a wooden match against his shoe, and puff away with maddening concentration until it finally took fire.

"I'm afraid you're going to have to excuse me now, Mr. Forbes. I'm already behind schedule. If you need any further clarification about Doctor Jaccard's credentials, I would suggest that you check with him yourself."

Garrett chose to ignore the note of irritation honing her voice. "Just one more question, Miss Leslie. Don't you find it kind of strange that within six months after receiving cell-injection therapy from Jaccard on Coral Key, one of his patients is dead, and another remains in deep coma at New York Hospital?"

Kate's eyes narrowed and she deliberately slipped on her horn-rimmed glasses. "You're a very distasteful man, Mr. Forbes, and not a very thorough investigative reporter, from what I've been able to observe. Fiona Van Zandt was dying of cancer before she even consulted with Doctor Jaccard. Three European doctors had already declared her to be in the final terminal stages of aplastic anemia. It's a wonder that Fiona survived as long as she did.

"And as far as Adrianna del Bario is concerned, her doctor told me he found traces of powerful drugs in her system after her collapse. He also discovered that she'd had a heart murmur since childhood. Adrianna's medical records at the Catholic orphanage in St. Louis where she was raised confirmed that."

Forbes coughed a hacking smokers' cough, and somehow managed to spew forth a cloud of smoke and burning shreds of tobacco. They fell upon the pale beige carpeting, where he ground them out beneath the heel of his scuffed brown loafer. "You'll have to excuse me, Miss Leslie, but I kind of get the idea that maybe there's something important that you don't even know."

"For instance. . . ?" Kate challenged.

"For instance, your friend Princess Shama didn't die of cancer," he informed her. "According to the Autopsy Report filed in the Southhampton Township court of records on July Fifteenth of this year she died of a massive cerebral hemorrhage. You see Miss Leslie, the Princess dedicated her body to science. They removed her vital organs before they buried her, and there was no sign of malignant cancer. She was clean on that score."

Kate felt something like a *frisson* circuiting up her spine, then started as the telephone buzzed directly behind her back. Gratefully she swung away from Garrett Forbes' pale, gray, questioning gaze and punched the glowing red button on the phone. "Yes, Iris, what is it?"

"Doctor Jaccard is on the line calling from Kennedy Airport. His flight for Jamaica leaves in twenty minutes, and he says it's urgent that he speak with you."

The call was on *conference* and Forbes clearly hadn't missed a word of it. He chuckled, and then removed the stub of his homemade cigarette from his mouth, holding it between his thumb and nicotine-stained forefinger. "I'll be pushing off now, Miss Leslie. I guess you and your friend Jaccard have a lot of things to talk over in private. Thanks for sparing me so much of your very valuable time, *Madame President*. You'll be hearing from me."

Kate waited until he had closed the door behind him before taking Andreas' call. She felt weak in the knees and sat down in her chair before picking up the phone. "Hello, Andreas," she said. Her features were as bland and noncommital as her voice. "Yes, I'm fine, thank you. The showing was a huge success. I think you should feel very pleased."

Then, choosing her words with extreme care, Kate went on to say, "I am concerned about what happened Friday night, Andreas. I think we both made a big mistake."

Kate sat listening to Andreas' deep, reassuring voice coming over the line. It was the *other* Andreas Jaccard. The one she had first come to know and trust on Coral Key.

Andreas spoke in low, measured tones. He explained that he and Ingrid were returning to Coral Key. Everything was now under control, he assured her. "Ingrid deeply regrets what happened. Now I don't want you to worry about a thing, Kate. I've already paid off the detectives and destroyed the original negatives.

"Just forget that any of it ever happened," Jaccard assured her just before signing off. And that was exactly what Kate intended to do, as she hung up the phone.

By that point all the technical people working on the photography session had long since packed up and left. Kate was alone in the boardroom. Alone with the sibilent whisper of the air-conditioning system and a powerful sense of needing at least a few minutes completely to herself. Sealed off from the outer clamor, and all that lay ahead of her that afternoon.

"Thank God," she murmured. The crisis was past and both of them had learned a valuable lesson. From that point on their relationship would have to remain strictly business, Kate vowed. There was simply too much at stake to allow herself to get emotionally involved with Andreas Jaccard.

But was it really going to be that easy? Kate wondered. Now Garrett Forbes had entered the picture, and he was acting like some kind of consumer advocate with a score to settle. There was something compellingly masculine about Forbes, but he frightened her as well.

For a few more minutes Kate sat alone in the silent conference room among the empty chairs, empty silver water carafes, and glaringly blank notepads. She felt the hot sting of tears. But she quickly steeled herself against the impulse to have a good cry, even though it would probably have done her a world of good.

At two o'clock she would be interviewed for a December

Time magazine profile of ''Women on the Move,'' and it just wasn't worth ruining her makeup.

Kate's lace-cuffed hands hung limply from the arms of her chair. She deliberately lifted her eyes to stare at the Jonathan Wainwright portrait of Paul Osborn hanging beyond the long, gleaming expanse of conference table at the far end of the room.

Then abruptly Kate rose, gathered her portfolio, straightened her skirt, and walked briskly from the room, closing the doors silently behind her.

Chapter Twenty-six

It was the typical Manhattan fashion crowd. Pampered women and exquisitely tended men with lots of gold jewelry and wasp-waisted Cardin suits. The tough-talking gimlet-eyed buyers with their hard faces and lethal tongues. The wire-service photographers and rag-trade columnists who never missed a showing.

Kate would have rather they had met anyplace else for lunch, but Celia had insisted. She had arrived back in New York over the weekend after spending two weeks on Coral Key. Kate was anxious to talk.

''Mrs. Randolph is waiting for you at her table,'' Michael the maître d' announced. ''If you'll please just follow me, Miss Leslie, the fashion show is going to begin in about fifteen minutes.''

Kate was no longer surprised at the stir her entrance invariably caused, and she was even beginning to get used to the swiveling heads when people happened to recognize her on the street or in stores and restaurants.

During the past weeks there had been a whirlwind round of TV talk shows, and a variety of magazine and newspaper interviews. Word had gotten around that Kate's picture was to grace the cover of *Time* magazine, for their "Women on the Move" issue. It was coming out in December, and she had already received dozens of requests for speaking engagements from prestigious women's groups across the country.

"Sorry to be late," Kate breathed as she slipped into the padded corner banquette. "Mondays always seem to have a curse on them. If I hadn't been dying to hear the latest report from Coral Key, I wouldn't have canceled a luncheon engagement with the president of the Chase Manhattan Bank."

They exchanged pecks on the cheek. "You know I'm a lot more fun to lunch with than some tiresome banker, and I've already ordered for you," Celia announced.

She waved a copy of the morning paper, folded to Cassandra Presley's column, and donned a pair of stylishly petite half-frame reading glasses. "Just listen to this," Celia crowed.

"Word is out that Caramour Cosmetics is on to something very big with their new Rejuvenal-12 skin-care line. While not yet available to the general public, laboratory testing on over one hundred women with varying types of skin has proven that with regular usage, RJ-12 quite literally gives your face a new lease on life. The years simply fall away almost overnight.

"The cosmetic rumor mill is buzzing. Word is now out that Katherine Leslie, Caramour's high-powered lady prexie has every intention of going on to build a rejuvenation empire, with Caramour Miracle Spas popping up in lots of chic places around the globe."

"Now get this," Celia prompted, "because it may be as

close as you're ever going to get to honest-to-God revenge in the most exquisite sense of the word.''

''Meanwhile, *mes enfants,*'' she continued reading, ''the million-dollar honeymoon of cosmetics tycoon Paul Osborn and beautiful cover girl Allison Jeffries is beginning to resemble another Bay of Pigs debacle.

''While making the rounds of various Mediterranean watering holes aboard Osborn's spectacular super yacht, the *Caramour II*, the loving couple are said to be screaming at each other like a couple of Sardinian fishmongers.

''It seems that the bride has developed an absolute passion for spending her new husband's millions even faster than he made them. Of course the groom is simply decades older than his beauteous young wife.

''But who ever said that being young, beautiful, and married to a dynamic and attractive man with more money than God was any guarantee of happiness? *Au contraire*. There are always bound to be a few flies in the Beluga caviar. I've been told it all has something to do with age having to pay so that youth can have its day . . .''

''Don't you just love it?'' Celia gushed.

''I hate it,'' Kate replied. ''Do you really think I find it amusing to see Paul openly humiliated by a tiresome scold like Cassandra Presley?''

''It sounds to me like you're still in love with him,'' Celia challenged.

Kate didn't respond immediately. Instead she opened her purse and took out a slim platinum lighter, hammered-gold cigarette case, and antique Etruscan compact, placing each item carefully on the white linen cloth. ''Now that would be absurd, wouldn't it, Celia? Functional masochism is not my favorite pastime. I have better things to do with my life.''

''With love you never know,'' Celia responded. ''I mean

there will no doubt be people who think it's absurd for a woman my age to even consider marrying a man forty years younger. But I'm not going to let that stop me from marrying Benny Valdez."

Kate choked on her vodka martini. "I guess I must be hearing things. I could have sworn that I just heard you say that you and Benny Valdez were going to be married."

"There's nothing wrong with your hearing." Celia beamed. "If a woman can find sex and love all wrapped up together in the same packaging, honey, she better put her brand on the merchandise before it gets snatched up by a comparison shopper."

"Are you sure you haven't OD'ed on Jaccard's cow ovaries? Look, Celia, you know I'm only interested in your happiness. So you think you're in love with the young man? I couldn't be more pleased, but marriage to someone like Benny Valdez . . ."

Celia regarded Kate languidly over the rim of her champagne cocktail. "You know, Katherine, I'm only doing publicly what a lot of women are doing on the sly. What about you, for instance? I know all about you and Andreas Jaccard."

Celia arched one finely penciled brow as Kate sat staring at her, totally at a loss for words. "And you were always so definite about not having an affair with a married man, weren't you?"

"Exactly *what* do you know?" Kate finally managed.

"Just what Andreas openly admitted. That you and he had a thing going. My impression was that it had been consummated during his fall visit to New York. He says he's going to ask Ingrid to give him a divorce."

Kate was both flushed and flustered. "Celia, you've got to believe me. There is absolutely nothing going on between us. Yes, of course, I felt a very strong physical attraction in the beginning. What woman doesn't feel that way about Andreas? But my God, I only slept with the man once. We've hardly got a 'steady thing' going, and I just can't understand why he told you we did. When he left for Jamaica, we both agreed that it wasn't going to happen again."

"You can relax, Katie. Frankly, I think that you and Andreas are a match made in heaven. I'm just a little miffed that you chose to keep me—your very dearest friend in the entire world—in the dark for so long. Then of course there's this business about committing Caramour to a multimillion-dollar investment in Coral Key. I mean, I am a board member after all, and I certainly wasn't consulted in the matter."

Very deliberately Kate tapped the ash off her cigarette. "I didn't bring the matter up before the board because it had to be handled fast and in complete secrecy. Considering the success of Rejuvenal thus far, Caramour might very well be franchising rejuvenation spas across the country within a couple of years. The profits from such a venture could be enormous. The bottom line was that I had to keep Andreas from selling out to our competitors. He offered me first refusal and I had no choice but to act fast."

"Well, I've been doing a little wheeling and dealing on my own," Celia announced smugly. "I was high bidder when the *Sultana* was put up for auction, and I still got her for a song. Now don't be mad at me, Katie, but I had to sell all my Caramour stock in order to make the deal. I mean after all, you have only your own success to blame. Who was I to refuse if someone was willing to pay a quarter-million-dollar bonus in order to get their hands on a big chunk of Caramour stock?"

Kate went pale. "Celia . . . you didn't?"

"Oh yes, I did. Andreas convinced me I could make a fortune by buying the *Sultana* and turning her into a floating gambling casino. I'm going to put her at anchor in the harbor at Porto Cristo, and Benny and I are going to live on board."

Kate's mind was racing as Celia rambled on, explaining that all of Fiona's art treasures had been auctioned off separately, and she was going to have to totally refurbish and redecorate the yacht.

"I've put everything on the market," she announced. "My Manhattan townhouse, my Easthampton estate, my decorating business . . . everything I own in the world. Andreas insists that Porto Cristo is going to boom. A lot of people are going to make a lot of big money fast, and I have every intention of being in on the ground floor. Tropicana resorts has already bought up half the town and is putting up a twelve-story hotel with a yachting marina. You simply aren't going to recognize—"

"Celia," Kate cut in. Her voice was startled, questioning. Her pulse was racing, but she tried very hard to keep her sudden panic under control. "I want you to tell me who was willing to pay a quarter-million-dollar premium to get hold of your Caramour stock. It's very important that I know."

"Oh, I have no idea of the name of the company," Celia declared with an airy wave of her hand. "My broker handled everything. All I did was to sign the necessary papers."

Kate was numb with apprehension as Celia went on to relate her latest amorous adventures with Benny Valdez. Their farewell encounter had been in a hammock strung between two palm trees on the beach, and according to Celia's glowing description, had turned out to be "a genuine grade-A Masters and Johnson peak orgasmic experience."

Kate scarcely heard a word she said, and was glad when the fashion show finally began, with long-legged models gliding down a wide Plexiglas stairway to sweep out among the tables in a sumptuously choreographed display of Jon-Claude Fabiani's latest creations. The music swelled as a trio of strolling violinists began to make the rounds, and a disembodied voice began to chant the designer's praises over the loudspeaker system. From a table on the other side of the room Cassandra Presley was staring across at her, but Kate refused to make eye contact.

"Excuse me, Miss Leslie, but there's an urgent call for you." Kate was so startled that she managed to spill part of her drink as Michael the maître d' placed a phone at her elbow and bent to plug it in beneath the table.

In spite of the noise and confusion created by the prancing mannequins as they paraded around the tables greeted by waves of enthusiastic applause, Kate immediately recognized the voice coming from the other end of the line. It was Garrett Forbes.

"Sorry to interrupt your fashion show," he drawled, "but I thought you might be interested in something I just picked up from UPI. It seems that your friend Jaccard is now a widower. His wife, Ingrid, was aboard a rented plane that exploded en route from Porto Cristo to Miami. There were no survivors."

Part Four

Winter Solstice—A Dark Star Rising

Chapter Twenty-seven

Max Drexel loosened the catch of his seat belt and let it fall away from his corpulent girth. Directly across the aisle, Kate repeated his performance, then dropped her head back against the seat as the piercing scream of the jet engines muted abruptly after taking off from La Guardia Airport.

Kate's eyes were veiled behind oversize dark glasses as she stared out the window toward the distant towers and spires of Manhattan rising to dominate the western skyline. She was, she realized, at the top—or almost the top—of the heap. But it hadn't come easy. She'd had to scheme and claw and fight her way up, every inch of the climb, and she had no intention of allowing anyone to take it away from her.

The Rejuvenal campaign had kicked off in late November, with full-page ads in all the major fashion magazines featuring a stunning closeup of Kate in her executive suite offices high atop the General Dynamics building.

Staring directly into the camera, she looked the very epitome of the New Corporate Woman. Coolly confident, elegantly casual, decidedly glamorous, and slightly bemused by it all. The ad copy read: THIS WOMAN IS OLD ENOUGH TO HAVE A PAST. SHE'S THE KIND OF WOMAN THE FRENCH CALL FAROUCHE. SHE HAS A LOOK ABOUT HER THAT IS UNIQUELY HER OWN. A CLARITY AND CANDOR THAT REFLECT A STRONG SENSE OF PERSONAL STYLE AND RADIANT LOVELINESS THAT GO FAR BEYOND THE DESIGNER CLOTHES AND SIX-FIGURE SALARY.

HER NAME IS KATHERINE LESLIE—THE CARAMOUR WOMAN.

The Lockheed Tri-Star Executive jet had by now reached cruising altitude, and beyond the windows was nothing but an endless cloudscape stretching as far as the eye could see. Kate and Max Drexel were the only passengers in the luxuriously appointed cabin, with its hidden galley and four comfortable reclining loungers equipped with small retractable desks. The cabin was soundproofed and separated from the pilot in the cockpit by a padded door. The interior of the passenger compartment was done entirely in soft mother-of-pearl gray upholstery.

It had been a cold and blustery December in Manhattan, but it had been a prosperous one as well. Long before the advent of Christmas week, Fifth Avenue had blossomed forth with festive holiday displays and a bevy of Caramour Beauty Reps. The milling, jostling throngs of Christmas shoppers were confronted almost everywhere with the distinctive midnight blue packaging, the silver serpents entwined in the form of the double helix that had become the Rejuvenal trademark, symbolizing the basic common denominator of all life.

Kate had known from the beginning that she was onto something big with RJ-12. But nothing could have prepared her for the massive public response to the Rejuvenal skin-care product line. The factory in New Jersey was deluged with unfilled orders, and stores across the country found it virtually impossible to keep Rejuvenal in stock. Everywhere sales were booming and testimonials continued to pour in, praising the products' effectiveness.

Caramour stock was already on the rise, and L'Immortal perfume had taken the fragrance market by storm, at one hundred and twenty-five dollars per ounce.

Kate's own corporate star was most definitely on the rise, and yet, as the company jet carried her south to preside over the opening of the new Caramour Rejuvenation Spa on Coral Key, she felt angry and frustrated; somehow cheated out of the recognition that was due her.

During a long-distance telephone conversation with Paul on the previous day, he had behaved like a petulant and fretful child. In spite of a glowing corporate financial picture and the astounding success of RJ-12, Paul was furious at her for going ahead with the acquisition of Coral Key without his prior approval.

For the first time in memory there had been an angry exchange between them, like the rattle of small arms fire. Rather than praising all Kate had been able to achieve in such a short time, Paul had sternly cautioned her about "moving much too fast on her own authority."

It was as if Paul resented her success, Kate felt. But she also realized that the jarring conversation had managed to achieve one thing for sure. And that was to steel her resolve to go her own way, without brooking any interference. Not from Paul . . . not from anyone. To hell with his precious masculine ego.

The sound of crumpling cellophane managed to bring Kate out of her reverie, as Max Drexel removed the wrapping from one of his torpedo-shaped El Supremo cigars. "I have asked you not to smoke those things in my presence." Kate's voice sharply intruded on the silence that had fallen between them ever since taking off from La Guardia some twenty minutes earlier.

"Getting kind of touchy, aren't you, Katherine," Drexel drawled. "Why don't you just relax and enjoy the rewards of your success. You know what they say about *sic transit gloria*."

"You have appalling bad manners, Max. You really ought to try and do something about them."

"And you, boss lady, have always given me the distinct impression that maybe I gave off some kind of bad smell, like dead fish. I always get this feeling that you don't really think I'm fit to share your presence." Drexel spoke with a cutting, sardonic edge to his voice.

"Our business arrangement has nothing to do with personal likes and dislikes," Kate reminded him. "You were a legacy left to me by Paul Osborn, and the simple truth of the matter is, I never would have been able to get Rejuvenal on the market within six months without your rather unique . . . shall we call it *expertise*."

"The only names that anyone ever remembers are those of the winners," Max informed her genially. "Sure, I got bad manners, but I get the job done. With friends like Celia Randolph, Katherine, you don't need enemies."

Only the barest flicker of an eyelid betrayed how successfully Drexel had pierced her glacial reserve. "Celia didn't know anything about this business with I.C.E. When they offered her broker a great deal more than her Caramour stock was worth at the time, she jumped at the chance to sell. She couldn't have the faintest idea what a dangerous position that would put the company in, or she never would have done it. There's just no point in trying to fix the blame on anyone, Max. It's simply a situation that has to be dealt with as quickly and quietly as possible."

"And just how do you intend to manage that?" he sneered. "Since the horse already appears to be out of the barn."

For a moment Kate stared at his brutal, florid face and felt herself being mirrored in the slush-colored eyes. Her stare was one of almost palpable dislike. "I wouldn't start getting any ideas about jumping ship just yet, Drexel. I have absolutely no intention of allowing I.C.E., and Henri Dayne, to reap the benefits of all I've worked to achieve."

"And what if they have managed to put enough stock together to force a stockholders' suit?" Drexel questioned. "What then? You know that Dayne is acting as I.C.E.'s point man, and Ted Baxley is just a clone. He'll do anything that Dayne tells him."

"I am not about to allow either one of them to sell Caramour out," Kate responded quietly.

With Drexel looking on, she removed two identical pale blue folders from the leather portfolio resting on her lap. "Do you recognize these?" she asked, handing them across to him.

"Sure. I'm the one who gave Paul the idea to keep files of corporate intelligence on anyone who might prove to be a problem."

Drexel casually scanned through the files on Dayne and Baxley, underlying various sections with a sausagelike index finger. He grunted and then laughed an ugly grating sound. "Well what do ya know about that? So old Teddie Baxley got picked up for propositioning an undercover vice-cop in the john of the Grayhound bus terminal a couple of years back. I never even suspected the guy was a fruit."

"I forbid you to use that particular information in any way," Kate warned him. "There's enough evidence of corporate malfeasance in both their files to put Dayne and Baxley behind bars. Your job is to convince them that if they should be so foolish as to vote their stock holdings with I.C.E. I will not hesitate to turn these dossiers over to the Manhattan District Attorney."

Drexel turned abruptly to stare across at her, and his tongue came out to lick his thick lips. "Well I gotta hand it to you, boss lady. Quite frankly, I didn't think you had the guts to actually use blackmail. I guess I underestimated you."

"Blackmail is such an ugly word," Kate informed him.

She held his starkly accusing gaze, refusing intimidation. "I believe that Paul used to refer to this sort of thing as 'applying corporate leverage.' In any case, that's the way I prefer to see it. I'm not happy about doing this, Max, but I really don't see that I have any choice in the matter."

"And just what do I stand to get out of this?" Max demanded.

"As soon as Henri Dayne is cut off at the knees, I'm going to appoint you Director of International Sales . . . with a percentage commission."

"It could work," Drexel shrugged. "Dayne is sure to resign before he'll allow me to move in and stake out his territory. But he isn't going to take a chance on going to jail. Baxley will shit bricks when I show him the numbers of his secret Swiss bank account. I don't think it should be too hard to convince him to take an early retirement for 'personal reasons.' But you should understand that it's only a question of buying yourself some extra time, Katherine. What I.C.E. wants, I.C.E. usually gets."

"What's your point, Max?"

He removed the copy of the *Wall Street Journal* that had been folded in his coat pocket. "I think you ought to take a look at just how hard the competition is willing to play. It might help to give you a wider perspective on just what it is you're up against."

Kate took the paper from his hand, and slipped on her

reading glasses. Then she allowed her eyes to travel down the front page to where the headline: JAMAICAN RESORT SLATED TO BECOME CARIBBEAN MONTE CARLO was circled in red pencil.

As she began reading, Kate started to experience a numbing chill. "Representatives of International Consortium Export today unveiled plans for a 500-million-dollar casino resort complex on the island of Jamaica.

"During an interview with the Jamaican Minister of Internal Affairs, lawyers for the huge conglomerate outlined the project, which will eventually include a luxurious gambling casino, hotels, and yacht marina to be developed at Porto Cristo on the island's northern shore.

"Representatives of I.C.E. indicated during the course of an orientation meeting with a variety of prominent government figures that they were currently in negotiation with Tropicana Resorts Ltd., who have already begun construction of a much smaller resort at the same site. Within twenty-four hours after the meeting with I.C.E.'s lawyers, the Jamaican legislature introduced legislation that would legalize gambling on the island, and approve the I.C.E. takeover of Tropicana Resorts Ltd."

The creeping numbness had spread to the remotest extremeties of her body by the time Kate finished reading the fourth paragraph, but she forced herself to continue reading as the *Journal* went on to describe I.C.E. as a "Mega-Conglomerate," whose financial interests had become inextricably woven throughout the economic fabric of dozens of countries around the globe.

In essence, I.C.E. was portrayed as great masses of money on the move. Money and power that flowed in endless directions, reaching out its tentacles to touch countless political and economic nerve centers throughout the world.

That was what she was up against, Kate realized.

* * *

Kate lay very still on the inflated raft floating near the center of the pool. It was very hot, and her eyes were closed against the blazing Caribbean sunlight.

Immediately upon arriving on Coral Key, the spell of the island had begun seeping into her consciousness: the quality of light and the purity of the sea air, the clouds floating across an azure sky, driven by warm offshore breezes.

Kate lay there with the warmth of the tropic sun burning into her skin, and allowed her mind to float lazily out to sea, as weightless as her body, stretched languidly upon the dark blue rubber raft, drifting effortlessly upon the clear aquamarine water.

The constant tensions that had been driving her so relentlessly in New York had become a web of conflicting interests and ambitions almost too complicated to negotiate. Kate had needed desperately to get away. In spite of her misgivings about coming face to face with Andreas Jaccard once again, Kate had come to Coral Key determined to make it a working vacation.

Yet no sooner had the Caramour executive jet touched down at the newly constructed Porto Cristo Airport, than she began to comprehend how greatly everything had changed.

The rutted, winding road leading along the rugged coastline from the airport had been newly paved and widened into a three-lane highway, while Porto Cristo itself had mushroomed into a bustling tourist mecca. There were cruise ships anchored in the harbor, and a flotilla of yachts and cabin cruisers dotted the beautiful crescent bay.

Newly fabricated pastel-colored villas had begun to climb the encircling green hills, while out on the point, below the old Spanish fortress, the starkly geometric skeleton of the new I.C.E. Intercontinental Hotel had begun to rise from a raw and gaping wound in the rust-red earth.

Porto Cristo shimmered and wilted in the blinding heat haze of early afternoon, and its narrow streets had become a garish calliope of honking horns, sing-song vendors' voices and the rhythmic pulsing of a Jamaican drum band playing for tourist coins in the central square.

Then they were skimming out across the water in a sleek new power launch emblazoned with the Caramour corporate logo—silver serpentine double helix against a field of midnight blue.

During Kate's seven-month absence from Coral Key there had been a great number of astonishing changes. The lagoon had been dredged to accommodate a new dock, and there was a floating helicopter pad moored in shallow water. A dozen new chalk-white villas of the rococo-Moorish persuasion rose like coral polyps from a verdant green sea of tropical vegetation. Even the old Great House had been totally restored to its turn-of-the-century magnificence.

From the moment that Kate set foot upon the island, Andreas Jaccard had totally taken charge. Her first official act as hostess of what was being billed as the Caramour Celebrity Gala was to preside over the dedication ceremony of the new laboratory wing. It had been added to the administration building in order to house Jaccard's greatly expanded laboratory facilities.

Together they stood there on the lawn, smiling as Kate snipped the ribbon. The encircling crowd clapped and cheered as cameras flashed.

Kate had decided to forgo the *al fresco* luncheon being served on the lawn. She was tired and needed time to think. But Andreas had insisted that she remain at his side. If Celia had been largely instrumental in putting the whole three-ring circus together, Andreas was clearly the unquestioned focus of all attention.

Once again he was the same handsome, brilliant, and

suavely sophisticated charmer who had so completely captured Kate's imagination upon her initial visit to Coral Key.

Together they moved among the guests, greeting local dignitaries and politicans while Andreas cleverly stage-managed the attendant press corps and seemed almost effortlessly to dazzle Celia's social celebrity friends with his style and wit.

It was as if he were in possession of some inexplicable and mysterious power that made him all but irresistible, Kate thought, as she shook hands, nodded agreement, and smiled until her face hurt.

The production had been superbly staged on the lawn of the Great House, with the verdant green mountains of Jamaica hanging in the background while the powder-sweet fragrance of flowering mimosa gently scented the air. But what of the other Andreas? Kate wondered. That dark medieval persona and ruthless ego. The slumbering violence only barely held in check, like the promise of some exquisite cruelty.

Celia seemed to be everywhere at once. She had flown down from New York the night before, accompanied by a dozen jet-set luminaries and a gaggle of newspaper columnists, including the gaunt and predatory figure of Cassandra Presley. All of them had been accommodated at the St. George Hotel in Porto Cristo, and there was no possible way of mistaking Celia's immediate entourage.

Those perpetually sun-bronzed sybarites, dressed to the nines with an eye to informal elegance and all the right labels. For the first time Kate realized that they were supremely gentile *in toto*, as well as serenely superior in their self-possession. With their perfect frozen smiles, they all had the look of people who expected to receive far more from life than they were prepared to give. All those golden-skinned women with searching huntress eyes and their lean, well-proportioned men for whom success appeared to have always been a *fâit accômpli*.

They seemed to exist within some kind of charmed circle, leading lives impressively redolent with pleasure and all manner of sensual gratification. While they invariably bored Kate to distraction, they were exactly the kind of people guaranteed to establish Coral Key as the rejuvenation spa of choice for that glittering international elite who traveled the world aboard their private planes and yachts like some rare species of migratory birds.

"I have to hand it to you, Katherine. You've surprised me, quite frankly, and a lot of other people as well."

The voice seemed to come out of nowhere. Kate opened her eyes and lifted her head from the pillow of her arms to see the chiaroscuro figure of Cassandra Presley standing beside the pool against a background of pure white light. She was enveloped in a bright orange Hawaiian muumuu while her face was largely obscured behind huge dark harlequin glasses, with a big floppy-brimmed straw hat.

Kate was drowsy with the heat, and the columnist appeared to be moving in and out of focus like some spectral figure captured on a negative film transparency.

"You've been giving quite a performance," Cassandra called out in her soft, insinuating Southern drawl. "In less than a year you've become the most powerful woman in the cosmetics industry, and stamped your own indelible imprint on Caramour like a brand. From where I stand, it looks as if Rejuvenal could turn out to be the miracle product of the age. And now there are rumors floating around that you and wondrous Doctor Jaccard are about to become the dynamic duo of the decade."

Cassandra sipped from her champagne glass and waved her long cigarette holder like a conjurer's wand.

"Of course you know what they say about still waters running deep. Oh, there's no point in bothering to deny it. I know all about your secret love affair with *young* Brian

Brophy, and I must admit that I'm extremely impressed. I mean after all, my dear—a Nobel Laureate and a gorgeous young lover worth two billion dollars. Maybe you don't realize it yet, but your life has become the stuff from which dreams are made."

Kate was exhausted. "I didn't fly you down here on this little celebrity junket in order to have you dissect my personal and professional life, Cassandra. Just what is it you're getting at?"

Cassandra's brittle laughter was unsettling. "You'll have to forgive me, Katherine. But I just can't help wondering what would happen if Paul Osborn were to suddenly reappear upon the scene. I think I'd give that little scenario some thought if I were you. Who knows, you might not be all that willing to give it all up. Paul's dumping Allison, by the way. He's cabled his lawyers to bail him out . . . at any price."

Chapter Twenty-eight

Kate stood in the rushing hot torrent with the steam clouding up about her naked body. It was past midnight, and she had just returned from Porto Cristo and the big celebrity gala dinner at the St. George Hotel.

The events of the evening remained with her like a series of vivid slide projections cast upon the screen of her mind. The St. George had been completely refurbished and totally redecorated by Celia Randolph in classic Art Deco. All the china, crystal, silver, and linen had been chosen to match the etched glass and Art Deco murals, which had been painted by local artists on the walls of the Lagoon Terrace dining room.

The tables had each been set for six, and huge silver candelabra had cast dancing reflections on each grouping of the bejeweled cast of characters playing in the evening's drama. Most were merely walk-ons, but there had also been a major attraction to add luster to the event.

The surprise arrival of Lady Brenda at the Caramour Celebrity Gala had sparked a sensation from the moment she appeared. The Duchess was dressed in mourning black, with a heavy emerald necklace and matching diamond and emerald earrings that hung halfway to her powdered white shoulders. She looked ghastly pale, and her darkly hennaed hair had been swept up in negligent disarray beneath the most impressive jeweled tiara Kate had ever seen.

As Kate moved forward to greet the Duchess, she saw the pale puffiness beneath the powdered makeup, the poached alcoholic glitter of the eyes, and the slight tremor of the extended hand. It was the first time that Lady Brenda had been seen in public since the burial of the Duke in Westminster Abbey some five years before.

Now she was standing there among them, ablaze with diamonds, emeralds, and rubies as big as goose eggs. So this was the legendary Duchess of Sutherland? For Kate, their meeting was accompanied by a startled sense of recognition reserved for those figures of ghostly celebrity who have somehow managed to survive the epic scandals of their past.

The promotional gala at the St. George turned out to be something less than a total success. There was the alien glitter of the New York crowd mingling uncomfortably with the black new-moneyed aristocracy of Jamaica, who actually came in a variety of shades from ebony to golden tan.

Andreas, however, had spared no expense in staging the affair. A twelve-piece orchestra had been imported from Montego Bay for the evening, while the Chef de Cuisine from the Caneel Bay Club had been helicoptered in to prepare an eight-course repast. It was definitely Creole *haut cuisine*, and accompanied by such vintner's rarities as a Romanee St. Vincent '45 and a magnificent Chambolle Musigny 1937.

There was lobster mousse, gallantine of duck, batins of black truffles, and asparagus tips as thin as broomstraws in a delicate butter cream sauce. Andreas was an exacting gourmand and had planned the entire meal, although Kate had scarcely touched a bite.

She had, however, drunk a large quantity of wine, and by the time that dinner was over, Kate felt herself to be at precisely the right point of inebriation. With the help of a couple of Wes' little yellow pills taken earlier in the evening, she had managed to anesthetize her emotions, while infusing her mind with vivid, crystalline clarity.

Throughout the day the sun had glared down mercilessly from a white-hot sky. The heat was almost palpable, and even the wooden-bladed fans circling slowly overhead scarcely managed to stir the torpid air.

Throughout dinner Kate felt dragged down into the quicksand of triviality as she hosted a table of Celia's guests. They talked of nothing but money, clothes, each other, and the oppressive heat. The orchestra played interminably, the centerpiece flowers drooped, and by the time that the after-dinner liqueurs were being served, Kate felt that the worst of the ordeal had been put behind her.

She was wrong. Perspiring profusely, Max Drexel insisted on leading Kate out onto the dance floor, and she didn't dare cause a scene by refusing, an unpleasant subtlety that he was obviously enjoying.

Max had blossomed with the hot weather in a white alpaca suit, and kept mopping his beefy red face with a crumpled linen handkerchief. There was a leering ironic smile on his thick, sensual lips, and Kate was revolted by the feel of his moistly pawing hands upon her body, but there was nothing she could do but submit.

"Why don't you try and loosen up?" Drexel growled, clearly relishing her discomfort. "Remember that we're playing on the same team, whether you like it or not." It was something of which she was all too painfully aware.

Then, looking across Drexel's shoulder, she saw Andreas working his way toward them across the dance floor and experienced a grateful sense of relief. He took her in his arms and Kate felt as if a crack had opened in an impenetrable wall of stifling predictability. Andreas was smiling down into her eyes, and Kate felt that somehow she had managed to slip through to the other side.

They danced in easy compatible harmony, turning and gliding around the floor as if they had been dancing together for years. The power of attraction between them was almost overwhelming. Yet Kate realized that she would have to stay very much in control of her emotions if she were not to be consumed.

As the fatigue and tensions generated by the evening just past began to drain away beneath the tingling rush of hot shower water, the bathroom lights dimmed, flickered, and went out, plunging the villa into darkness.

Kate stood listening in the dark tropic night to the ratcheting chorus of the ciccadia. Then came the sudden violent shriek of a fruit bat, underlain by the shrill and ever constant piping of millions of tree frogs.

Kate had just finished drying herself with a big fluffy towel when she heard a different kind of sound, a soft clattering noise as if someone had passed through the beaded glass curtains hanging in the doorway of the living room.

Kate's heart was beating rapidly as she quickly tied the sash of a long silk dressing gown about her waist. Scarcely daring to breathe, she opened the bathroom door and stepped into the outer room. "Is someone there . . . ?" she called. Her voice was softly tentative.

There was an instant of distilled silence. Then a silhouette materialized against the faint light sifting in through the latticed jalousies. A match was struck and a candle took flame, illuminating the room with a pale sheen of light. "I'm sorry if I startled you," Andreas said. "The generators are out."

"I was taking a shower," Kate automatically recited. "I wasn't expecting visitors."

Kate hoped the tone of her voice would place some distance between them, but Andreas appeared not to notice. "Why did you disappear after we danced together tonight? I looked for you."

"I was very tired, and Celia was getting sloshed. I talked Benny into bringing us back to the island in his boat. I'm afraid it's been a very long day for me, Andreas. All I want to do is fall into bed. I'll be leaving for New York at seven in the morning. Benny has promised to take me to the airport."

Kate circled the room as she spoke, touching a match to the candles standing in tall wrought-iron candelabra. The decor was Moorish baroque, with moving shadows cast upon the rough white plaster walls. The smooth terra cotta tiles beneath her bare feet seemed to draw the light with a burnished luster. Very cool and smooth.

"Would you like a nightcap?" she asked, trying to keep her voice as light as possible. "I brought a bottle of Courvoisier down with me in my luggage, just in case."

Andreas chuckled deeply, amused. "You know what your friend Celia always says about rules not being any fun unless you can break them once in awhile."

Kate could feel his eyes upon her as she crossed the room to remove two glasses from the cupboard in the small kitchenette. After pouring each of them a drink, she returned to the sunken conversation pit, where Andreas had taken off his jacket and settled comfortably against the huge batik cushions.

Their glasses touched briefly. Then Kate quickly turned away to settle herself on the other side of the low glass coffee table. It was at least slightly comforting to have some solid and reassuringly familiar object between them. Kate never quite knew what to expect from Andreas, or which of his many different masks he might be wearing.

"I was terribly sorry to hear about Ingrid," Kate ventured, groping for words. For some oblique thread of mutual understanding.

Andreas' face in the candlelight was dominated by his piercing dark eyes, conveying a mixture of intensity and perfect calm repose. He seemed to fill the room, both with his physical dominance and the air of controlled tension that emanated from him. "Ingrid was leaving me when it happened," he said without the slightest change of expression. "She had agreed to give me a divorce."

"I can't tell you how awful I felt about . . . well, you know. About what happened that night in that ghastly hotel. I imagine it must have had something to do with the end of your marriage."

"It hadn't been a real marriage for a long time. You see, Ingrid was pathologically jealous. She suspected me of sleeping with every attractive female who came to Coral Key, including Solange Wilkerson. It was Ingrid who drove the girl away. I lied when I told you she had run off with someone. My wife was convinced that we were lovers. In case you're still interested, Solange is living in Montego Bay. She's become a prostitute."

Kate just left it there, moving swiftly to change the subject because she just didn't want to know. "You said when we were dancing that you had something important you wanted to talk to me about, Andreas?" It was a question rather than a statement.

Andreas nodded. "I must say that I've been suitably impressed with the way you've managed to finesse our current arrangement. You're to be congratulated, but then I always knew that you had a lot of special qualities."

Kate regarded him levelly. "Andreas, I'm going to speak quite frankly. You must realize that I've far exceeded my authority. There are bound to be repercussions."

"That's what I like about you, Kate, *modesty.* I happen to know that you've already taken steps to solve that problem. At least that's what Max Drexel tells me."

Kate blanched. "He had no right to tell you about that," she flared. "Of course, I did what I had to do. It's a shabby maneuver, and I'm not going to make any excuses. Drexel is right about one thing. Blackmailing Baxley and Dayne is only a stalling action. One way or another, I am legally bound to call another board meeting within the next sixty days. Make no mistake about it, International Consortium Export is bound to be tops on the agenda."

"Then I strongly advise that you waste no time whatsoever in appointing me to the Caramour board of directors. Celia has decided to resign her seat, and the simple truth of the matter is that you're going to need all the firepower you can get when I.C.E. moves in for the kill."

Kate answered in a sharply defensive voice. It was hard and metallic. "I want you to understand my position clearly, Andreas. I cannot continue to run Caramour indefinitely by executive fiat. It's just not in my nature to deliberately abuse my authority."

His laugh was full of soft irony. "You might as well face up to it, Katherine. You've already joined the club, whether you like it or not."

"I want you to be honest with me," Kate said. "What exactly does all this mean to you, Andreas? Where is it all heading?"

"Fame, riches, and *my own* Nobel Prize," he pronounced

without the slightest trace of equivocation. "I need you as much as you need me. Neither one of us is going to be able to make it alone without being torn to pieces. Together we form a powerful team, and if the results of my latest series of RJ-12 experiments prove to be positive, well, I guess we can begin talking about franchising Caramour Rejuvenation Spas all over the world."

Kate rose and paced restlessly to the breakfast bar, where she splashed some more brandy into her glass. "How soon can we petition the FDA for approval of cell-injection therapy?"

"I'm not quite ready yet," Andreas responded. "There are still problems that have to be resolved. But when I am ready, it is essential that you are powerful and secure enough in your position to throw all of Caramour's resources into going public with RJ-12."

"That is going to take far greater resources than I have at my disposal," Kate informed him.

Andreas got up and slowly paced to where she stood. He took the drink from her hand and placed it on the counter of the breakfast bar. Then he bent to kiss her throat; high up, just below her ear lobe.

Kate stirred to the muscular hardness of his body as Andreas' arms remained strong about her. He sought her mouth, and Kate was suddenly overcome by a seething rush of desire.

She wanted him to make love to her. But not the kind of well-groomed lovemaking that required carefully orchestrated movements and politely murmured endearments. Kate wanted him in a way that made totally irrelevant all other considerations beyond the present moment.

Chapter Twenty-nine

The Checker taxi that had transported Kate from La Guardia Airport sped across the Triborough Bridge, with the Manhattan skyline etched against a gray and wintry sky. Snow had fallen earlier in the day, and, as the cab turned off the exit ramp onto Second Avenue and headed south, the uptown streets had a white and crumpled look, with cars, trucks, and people seeming to move past in laborious slow motion.

The temperature was somewhere in the low thirties, and the windows of the taxi were frosted with silvery patterns of moisture that appeared to be highly sensual from Kate's own perspective. Making love to Andreas just before he took her to the Porto Cristo Airport had been the total release of raw, omnivorous passions that, even in retrospect, caused Kate's limbs to feel fuller and stronger.

In fact just thinking about their impassioned physical mat-ing caused her blood to course more swiftly through her veins, while every muscle and sinew strained with her own female potency. In that moment, her relationship with Andreas Jaccard seemed to be governed solely by its lack of predictability.

Each time they met was like throwing a pair of dice into the air and watching them fall back into ever new patterns and configurations.

Kate remained immersed in her thoughts about Andreas as the Checker turned east on Eighty-sixth Street, cruised toward the river for several blocks, and then swung left on East End Avenue to finally pull up in front of River House across from Gracie Mansion.

As soon as she stepped inside her apartment and switched on the light in the foyer, Kate sensed that something was wrong. It wasn't anything she could immediately identify, but rather a vague sense of violation. Some as yet undetermined intrusion upon her privacy and her person.

For over a decade Kate had lived in the Jacobean-style duplex overlooking the East River, with its richly panelled walls, pewter sconces, two marble fireplaces, and nineteen-foot ceilings with oaken crossbeams. All her furnishings were comfortably eclectic.

While nothing really looked any different as she crossed the foyer and moved down the steps into the sunken living room, Kate's sense of something being terribly amiss continued.

After climbing the carpeted stairs to her bedroom on the upper floor of the duplex, Kate switched on the overhead chandelier and stood looking around the room.

Maria-Luz, the middle-aged Cuban woman who cleaned, shopped for food, and generally kept Kate's domestic life well ordered and neatly predictable, had been visiting relatives in Miami for the past two weeks. No one should have been in the apartment during Kate's absence. And while the bedroom appeared to be exactly as she had left it, there was a subtle sense of difference.

Crossing to her rosewood desk, Kate opened the top drawer to find that the papers within had been shifted ever so slightly. From there she tried the drawers of her bureau in the dressing room, only to discover that some anonymous hand had rifled through her most intimate belongings.

A more thorough check indicated that nothing appeared to be missing. Her jewelry was intact in her jewel case, as was several hundred dollars in mad money that Kate always kept on hand in a china pot.

As she made her way back down the stairs, Kate had the feeling of having been violated. Although she hadn't a clue as to what the clandestine intruders had been searching for or who they might have been, Kate knew as well that it was not a matter for the police.

After double-locking the front door of the apartment and turning on all the lights, she returned to the living room just as the phone began to ring. Kate had been expecting a call from Brian, and as soon as she heard his deep, comforting voice on the other end of the line she blurted out that someone had broken into her apartment.

Skip was clearly startled by her announcement. "Jesus, Katie . . . are you sure you're all right . . . was there anything of value stolen?"

Clutching the phone to her ear, Kate sank down on the couch. "No . . . it wasn't that kind of a break-in. It's something else."

He was silent for a moment. "It'll take me about two hours to drive in," he said, with concern engraving his voice. "I know this has been a terrible shock, and I don't want you to be alone."

"No . . . please," Kate protested. "It's not really necessary tonight. I just got back from Jamaica and I'm worn out. All I want to do is have a long soak in a hot tub, take two Valiums, and get a good night's sleep. Why don't you come into town tomorrow evening? I know you've had some training in electronics, and to tell you the truth . . . I'm afraid that my apartment may have been bugged."

The following evening Kate left her office promptly at seven, in order to meet Brian at the Sign of the Dove on Third Avenue. It was the first time that he had entered Kate's other world, and both of them were clearly uncomfortable with the arrangement from the very beginning.

Kate had deliberately chosen the chic Upper East Side restaurant because she didn't think that she'd be recognized. But no sooner had they been shown to their reserved table in the glass-enclosed garden-patio, than diners at nearby tables began to stare and lean confidentially together in whispered conversation.

Throughout the meal, Kate and Skip sat silently across from one another like store display mannequins. Something, she realized, had come to an end. But Kate was not entirely sure exactly what it was.

Then as they left the restaurant, they were suddenly surrounded by a half-dozen photographers who pressed and crowded them relentlessly as they sought to hail a cab. On the following day, their photograph would appear in the New York *Daily News* beneath the headline caption RELUCTANT BILLIONAIRE TRYSTS WITH BEAUTY TYCOON.

Immediately upon entering her apartment, Skip began checking for the suspected bugging device Kate feared had been planted.

She stood watching apprehensively as he ran his hands beneath the edge of the carpet, checked behind picture frames, looked under the furniture, and finally dismantled the phone.

"You were right," Skip said. He produced a small amplifying device no larger than a martini olive, and placed it in Kate's hand, after deftly rendering the unit incapable of transmission with a penknife.

"I can scarcely believe this is happening," she said, staring down at the bug as if it were some lethal explosive device. Her voice was strained. "This must mean that my office phones are being monitored as well."

"And probably your bedroom," Skip volunteered. "This has the look of a very professional and thorough job to me."

The color swiftly drained from Kate's face as the impact of his words sunk in and the implications took hold. Skipper was staring at her in the strangest way. "In that case," she offered rather sharply, "I guess you'd better have a look."

Upstairs Skip circled the bed, feeling beneath the frame with his fingers while Kate stood staring out of the bedroom window. Her arms were folded stiffly across her breasts. She stared out at the wintry hunter's moon hanging pale and immense over the East River. The maple trees looked starkly brittle in the incandescent light of the street lamps, while in the park beyond the snow drifts lay deep on the ground, where they bulked up against the rocks and trees like glistening white sand dunes.

It was eleven .. by the watch on her wrist, and Kate felt suddenly chilled. In fact she always seemed to be cold of late, and no amount of Codine seemed to give relief from the insistent migraines, accompanied by dizziness and nausea.

"Here's another one," Skip said as he tossed an additional small bugging device onto the satin bedspread. "It looks to me like a very professional job, all the way around. Whoever hired this done must want to get something on you pretty bad."

Kate turned, and her eyes flashed angrily. "Just what is it you're getting at . . . what are you trying to say?"

Skip was staring across the bed at her, with the device lying there between them like a grenade that might explode at any moment. "I think you'd better call the police," he said simply. "This doesn't look like something you should fool around with."

Kate stubbornly shook her head. "That wouldn't help. It's already gone too far for that."

"Do you want to tell me what this is all about?" he questioned.

Kate tried desperately to remain in control of her emotions; the anger, frustration, and humiliation. It was all so ugly, so debased, and suddenly she couldn't bear to have him staring at her that way.

Skipper's gaze was clear and questioning, yet without judgment of any kind. But there was something else in his eyes as well. There was pain, confusion, and a depth of concern.

"Look, Katie, I already know that something has been going on between you and Andreas Jaccard," he informed her quietly. "I've sensed it ever since last fall when he showed up in New York for the gallery showing. Like tonight, you're always different right after you've been with him. You know that I care for you very, very much, Kate. But the simple truth of the matter is that three is just one too many of us."

Brian's candid appraisal of her affair with Andreas Jaccard was more than Kate was able to handle. Abruptly she turned away from him and bolted through the bathroom door, slamming and locking it behind her.

Her head was spinning, and to keep herself from falling Kate braced against the wash basin, resisting the urge to vomit. The bathroom whirled and spun about her in a sickening kaleidoscope of pink pastel tiles, yellow monogrammed towels, and hand-painted porcelain fixtures. Kate's head was throbbing with an onrushing migraine, and the overhead light seemed unnaturally harsh and scorching against her eyes.

Skip was right about her being different after she had been with Andreas, Kate realized. Just thinking about him was like being possessed by some subtle psychic force. The sense of sexual possession was like a restless moontide, curling about her to drain away her vital energies and weaken her will to resist.

The passion that Andreas had aroused within her was like the steady, deadly pull of an ocean undertow. It ran like fever in her veins and she had discovered levels of her own sexuality that she had never even imagined to exist.

Together she and Andreas had traveled to strange, wild heights, exploding finally in a rough and stunning climax that left her physically spent and emotionally exhausted. Straining and writhing like a creature possessed in those final frantic moments of wanton, convulsive release.

Now, back on her own home turf, there was a fragility in her bones. Kate felt the awareness of having tasted too deeply. Of having trespassed into an emotional wilderness where life was very close to death, and Doctor Andreas Jaccard was unequaled master of the revels.

Twenty minutes later, the sound of a door closing along the upper gallery caused Brian to turn from the fireplace and look up. Kate was moving slowly down the stairs in a sheer sky-blue caftan edged with gold embroidery. Her hair was loose and flowing about her shoulders, burnished with the firelight that filled the room, yet her features were tightly drawn, with damaged eyes and ashen pallor that belied the fresh application of lipstick.

"I need a drink," Kate said as she crossed to the rolling liquor cart and poured herself a brandy. Then she turned to face him, and her features seemed to dissolve into a smoothly stylized mask as perfectly composed as the face of a Dresden china doll.

"And now Mr. Brian Brophy, I think you deserve an explanation. Let's just say that I've been forced to do certain things of which I'm not very proud, and of which you, with your lofty spiritual values, would definitely not approve. How does the word *blackmail* strike you?"

"I have no intention of making any judgments, Kate. It's not difficult to see what you're trying very hard to become, but I know it isn't really you. It's only a mask.

"I'm going to give it to you straight," he flared. "I don't care what you've done, or how you were able to justify it. All I know is that you sold out cheap, whatever it was. You didn't need any sleazy tricks to make it, Katie. You already had everything it took. Look, you're a whole lot better than what you're trying so hard to become, and you know it. You don't have to go on living like this. You do have alternatives."

Kate swirled the brandy in her glass and restlessly began to prowl back and forth on the rug before the fire. "And just what would you suggest that I do?"

"I would suggest that you go upstairs, pack a bag and come with me. Now. Tonight." Skip reached out to place both hands lightly on her shoulders.

"Hasn't the light begun to dawn on you yet? Can't you see what you're doing? You're running Paul Osborn's company, riding in his limousine, wearing his fur coat, and fighting his battles. He's still using you Kate, can't you see it? You're one hell of a surrogate, I have to admit. But Paul knew that all along. He knew exactly what buttons to press, and he's still having it all his way."

His words struck her like dull physical blows, and Kate's eyes turned to cool gray slate in the flickering firelight. "Take your hands off me," she said with quiet, icy precision.

Skip's hands fell away and Kate leaned back against the

carved marble mantelpiece. The atmosphere in the room had polarized. Suddenly it was like a dangerously mined terrain where a single word or gesture might trigger an explosion.

"Since straight talk appears to be in vogue tonight, I've got a few honest but painful observations of my own," Kate said. "It's all very well and good for you to talk about just packing up and walking out. I mean, after all, you've never had to take responsibility for anyone but yourself. You were always the son of one of the world's richest women, with every privilege that conveyed."

"I never wanted any part of my mother's fortune. I was never willing to accept the responsibility of having that much money. It's too easy to begin seeing people and things with a price tag attached."

"So you always kept a bail-out bag packed," Kate accused. "So you could just *split the scene* when it got too *heavy* for you. Well, my life has been quite different from yours, Mr. Brophy. I always had to work to earn my way, and nobody ever gave me anything. Now let's just get *straight* with the facts.

"Number one," Kate ticked off with her extended forefinger, "I happen to be the chief operating officer of a very large and very successful corporation. Every decision I make affects the lives of thousands of people, and often involves many millions of dollars of other people's money. How utterly smug of you to talk as if I were some kind of corporate whore."

"I never said or even remotely suggested anything like that. Don't you see, Kate? It's you. You're starting to see yourself in those terms."

"Isn't it more likely," she challenged, "that you'd resent any woman who's made a success of her life?

"When it comes right down to it, Skipper my lad, you're just like all the rest of them. Your precious male ego simply can't stand the thought that I just might have the ambition to make something of myself. You're nothing but an escapist. You couldn't possibly even begin to appreciate what I've been able to achieve."

Skip slowly shook his head, and when he spoke there was not the slightest hint of censure in his deep baritone voice. "I've never been willing to buy success at the expense of my own values, if that's what you mean. At least not at the cost of living my life in a humane way. Sure I'm an escapist, someone searching for the best, for the most productive and honest way to live my life. And I'll go on searching and sorting out ideas, until only the truth is left. But don't you see that you're searching too, Kate? Andreas Jaccard and this whole rejuvenation business has somehow warped your values until you don't even know who you are anymore . . . or even *what* you are."

Skipper was silent for a moment, entreating her with his clear blue gaze. He reached out to brush her cheek with his fingertips, then made a shrugging, helpless gesture. "Jesus, Kate. Don't you realize how much I care about you? We need each other, and we're right for each other in a thousand different ways. It doesn't have to get complicated. Let's just go away and be together for awhile."

Kate turned away, staring down into the flames that had burned low in the grate. "Andreas has asked me to marry him," she announced in a very still, small voice. "I've decided to say yes."

Skip's hands fell away into the shadows, and Kate heard him exhale a deep, shuddery breath. Then he placed his arms gently about her waist and, pressing close, he kissed the part in her hair. "I guess it's about time for me to bail out," he said. Kate could feel the warmth of his breath against her cheek, but she couldn't bear to look into the somber, saddened countenance hovering above her.

"I've already sold the *Westwind,*" he said. "I'll be leaving for India in a couple of days."

Kate stood listening to Skipper's familiar, retreating foot-steps moving off down the hall against the polished parquet. How hollow and empty his steps sounded. And how final the click of the front door, closing on the silence.

He was gone, and Kate knew that she was going to miss him terribly. In so many, many ways, Skip Brophy had made her feel good about herself.

Chapter Thirty

It was nearly dawn when Kate awoke with her heart pounding and the satin bedsheets drenched with perspiration. For several moments she lay in the darkness, trying to locate herself in time and space. Trying to exorcise the nightmare from which she had just awakened.

Kate had dreamed of Adrianna. She had seen her dancing there in that very room, just as she had danced at her final performance at Lincoln Center. While her figure remained hazy and insubstantial, Adrianna seemed to move in fluid slow motion through her magnificent solo number from *Les Emerauds de la Reine*.

She was like a drifting pillar of smoke wafted by a gentle breath of wind. Shrouded in vaporous white veils that clung and flowed about her long stalk of a body, Adrianna's tossing mane of fiery hair was starkly molten against skin as pale as Chinese porcelain.

Adrianna's features looked waxen and ghostly in the faint light; as lifeless as a death mask, gradually evaporating into nothingness.

Kate sat bolt upright as the phone suddenly shrilled beside the bed. She reached out to place her hand upon the receiver, feeling sick and trembling with dread.

For a long time Kate remained frozen as the phone kept up its incessant ringing, with each ring growing successively more shrill and urgently demanding.

Then, on the tenth ring, Kate released the breath she had been holding. She lifted the instrument to her ear and heard a sudden crash of static, coupled with distant voices speaking in garbled bursts of French. There were a series of strange sonarlike blips that quickly escalated into a piercing metallic scream.

"Hello . . . hello . . . ?" Kate said. "Is someone there?"

"I am trying to place a collect call to Miss Katherine Leslie, from a Mrs. Paul Osborn in Beirut, Lebanon."

"Yes, of course, operator," Kate responded breathlessly. "Please put the call through immediately."

Suddenly everything was silent except for the sound of softly muffled weeping from the other end of the line. "Allison . . .?" Kate questioned in a tentative voice.

"Oh Christ, Kate . . . thank God it's you. I thought I'd never be able to get through. I've been trying for hours, but the goddamned phones have been out because of the fucking revolution. Can you imagine these assholes are actually shelling the goddamned Beirut Hilton? Here we are stuck right in the middle of some kind of asshole revolution, and Paul had to go and have a fucking coronary."

"Allison . . ." Kate's voice was sharp and tautly commanding. "Get hold of yourself, and tell me about Paul. How is he now? What's happened to him, Allison?"

Once again there came the sound of weeping, coupled with

the distant banshee wail of air raid sirens, and the rapid, crackling tattoo of automatic weapons fire. Then a moment of distilled silence, during which Kate could hear her own heart beating.

"Allison?" Kate demanded with a desperate edge honing her voice. "Is Paul dead . . . ?"

"He's in pretty bad shape," Allison snuffed in a tearful plaint. "Paul's in the intensive care unit at the hospital. The doctors don't know yet if he's going to make it."

Chapter Thirty-one

Fate had once again dealt a sickeningly cruel blow. Kate was shattered by news of Paul's heart attack. But work as always had been her salvation. Only by driving herself beyond the point of mental and physical exhaustion was she able to cope with the crushing burdens that seemed to have descended upon her so swiftly and unexpectedly.

If there was such a thing as her own personal universe, then Kate's office was definitely the heart and center. For it was there that the well-ordered complexity, the controlled industry of herself and her staff, could be readily visualized as a reliable functioning structure of which she herself was totally in command.

Kate had been dreading her visit to the New Jersey factory, and had been putting it off for the past several weeks. But now, after receiving a sternly reprimanding memo from Scotty

McPherson, Kate reluctantly decided to make the trip across the river to New Jersey on the first Monday in March.

It was a dreary gray day, and the sprawling, slightly dilapidated factory complex, begun thirty years ago by Colin Leslie along the heavily industrialized Trenton River, could not have looked any more depressing.

Immediately upon her arrival that afternoon, there had been the obligatory tour of the factory, storage, and shipping facilities. It was Kate's first visit since becoming president of the company, and she couldn't help but marvel at how her father's original operation had mushroomed over the intervening years to include a dozen large structures, located upon sixty acres of prime industrial parkland.

The original name peeling from the front of the main building still read LESLIE CHEMICAL COMPANY LTD. And her father's old office was exactly as Kate remembered it from many years before, rather cramped and comfortably worn, with a rag-tag assortment of outdated office furnishings, while the knotty-pine walls were still covered with her father's hunting and fishing trophies.

Even now his portrait still hung behind the big scarred oaken desk. His faded features were as stern and uncompromising as Kate remembered. Even now, after all these years, he still seemed to be scrutinizing her like a judge about to deliver sentence.

"This will take the chill out of your bones," Scotty announced as he placed two big mugs of steaming black coffee on the edge of the desk, and proceeded to fill each of them to the brim from a bottle of Irish whisky.

Kate tried to smile at him as she took one of the steaming mugs in both hands, as if warming herself with the brew. Coffee with a generous slug of Irish whisky had always been her father's way of announcing that there were serious problems afoot, and the time had come to solve them with straight, tough talk.

"Well now . . ." Scotty began as he settled into the scuffed leather chair that Kate remembered so well. "It's been quite a while since we last talked. What's the latest news on Paul Osborn?"

"He's been flown out of Beirut and taken to the American Hospital in Rome," Kate informed him. "Paul's no longer on the critical list, Scotty. But he is still a very sick man. After all, they had to do a triple bypass in open-heart surgery. Paul was just lucky to survive."

Scotty sipped his scalding coffee, and then shook his head from side to side. "You know it's a damn shame that Paul went off half-cocked and married that Jeffries girl. She'll end up putting him in his grave."

The ensuing silence between them was strained and uncomfortable. Kate could hear the loud ticking of the old ship's clock, and, to escape Scotty's uncompromising gaze, she concentrated her attention upon the huge map of the United States that dominated the far wall.

It wasn't difficult to recall the same map when there had been no more than a handful of color-coded pins dotting the northeastern part of the country. But that had been over twenty years before, and now there were thousands everywhere.

Kate finally turned back to Scotty, who was patiently cleaning out the bowl of his pipe with a penknife and knocking the cinders into a nearby ashtray. "You said that you had something important you needed to discuss with me," Kate reminded him. "Something so important that you refused to even discuss it with me on the phone." Kate paused to glance down at the platinum Piaget on her wrist. "I have to be back in Manhattan for a cocktail appointment, Scotty. So we really don't have much time."

Refusing to be rushed, McPherson proceeded to sip his coffee and deliberately scrutinize Kate from the depths of her father's old straight-backed leather chair.

"We don't get to see very much of you around here anymore, Katherine. Except maybe in the magazine ads or on the TV."

"Running Caramour is a full-time job," she responded matter-of-factly. "Besides, Mac, you know everything there is to know about running the company from this end. You don't need me to tell you your business."

"I guess you noticed when you drove up in that big, swell white car of yours that the name *Leslie* is still out in front. As long as I'm around to have any say in the matter, it's goin' to stay there. You see, Katherine, it's a name that's always gotten a lot of respect in this business."

"What is it you're trying to say, Mac?"

"Just that there's something mighty damn fishy going on, and I have a hunch that you may find yourself right smack in the middle of the biggest scandal to hit the cosmetics industry in the last decade. Caramour's in trouble, Katherine. Big trouble."

Kate's brow furrowed. "What kind of trouble?"

"Government trouble," he said dourly. "It's your boy Drexel. He's been involving himself in some mighty strange goings-on, and that's for damn sure."

Kate sat watching in an agony of apprehension as Scotty removed a scorched briar pipe from the pocket of his baggy maroon sweater. Slowly he tamped it full of Prince Albert pipe tobacco from the humidor he had kept on the corner of his desk for as long as she could remember.

Then, striking a match against the sole of his shoe, he began puffing away with maddening concentration until the tobacco finally began to burn. Kate was ready to scream with impatience, but the rich, dark smell of Prince Albert tobacco immediately calmed her with memories of another day. She sipped deliberately from her mug of coffee and realized that she had almost entirely forgotten the taste of good Irish whisky.

"How many women has Drexel got working for him in that pussy brigade of his?"

"We prefer to call them Beauty Reps," Kate informed him patiently. "And there are over a thousand, nationwide. About half of them will be in New York all this week for the annual sales convention."

"I'm gonna give it to you straight," Scotty advised. "Ever since you put Rejuvenal on the market, your Reps have been offering certain wholesalers much lower prices than our major customers are getting. On the face of it the scheme accounts for very strong sales figures, since they place a lot bigger orders. You don't know it yet, because all the figures are still in the computer, but you are going to have a serious accounts receivables problem in the very near future."

Scotty sat there in her father's chair with his head wreathed in a drifting haze of smoke. "I suppose you're already aware that this kind of chicanery is illegal under the Robinson-Patman Act? The law clearly states that every account sold by a cosmetic manufacturer has to receive equal treatment."

"But you know as well as I do, Mac, that most companies violate the law regularly by giving volumn discounts in the form of equivalent promotional benefits. In most cases, the discounts are entirely justified in order to meet competition."

McPherson shook his head, gripping his pipe tightly between his teeth as he spoke. "What Drexel has been doing is a very different kettle of fish. He has authorized the Reps to make sizable under-the-table deals with any wholesaler who agreed to push Rejuvenal. The Reps just signed a letter on Caramour stationery authorizing X number of dollars, to be spent for so-called promotion and advertising the product.

Then the wholesaler kicked back twenty percent and subtracted as much as forty-five percent from what they owed us. The problem we now have is that hundreds of small to medium-sized wholesalers are refusing to pay up because they know they have us by the balls. What Drexel did is so clearly illegal that most of them are counting on us not pressing them too hard."

Kate was angry and exasperated, but she was puzzled as well. "But why would Drexel take such a chance? He must have known that it would show up eventually in accounts receivable. What made him stick his neck out like that?"

"From what I've been able to determine, the Beauty Reps were kicking back at least ten percent to Drexel, and it's almost impossible to pin anything directly on him. I guess he was betting on the fact that as long as sales were way up nobody was going to make waves."

Kate rose abruptly from her chair and restlessly paced the room to stand before the window, looking out. Across the way in the distribution depot, a half-dozen huge diesels were backed up to the loading docks. Beyond was the Trenton River, with a lone tug sliding through the oily black water with a heavy barge in tow.

When she was growing up, Kate recalled, there had been trees and grass, and family picnics along the riverbank. She stood in profile with the light washing in through the windows to softly illuminate her features. Kate's eyes were haunted and smoky with the past.

"What do you think the accounts receivables will add up to in the final analysis?" she finally asked.

"There's no real way of being certain," Scotty responded. "But my best guess would be somewhere around five to seven million dollars. Of course you can have your legal eagles over at that fancy company headquarters of yours write it off as a tax loss. But there's no way that you can square it with the SEC. After all, Caramour stock is up ten points on the market in just eight months. The SEC takes a very dim view of falsely inflating corporate profits as you very well know. I've still got a few connections in Washington, and from what I've been able to determine, someone has deliberately blown the whistle in order to instigate a top-level government investigation."

The culprit was only too obvious, Kate realized. It was I.C.E., with Henri Dayne directing the entire scenario from behind the scenes. If an SEC investigation were launched, they would inevitably step in to buy up all the Caramour stock they could lay their hands on at bargain basement prices.

McPherson came forward in his chair to spew forth a cloud of smoke and cinders from the bowl of his pipe. Then he banged the bowl several times on the bottom of his shoe, and once again began tamping the pipe full of fresh tobacco. "While you've been running around with your rich friends in your chauffeured limo, and flying back and forth to the Caribbean in the company jet, someone has been workin' overtime to try and destroy everything that your father and Paul Osborn spent their lives building up. Frankly, I hate to be the one to have to tell you this, Katherine. But if the wholesalers decide to turn state's evidence—and well they might if it's a question of savin' their own necks—you could suddenly find yourself under indictment along with Max Drexel."

Kate was aghast, but she was angry as well. "Surely no one could possibly believe that I had any hand in engineering this whole sleazy business about kickbacks; or that my saleswomen are screwing to meet unreasonable sales quotas at my bequest. I mean, my reputation has got to stand for something in this business, after all these years."

Scotty removed the scorched briar pipe from his tightly

clenched teeth and pointed it in Kate's direction like a naked accusation.

"Money talks," Scotty dourly intoned, "and money walks. Surely you can't be so naive that it hasn't occurred to you that if you were to unload your Caramour stock holdings on today's market, you would suddenly find yourself to be a very, very rich woman. You'd better give that some thought, Katherine. An astute prosecutor might just find that a compelling argument for conviction."

Chapter Thirty-two

It was after six o'clock in the evening, with a heavy spring rain streaking and running against her office windows. Her sable coat thrown across her shoulders, Kate sat behind the gleaming expanse of her desk, with a light blue folder before her marked DREXEL, MAXMILIAN WALTER. HIGHLY CONFIDENTIAL. Next to it lay Paul's Second World War service revolver. Kate had discovered it inside the locked file cabinet. Taking a deep breath, Kate slowly opened the folder and carefully aligned the sheets before her, which documented Max Drexel's general background, his accounts in a variety of banks, as well as his outstanding stock and security holdings. Then, with meticulous care, Kate began to trace Drexel's various financial transactions from a date five years earlier, when he had first joined Caramour as Domestic Sales Manager.

Kate worked with total concentration and attention to

detail, while scribbling notes on a nearby pad and making various calculations on a small electronic computer.

It took her about an hour to follow the labyrinthine twistings and turnings of Drexel's myriad financial transactions and transfers of capital from one bank account to another. But as she worked, a shadowy picture began to emerge that perfectly coincided with an accompanying outline provided by a crack team of private investigators hired by Paul Osborn.

Of particular interest was a single fluid account that Drexel kept in the Grand Bahama Bank in Nassau, which seemed to be a funnel leading eventually to a secret bank account at Credit Suisse in Zurich. In the margin of the report the number (36X-2879) appeared in Paul's own hand.

Feeling both tense and drained, Kate leaned back in her chair with her fingers clasped beneath her chin. There was plenty of additional information of a highly personal nature, but Kate had seen enough. It was already eminently clear that Drexel had been working the kickback scheme through his Beauty Reps from the very beginning, and Paul had known all about it.

For over five years, Kate realized, Caramour had been consistently involved in the practice of illegal price discrimination, which was prohibited by the Robinson-Patman Act. Paul had obviously kept close tabs on the operation. But he had done absolutely nothing to put a stop to it just as long as the sales figures kept climbing, and the legal department was somehow able to write off the losses or bury them somewhere in the annual stockholders' report.

Feeling chilled to the bone, Kate stroked the sleeves of her fur coat as she considered the gravity of her situation. There was something vaguely reassuring about the feel of the opulent animal pelts, and reassurance was exactly what she needed most.

Never in her life had Kate felt more isolated and alone.

Always in the back of her mind throughout the past year had been the reassuring knowledge that if things ever got too rough, she could send out an SOS to Paul for reinforcement.

But now Paul Osborn was a broken man, lying in an oxygen tent in a Rome hospital. He had created a monster in Max Drexel, and now Kate herself had been left to deal with the consequences. The crisis consumed her.

But at that critical point in the game, Kate realized that she didn't dare loose her nerve. She would have to most definitely keep her wits about her if both she and Caramour were to survive. Considering the desperate drift of her present circumstances, Kate had become convinced that there was now only one course of action open to her.

Drexel had turned everything she had worked so hard to achieve into fraud and sham. Kate loathed and despised him for it, and the idea of venting her vengeance and her anger was eminently appealing on a variety of levels. Max Drexel was going to have to take a fall.

Kate felt like a huntress tracking powerful prey. But she would have to act swiftly to bring criminal charges against him by turning the blue file over to the State Attorney General. Kate was also willing to offer her complete cooperation in the case, which ran the chance of destroying, or at least derailing, her own career in the process.

Still, she didn't really see that she had any choice but to go after Drexel, in hope of stalling the SEC investigation. What she needed was time in order to consolidate her power base and establish the legitimacy of the cell-rejuvenation concept in the public mind. Max Drexel's indictment for criminal fraud might take years to make its way through the courts.

Whatever the outcome, Kate realized that she was also losing a powerful, if entirely mercenary, ally. However virulent and abrasive his personality, Max Drexel had been able to deliver the goods when it counted. Without him she stood totally alone, and there was no longer the slightest doubt in Kate's mind but that I.C.E. would stop at nothing in order to prevail.

Nor did she any longer doubt that she was being followed twenty-four hours a day. Upon entering the lobby that morning, she had recognized one of the men who had been shadowing her around the clock. The man lingering in the lobby phone booth was the same man she had seen several days earlier talking nonchalantly to the doorman of the building next door to where she lived.

It had begun to seem to Kate that she was surrounded by enemies on every side. That afternoon a sealed manila envelope had been delivered by a messenger from the editorial offices of *Cosmetology Today.* It was a typescript of Garrett Forbes' second article on Caramour, Inc., and until that very moment Kate had been unwilling to discover what new and devastating disclosures might lie within.

A LEGEND IN THE MAKING

by
Garrett Forbes

When a woman by the name of Katherine Leslie was named president of Caramour Cosmetics early last May, more than a few eyebrows were raised. Paul Osborn, whose corporate savvy and sheer dynamism had nurtured the company to a competitive edge in the cosmetics industry, was admittedly a hard act to follow. But it was more than that.

At first many people in the business found it difficult to take Miss Leslie's elevated status all that seriously. It was assumed that due to their long and some suggested *intimate* association, the retiring Osborn would continue to call the shots.

Cosmetics can after all be a very cynical business, and shortly after Katherine Leslie's appointment to the presidency, Senior Vice President Henri Dayne was quoted as saying that the cushy title was little more than a "token gesture" that was "relatively meaningless" in the larger corporate scheme of things.

Since that time, the same Henri Dayne has been summarily demoted if not actually deposed by some very slick maneuvering on the part of Caramour's new lady president. The question is no longer whether or not Katherine Leslie is fully in command.

But rather whether or not the company can survive her endless, restless ambition, which during the past ten months has made her a formidable force to be reckoned with in the cosmetics industry.

In questioning those who have been associated with her, it seems that no one can manage to supply any but the scantiest personal details. Katherine Leslie would appear to be a very private woman indeed, even though all seem to be highly impressed by her obsessive commitment to Caramour, her career, and Paul Osborn. There seems to be general admiration for her business acumen, creativity, and high intelligence, while even her most vociferous critics cannot help but be impressed by the breadth and swiftness of her unparalleled success.

According to media whiz Shanga Duprez, who has worked closely with Miss Leslie on the Rejuvenal promotion, she is "a brilliant package of creative and managerial skills, who also just happens to be highly attractive, extremely intelligent, and not even remotely interested in the pursuit of power for its own sake."

Yet there are others in the cosmetics industry who picture Katherine Leslie as coldly ambitious, ruthless, hard, and unfulfilled. She seems to be something of an enigma, although the preponderant evidence points to a succession of bruised male egos and career casualties along the road to her own vision of how a cosmetics company should be run.

While never an ardent feminist, Katherine Leslie moved ahead in corporate management by playing all sides against the middle. For the most part, the lower-level managerial staff at Caramour has been replaced by women, who all report directly to the president's office. The board of directors has not met in almost nine months, and Miss Leslie continues to run the company by executive fiat.

There are of course the rumors about kickbacks, flesh peddling, and a pending investigation by the SEC. Nor is there the remotest doubt that Miss Leslie knows where all the bodies are buried, and has not the slightest compunction about going straight for the jugular.

According to Theodore Baxley, who recently retired from the Caramour board for unstipulated reasons of "ill health," "Katherine Leslie is a velvet-gloved castrator, who has done her level best to emasculate any man in the company she considers a threat to her own ambitions."

Another Leslie critic who prefers to remain anonymous says, "She is the kind of woman who makes any real friendship all but impossible. A woman who seems to trust no one, and remains largely inaccessible behind a shield of opaque and steely self-assurance."

In spite of her astounding success in conceiving and marketing the Rejuvenal skin-care products line, many questions about Katherine Leslie remain unanswered. With Caramour's projected entrance into the rejuvenation spa business, a lot of people would like to know more about Doctor Andreas Jaccard.

He is the controversial Nobel-Award-winning researcher who formulated the highly touted youth drug called Rejuvenal-12. Is cell rejuvenation therapy an idea whose time has come? Or is the "eternal youth syndrome" a very dangerous and questionable medical hoax, capable of causing serious disability or even death?

These are the questions that will be examined in a future edition of *Cosmetology Today.*

As Kate finished reading, there was a brief knock on her office door, and Wes popped his head inside. "Have you ever heard of a place called Dante's Inferno?" he asked.

Kate looked blank, then puzzled, motioning for him to come inside with a wave of her cigarette. Considering what she had just read, she was glad of any distraction. Deftly she covered Paul's service revolver with Drexel's blue file, and slipped both of them into the top drawer of her desk. "From what I've heard, it's some sort of swinging singles disco, considered to be definitely too far out for words. Isn't it one of those sex-swapping palaces?" Kate questioned.

"That and a few other things too sordid to mention."

Wes came over to perch himself on the corner of Kate's desk. "And while we're on the subject of things too sordid to mention . . . I was over at the convention late this afternoon, and the word going around is that Max Drexel has rented the place out for the night, and invited about a hundred top salesmen from the cosmetic wholesalers convention at the Hilton."

Wes reached into the pocket of his blazer and withdrew a golden key hanging from a heavy gold chain. Dangling it before her questioning gaze, he said, "What you see before you is 'the key to the kingdom.' At least that was what Max Drexel was telling your beauty reps when he passed them out this afternoon—to a select group known for great knockers, round heels, and terrific sales figures.

"You can take my word for it, Katherine, they don't call them the pussy brigade for nothing."

Chapter Thirty-three

As the cab pulled up to the curb in front of Dante's Inferno, Wes reached over to clasp Kate's hand. "Are you sure that you want to go through with this?"

"I have to know," she said quietly.

Suddenly conscious of the driver's eyes fixed upon her in the rearview mirror, Kate realized that it was not her real self he was seeing. It was rather her impersonation of a flashy-looking blonde in a skimpy clinging jersey dress, ranch mink chubby, and high stiletto heels. They clattered on the wet cement as she climbed from the cab and crossed the sidewalk to wait while Wes paid the driver.

The street was nearly empty of traffic, and the lights of the Jersey shoreline glittered across the cold black water of New York harbor like a gaudy rhinestone necklace. The heavy rain earlier in the evening had washed everything clean, and the breeze sweeping in from the Verrazano Narrows Bridge smelled fresh and briny—of the sea.

"That guy just offered me fifty bucks to sleep with you." Wes grinned. "I guess that means your disguise is a success."

Taking her by the arm, Wes drew Kate back into a shadowed doorway. "Fortunately for you, I just happen to have some Grade A *numero uno* snorting stuff that's gonna take you right up there to where you need to go. I mean you'd have to be a certified masochist, walking into that seething slough of sexuality cold turkey."

Kate started to protest as Wes poured a small mound of white powder onto his thumbnail and quickly applied it to each nostril in turn. He inhaled with several short snorts, and then licked the crystalline dust from his thumbnail with a quick, practiced flick of his tongue. "Have I ever steered you wrong in a tight spot?" he questioned with the exaggerated patience of someone continually forced to explain the obvious.

"Go ahead and take a couple of good snorts," he commanded. Wes spilled some more white powder onto his thumbnail and presented her with a crisp one-hundred-dollar bill rolled into a tube. "You can take my word for it, Katherine, all this is going to look a lot more reasonable if you're stoned out of your gourd. It's the only way to fly."

Kate hesitated only briefly. Wes was right. She desperately needed something to pick her up, and the magical promise of the white crystalline powder quickly overcame any qualms she might have otherwise had.

Repeating Wes' bravura performance, she sniffed hard several times in quick succession, and then blinked rapidly as brightly luminous waves seemed to wash over her mind with a cleansing purity.

Arm in arm they moved back out onto the sidewalk and started walking toward Dante's Inferno. "What did you tell the driver when he offered you fifty dollars to sleep with me?" Kate teased in a lightly bantering voice.

"I informed him that your time was worth something in the neighborhood of two thousand dollars an hour. But I don't think that he believed me."

After being queried through a grilled aperture in the door, Kate and Wes were finally admitted by a fiftyish-looking dyke with a brusque manner and immobile features that spoke of either terminal boredom or totally jaded sophistication. Kate wore the golden key of admission about her neck, and it fell into the deep cleavage of her dress.

They were presented with black satin eye masks and finally buzzed through an electronically controlled inner door to be confronted with a solid wall of noise. Quite obviously the party had been in progress for some time, with nearly everyone at a different stage of undress.

"Why don't you wait for me here?" Wes suggested, leading Kate over to a relatively secluded nook close by the heated pool. "I'll check our coats, and pop over to the bar for a couple of drinks."

Kate just nodded, scarcely trusting herself to speak, as she sank gratefully down on the edge of a padded lounger. The coke was beginning to work on her head with changing hues and colors. The huge basement room seemed to be whirling slowly about her, while her vision alternately faded and then refocused with brilliant clarity and sharp definition.

Everything seemed slightly exaggerated, larger than life and vividly technicolor. Wes made a thumbs-up gesture, and then disappeared into the crowd thronging the dance floor. Flashing strobe lights seemed to ricochet from the turning mirrored ball hanging above all the variously clad bodies, writhing and twisting to a blaring disco beat. Everybody was wearing the same black satin eye masks, which succeeded in endowing the proceedings with an aura of forbidden and anonymous sexuality.

The air was close, moist, and redolent with the sweet, dark, insinuating smell of burning hashish. While from a tinted plastic bubble high above the illuminated Plexiglas dance floor, a twentieth-century pied piper steadily upgraded the stereophonic frenzy quotient. The dancers appeared to Kate to be hurling themselves at the silver mylar walls like swarming locusts flying headlong into onrushing headlights.

Kate was not exactly sure at that point just what it was she had been expecting. But certainly it was not the full-fledged bacchanal so uproariously in progress. Shadowy figures moved together in the dimness of pillowed nooks, while others openly kissed, fondled, and caressed in the heated pool, which clouded the air with a perfumed mist.

There was a veritable jungle of synthetic plants adorned with twinkling Italian lights. No one seemed to mind the heat or the crush or all the close bodily contact. Most of the men wore little more than towels draped sarong-style about the waist, the women were more distinctively attired, in lace teddies, sheer bikini briefs, and high-heeled mules.

Kate had by now lost all track of time. It seemed ages since Wes had gone for drinks. But it could have been only a matter of minutes until she was almost startled out of her wits by a hand clasping her breast from behind.

"Hey there, sweetheart. What's a looker like you doing hiding out over here all by herself?"

Kate spun about to confront a husky six-footer draped in a pink towel. His drawl was pure Texas Panhandle, and he reeked of Scotch and strong cologne as he pulled her hard against him.

The sharp slap she gave him was a purely reflex action. As the Texan staggered backward in shocked surprise, Kate turned on her heel and bolted out onto the dance floor, where she was immediately engulfed in a sea of dancers who twisted and turned to the thundering beat of the throbbing disco music.

Somehow she made it through the wildly swinging, swaying, and jiggling crush of bodies, only to find herself inside a room with wall-to-wall mattresses, illuminated by an eerie blue luminescence. The room was filled with people; a flowing, moving, montage of breasts, thighs, backs, arms, heads, and genitals.

Kate remained pressed and frozen against the wall. It was like viewing an aquarium swarming with slow, amorphic underwater movements. Outside the music was still blaring, but now it seemed to come from a great distance. There in the dimness, the sounds were soft, and caressing hands seemed to move in slow, freeze-frame motion, over naked limbs and torsos, that kept dissolving and materializing like erotic shadows cast upon a luminous screen.

She fled the mat room, possessed by a kind of blind urgency that carried her along a maze of narrow hallways with individual cubicles opening off on either side. Kate could only imagine what might be going on behind the closed doors, and breathed an enormous sigh of relief when she finally reached the ladies' lounge, marked by a red neon sign.

Inside, the room's mirrored walls provided a reflective kaleidoscopic image of a woman Kate scarcely recognized. She tore the blonde wig from her head, and pulled wads of toilet paper from the dispenser inside one of the cubicles. Then Kate slumped down on a padded stool before the mirrored makeup table, surrounded by pink vanity bulbs, and began to wipe the heavy cosmetic mask from her face.

Suddenly the door swung open and Max Drexel stormed inside, accompanied by a blast of the endlessly throbbing disco beat, a bust of shrill teasing laughter, and the sound of breaking glass. He slammed the door shut behind him and jammed a straight-backed chair beneath the handle before turning to confront her.

Kate had not moved, nor did she turn around. Their eyes met and dueled in the reflective surface of the mirror. Her features appeared totally blank in the harsh flourescent lighting. Her mascara was caked and running, while her lipstick had become a bright red smear across her chalk-white face.

"I want you to turn around and go back out there, to put an end to what's going on," she instructed in a coldly commanding voice. "You're scum, Max, and everything you touch becomes infected. I suppose I actually had to see this with my own eyes in order to do what I have to do."

More composed now, Drexel began pacing slowly toward her. He was chewing on the ragged end of a half-smoked cigar and clutching a bottle of bourbon in one hand like a grenade. Max was wearing a monogrammed dressing gown of wine-red satin, and his bare feet were slippered in snakeskin.

Kate saw something in his eyes that bordered on the inhuman, a hooded, piercing look. As he came toward her Drexel seemed to exude a mindless ferocity, as palpable as a massive electric charge. Something about him terrified her, but Kate knew that the one thing she could not afford to do was lose her nerve.

"And just what is it you intend to do?" Drexel challenged.

Kate reached into her bag, removed a tube of lipstick, and swiftly scrawled the numbers *36X-2879*. "Does that mean anything to you? For instance, does it remind you of a secret numbered Swiss bank account?"

She swung around to face him directly. "I'm turning your blue file over to the Manhattan District Attorney's office, Max. You see, the SEC is going to investigate Caramour. Someone tipped them off about your kickback scheme. Who knows, they probably even know about your stable of whores out there—the whole ugly disgusting business."

Max Drexel was breathing heavily as he stood looming over her. He laughed harshly; drunk, dissolute, and blatantly unrepentant. "And just where do you think all that will get you?" he sneered. "You wanted big sales figures in the first six weeks after Rejuvenal was launched, and that's exactly what you got, with a built-in bonus. I made you, sister. And if you want to know why those men are out there tonight, banging your top salesladies, I'll tell you that too. Those guys account for over one-fourth of all sales at the wholesale level."

He leaned closer, and Kate could smell the liquor flaming on his breath. "Excuse me all to hell, madame lily white, but I didn't hear any complaints from you as long as the big bucks kept rolling into the corporate till, and the price of Caramour stock went right straight through the ceiling."

Max paused to exhale a single perfect smoke ring, billowing directly in her face. "*Blackmail* is such an ugly word, isn't it, Katherine?"

Kate turned sharply back to the mirror, and, taking a comb from her purse, she began running it through her hair in short, attacking strokes. "I made a serious mistake," she admitted.

Drexel tilted the bottle of bourbon to his lips and swilled deeply. Then he wiped his mouth with the back of his beefy hand, and held her firmly with his eyes.

Glancing at his reflection in the mirror, Kate realized he was gauging her somehow. Measuring her, as if trying to find the place where she would be most painfully vulnerable.

"Ya know, I really gotta hand it to you, Katherine. Sometimes I get amazed at what a terrific little actress you are. I mean, you're sitting here talking to me like you were pure as the driven snow or something."

Drexel's jaw muscles twitched, and his eyes were as hard as stones. "I know all about you," he said. "All about you and Jaccard, and the way he got rid of his wife."

Kate tried to rise, but Drexel gripped her roughly by the arm and forced her to sit back down abruptly. "A very convenient accident, wouldn't you agree, Katherine? Now the two of you are free to marry."

All expression had drained from Kate's face as though wiped clean by an unseen hand. "What are you talking about?" she demanded.

"I'm talking about the dynamite that somebody put in Ingrid Jaccard's luggage—or didn't you know about that?"

For several moments they continued to stare into each other's eyes, yet neither was willing to yield. Then Drexel smiled and released the grip of his fingers biting into her arm. It was a hungry, wolflike smile.

Picking up the blonde wig that Kate had been wearing, he hoisted himself into a sitting position on the edge of the makeup table, and slowly began to wipe and smear away the numbers she had written upon the mirror. "Now me, I'm a student of human nature so to speak. For instance, I picked you for a wild card from the very beginning, and decided that I was going to need some insurance."

"Insurance . . . ?" Kate repeated, staring into the messy red smear of lipstick.

"Yeah, *insurance*. You know the kind of stuff—tapes and pictures. I've had you followed for months, Katherine. I've had a tap on your phone . . . at the office . . . your apartment . . . your place out in Amagansett. I even had the foresight to stick a bug in your villa on Coral Key the night Jaccard paid you a visit during the blackout. Hell, I even tracked those gumshoes down who pulled the raid on you and Jaccard at the Hotel Victoria. I got the pictures for five hundred bucks, and I'm pretty sure it's going to turn out to be a good investment. Wouldn't you say so, Katherine?''

Kate was numb with shock, suddenly exhausted by a game that seemed to go on and on with no clear victories or winners. Time was running out on her, and it was beginning to take more energy than she had just to stay even.

Max Drexel removed the cigar from between his teeth and slowly ground it out among the cosmetics that had spilled out into the formica counter from her open purse. Her lipstick lay there between them, with its glossy red tip gently molded by her lips. Drexel picked it up, carefully put on the cap, and then slipped it into his pocket.

''Now me, I'm a reasonable sort of guy, and I just happen to have a solution to all your problems.''

Drexel removed a wad of crisp new one-hundred-dollar bills from the pocket of his dressing gown, and lovingly riffled through the currency with his thumb. ''You know what, Katherine, a lot of people talk about money as cold, hard cash. Now doesn't that just sound like about the silliest thing you ever heard? But then I guess a lot of people look at money the wrong way.''

Once again the wad of money crackled to his touch. ''Money's soft,'' he cooed, ''and it's a very practical color, don't you think? I mean, it does go with anything you've got, doesn't it? And the more you've got of it, the better it's gonna go.''

A question shimmered in Kate's eyes, but she didn't move a muscle. Not the slightest flicker of an eyelash.

''Trust me, Katherine,'' Drexel said. ''There isn't going to be any SEC investigation, and you're not going to turn that file over to anyone. Just remember! There are a lot of people who have a lot to lose if you should start to get . . . let's just say . . . self-destructive. This is the big leagues, and we play for keeps.''

Chapter Thirty-four

The chopper lifted effortlessly into the clear, bright spring air above midtown Manhattan and fluttered skyward across the East River, glinting silver in the morning sunlight.

Kate didn't bother to unfasten her seat belt, since it was only going to be a short hop. Instead she leaned her head back against the seat rest and closed her eyes against the spectacular panorama of the world's greatest city spread out below her. Leaving Manhattan on that particular Sunday morning was more like a strategic retreat. In New York her life had become a jeweled web spun with gold and platinum lies. With each new and unexpected contraction of events, the glittering mesh had begun to tighten; to suffocate and to entrap. With an unsettling sense of dire premonition, Kate had begun to believe that even more ghastly revelations were yet to come.

In twenty minutes they would be setting down at the

Westchester Airport, where the Caramour corporate jet was waiting to fly her off to the island of Bermuda. To Celia Randolph's wedding to Benny Valdez aboard the newly refurbished yacht *Sultana*.

Ever since her soul shattering confrontation with Drexel at Dante's Inferno the week before, Kate had been consumed by one crisis after another.

On Monday the *Wall Street Journal* had come out with a front-page headline that blared: SEC INVESTIGATES BEAUTY BONANZA. It was enough to raise a specter—the glare of ugly publicity. By the time the Stock Exchange closed for business on Tuesday, the price of Caramour stock had already slipped two points.

On Wednesday Kate received a registered letter from Washington that had been waiting for her when she arrived at her office. It was from the Ethics Subcommittee of the Security Exchange Commission, and requested a visit to Washington at her earliest convenience, in order that Kate might share any knowledge she might have relevant to the sudden and quite spectacular rise in the price of Caramour stock.

It had been one of the longest working days of her life, but for the first time her work did not manage to distract her. It was in fact impossible to concentrate on anything but the forthcoming hearings and the impact they would undoubtedly have upon her career and her life. Kate was frantic at the thought of being dragged through the muck of a high-level investigation, which was guaranteed to expose her to the glare of public scrutiny.

By the close of the working day on Thursday, the pending investigation had begun to cause cancellation of major wholesaler contracts. There was talk throughout the industry of little else beside the Beautygate Scandal, which managed to elevate even the most spurious gossip to the level of factual information.

The storm clouds were gathering rather more rapidly than Kate could have possibly imagined, and there were times when she felt as if she were balancing on a razor's edge. Within a twenty-four-hour period, Kate made over two hundred phone calls in order to reassure restive creditors, wholesalers, important stock market arbiters, and various banking moneymen. She also called in every IOU she held outstanding, and by five o'clock on Friday evening the downward slide of Caramour stock had stabilized, at least for the time being.

Reading the *New York Times* over breakfast on Saturday morning, Kate was further shocked to discover that Theodore Baxley had been rushed to a Palm Springs hospital after an abortive attempt at drowning himself in his own swimming pool.

According to the article, word of his secret homoerotic activities and subsequent arrest had been leaked to a West Coast scandal sheet known for scavenging the lives of prominent people. Kate felt awful about what had happened to Baxley, but she was also very much aware that it was Max Drexel's way of putting her on notice. Of warning her that if she had any thought of crossing him, he was perfectly willing to play rough.

If it had accomplished nothing else, her confrontation with Drexel had the effect of jolting Kate awake to her predicament with stunning clarity. She had been forced to face an entire spectrum of new emotions—anger, bitterness, and resentment. Overall, the terrible frustration of seeing all she had worked so hard to achieve threatened by imminent destruction.

It was like riding a roller coaster running wildly out of control, and there seemed to be absolutely nothing she could do to stop it.

Kate knew now that she had been lying to herself for as

long as she could remember. She had lived her life as little more than an interested observer, and always from a safe distance.

Now she had come to that place where she had never intended to go, and there was no turning back, because the journey had changed her irrevocably and forever. Kate had no choice but to confront the truth about herself, and the only thing that really kept her going was the belief that somehow she could manage to cross over—to break through to the other side. To that place where she would never again have to be afraid. Not of age or loss or even death.

As the helicopter clattered across the sky, Kate didn't even bother to look back. Earlier in the week she had received a letter from Skipper. The postmark read Bombay-India, but Kate had not been able to bring herself to open it. At least not until that moment, with the combat zone receding in her wake.

Now she slid her nail beneath the flap of the envelope and drew out a short single-page letter accompanied by a polaroid photograph.

Kate sat staring down at Skipper's boyishly beguiling features. His skin was very tan and his hair very blond, as if from spending a lot of time in the sun. The photo had been snapped by some anonymous polaroid, and Brian had been captured standing on the bank of a river. There was an ancient stone temple silhouetted against a sky of brilliant postcard blue, and he was smiling that old familiar smile she knew so well.

For over seven months Brian Brophy had been like ballast in her life, and there were times when Kate missed him desperately.

His letter read:

> Salutations from Shangri-la. I am living at Ganeshpuri, where Baba's ashram is located in a beautiful valley

surrounded by mountains. Everything is very lush and green at this time of year, with rice paddies mirroring the sky, browsing water buffalo, and the sacred Saraswati River winding through the valley like a silver serpent.

There is something marvelous here, Kate, if I can only attain it. Just to sit in Baba's presence each day in the sunlit marble courtyard of the ashram is something very high, and not at all within the realm of my ordinary comprehension. Words seem to be entirely unnecessary. Just looking into his eyes is to receive a moment of truth and clarity that is often very hard to bear.

Being here with Baba has come to mean many things to me. It means converting my energies to something higher. It means awakening to my own inner experience, and coming to know my relationship to everything and everyone that is. It means being totally present within each passing moment. But perhaps most of all, it means feeling like a more natural and authentic human being.

P.S. By the way, I'll bet you would like to know how I knew you were crazy for soft-shelled crabs.

The handwriting blurred before her eyes. How utterly ridiculous, Kate thought, blinking rapidly. Was it possible that she'd actually allowed herself to fall in love with a postadolescent called *Skipper*? A wonderful, beautiful, insanely rational dreamer, who had suddenly become her only link to some ultimate reality.

At least she knew that he was out there somewhere, Kate thought with a twinge of desperation. And that he still cared.

Celia had chosen a seductive panorama against which to stage her marriage to Benny Valdez. White sails, azure, sun-sparkled water, and a chain of lush, green islands with pink sand beaches and softly curling hills peaking up to gently caress a clear and cloudless sky.

Even from a distance Kate immediately recognized the dazzling white superstructure of the *Sultana*.

The yacht totally dominated the outer harbor at Hamilton with her highly polished teak decks, towering masts, and shimmering brasswork.

As the Bermudair helicopter came clattering down out of the sky to settle lightly onto the yacht's new heli-pad, Kate stepped from the cockpit and ducked down beneath the backwash of the whirling rotor-blades. She was carrying a single piece of Vuitton luggage and her briefcase.

Benny Valdez was waiting to greet her. With his handsome bronzed features, shorter hair style, open body shirt, and white Cardin suit, he managed to look so casually right that it was not in the least difficult for Kate to imagine that he had been greeting people arriving aboard yachts forever.

Benny informed her that the "usual crowd" was already aboard for the festivities. There were gardenias floating in the swimming pool, orchids strung along the railings, and white-coated stewards setting out china, silver, and crystal along a shimmering white linen table set up beneath the striped awning on the afterdeck.

The nuptial vows were to be exchanged at precisely sunset, and the ceremony was to be conducted by the ship's captain.

One hour later Kate was just about to rap on the door of the Donatello Suite when the ornately carved doors were thrown open and a crisply uniformed negro maid bolted past Kate and ran off sobbing down the companionway.

"Thank God you finally arrived. That just goes to prove that there is still some power in prayer."

Kate turned to find Jon-Claude Fabiani advancing toward her across the familiar Bohkara carpeting. She had never liked Celia's designer in residence, even though she wore many of his clothes. Jon-Claude was of course attractive in his own sly-featured way, but Kate had always distrusted him instinctively. He was far too sure of his social cachet and the rich neurotic women who fawned over him in such a wildly extravagant manner.

"It's probably just a case of bridal nerves," Kate said with more conviction than she felt. "I'm sure Celia will lighten up once she gets all tarted up for the ceremony."

Jon-Claude looked extremely dubious as he lifted her hand and brushed it lightly with his lips. "Anyway, *ma cherie,* I'm dumping the whole mess in your lap. I've got to dash off and zip up the Principessa. Since *your* Doctor Jaccard wasn't able to make the wedding, Wonder Woman has pressed me into service as best man."

Before Kate could think of anything even remotely appropriate to respond, he was gone, trailing the scent of his highly successful Fabiani Unisex cologne.

Kate moved across the carpeted foyer and into Celia's boudoir to find her in the process of dressing behind a Renaissance tapestry screen. "Where the hell have you been?" Celia demanded crossly. "Do you have any idea what it's like trying to keep dry under the arms when your maid of honor hasn't shown up for the ceremony?"

"Something important came up," Kate responded in measured tones. Since purchasing the *Sultana* at auction, Celia had converted the yacht into a virtual floating *palazzo.*

What had previously been Fiona's luxurious silken seraglia was now completely refurnished with eighteenth-century Venetian antiques. In the adjoining bathroom Kate discovered delicate mosaic flooring of Sienna marble, gold-plated faucets, and a sunken tub decorated with the most exquisite inlaid tiles of dolphins and flying fish.

Crossing to the wash basin, Kate ran herself a glass of water and gulped down two little yellow pills from an enameled pillbox. Then, with Celia's voice prattling on from the next room, Kate stood staring at her own reflection. She wore a summery pastel garden-party dress the color of morning sunlight, and her hair gleamed in burnished auburn waves as it fell to her shoulders, giving her a casual rather than a studied formal-wedding look.

Kate was surprised to see that her features appeared smoothly composed. Her complexion looked fresh and radiantly clear, with no visible signs of the intense emotional strain she had been undergoing over the past several weeks.

It was almost eerie, Kate thought. There wasn't a sign of the pills, the alcohol, the three packs of cigarettes a day, and the long sleepless nights.

"Kate darling," Celia called out. "You haven't said a word out there. What do you think of the *CeliaMar*? Of course it cost me an arm and a leg to do the whole ship over, but then who can put a price tag on the Italian Renaissance."

Kate returned to the bedroom. "The *CeliaMar* . . . ?" she repeated. "It sounds like some kind of dairy creamer."

From behind the brocaded screen there was a flutter of white arms thrusting upward through some lacy garment with trailing ribbons.

Celia pretended not to have heard the comment. "I guess you didn't know that I rechristened the *Sultana*. Oh I know it's supposed to be something like fifty years of bad luck, but I simply couldn't resist. Isn't it perfect? Celia Mar was the stage name I used as a Ziegfeld Girl over forty-five years ago."

Kate began to wander about the room, trying to shake the uneasy sense of treading on quicksand. She reached out to touch a sheer scarf, a satin dancing slipper, a jeweled belt. They were all Celia's possessions, as was everything in the room, and yet Kate could not seem to exorcise the powerful sense of Fiona's presence, as if she had just stepped out the door only moments before her own arrival.

"Will you get me my bridal bouquet from the florist's box on the bed?" Celia called. "I'm almost ready to make my grand entrance."

Kate did as she asked, but as she threw back the embroidered Toronini hangings she realized with a startled gasp that Fiona's huge gilded swan bed was still in place.

For just a moment, Kate thought she could even smell the cloying and familiar sickly sweet stench of cancer.

"Well, darling, what do you think of my *robe de mariage*? That flaming fruitcake Fabiani only finished basting me into it fifteen minutes ago, and I can scarcely get my breath."

Kate hardly knew what to say. Celia's wedding dress was a truly indescribable bubbling white confection, with butterfly sleeves, a floating hemline, and a towering trellis of lace veiling falling over a mass of lacquered golden ringlets.

"I had no idea you were going all out," Kate finally managed. "I mean . . . a formal white lace wedding dress, Celia . . . ?"

Celia took the bouquet of white lilies from her hand, and struck a typically demure bridal pose in front of the gilded pier glass. "I either got carried away by the idea of getting married again, or went bananas when I discovered that this lace was embroidered by cloistered eighteenth-century nuns on a small island in Lake Como. I mean, after all darling, this is going to be my last time out, on a very fast and slippery track. You can hardly blame me for wanting to make the most of it."

Celia busied about, pouring each of them a glass of Tattinger '59 from a champagne bottle chilling in a silver urn. "We've only got about fifteen minutes before sunset, so there isn't much time. Everyone else is already up on deck."

"Why did you decide to be married at sunset?" Kate questioned.

"It had something to do with my Virgo being in transit through Benny's Uranus. According to my latest I Ching reading, there won't be another time quite as auspicious until 1996. And I'm not at all sure that I'll still be around by then. One has to get it, so to speak, while the getting's good. *N' est-ce pas, cherie*?"

Celia lifted her glass. "Let's drink to the man who's responsible for everything. Here's to Doctor Andreas Jaccard. He has performed miracles in both our lives."

They toasted and drank, but a shadow had fallen across Kate's features.

"There's something I have to talk to you about," she ventured tentatively. "This morning I went to visit Adrianna in the hospital. That's why I was so late in arriving.

"Her doctor, Doctor Charboneau, told me that José del Bario has agreed to have Adrianna transferred down to Coral Key. Andreas has persuaded him that she should be under his exclusive care."

Celia pursed her painted rosebud lips. "Oh, Katie. Why are you still torturing yourself with those morbid hospital visits? Surely you must have been convinced by now that Adrianna is never going to be . . . well, not going to be *right* again. Who knows whether she could even survive without all those tubes and bottles and machines?"

"She's not like that anymore," Kate interjected shortly. "Adrianna has been surviving on her own, *without* the machines, ever since Christmas. If you had ever bothered to go and see her, you would realize that her condition is very much improved."

Celia sighed deeply, drank off her champagne in a gulp, and quickly refilled her glass. "Now let's try not to get overemotional about this thing," Celia patiently recited. "Have you actually seen Adrianna make one single voluntary move? Has she even wiggled a finger or a toe?"

Kate shook her head regretfully. "No, nothing like that. You're just going to have to take my word for it. There have been times lately when I knew that Adrianna realized I was there." By now Kate was imploring Celia with her eyes, and, reaching out, she clasped her hand, pressing it fervently.

"Just do one simple thing for me, Celia. You know José del Bario much better than I do. You've got to convince him not to send Adrianna to Coral Key. At least not yet."

Clearly out of patience, Celia pulled her hand away. "I will do no such thing, and I've heard quite enough of this dreadful morbidity. This is my wedding day after all, Katherine, and I have absolutely no intention of listening to one more depressing word—from you or from anyone else. Now have I made myself entirely clear?"

Kate appeared chagrined and profusely apologetic. "You're absolutely right, Celia. It was awful of me to drop that on you right out of the blue, like that." Her voice was low and slightly shaky. "I'm not myself lately. Quite frankly, I'm terrified about this government investigation and what it is likely to turn up. I feel so confused . . . so vulnerable. If only I could talk to Paul, if only he were well enough to stand the strain."

Celia's laughter was brittle and short. "Unless I'm terribly mistaken, *vulnerable* is not exactly the word most frequently used to describe you, Katherine. I've heard *ruthless* and *calculating*, but *vulnerable* hasn't cropped up once."

Kate stared at Celia in disbelief, not wanting to believe her ears. "At least I'm not just another middle-aged woman grasping and clawing after younger men." As soon as the words were out of her mouth, Kate regretted having said them. But Celia had already turned deliberately away.

"This is neither the time nor the place to continue this

conversation,'' Celia snapped. ''We have about five minutes. I suggest you have another drink and try and pull yourself together, while I put the finishing touches on my makeup.''

Kate spoke softly and with deep regret. ''I didn't mean that the way it sounded, Celia. I'd hate for you to think that I did.''

Celia's response was brightly metallic. ''Of course you didn't mean it—at least not like that. But don't think I'm not aware of your views about Benny and me. I suppose there might even be those who would consider you something of a hypocrite. I mean after all, there you were last year carrying on affairs with a twenty-six-year-old billionaire and a very much married doctor.''

''My, but you were a busy girl, weren't you, Katie? I often wonder how you manage to keep your stories straight.''

With that Celia bustled into the bathroom and closed the door behind her. Kate could hear water running as she stood staring out the porthole. The sun was dying in the west, and the sea was shimmering with a skein of molten light.

Suddenly the phone was ringing and someone was knocking.

''Celia,'' Kate called, crossing to rap lightly on the bathroom door. ''It's time . . . we have to go on deck.''

The only response from inside was the crash of shattering glass. Leaning close against the door, Kate thought she heard a muffled cry followed by a soft thud. Like the sound a human body would make falling hard against cold marble tiles.

Chapter Thirty-five

Miami International Air Terminal wavered like a mirage in the sun-blasted afternoon. Out on the tarmac, the Air Jamaica 707 shimmered in the heat haze like a ghostly silver projectile. The flight had originated in New York that morning, and had set down in Miami only long enough to refuel for the long flight south to Montego Bay.

It was dim and cool inside the first-class cabin. A pretty black stewardess was handing out the latest Miami newspapers, while the air filtration system played like a sibilant whisper in the background. In the galley at the front of the plane, a white-coated steward was preparing to serve a luncheon of Russian caviar and fresh cracked crab, along with a light, dry Pouilly Fuissé.

Kate sat alone in the last row of seats before cabin class. She had requested a window seat. The flight was lightly booked, and she was dressed in a belted trench coat, slacks, sweater, low, comfortable walking shoes, a floppy-brimmed felt hat, and oversize sunglasses that largely obscured her features. There was an unlit cigarette poised between her fingers, while a glass of white wine stood untouched on the white linen cloth.

Celia's death had come with stunning suddenness. After suffering what doctors later described as a massive cerebral embolism, she had been ferried by helicopter to a hospital in Hamilton, Bermuda. And it was there that Kate had kept a desperate twenty-four-hour vigil, praying for Celia to regain consciousness.

Then she was dead, and Kate was left stunned by the swiftness of her passing. Yet out of her ordeal had come the terrible awareness that Adrianna, Fiona, and now Celia had all been struck down in exactly the same manner. The sudden clotting and bursting of a blood vessel inside the head. Doctor Charboneau had described it as "a massive cerebral contusion," like a small grenade exploding inside the human brain.

Celia had been buried on a sparkling spring day that was sharply clear and warm in the sun.

Cameras flashed as Kate emerged from the church flanked by Shanga and Wes, and was handed into the back seat of her waiting Rolls. Then, just as the car was about to pull away from the curb for the short drive to the cemetery, Garrett Forbes came shoving his way through the crowd to thrust a letter through the open car window into Kate's gloved hand.

"I think you'd better have a look at this, Miss Leslie. It's from Doctor Meyerhof in Geneva. It's about Jaccard."

The words had been spoken like an indictment. But at the time Kate was still too benumbed by grief to pay more than nominal attention, and simply slipped the letter into her purse.

But later that evening, after returning to Manhattan and the privacy and seclusion of her River House apartment, her worst fears had been confirmed.

Whatever the cost, Kate realized, she no longer had any choice but to fly to Jamaica and uncover the whole truth.

"Would you like to see a copy of the Miami *Herald*?" It was the voice of the stewardess, bright and lilting with a West Indian accent.

Kate reached to take the paper from the girl's outstretched hand. Then her eyes moved to the name tag on the girl's shoulder. Kate smiled. "Thank you, Miss Livingston. And by the way, one of the pursers brought aboard a case of high-speed film for me. I'm shooting an advertising layout in Jamaica, so I didn't want to take any chances on having the film ruined in your security X-ray machine."

"I'll bring it to your seat as soon as we're airborne, Miss Leslie." The stewardess' ingratiating smile was suddenly dazzling in her café au lait face. "I saw your picture on the cover of *Time* magazine, Miss Leslie, and I have to say that it didn't nearly do you justice."

With that she returned to the front of the plane and Kate buckled herself into a seat for takeoff.

One by one the massive 707 engines came shrieking to life and the plane began taxiing slowly along the runway. Then, ever more swiftly, the huge jet continued to gather speed until finally lifting off the macadam airstrip to climb effortlessly into the pure blue sky.

As Kate waited impatiently for the NO SMOKING sign to be switched off, her eyes turned restlessly to scan the headline copy of the Miami *Herald*. DUCHESS OF SUTHERLAND DEAD. The words seemed to fairly leap out at her, and the accompanying photograph was from the Caramour beauty spa gala at the St. George Hotel.

Lady Brenda had died within forty-eight hours of Celia Randolph, Kate discovered as she feverishly scanned the print. Both had died after suffering massive cerebral embolisms, and both had left everything to the Jaccard Foundation for Life Extension Research.

Kate lurched forward in her seat as the stewardess lightly tapped her on the shoulder. "Here is your camera case, Miss Leslie. But you know that the purser could have gotten in a lot of trouble carrying it through for you. Security is pretty strict with all these hijackings to Cuba."

Kate summoned her most glamorous celebrity smile and took the camera case into her lap. "Now, really, Miss Livingston. Do I look like the kind of woman who would be smuggling something lethal aboard?"

For a long time after the stewardess had brought her double vodka on the rocks, and Kate had declined her offer of the first-class gourmet luncheon, Kate sat staring into the outer emptiness.

"Our lives are but a spark of light, between one darkness and another." It was the opening line of Celia's eulogy, and Kate could not seem to get it out of her mind. Ever since the funeral, the words had been darting and racing like some small, scared, and terribly vulnerable creatures trapped forever in an experimental maze.

Taking a key from her purse, Kate unlocked the camera bag in her lap and slipped her hand inside. Paul Osborn's service revolver was wrapped in a Valentino scarf, and for just an instant Kate caught the heady scent of L'Immortal perfume. Kate had removed the weapon from the blue file early that morning as she was sending Drexel's incriminating dossier to the State Attorney General's office by special bonded messenger.

Slowly Kate's fingers traced the cold metal outlines. Then she lifted it slightly to test the deadly weight and feel of the weapon in her hand.

Now she was the only one left, Kate realized. Lightly she caressed the trigger. The sole survivor of the Newborns.

PART FIVE

A Point of Light—And Beyond

Chapter Thirty-six

For several hours before the murder trial of Katherine Leslie was to begin, the old Montego Bay courthouse on Britannia Street was overflowing with spectators. The trial was to be held in the large judicial chamber on the first floor, and corridors throughout the building were under heavy police guard.

Newspaper correspondents, photographers, and wire service stringers were everywhere, and passes to the trial were being scalped at outrageous prices in the most prestigious hotel lobbies in Montego Bay.

When Kate entered the courtroom for the first time, she found herself in a commodious wood-panelled chamber with the seats divided in rows of wooden benches. At the front of the room was a raised platform upon which stood the judicial bench, with a high-backed leather chair for the presiding magistrate.

Robbed entirely in black, and wearing a traditional white peruke, he was the right honorable Sir Malcome Wingate, an impressive-looking Jamaican with heavy African features and imposing stature.

After being shown to her seat at the defendant's table fronting the courtroom, Kate turned immediately to scan the jury box, from which she in turn was being observed by twelve coldly hostile dark faces. Four women and eight men who all appeared to be staring at her as if she were some kind of deadly specimen being presented for scrutiny beneath the powerful microscope of the High Court inquiry.

It was crowded, close, and humid inside the courtroom, and the slowly turning ceiling fans did little more than faintly stir the torpid air.

Kate was dressed simply, with little makeup and no adornment whatever. She looked tense and withdrawn. Yet as soon as she had been led into the courtroom by two strapping six-foot Jamaican marshals, a wave of excited whisperings swept the chamber.

After six weeks of incarceration in a Jamaican prison, Kate looked thinner. But the leanness only served to accentuate the strongly sculpted bone structure and to endow her features with a haunted and vulnerable quality that had not been there before.

Seated at Kate's left was the hugely corpulent figure of Tyler Grayson, her lawyer. They were leaning together in urgent whispered conversation as the proceedings began to get under way.

Grayson was widely acknowledged to be one of the most successful criminal lawyers in America. He was a highly theatrical man, the very personification of a Kentucky colonel, who combined a deceptively easygoing Southern gentility with ferocious fealty to his clients, and, some said, extremely elastic ethics.

While his style was exceedingly leisurely and relaxed, Tyler Grayson was known for his ability to wither prosecution witnesses under cross-examination. His forte, however, was intimidating public prosecutors, and his approach to the jury was invariably one of courtly deference.

Grayson had never lost a major case. But neither had he previously defended a client against first-degree murder charges in such a pervasively hostile atmosphere.

At the prosecution table, on the other side of the aisle, Justin Marley sat huddled with his staff lawyers. The prosecutor was a distinguished-looking mulatto whose upper lip was neatly mustached and whose skin was a light tobacco hue.

Marley was a crisp, incisive speaker who had been schooled at Oxford, and had a consummate mastery of the English language. He spoke and wrote at least a dozen other languages as well and was often called to lecture upon the British system of jurisprudence to groups of jurists around the world.

Few who faced him in court were not immediately intimidated by his sharply inquisitive stare. The brooding saturnine features and lofty brow were capped with patent-leather black hair slicked back sleekly against his skull. The sideburns were crisply graying, worn stylishly long, and perfectly barbered.

The Jaccard murder case was perceived by many as exactly the vehicle that Justin Marley needed to catapult him to instant international judicial acclaim. No other event in memory had drawn so many foreign newspaper correspondents and newsreel cameramen to Jamaica. It was no secret that Marley had long entertained high political aspirations.

On the local front the trial was headline news, and had succeeded in arousing a torrent of antiwhite sentiment among the general populace. Jaccard had been highly renowned in Jamaica, and Kate Leslie was tried and found guilty almost daily by the press as some new and ever more sensational aspect of the case came to light.

Had they been asked, most of the islanders would have voted for a verdict of guilty, and professional gamblers frequenting the posh casinos were offering odds of fifty to one that Kate would be convicted of first-degree murder.

The trial was about to begin. The presiding judge banged his gavel, and the courtroom came gradually to order.

The prosecutor rose and walked to the jury box. His movements were marked by a quick, feline grace. In his right hand Marley carried a fly whisk, which he habitually switched along his well-tailored thigh, or used to punctuate his crisply declarative style of speaking.

As Justin Marley began his opening statement, there were many present in the courtroom who were convinced that he had set his sights on running for prime minister in the coming election year. If such were the case, the Jaccard murder trial was precisely the vehicle through which to extend his already formidable reputation for having a "jugular mystique."

"The Jaccard affair," he informed the packed courtroom, "was the case that had everything. Passion, glamor, betrayal, and, ultimately, a grisly murder."

Marley went on to describe the principal cast of characters as "globe-trotting narcissists, white Norte-Americanos of the rich and privileged persuasion. Those who see the world as a mirror, that exists solely in order to reflect their own celebrity, wealth, and power."

The jury sat spellbound as Marley continued speaking in his tightly clipped British accent. He gave every indication of having an airtight evidential case. Crisp and well tailored, he was perfectly composed.

Then Marley was moving toward Kate with slow deliberation. He flicked his cuffs and leaned forward against the smooth wooden railing encircling the judicial arena at the front of the courtroom.

Kate refused intimidation as he pointed one finely manicured finger directly at her. "Before the close of this trial," he pronounced, "I intend to demonstrate to this court that this woman cold-bloodedly planned and executed the murder of one of Jamaica's most esteemed men of science. And that she committed this brutal act with both malice and forethought."

Prosecutor Marley dropped his accusing pose, and his voice became dangerously soft. "By her own admission, Katherine Leslie was at the scene of this . . . heinous butchery. And I shall demonstrate beyond the slightest shadow of doubt that she had the motive, occasion, and fully premeditated intention of terminating the life of Doctor Andreas Jaccard."

Chapter Thirty-seven

During a short recess, Grayson handed Kate a copy of *Cosmetology Today* bearing the headline: YOUTH DRUG MANIA ROCKETS BEAUTY STOCK SKYWARD.

As the dramatic murder trial of beauty tycoon Katherine Leslie gets under way in Jamaica, International Consortium Export has won a stunning victory for control of the company she formerly headed. And yet the latest revelations of shady dealings in high places seem only to have increased the public demand for Caramour's controversial skin-care line.

Thus far, Rejuvenal-12 has launched several government investigations in the United States, as well as a sensational murder trial in Jamaica investigating the circumstances surrounding the violent death of Doctor Andreas Jaccard, the Nobel-winning medical scientist known for his pioneering work in cell-rejuvenation therapy.

While Miss Leslie, Caramour's former president and reportedly Jaccard's mistress, is on trial for her life in Montego Bay, Henri Dayne, acting as spokesman for I.C.E.-Caramour, Inc., indicates that it has been impossible for the company to keep up with the unprecedented public demand for Rejuvenal-12 in topical form.

A flourishing black market is now reportedly in operation, with wealthy middle-aged women willing to pay huge finders' fees in order to secure the product.

In response to our recent series of articles questioning the efficacy of RJ-12, letters have been flooding into the editorial office of *Cosmetology Today,* attesting to near miraculous results. According to Henri Dayne, who is currently acting president of I.C.E.-Caramour, Inc., the company will soon be expanding the total rejuvenation concept into a chain of beauty spas around the world.

Following the thirty-minute recess, the trial reconvened with Prosecutor Marley immediately going on the offensive. "The question with which you are faced, ladies and gentlemen of the jury, is not whether Katherine Leslie killed Andreas Jaccard . . . but rather why she killed him."

Marley was slowly circling the judicial arena with his hands tightly clasped behind his back. "I would submit to you that the defendant murdered Jaccard because she discovered that he intended to break off their relationship."

Marley shrugged expressively. "Of course Jaccard was known to be a womanizer, and he was nothing if not a very slick opportunist. The man was many things, but he was certainly not the monster the defence is attempting to portray."

Marley came to an abrupt halt directly facing the jury. "Now let me ask you this question. Why was it that Miss

Leslie went to the trouble of secreting a weapon in her camera case on her clandestine visit to Coral Key, when she didn't even bother to bring luggage? If Jaccard's murder was not in fact premeditated, then why would she have gone to so much trouble to smuggle a gun through airport security?

"The fact is, ladies and gentlemen of the jury, the woman we are dealing with here today in this courtroom is someone who knows exactly what she's doing, as you will soon see for yourselves."

Marley turned his accusing gaze upon Kate. "What it really comes down to is that this woman is asking us to believe the unbelievable. That a highly respected medical scientist of worldwide repute was engaged in conducting a macabre experiment on a group of well-known and, for the most part, very rich women. But to show you how utterly preposterous her charges actually are, you have only to consider the facts.

"Fiona Van Zandt had already been diagnosed as having terminal cancer. The Duchess of Sutherland was nearly senile and close to ninety years of age, while Mrs. Randolph was a middle-aged alcoholic virago, lusting after virile young males. As for Adrianna del Bario, I have in my possession written testimony from her physician that she was heavily barbiturated at the time of her collapse into coma, and had a history of heart disease as a child."

Marley gestured eloquently with both hands. "As you can see, Miss Leslie herself appears to be in the very best of health. And as for the records she claims could have documented this mad and fanciful experiment . . . quite conveniently they have simply ceased to exist. We are being asked to take her word for the fact that Doctor Jaccard burned them himself in order to eliminate the only existing evidence of his own guilt."

Turning his full attention once again to the jury, Marley pressed his meticulously manicured fingertips together, and tapped them lightly in a highly characteristic gesture.

"Perhaps the most bizarre claim made by Miss Leslie in this ludicrous scenario is that we are asked to believe that Jaccard was about to inject her with some mysterious, and, she believed, *deadly* substance, when the defendant decided to slit his throat with a razor-sharp scalpel she just happened to find handy.

"The man was of course a medical doctor, trying to sedate an hysterical and dangerously paranoid woman. Undoubtedly she did get roughed up a bit by Jaccard after pulling a gun on him. And why not, since she had obviously come to the island and broken into his laboratory in order to take his life!

"Jaccard was merely defending himself, and no doubt trying his best to keep Miss Leslie—his patient—from inflicting serious physical injury upon him or upon herself. It was as simple as that, and I would postulate as well that Jaccard had reason enough to fear the wrath of the woman he fully intended to repudiate."

Marley wagged a finger and gently tapped his handsome head.

"The truth was that Jaccard had already been approached by the conglomerate giant seeking to take control of Caramour Cosmetics. And as I shall subsequently demonstrate, he had already agreed in principle to throw his full support behind a corporate takeover by International Consortium Export, who were committed to franchising Rejuvenal Beauty Spas around the world."

Once again he turned to Kate. "The woman you see before you was desperate—on the verge of losing everything. Katherine Leslie came to Jamaica for only one reason, and that was to murder Doctor Andreas Jaccard in cold blood."

The first prosecution witness was called to the stand.

"Will you state your full name and position," Marley instructed, "and briefly inform the court of just how you happen to be in your present position of authority."

"My name is Henri Wadsworth Dayne, and I am presently the acting president of Caramour Cosmetics Company. Following Miss Leslie's arrest, I was appointed to my present position by a Federal court judge, who is presiding over the currently pending stockholders' suit."

"When was the last time that you saw Doctor Andreas Jaccard alive?"

"One week previous to his death," Dayne responded. "I flew down to Jamaica as a representative of International Consortium Export. It was I.C.E. who initiated the present legal action against Caramour that I spoke of, and my sole purpose in requesting a meeting with Jaccard was to solicit his support of the I.C.E. takeover. Miss Leslie had recently appointed Jaccard to the Caramour board of directors, and his vote was going to be crucial to the ultimate resolution of the stockholders' suit. We met in a room at the St. George Hotel in Porto Cristo."

"And what was Jaccard's response?"

"He agreed to join us."

"I assume that during your meeting with the doctor, that Miss Leslie's name was brought up?"

"That's correct. She was, in fact . . . discussed at length."

"Can you be more specific in that regard? What exactly was it that Jaccard had to say about Miss Leslie?"

"He informed me that he had decided to break off his relationship with Miss Leslie. Jaccard told me that she was becoming increasingly demanding and emotionally unstable. To be precise, he said that he was flying up to New York within the week to inform her of his decision. After that, he was going to go public in his support of the I.C.E. takeover."

"I must assume that you were not entirely satisfied with

the manner in which Miss Leslie was running Caramour Cosmetics.'' It was less a question than a statement of fact.

''In that you are entirely correct,'' Dayne said stiffly.

''For the benefit of the jury, Mr. Dayne, would you try and characterize your dissatisfaction.''

Dayne cleared his throat, picked a speck of lint from his faultlessly tailored pinstripe, and began speaking in short, biting terms. ''During the ten years that I worked with Katherine I found her to be a cynical man hater; ruthless, self-serving, and ultimately false. She was never even remotely qualified to hold such a position of power, and I firmly believe she only got the job because she was Paul Osborn's mistress.''

Tyler Grayson was on his feet with surprising alacrity. ''Your honor, I must object most heartily, unless the witness is prepared to prove his accusation before the court.''

''Objection sustained,'' the judge concurred. ''Mr. Dayne, I must ask you to stick with the facts and respond only to those questions put directly to you by the prosecutor.'' He nodded for Marley to continue, then sat back in his chair to mop his perspiring brow with a white handkerchief.

Outside it was a searing one hundred degrees in the shade, and the courtroom was stifling, in spite of the slowly circling ceiling fans that scarcely seemed to stir the torpid air.

''And now, Mr. Dayne,'' Marley commenced once again, ''after twelve months under Miss Leslie's stewardship, can you describe to us the present conditions prevailing at Caramour?''

''Most simply put,'' Dayne barked, ''the company is presently under investigation by the Security Exchange Commission, while Miss Leslie's second in command has been indicted on one hundred and twelve counts of Gross Fraud and Grand Larceny Fraudulent Misuse of Corporate Funds. It is now a matter of court record that a goodly number of

Caramour sales representatives were greatly inflating sales figures by peddling their sex and kicking back huge sums to Max Drexel. And I quite frankly wouldn't be a bit surprised to find out that our former president was behind the whole thing from the very beginning."

"Objection." Tyler Grayson was on his feet once again. "Your honor, the witness clearly shows a strong personal bias against my client that quite obviously goes far beyond the just resolution of this case."

"Objection sustained. Will you please move along with your questioning, Mr. Marley? This line of inquiry appears to be going nowhere."

"Very well, your honor," Marley conceded. "Just one further question. In simplest terms, Mr. Dayne, how would you sum up Miss Leslie's twelve-month reign as president of Caramour Cosmetics?"

For several moments Dayne remained thoughtfully poised, like an actor about to deliver his best line. Then he said, "Most simply put, Katherine Leslie was a woman possessed by a ravening greed for power."

Chapter Thirty-eight

On the second day of Kate's trial, Tyler Grayson took the floor for the defense.

After gathering together some papers in a rather absent fashion, he got to his feet and ambled slowly across to the jury box, peering myopically through his old-fashioned wire-frame spectacles.

Grayson deliberately prolonged the suspense by removing an antique timepiece from the pocket of his rumpled suit. He carefully noted the time, murmured something to himself, and then lifted his rheumy eyes to scan the double rows of shining dark faces so stonily arrayed before him.

His manner was faintly hesitant as Grayson started speaking, and the members of the jury were immediately forced to strain ever so slightly forward in order to catch his faltering words. In his mind Tyler Grayson clasped a small, worn leather Bible.

"The woman on trial in this court today has been accused of the most heinous offense against humanity. Katherine Leslie stands accused of deliberately snuffing out a man's life, with malice aforethought and premeditation."

Grayson lifted his Bible and waved it aloft. "There is no doubt in my mind but that each one of you seated there in that jury box is familiar with the biblical injunction—*thou shalt not kill!* Society has forbidden us to kill, and yet we send our sons to war because in certain situations the act of murder is readily condoned and often even highly acclaimed.

"We are forbidden to kill, ladies and gentlemen of the jury, and society itself has placed you in that jury box in order to judge who is guilty. Who is to live and who to die, for the adjudged act of illegal murder must be punished.

"But then murder, my friends," Grayson continued, "is not really what this trial is all about. It is about the act of self-preservation. This woman sitting here before you on trial for her life is actually being tried for defending her own existence against a pathological killer, who gave every indication that he intended her serious bodily harm."

Grayson spread his hands and smiled benignly. "My client has been accused by the prosecution of plotting and executing the murder of Andreas Jaccard because she was desperately in love with him and feared rejection."

Tyler Grayson removed his glasses and began wiping the lenses. "But did she love him? That is the question that each of you will have to decide for yourselves. And it is that decision upon which the outcome of this trial and the fate of this woman will ultimately hinge."

Grayson turned to the judge. "Your honor, as the first witness for the defense in this proceeding . . . I would like to call Miss Katherine Leslie to the stand."

The judge was forced to bang his gavel for order as Kate took her place in the witness box to the right of the judicial bench, and it was at least a full minute before order was restored.

"Miss Leslie," Grayson began, with one hand resting upon the lectern, "I want you to reflect very carefully on the testimony you are about to give to this court. Remember that the truth and sincerity of your answers will no doubt determine your fate in the eyes of these twelve good people who have been called upon to render judgment."

"Now," Grayson continued with almost grandfatherly affability, "in your pretrial statement, you said that you flew from New York to Jamaica several days after Celia Randolph's funeral in order to find evidence proving that Doctor Andreas Jaccard was engaged in some kind of illegal medical experiment, to which you believed that you and a select group of other women had been subjected.

"Now, Miss Leslie . . . in your own words, will you tell the jury what it was that so suddenly convinced you that such an experiment had been performed."

Kate responded in a clear, firm voice. "At Celia Randolph's funeral, I was approached by a journalist named Garrett Forbes. He had already informed me that he intended to research Jaccard's background, and he handed me a letter he claimed to have received from Doctor Anton Meyerhof, a man considered to be the foremost expert in the field of cell-rejuvenation therapy. It was after reading that letter that I decided I had no choice but to go to Coral Key in order to discover the truth about Andreas Jaccard."

Grayson turned to the judge, whose shining black features were gleaming with perspiration. It was very hot, muggy, and close, and many spectators present in the courtroom were fluttering palmetto fans or wafting the air with folded newspapers.

Meanwhile the crowd gathered outside in front of the courthouse was angry and bristling. The faces were mostly black, and a mood of sullen hostility prevailed as oppressively as the heat itself. Upon Kate's arrival at the courthouse that morning, the crowd had surged forward to surround her car, with jeering, hostile faces pressing up against the windows.

"Your honor," Grayson addressed the bench, "I would like to ask that the letter in question be placed in evidence, after having been read to the court."

"Your request is so granted, counselor," the judge responded. A transcript of closely typed pages was handed across to the court reporter, who then rose and began reading aloud with a monotonous, sing-song cadence.

"*. . . In response to your recent query about my former protegé, Doctor Andreas Jaccard, I hasten to reply with full truth and candor.*

"*I first encountered Jaccard at a scientific symposium in Paris over fifteen years ago. Along with a great many other people present, I was greatly impressed by both the man himself and by a paper he presented, detailing his recent research into genetic coding. It was on the basis of this that I invited Jaccard to work with me in Geneva, where I put my own research and laboratory entirely at his disposal. At the time I trusted him enough to give him the hand of my only daughter, Angelique, in marriage.*

"*When we first met, I fully believed that Andreas Jaccard stood on the brink of altering human life itself, through the process of what is known in molecular biology as gene splicing.*

"*Andreas was perhaps one of only a handful of scientists in the world who stood in the forefront of a great biological revoluation, which would inevitably give science the ability to manipulate and possibly even control human genes.*

"*Jaccard had become convinced after several years of intense research that somatotropin, or what is known in science as HGH, held the key. It is a substance produced by the pituitary gland at the base of the brain stem. It promotes and regulates normal physical growth.*

"Because HGH had proven to be promising in treating certain forms of dwarfism, Jaccard was convinced that it ultimately held great promise in the science of promoting human longevity. The supply, however, had always been severely limited, since it could only be obtained in minute quantities from cadavers. At the time, I considered Andreas to be a scientific genius, and I encouraged his research into what was to become a most controversial genetic engineering technique known as recombinant DNA.

"Jaccard's experimental thesis was unquestionably brilliant. By using human pituitary tissue, he set out to construct a prototype DNA gene segment that would be capable of producing somatotropin by implanting artificial genes in a laboratory strain of common bacterium.

"It took several years of experimentation, but eventually Jaccard was successful beyond his own furthest expectations. In the interim, however, there were at least two other scientists who had come up with practically the same results. Nevertheless, I myself was so impressed with Andreas' work that I nominated him for the Nobel Prize in Medical Research, which he eventually was forced to share.

"Andreas was extremely bitter about the outcome, and threw himself into his work with something very close to obsession. Then, about a year later, I discovered to my horror that Jaccard had succeeded in combining somatotropin with a cellular-revitalization serum that he called Rejuvenal. He was testing the substance on living human beings, in hopes of discovering a veritable panacea or miracle drug. One that would ultimately cure cancer, restore sexual vigor and vitality, retard the onset of senility, reduce emotional strain, and quite literally rejuvenate the body's entire organic structure.

"There had always been considerable fear of course in the scientific circles regarding manmade genetic hormones. But on the other hand, Andreas was right that the very same process that could populate the world with clones might very well lead to the cure of dozens or perhaps even hundreds of diseases plaguing mankind."

By this point, the voice of the court reporter had almost been drowned out by the melée that had suddenly erupted outside the courthouse.

It was over almost as quickly as it had begun. But reports of the Montego Bay courthouse riot would appear via satellite on the major American news networks that same evening. The frenzied rout. The roiling mass of Jamaicans, surging this way and that, amid searing clouds of tear gas, flashing red lights, and screaming police sirens.

It took several minutes for the judge to restore order in the courtroom itself. But finally the court reporter was once again ordered to continue reading the letter from Doctor Meyerhof to a charged and expectant audience. He began where he had left off. But there was a nervous edge to his voice now, and no one was exactly sure just what was going to happen next.

"I confronted Andreas with the records he had kept on his latest experimentation. I warned him that what he was attempting to do could lead to the possibility of altering the nature of human life on this planet. But he would have none of it. He justified everything that he had done in the name of scientific advancement. Jaccard manifested a complete lack of compassion or remorse for the victims of his experiments, and appeared fundamentally unable to appreciate the gross criminality of his conduct.

The experiment itself involved a half-dozen inmates at the local insane asylum where Jaccard did volunteer medical work. It was a disaster, and several of his patients died, while others collapsed into a state of suspended animation, or deep coma.

"It shall be to my eternal shame that I took no action against him after discovering the truth. I feared the effect the inevitable scandal would have on my own research into cell-rejuvenation therapy, and I also feared for my daughter's safety at the hands of such a man.

"Jaccard agreed to leave Europe and divorce my daughter. In return, I agreed to destroy the evidence of his experimentation, and say nothing about what had taken place, although I had previously threatened to expose him for what he was to the Swiss authorities, and report his activities to the Nobel Scientific Commission in Stockholm.

"Needless to say, I did none of these things. Three weeks later Jaccard was gone, my daughter was dead in a freak boating accident, and the local insane asylum where Jaccard had conducted his experiments had mysteriously burned to the ground.

"In your letter you have asked me to evaluate Jaccard in terms of his general psychological profile, but I believe I can be more specific. Andreas Jaccard is in my opinion a severely disturbed man who appears to be normal, but totally lacks the ability to feel empathy or even ordinary concern for others."

The court reporter returned to his seat upon completion of his recitation, while Grayson proceeded to prolong the suspense the way a great actor holds his audience enthralled through instinctive timing. The revelations thus rendered had been damning indeed, and the stage was fully set.

"And now ladies and gentlemen of the jury," he finally injected, "I would like you to hear my client's story in her own words."

He turned to Kate sitting very erect in the witness chair with her hands tightly clasped in her lap. "Miss Leslie . . . will you be good enough to tell us as clearly as you can exactly what happened after you read the letter from Doctor Meyerhof. What exactly was your reaction?''

''After reading his letter,'' Kate began in a faltering voice, ''I knew it would be useless to report my suspicions to the authorities until I was able to prove what I suspected beyond the slightest trace of a doubt. Andreas had acquired very powerful political connections, and I realized that I had no choice but to go to Coral Key and find out the truth for myself.

''It was already dark by the time I arrived in Montego Bay. I didn't want Andreas to be alerted to my visit, and so I rented a car at the airport and drove across the island to Porto Cristo. I found Benny Valdez drinking in the bar of the St. George Hotel. He was heartbroken over Celia's passing, and he didn't really seem to be surprised when I explained my suspicions that she hadn't died of natural causes.

''We went out to Coral Key in Benny's outboard, and landed on a secluded stretch of beach on the island's leeward side. From there we followed a path leading up through the gardens to the administration building. We didn't see anyone about on the way, but we could hear the guard dogs barking as we got closer. It was almost one o'clock, and Benny said he needed at least fifteen minutes for the drugged meat we had brought along to fully subdue the dogs.

''The lights were out in all the villas. I waited in a cabaña by the swimming pool. Then, using the flashlight I had brought along, I went up the gravel path past the tennis courts and across the lawn to the Great House. Benny had already told me that Andreas kept the key ring for the lab in the desk in his study. He also said that the French doors opening off the study onto the veranda were never locked. It was no problem at all finding the keys . . . and then . . . getting inside the . . . lab.''

Kate's voice faltered. Her eyes fell, and her hands clenched tightly in her lap as if the steely self-control she had thus far exhibited was beginning to come unraveled.

"And once you had gained entrance to Jaccard's inner sanctum sanctorum," Grayson prodded, "what was it you found there? Try and describe to us exactly what it was like."

His voice seemed to bring Kate back from the shadows. She looked up, nodded faintly, and then proceeded to relate her story. Once again her voice was firm and clear, as she addressed herself directly to the jury box with its twelve coldly hostile faces.

"The laboratory was almost clinically austere, totally depersonalized. I remember thinking that it reminded me of an operating theater. There were no windows, nothing to break the monotony of sterile white walls and ceiling. It was very warm, and smelled strongly of formaldehyde.

"I had come to Jamaica counting on Jaccard's meticulous professionalism. If such an experiment as Dr. Meyerhof reported had indeed taken place, Andreas would have documented it fully. As soon as I was able to determine the proper key, I unlocked Andreas' medical file cabinet and removed the files I had come to find. Then I spread them out on the white enamel dissection table in the center of the room, and began photographing all of Celia Randolph's medical records for the past five years. Immediately my worst fears were confirmed.

"It was all there meticulously notated in Jaccard's own hand. Page after page of detailed notes, records, and analyses. There were charts, graphs, and computer printouts. All of it dealing with the series of injections that Celia had received the previous spring, along with myself, Adrianna del Bario, Fiona Van Zandt, and the Duchess of Sutherland.

"Meyerhof had been right. The records clearly showed that, compared to her previous visits, Celia's rejuvenal dosage had been greatly escalated, in conjunction with additional injections of procane and somatotropin.

"I had just begun to photograph the others' files when the door to the lab opened, and I looked up to see Andreas standing in the doorway. He appeared to be as surprised to find me there as I was startled by his unexpected appearance in the lab at that hour of the night.

"Then his eyes moved past me to the files spread out on the dissection table. He saw my camera and flashlight. And when he looked back at me, there was something in his eyes that confirmed—at least in my own mind—that he would never allow me to leave that room alive."

Then, intruding suddenly upon the scene came a voice that was honed to a razor's edge. It came from a spectrally thin young woman who had leapt to her feet to shriek, "She's a lying murderess! A demoness of satan! Don't you understand, Andreas Jaccard wanted to give us all eternal life!"

The woman with the ravaged face and vengeful eyes pointed a spectral finger directly at Kate. "She has murdered the new messiah, and must die for her sin."

Within moments the judge was pounding his gavel, and the entire courtroom erupted into chaos as the hysterically sobbing woman was carried bodily from the chamber by uniformed marshals.

A recess was immediately called, and it wasn't until some thirty minutes later that Kate returned to the witness chair to continue her recitation. She looked pale and shaken, as once again she began to speak.

"Once he realized why I had come, Andreas didn't waste any time in destroying the evidence. He gathered up the incriminating medical file folders and burnt them in a metal basin with a bottle of sulphuric acid.

"Then he exposed the film in my camera. He said that he was sorry I had discovered the truth. He admitted that the experiment had been a failure, but I was wrong that only five of us had participated. Solange Wilkerson had been the sixth.

"Andreas told me she had died, just like the others. Then he proceeded to show me her body in a refrigerated drawer. Solange had been grotesquely mutilated during the autopsy that Andreas had done on her. And I could scarcely relate the butchery I saw with someone I had actually known. With a living human being.

"Then . . . I had the gun in my hand. I told Andreas that I would shoot him if he moved. That I would kill him, the way a mad dog has to be destroyed. Never in my life can I remember feeling such anger . . . such rage and, yes, I suppose . . . hatred. I warned him again, but he kept coming at me. His eyes were terrifying, and I realized suddenly that he had crossed over. That he had actually become that other persona that Meyerhof had described. Someone without the slightest trace of humanity or compassion."

Kate faltered momentarily, and paused to sip a glass of water that Grayson had poured. Her hand trembled slightly as she lifted the glass to her lips, while the courtroom remained completely silent. Then someone sneezed, and it was like a gunshot shattering the simmering hush.

"Please continue," Grayson encouraged. "What did Jaccard do next?"

"Andreas kept coming at me, taking one step after another. He said that I couldn't possibly pull the trigger, and he was right. My hands were shaking so badly that I could scarcely slip off the safety catch before he was on me like some snarling, enraged animal.

"It all happened so fast," she went on in a scarcely audible voice that caused everyone to lean forward in their seats. "Andreas slapped me brutally across the face. Then I felt myself being slammed up against a glass-enclosed cabinet full of surgical instruments. By now he had the muzzle of my revolver pressed hard against my throat. He hit me again and again with his naked fists until I finally pitched forward onto the floor, where he shoved the metal cabinet crashing down on top of me."

Kate brushed one hand across her eyes, clearly making an effort to continue. "I must have blacked out for a space of time. I have no recollection of how long. All I know is that after I began to regain consciousness, I saw Andreas standing over me holding a hypodermic syringe up to the light." She paused, fighting for composure.

Grayson's voice was soft. "Can you tell us what happened next?"

"It was all so confused . . . such a nightmare experience. Andreas was leaning over me trying to find the vein in my arm, and I almost didn't care anymore. I felt so cold inside . . . sick, and in pain. He was looking into my eyes and smiling. Then I felt something cold and sharp touch my fingers. It was a scapel I think . . . that had fallen from the cabinet along with everything else.

"But then I didn't really stop to think, or to reason, or even to feel anything. I'm not even sure just how it happened. The next thing I knew I was slashing and stabbing at his throat, and Andreas was staggering backward, making a terrible choking sound.

"He was clutching his throat, and his hands were running with blood. Andreas tried to speak, but . . . there was only an awful gasping sound," Kate recited in a scarcely audible voice.

"His eyes were wide . . . disbelieving . . . staring at me as if he had thought he would live forever."

Chapter Thirty-nine

After the courtroom had been called into session on the third day of Kate's trial, Tyler Grayson called Benny Valdez to the stand as witness for the defense.

But just as the court bailiff was swearing him in, there was a stir at the rear of the courtroom and heads began to swivel around to stare toward the huge double doors at the rear of the chamber.

Leaning heavily on the arm of a burly white-uniformed male nurse, Paul Osborn had entered. And as he slowly made his way down the aisle, Kate's features bore a startled, tortured look. It was the first time that she had openly betrayed her emotions since the start of the trial.

Paul had aged at least a decade since the last time Kate had seen him. He looked gray faced and haggard, while his clothes hung loosely against his gaunt frame. Kate finally was forced to turn away from the eyes that seemed to be entreating her from across some enormous void.

Then once again the judge was banging his gavel for order, and Tyler Grayson approached the witness box in order to address his first question to Benny Valdez.

"Tell me, Mr. Valdez, what exactly occurred at your meeting with Miss Leslie at the bar of the St. George Hotel on the night of Andreas Jaccard's death?"

"She gave me a letter to read from Doctor Meyerhof in Switzerland. Miss Leslie said that she believed Jaccard was responsible for Celia . . . Mrs. Randolph's death. She asked me to take her out to the island, because she wanted to try and locate some medical files documenting some experiment Jaccard was supposed to have conducted."

"Were you surprised when she told you of her suspicions?"

"No, I wasn't surprised. I worked for that dude over two years. I knew he was always hustling. Jaccard was always on the make, but real cool like, ya know? He had a lotta irons in the fire, and was always lookin' out for the big score."

"Can you be more specific?" Grayson asked patiently.

"It was Jaccard who paid me in the beginning to hustle up to Mrs. Randolph. He gave me five hundred bucks the first day she arrived on Coral Key. Jaccard said to be extra nice to her. He told me to make her feel attractive . . . desirable."

Benny Valdez had changed greatly since that first day Kate had met him at the Porto Cristo Airport. He sat in the witness box looking more youthfully attractive than ever, and wearing a look of suave sophistication in his navy blue blazer, gray slacks, Gucci loafers, and open-neck polo shirt.

The transformation from local tennis pro to suavely polished sophisticate was still something less than complete. Yet Benny's own natural sense of self-assurance and boyish charm made him an impressive witness. He was totally unaffected and extremely likeable, and the jury was paying close attention to his testimony. It was not in the least difficult to see how a Celia might have been swept off her feet.

"In your opinion, Mr. Valdez, what was it Jaccard was trying to accomplish?"

"Jaccard wanted me to convince Celia . . . Mrs. Randolph, to sell out all her holdings in New York, and invest down here. When the *Sultana* was up for auction, he sold a lot of local politicos on the idea of turning it into a gambling ship anchored in the harbor at Porto Cristo. Celia fronted the deal without knowing that there were a lot of other people going to be in on the take. Andreas was hustling Celia Randolph from the first day she set foot on Coral Key."

"Tell us, Mr. Valdez. How did you feel about *shilling* for Jaccard, so to speak?"

"Jaccard used everybody," Benny responded evenly. "At first I didn't really mind. He paid well, and I wasn't doing anything else with my time. Besides, Celia . . . she seemed happy with the arrangement, and I didn't see how it could cause any trouble for anyone. Like Andreas said, everybody was getting exactly what they wanted. Then later, when Celia began to get serious about the idea of getting married, I wanted to tell her everything, but Jaccard wouldn't let me. He said if I did, he'd have the Haitians who worked for him 'deep six me.' You know—eliminate me by cutting my air hose while I was diving, or something like that."

"And were you intimidated by this threat?"

Benny pondered. "Not at first I wasn't. Then about a week later Doctor Jaccard's wife, Ingrid, was killed in the midair explosion of a rented plane flying her to Miami. The same day I discovered that three sticks of dynamite were missing from a storeroom on the island. We'd been using the explosives to blow up coral heads in the lagoon."

"Did you tell Doctor Jaccard about the missing explosives?"

"Yes I did," Benny admitted. "He slipped me ten brand

new one-hundred-dollar bills, and told me to forget it. He said the Haitians had been using the dynamite illegally, to blow up schools of fish."

In the wake of his accusation, a wave of whispered speculation swept through the courtroom, and Justin Marley was immediately on his feet. "Your honor, I must object. This is nothing but unfounded and scurrilous accusation against a man who is quite unable to defend himself on this side of the grave."

Marley paused to allow his gaze to cut like a whip over the defense table. "If there is one single shred of hard evidence to prove that Andreas Jaccard was the psychopathic monster that the defense is trying to portray, I demand that it be presented to the court."

"If I may be permitted the court's indulgence, your honor." It was Tyler Grayson, standing at the defense table holding a sealed manila envelope in his hand. "There is no better way to demonstrate exactly the proof my colleague demands than to recount my discovery of the single most definitive piece of evidence as yet presented to this court."

"If such evidence is pertinent to the speedy resolution of this proceeding, then so be it," the judge pronounced.

For several lingering moments Tyler Grayson remained poised before the jury box, rocking slightly back and forth on the balls of his surprisingly small feet. One hand was plunged deeply into the pocket of his baggy white linen suit, while in the other the sealed manila folder tapped absently against the scarred ebony railing enclosing the jurors.

Then, very softly at first, Grayson began to speak, his languid, drawling voice rising and falling gently. His delivery was sonorously grandiloquent in a casually insinuating way, while from the very beginning, Tyler Grayson's audience remained rapt and straining, so as not to miss a single word.

"Yesterday afternoon—after this court went into recess—I

was able to convince Benny Valdez to accompany me on a visit to the island of Coral Key. Somehow I had become convinced that in order to truly understand what had really taken place it would be necessary for me to retrace the same steps that Katherine Leslie had herself taken on that fatal night when Doctor Andreas Jaccard met his rendezvous with death.''

Very carefully and methodically, Grayson removed his silver-frame spectacles and proceeded to clean and polish the lenses with a crumpled white linen handkerchief. Then, after absently returning the manila envelope to his pocket, he continued his story. ''It was dark by the time we arrived, and I couldn't help wondering exactly what it was that Katherine Leslie must have felt when she herself stepped ashore on that strange and lovely tropical island, determined to discover the truth, no matter what the cost.

''For as everyone here in this courtroom is already aware, out of the five women who had undergone cellular therapy along with her that previous spring, my client was by then the only survivor. There could have been no possible doubt in her mind as to what was at stake, if her suspicions of Jaccard proved to be correct. Everything hung in the balance. Her career . . . her personal freedom . . . and perhaps . . . even her life.''

Tyler Grayson paced ponderously back and forth for several moments before the jury box, stroking his courtly Van Dyke and fingering his gold watch chain. In the stifling air inside the overcrowded courtroom, there was absolute silence.

''I persuaded one of the Haitian caretakers to let me into the sanctum sanctorum of Jaccard's multimillion-dollar laboratory,'' Grayson went on to relate, ''although he did so only after the receipt of a generous inducement in the form of hard Yankee cash.''

There was a nervous twitter of laughter from somewhere in

the courtroom, and Grayson once again took the opportunity to remove a large crumpled handkerchief and absently mop his perspiring brow. "My client has testified before you that she came to Coral Key to verify an accusation concerning Andreas Jaccard's professionalism as a scientific researcher. Indeed, after unlocking his medical file cabinet, she has claimed under oath . . . that all her worst fears were immediately confirmed.

"It was all there," he said gravely. "Every single detail of the experiment had been carefully recorded in Doctor Jaccard's own handwriting. Page after page of detailed notes, records, and analyses pertaining to the series of injections he had administered to Katherine Leslie, Celia Randolph, Adrianna del Bario, Fiona Van Zandt, and the Duchess of Sutherland the previous spring.

"It was at that point in her investigation that my client realized that Meyerhof had been right. Andreas Jaccard was a dangerous psychotic, totally irresponsible in his experiments on other human beings. And only moments later, when the said Doctor Jaccard suddenly burst unexpectedly upon the scene, Katherine Leslie also realized that he would never allow her to leave the island of Coral Key alive." Grayson paused and regarded the jury.

"As you might well imagine," he continued, "Jaccard wasted no time whatsoever in destroying the incriminating file folders that Miss Leslie had been attempting to photgraph. He even went so far as to admit, ladies and gentlemen, that the experiment itself had indeed been a failure. And that there had been six rather than five participants, as Miss Leslie had previously supposed.

"Now what would you have done in her place?" Tyler Grayson questioned in a voice as seductively veiled as hanging Spanish moss. "To be sadistically forced to look upon the mutilated remains of someone you had known. Someone who was now being kept in a refrigerated drawer by a madman, fully imbued with a sense of his own godlike omnipotence.

"Yes, it's true that Katherine Leslie had a gun in her purse," he added hurriedly. "And she admitted to you herself that she threatened to shoot Jaccard if he made a move to molest her in any way at all. But alas," Grayson lamented, "it was all to no avail. Because before she was able to properly defend herself, Jaccard was on her like some snarling, enraged beast. You, present in this courtroom today, have already seen photographic evidence that Miss Leslie had been beaten into unconsciousness. And she herself has testified that she awakened to find Andreas Jaccard leaning over her with a hypodermic syringe in his hand.

"But by that point, ladies and gentlemen of the jury, Katherine Leslie was completely beyond any coherent thought. All she felt was the fiercely primal will to survive, and in the very next moment she found herself slashing and stabbing at Andreas Jaccard's throat with a sharp-edged instrument that had fallen to the floor during their earlier struggle. Then Jaccard was staggering backward clutching his throat . . . and his hands were running with blood."

The courtroom was utterly silent as Grayson finally removed the mysterious manila envelope from his baggy jacket pocket, and slowly waved it back and forth before the jury like a conjurer's potion. "Inside this envelope is a portion of tape recording I recovered from Andreas Jaccard's laboratory, after discovering that he had installed a voice-activated taping system during the recent renovation. In its entirety, the original tape was used by Jaccard to record his findings in the autopsy of Solange Wilkerson. I believe it is time, ladies and gentlemen of the jury, to let Doctor Andreas Jaccard speak for himself."

Prosecutor Marley was immediately on his feet. "Your honor, I must object!" he shouted, with his voice crackling from the loudspeaker system.

The judge banged his gavel several times in order to quell the steadily rising tide of speculation sweeping the courtroom. "Objection overruled, Mr. Prosecutor. May the tape recording in question be admitted into evidence, and forthwith played for the court's instruction."

By this point the temper of the courtroom was like a grenade with the pin already pulled. The sudden silence was awesome, and Grayson proceeded to prolong the terrible, sweltering tension by fiddling at length with a battered portable tape recorder he couldn't seem to get to work.

As the seconds dragged past on the courtroom clock, there wasn't a sound from the packed benches of spectators. Everyone seemed to be holding their collective breath. Not a cough or a whisper until finally Grayson pressed the button, and the voice of Andreas Jaccard began to spool eerily out into the simmering hush.

"Katherine . . . ?" Jaccard's voice demanded. "What are you doing here?"

"I read a letter from Doctor Meyerhof," came Kate's surprisingly measured response. "I know all about the experiment, Andreas. I know the truth."

"And the truth is . . . ?"

"That you're a medical outlaw, without the slightest shred of human compassion. You knew all along that what you were doing might cost all of us our lives, or at the very least some serious disability. You used us like experimental animals."

"I'm sorry about Celia and the others, Katherine. Something went terribly wrong with the artificial hormones. But try and see it as it is. Their lives were only shortened. We all die sooner or later."

"To be sorry you have to be able to feel, and you're not

really capable of feeling anything, for anyone . . . are you, Andreas?''

''In science, Katherine, the only names that anyone ever remembers are those of the winners. Nobody cares a damn about someone who had to share a Nobel Prize. Yes, of course I took a chance on doing the experiment. But it wasn't a total failure. Millions of women will benefit from Rejuvenal-12 in its topical form. It more than fulfills its promise in rejuvenating the outer skin, and it's only a question of time before RJ-12 injections become as commonplace as B-12 shots. Further experiments will eventually work out the kinks.''

''What are you doing?'' Kate's voice was sharply questioning.

There was a sudden sizzling eruption on the tape, followed by the sound of water running in a metal basin. ''Unfortunately for both of us, Katherine, you have made it necessary for me to destroy the only evidence that could have possibly proven that such an experiment ever really took place.''

''Benny is waiting for me at the boat. He knows why I've come, and if I don't return within the hour, I've instructed him to go straight to the police.''

''You should have realized by now that the local police work for me. And as for Benny Valdez . . . well, that young man can be dealt with in any number of ways. Benny is nothing, no one. But you, Miss Katherine Leslie, are a very different matter. Surely you realize I can't possibly allow you to jeopardize my life's work. There is not a single medical breakthrough that hasn't been accompanied by the loss of life.''

''You aren't really trying to tell me the ends justify the means?''

''I waited ten years in order to conduct the experiment in which you and the others were unknowing participants. From the very beginning, it was an elegant postulate. The perfect quintessential opportunity to see exactly what RJ-12 could do under the widest possible variety of conditions. The restoration of sexual libido for a woman well past menopause. Extended life for a woman dying of terminal cancer, and a great ballerina restored to her physical and creative prime. Then of course there was the octogenarian who wanted to live forever. Since she had no one to leave her fortune to, the Duchess wasn't going to be satisfied with anything short of immortality."

"And what about me," Kate demanded. "Just which role did I play in your murderous scenario?"

Jaccard laughed deep in his throat. "What else," he said, "besides the insecure, fearful, and increasingly neurotic woman in the throes of a full-blown midlife crisis. Together the six of you probably made up the most perfect test group imaginable. And, for a time at least, there's no denying that you all got exactly what you came here after."

"I didn't come to Coral Key last spring because I wanted to die, Andreas. I came here because I wanted to live."

"Whatever you may die of, Katherine, it won't be from RJ-12 injections. In spite of what happened to the others, you have absolutely nothing to fear. You see, at the very beginning I selected you as the experimental control."

"Experimental control," Kate repeated blankly. "I don't understand you."

"It's all very simple, really. All you received were placebo injections of a simple saline solution that is proven to be pharmacologically inert. Studies have repeatedly shown that placebos given in double blind testing situations under laboratory conditions benefit thirty to forty percent of all patients, whether they're afflicted with cancer or insomnia. The injections I gave you were basically incapable of eliciting any physical response beyond a few symptoms that are closely akin to the twenty-four-hour flu."

"But that's not possible," Kate insisted. "If I received

nothing then . . . how . . . what happened to change me? Everyone saw it from the moment I returned from Coral Key. We had all changed. We even called ourselves the Sisterhood of the Reborns.''

''You actually were reborn,'' Andreas responded. ''Not through any injections, but through something equally miraculous. A completely mysterious process that may be inherent in your own psychology, or perhaps even in your genetic coding.

''Through some form of psychic biostimulus, you were able to totally transform yourself simply by willing it. You saw what you considered to be miraculous results taking place all around you here on Coral Key. By simply believing . . . something got triggered, and you did the rest yourself.''

Kate's voice was poised on the very edge of disbelief. ''Why did you say that there were six women involved in the experiment?''

''Because there were six of you. In fact I came down here to the lab tonight in order to complete the autopsy on the sixth member of our test group. She received the same series of cell injections as everyone else. But with her youth and vibrant good health, I had hoped to try and slow down the aging clock almost indefinitely.''

There was a metallic sound like metal wheels moving along greased ball-bearing tracks. ''*Autopsia* is a Greek word meaning the act of seeing with one's own eyes. But I'm afraid you'll have to excuse the way she looks.''

''Solange . . .'' Kate gasped.

''Yes . . . Solange. The police found her body in an alley in Porto Cristo the night before last. She has needle tracks on her arms, and so they assumed she died of a heroin overdose. But the autopsy showed she succumbed like the others. Severe trauma, hypoxia, and massive intercranial bleeding.''

''That's why you wanted Adrianna placed in your care,

wasn't it?'' By now Kate's voice was honed with a razor's edge. ''You intended to perform even more experiments on her . . . wasn't that it, Andreas?''

''If medical science is to advance, it is entirely necessary to determine why it is that experiments fail. The fact that Adrianna del Bario is still alive offers me an excellent opportunity to discover just what went wrong.''

There was the sound of the heavy metal trolley once again, followed by the pneumatic slam of a refrigerated door. Then after a long moment of distilled silence, Andreas' voice came clear and questioning. ''What are you doing with that gun, Katherine? Just what is it you hope to accomplish?''

''I don't care what you say . . . you're a murderer, Andreas, without the slightest shred of feeling or compassion. What I intend to do is stop you before you destroy any more lives.''

Kate's voice had become progressively more high pitched, poised on the edge of hysteria, while Jaccard's remained cool and deliberately soothing.

''Nothing needs to change between us, Katherine. It's just that now we've both gotten to know each other somewhat better . . . that's all. Certainly you're not going to throw everything away in order to achieve some absurd kind of stupid female vengeance.''

''Don't take another step, Andreas. I am perfectly capable of pulling the trigger of this gun.''

''Stop acting like a little fool,'' his voice continued in the same soft, mesmerizing tones. ''We make a winning team, and we still have it all ahead of us.''

''Not another step,'' her voice shrilled.

''I'm calling your bluff, Katherine. You see, I happen to know that you are totally incapable of shooting me in cold blood . . .''

The tape ended with a scream that left the entire courtroom sitting in stunned silence. ''If it may please the court,'' Tyler

Grayson's voice finally intoned, "I would like to place into evidence the medical file of Solange Wilkerson. It will corroborate everything my client has told this court."

Grayson passed the only surviving file to the court bailiff, and then turned to confront the jury. "The truth is that Andreas Jaccard *was* a monster, ladies and gentlemen. Somebody had to stop him, and Katherine Leslie was the only one who could."

Chapter Forty

Out of the ashes, it had all come together.

On the fourth day of her trial for the murder of Andreas Jaccard, Kate had been acquitted on a reduced charge of "Justifiable Homicide." The nightmare was finally over, and she felt strengthened by the soul-searing experience. As if she had come through a cleansing fire, irrevocably tempered by all that had transpired.

Kate stood on the sidewalk in front of the Plaza Hotel, staring up at a glossy window vitrine fronting on Central Park South. It displayed her own facial profile, viewed behind the wheel of a sleek bright red Ferrari.

The copy read: THE CARAMOUR WOMAN KNOWS WHERE SHE'S GOING AND EXACTLY HOW SHE'S GOING TO GET THERE. FOR YOUTH AND BEAUTY FOREVERMORE, IT'S REJUVENAL BY CARAMOUR.

No woman who ever fell in love with Paul Osborn was

ever quite the same again, Kate realized. And she herself had been no exception. The only difference was that for her it no longer mattered.

The last thing that Kate had ever expected to feel for Paul was pity, and it pained her deeply to see him looking so old and ill. So completely drained of the power and vitality that had once defined his personality with such vividness and clarity.

Where there had once been incandescence, there was now little left but the empty shell of a man. The Paul Osborn she had always known had changed. The powerful inner radiance had guttered down to little more than a feeble glow.

They were both very different people now, Kate realized, and their paths were leading them inevitably apart.

Deliberately she put such thoughts from her mind as she purchased a bouquet of pastel-colored peonies in the Plaza florist shop and then hurried her steps. It was twenty minutes after ten o'clock in the morning on her first day back in New York, and Kate dashed across Fifth Avenue in order to catch the green light.

Directly ahead of her the General Dynamics building rose gleaming in the bright morning sunlight from its broad plaza of silvery reflecting pools and splashing fountains. As always, Kate felt a thrill as she allowed her eyes to travel upward. Following the shimmering sheath of marble, glass, and chromium steel to where it seemed to pierce the Manhattan skyline with an effortless sculptural thrust.

As she whirled through the spinning glass doors, Kate caught sight of the newspaper headlines blaring BEAUTYGATE SVENGALI TAKES A FALL. Max Drexel had been found guilty of Grand Larceny and sentenced to five years' imprisonment.

Kate paused only briefly to scan the printed copy. Then she

turned briskly on her heel and crossed the marble rotunda toward the double banks of elevators at the rear.

"Well, good morning, Miss Leslie . . . Gee . . . it's terrific to see you back."

It was Max, the garrulous elevator Starter, and Kate rewarded him with a warm smile as she stepped inside the elevator and pressed the softly glowing button inscribed: I.C.E.-CARAMOUR COSMETICS.

The doors slid silently closed behind her, and then Kate was rising upward in a soundless vacuum, while pondering the urgent summons she had received from Henri Dayne.

It was of course her stock that they were after. The last link to all that Kate had built up over the years to a pinnacle of stunning success. It was now worth somewhere in the neighborhood of five million dollars, and Kate was willing enough to sell if she would never again have to enter the building on Fifth Avenue where so many of her highest aspirations had been fulfilled.

No regrets and no looking back, Kate reminded herself as a soft, chiming note brought her back to the moment.

The elevator had come to a halt at the penthouse floor, and Kate mentally composed herself for the impending encounter with Henri Dayne. Strangely enough, after all that she had endured she felt perfectly calm and almost icily composed.

As the elevator doors slid open to the luxuriously appointed reception area, subliminal strains of Muzak played in the background like gently falling rain. Across the richly carpeted foyer, a remarkably beautiful and extremely familiar young woman sat behind the Louis XIV reception desk.

There was a vase of long-stemmed red roses at her elbow, while from overhead the Venetian crystal chandelier cast a muted aura of opulence over the ivory gilt and dusky rose foyer.

Beverly Farrell was seated behind the desk gently blowing on her freshly lacquered nails, and her eyes came up to meet Kate's coolly appraising glance. "I was told to be expecting you," she pronounced, holding up one freshly lacquered hand to display long, perfectly shaped nails painted a bright geranium red. It was the same shade of red as the longstemmed roses reposing in the crystal vase at her elbow.

"What do you think about the color match?" she questioned in a softly gloating voice. "Henri—I mean Mr. Dayne—insists that I always be color coordinated."

Kate ignored the all too obvious innuendo.

"I'd like to give these flowers to Iris Quaid before my appointment with Mr. Dayne," she announced in a deliberately brisk and businesslike voice.

Beverly Farrell shrugged prettily. "I'm afraid that won't be possible, Miss Leslie. You see, Iris is no longer with the company. She more or less retired when Henri . . . when Mr. Dayne became president."

"Acting president," Kate reminded her. "It's my understanding that the board of directors has not yet confirmed his appointment. And by the way, Miss Farrell, how is your acting career coming along? You still seem to be more or less between jobs. Perhaps just to be on the safe side, you really *should* learn typing and steno. Who knows, they might come in handy."

Beverly flushed, and her voice was sharply biting as she said, "The board of directors has been waiting for you to show up since ten A.M." She rose and circled the reception desk. "Mr. Dayne said to show you in just as soon as you arrived."

"How patient of them to wait." Kate's smile was beatific. "It's good of you to offer, but you needn't bother to escort me to the boardroom, Miss Farrell. I still know my way around."

They were gathered in the Caramour boardroom with its deep brown lacquered walls, pale beige carpeting, Chippendale mirrors, and long glass and chrome conference table with Henri Dayne seated at its head.

To his left was Theodore Baxley, while seated around the table were the four new board members, who had been appointed by I.C.E. They were all dark-suited conglomerate types with blandly undemonstrative features who appeared to have been pressed from the same mold.

At precisely ten twenty-five Kate made her entrance into the boardroom, and all those present rose to greet her. "Good morning, Katherine," Henri Dayne addressed her somewhat grudgingly. "I must say that you're looking exceedingly well considering what you've just been through. Congratulations, by the way, on your acquittal."

"Thank you," Kate replied lightly. "Though perhaps you would have been happier to see them hang me, isn't that right, Henri?"

"I'm sure that Henri had no such desire," Ted Baxley cut in with a soft clucking sound. "In any case, the past is behind us, and we're all here today to discuss the future."

After Kate had taken a seat on Henri Dayne's right, Ted Baxley went on to make the necessary introductions, and the meeting was hastily called to order.

"We will first have the minutes of the previous meeting read," Dayne said with a nod toward the attractive young stenotypist who had taken Iris Quaid's place. The girl was a glossy-looking, green-eyed blonde who crossed her long legs with a flash of silken thigh, and had the most extraordinary breasts imaginable.

Henri Dayne's demeanor came as a complete surprise to Kate. Instead of acting overbearing and arrogant in victory, he appeared extremely subdued, and there was something brooding and bitterly resentful in his attitude.

The girl began reading in a seductively soft Southern accent. Seated directly across the conference table from Kate, Basil St. John, the I.C.E. superlawyer, impatiently drummed his neatly manicured fingers for several moments, then suddenly motioned the girl to silence with an imperious wave of his hand.

From the first instant she had entered the room, Kate had been intensely aware of his pale, unblinking eyes licking over her like laser beams from behind heavy horn-rimmed glasses.

"In order to save time," St. John cut in, "we will dispense with the usual formalities. We're already running behind schedule, and the matter requiring discussion is urgent to the financial well-being of this company."

Basil St. John spoke in clipped Harvard accents. "I might even go so far as to say that the financial well-being of this company hangs in precarious balance. And it is to this grievous misalignment of corporate talent that we must now address ourselves."

For a moment St. John paused and allowed his highly magnified gaze to travel around the table until coming finally to rest upon the face of Henri Dayne. As always, Dayne was immaculately attired. Yet his posture was no longer erect and commanding. He had the look, Kate suddenly realized, of someone running scared.

Dayne and Baxley exchanged a warning glance, as Basil St. John sat back and spread his hands with a benign smile that failed to reach his eyes. "There is simply too much at stake for us to allow Caramour to flounder under . . . shall we say . . . inexpert leadership," he finally pronounced. "Something has to be done . . . and fast."

Henri appeared to be unnerved by the close scrutiny of Basil St. John, but was obviously holding himself in check. "Of course the powers that be back at I.C.E. headquarters are aware of Miss Leslie's proven ability to perform effectively in a role that required firm, executive leadership and a certain amount of calculated daring."

"Excuse me, Mr. St. John," Kate cut in rather sharply. "This is rather a busy day for me, and I have a lot of things to accomplish. Why don't you just get to the point? I assume you called me here to make an offer for my stock? I really can't say that I'm surprised you want to get me out of the picture as quickly as possible."

St. John's immediate response was a frosty smile. "Quite the contrary, Miss Leslie. In fact, I have been empowered by my superiors to offer you the presidency of Caramour and chairmanship of the board. We are prepared to make you a financial offer you can't afford to refuse."

Although Kate's features betrayed no more than mild surprise, she felt as if she had been slapped. St. John's offer, coming as it did right out of the blue, was a terrific shock, and it took an act of will to pull herself together.

Kate's hands tightened slightly around the floral bouquet she had brought for Iris Quaid. She had forgotten that she still had it in her lap. There, in the distilled silence broken only by the keys of the stenotype machine clacking softly away in the background, Kate desperately needed something to moor herself to.

The familiar and comforting presence of Iris Quaid was no longer in attendance, but the flowers Kate had brought to give her ultimately proved to be a perfect stage prop. She lifted them to sniff delicately their fragrance, and then turned her questing, smoky gaze upon the brooding leonine profile of Henri Dayne. "Well, Henri? Just how do you feel about this unexpected turn of events? I assumed they had promised you corporate immortality for bringing off the stockholders' suit in favor of I.C.E."

"Let's face it, Katherine," Dayne responded, still without looking directly at her. "You hit the jackpot with Rejuvenal-12. It's a tough act to follow."

"Perhaps I can be more specific," St. John put in. "Production is down, and costs are up. Scotty McPherson walked out the day we took over, and the Beauty Reps disbanded *en masse* as soon as Max Drexel was indicted. Under the present management we are losing potential sales running into multimillions. The prospective printout indicates that we've got the hottest product line to hit the cosmetic market in a decade. And you, Katherine Leslie, are the only one who can possibly put all the pieces back together again."

"Under the circumstances, just what makes you think that I'd be willing to do that?" Kate questioned.

"For several reasons," St. John responded. "But for one thing, we are prepared to make you the highest-paid woman executive in America. And for another, I.C.E. is ready to move ahead on your plan to franchise Caramour Beauty Spas around the world. Just name your price, and you don't have to worry about the FDA, SEC, or AMA. They can all be taken care of."

Kate leaned back in her chair, regarding St. John with a look of coolly impersonal consideration. "Just for the record, Mr. St. John, exactly how permanent a fixture is Mr. Dayne around here? You see, this is the same man who recently lied to a jury that held my fate in its hands. I'm more than ready to forgive . . . but it just wouldn't be smart to forget."

"I take your point." St. John nodded. "And for all practical purposes, you may consider Mr. Dayne to be expendable. Performance is the operative word with I.C.E., and Mr. Dayne is no longer considered to be as important to our interests as he once was."

Epilogue

It was four A.M. in the morning, and the human tide that perpetually ebbed and flowed throughout airports around the world had slackened to the merest trickle in the hour before dawn.

Paul had asked to drive Kate out to Kennedy, but she had steadfastly refused. The last thing she wanted was a poignant final farewell in some cavernously empty departure lounge.

It pained her deeply to see him looking so frail, so old and ill. As if something had already died inside him, leaving nothing beyond the empty shell of what had once been a magnificent man. All the power, charisma, and vitality had been drained away, and there was now a male nurse in constant twenty-four-hour attendance.

With her camera bag slung across her shoulder, Kate's footsteps echoed hollowly against the marble flooring as she crossed the international departure lounge toward gate number twelve.

More than anything else, Kate felt a swelling tide of relief that once again her life was hers to command. No longer was she responsible to Paul or to Caramour, or to the dozens of staff people who wrote her speeches, did her market research, remembered her appointments, made travel arrangements for her, paid her bills, answered her telephone, drove her car, opened doors and mail, and even bought gifts in her name for birthdays of other people's children.

At last her life was her own, and she was free to do with it whatever she chose.

For too long, Kate felt as if she had been operating strictly on automatic pilot. Then, following her acquittal in the death of Andreas Jaccard, she had received another letter from Skip in India. After that her path was clear, and there were no longer any doubts.

There had in fact been something transcendental and very powerful in Kate's innermost awareness that perhaps this was how it was always meant to be. That was all that really mattered. All the rest of it was past history.

As Kate made her way across the nearly empty and echoing rotunda, her steps faltered suddenly and then stopped. She stood staring up toward a huge illuminated photograph the size of a motion picture screen.

THIS WOMAN IS OLD ENOUGH TO HAVE A PAST, the ad copy read. FOR YOUTH AND BEAUTY FOREVERMORE—IT'S REJUVENAL BY CARAMOUR. Surrounding the advertisement was a skeletal metal scaffolding, and two workmen had already begun the task of dismantling the huge photographic panels.

For several long moments Kate stood staring up at her own image, hugely magnified upon the illuminated screen. Then, blaring out over the loudspeaker system, her flight to India was announced, and once again Kate's feet were set in motion.

It had been a rainy blustery night, but as Kate presented her ticket to the attractive young airline attendant awaiting her at gate number twelve, the air was fresh with the dawn, and there was already a pale luminous streak of light tracing the eastern horizon.

"You're the last passenger to go on board," the gate attendant informed her. "I was just about to mark you off as a no-show."

"How long will it take to get to India?" Kate inquired a bit breathlessly.

"Thirty-four hours, by way of London, Paris, Rome, Abu Dabi, Teheran, and Kabul. You should be able to see the Himalayas before landing at New Delhi."

"That sounds like a long way," Kate said, staring off toward the red and silver Air India 747 standing on the field with its cabin windows alight.

The young man nodded cheerfully. "Halfway around the world. Just about as far as you can go before you have to start coming back."

He removed the initial portion of Kate's airline ticket, then did a fast double-take as he returned it to her. "Excuse me, but I have the feeling that I've seen your picture just about everywhere."

His smile flashed in his handsome face, youthfully beguiling with open admiration. "Aren't you the Caramour Woman?"

Kate's gloved fingers closed over the ticket he had placed in her hand as she returned the smile. "You know . . . a lot of people ask me that," she informed him. "But the lady and I bear only a passing resemblance."

Before he could say another word, Kate hurried through the departure gate and out onto the glistening tarmac. Without a backward glance, she lifted her hand to wave, and then she was gone.